DARKNESS

STEPHANY BRANDT

VICIOUS BUNNY PRESS

Published in the United States by Vicious Bunny Press, LLC

viciousbunnypress.com

Cover Design Copyright 2019 by Ida Jansson, Amygdala Design.

http://www.amygdaladesign.net/

ISBN: 978-0-9987093-2-1

ISBN: 978-0-9987093-3-8 (ebook)

For Everyone Who Has Helped Me On The Way:
Jean, Mom, Dad, Grandma, and Tobin

ONE

EMERGENCY SIRENS BLARED as Captain Stuart sprinted towards the shuttle hatch. Behind her, First Mate Haddad furiously grabbed the medical supply boxes as the rest of the crew ran ahead. The countdown to launch screamed over the last functioning loudspeaker.

Haddad stumbled as the side of his bulky space suit hit the doorway leading to the launch craft. The impact threw his trim body backwards and he scrambled to regain his footing as Stuart turned and grabbed his jumpsuit sleeve, steadying him before he hit the floor. Their sights locked and Haddad saw terror hiding in her almond-shaped eyes, something she hid well from the rest of the crew.

Haddad stood back up and Stuart observed how pale his tan skin had gotten, making his cheeks look like the color of old oatmeal. They scuttled through the hatch door, one following the other, as the sterile female voice of the auto-launch sequence counted down from three minutes, against the growing feedback whine.

Ahead of them were the eight other crew members: the three women and five men struggled to get to their assigned seats without the normal assistance from the ground team, bumping bodies and helmets along the way. They hurried up the ladder extending vertically from the entry door to the tip of the cockpit, standing on a back wall that was in a temporarily-vertical position. There were two seats on either side of the aisle, arranged in two rows behind the cockpit; the captain's and co-pilot's seats faced the control display inside the cockpit proper.

Tears trickled from Dr. Galloway's eyes as he fumbled with the shoulder straps on his seat harness, something his surgical training had not prepared him for. He craned his head trying to see through the fog coating his helmet visor, and struggled to get one of the nylon straps out from the crack between his seat and the wall. Sweat dripped from his graying sideburns as he furiously tried hooking his shoulder straps into the center buckle, but one wouldn't go in. Yelping in a panic he tried again —this time the buckle made a satisfying click. His tears streamed down his face, but he had no way to wipe them.

Galloway's co-surgeon, Dr. Wren, took the seat next to him and fastened her harness quickly. Her auburn hair was tied up in a frizzy ponytail, covered underneath her helmet and safety cap. She craned her head back and forth in the cumbersome helmet, trying to get a better view as she pulled the straps over her chest, grabbing the leg pieces from below her crotch and jamming them all together in the center piece. She heard the loud click through her helmet, then wrapped her hand around Galloway's as he pulled her fingers tightly to his.

Engine officer Schwartz was first on board the craft; his smooth skin bore a slight sheen under his facemask. He'd raced up the ladder ahead of the others like a monkey to the seat right behind Haddad's, then confidently buckled his harness like he'd done the drill a thousand times before. Schwartz stared forward at the back of the co-pilot's seat, his blue eyes blank like he was staring at a video game screen. He didn't make eye contact with any of his crew mates.

Forester, the mission botanist, was up next behind Schwartz and he took the last chair just inside the entry doorway. He wished he could wipe the sweat trickling down his torso from both the exertion and his natural fear but the space suit fabric was stubbornly in the way. Forester managed his harness with shaking hands, his fingers jittering and fumbling through the launch suit gloves, as he clipped the five yellow belts of the safety harness into the center clip below his navel. His fingers scratched at the outside of his gloves, desperate to get at his cuticles entombed inside.

Patel was already sitting in the seat next to Forester. The petite biologist from Jaipur looked out the window and watched the atmosphere above the launch craft shimmer, her ebony eyes widening. She gasped suddenly as the neighboring launch pad seemed to waver and started shimmering too—a sign the impact was imminent. Patel turned her head away and stared at her hands, wringing them tightly through the suit gloves while she hummed softly.

Williams, the head of security and the lead engineer, held back and waited at the door until he could usher the navigators Gutierrez and Simon in before him. As soon as they were up the ladder, he made eye contact with Stuart, nodded at her, then climbed up the ladder himself. Williams took the seat next to Schwartz, looking at Gutierrez across the aisle and giving her a strained smile.

Stuart and Haddad secured the door hatch, then climbed up the ladder to their seats like gymnasts. Each buckled in like they were born in their space suits, and their hands moved in tandem as they flipped the switches to initiate launch. The language between them was like a symphony of codes and numbers, but their voices remained calm; the sound of their startup sequence was the only thing breaking the human silence in the cabin.

Haddad prepared the last of his control board. "Ignition ready."

"Launch initiated," answered Stuart as she pressed the button releasing the massive booster rockets, which suddenly rose to a deafening howl that reached above the growing rumble of the doomed planet. The launch force drove the crew back in their seats, their heads pressed against the headrests like they were glued down. Galloway felt his cheeks jiggle and press back against his skull.

Despite the force of the takeoff, Wren turned her head to the left and looked out the tiny hatch window. She thought she saw the shadow of the comet pass over the horizon, but wasn't sure if that was real or just her eyes playing tricks. An itch stubbornly crawled under the suit on her right arm, but the takeoff force was so hard she couldn't lift her hand to scratch it.

Stuart focused on the control panel in front of her. All engines were on-line and functioning, and from the looks of things it was your everyday average launch—except for the abandoned facilities falling away on the ground behind them.

Haddad looked briefly over at Stuart and saw the deep furrow crossing an otherwise smooth face, adding temporary years to her visage. He listened for the cacophony of voices down in mission control telling him what to do, but heard only blank silence return from the speakers. Haddad checked the cabin life support panel out of habit, and inwardly thanked all the people who had trained him. All functions still looked intact, and he continued with the launch routine he'd memorized months earlier.

The craft rose with the power that all great spaceships have on liftoff: the engines were blindingly bright, but the incoming comet's trail was even brighter. The ship jolted as the two initial booster rockets fell away towards the planet, and the spaceship continued upward on the power of the secondary set. Within minutes they were piercing the cool darkness of the upper atmosphere.

That was when they saw the impact: the giant comet made

contact with the plains of Argentina just as the launch craft pulled clear of Earth's atmosphere. Massive curtains of soil and comet debris, already glowing bright red and orange from the power of their own combustion, launched into the heavens like a sick confetti. Stuart's heart stood frozen in her chest as she watched the impact wave spread across the entire planet, carrying a devastating wall of fire with it. Within minutes, all the areas closest to the impact zone were on fire, and that fire greedily consumed anything and everything in its path.

Stuart could only wonder if there would ever be any life on Earth again.

STUART'S dark eyes were still focused on the instrument readings in front of her when the first alarm buzzer rang, the light flashing on the panel: COLLISION IMPACT WARNING. She looked to the craft windows and saw an ominous small object hovering above the burning planet's horizon; radar confirmed it was a satellite pushed disastrously off course by the comet's impact.

"Debris ahead," crackled Haddad's voice over the tiny speaker in Stuart's headset.

"Got it," she replied coolly. Her instincts called to change the trajectory of the launch pod, so she fired a tiny burst of rockets that pushed the spaceship just enough out of the way. She breathed for what seemed like the first time as the rogue satellite passed behind them, on a course servicing a planet inhabited by burned corpses.

"What was that?" uttered Patel over the intercom.

"Nothing to be worried about," returned Stuart, trying to sound soothing. "We used thrusters to avoid the path of an oncoming satellite. The comet sent it rogue."

"Are there more?" Schwartz spoke up with a slightly worried

tone, a wisp of smooth brown hair sticking out from the cap covering his head. The others felt a knot of fear drop in their bellies when they heard trepidation in his voice, instead of his usual gung-ho bossiness.

"Most likely," interjected Gutierrez. Her voice sounded calm, but her coffee-colored skin had gone ashy. "The impact created an energy wave that hit the whole planet, passed in the upper atmosphere too. All the satellites that weren't burned up probably got pushed away from the impact zone."

"Yup," agreed Stuart. "I've checked our path to the ship, and we've got a clean flight to the dock zone now." The crew breathed almost in unison.

Forester and Patel looked at each other and Patel offered Forester a wan smile, her round cheeks creasing into dimples at the corner. He couldn't bring himself to smile back at her, but Patel took Forester's hand and held it tight.

Forester turned his head away from Patel and looked out the window to his right, wishing he could clean the fog from his glasses. The planet below them burned: every city and continent glowed an equal shade of orange as the terrain consumed itself to nothingness. The oceans boiled but the steam from them did not create clouds; it streamed into outer space, released from the confines of the atmosphere as the ocean beds blazed.

Tiny fireworks exploded in the sky below the spacecraft. Each burst of sparks seemed bigger than the next, as hundreds of satellites pushed out of orbit collided, and their nuclear reactors reached critical temperature. What came next was what nuclear reactors did when they got too hot: they went boom.

Stuart focused on the end of the launch craft's nose: ahead was a tiny speck, bright against the firelight. The ship continued advancing and the speck grew to a larger dot, then something the shape of a stick. Each second the approaching vehicle grew exponentially in size, until it loomed ahead of the launch craft.

Overhead stretched a long expanse of white tiled skin. Black patches lined all sides of the craft, the solar panels within glinting in the sun and firelight. The wedge-shaped nose of the hull tapered back in equal angles, creating a smooth line from the tip of the nose to the point of each wing. It made the craft look like a fat boomerang, or a very narrow arrow, that was about the size of two large submarines placed nose-to-nose.

A docking arm extended from spacecraft's rear, looking like a tentacle dangling from some forlorn space jellyfish. Stuart fired a small thruster blast and the launch craft nudged forward, closing in on the waiting arm.

Haddad spoke up. "We're moving at ninety klicks. Deceleration is advisable."

"Wait," answered Stuart. She flinched from the disturbance during her docking maneuvers, almost like she'd been slapped. Stuart refocused on her work and didn't utter another word to Haddad; Haddad knew the drill, he shut up.

"Eight hundred meters to approach zone," Haddad piped up after five endless minutes of silence, punctuated with the whooshing noise of thruster rockets.

"Decreasing approach," answered Stuart. She touched the screen in front of her and began making a slow drawing motion down the screen—the rocket engines answered and a new bank of thrusters pushed back directly from the nose. The approach slowed, and the docking arm suddenly seemed farther away again.

Stuart worked her left hand over another screen. This hand controlled thrusters on either side of the craft, which she hit in tiny bursts intermittently. Each burst narrowed the ship in on its target, until the launch craft's side was parallel to the docking arm. She looked like a concert pianist performing Rachmaninoff, only it was the ship's thrusters she made music with.

Stuart's eyes squinted and her unkempt brows furrowed, she pursed her lips as she focused on the dock zone. As the arm approached the lock, she fired another tiny burst of rockets from the nose; the craft slowed and the homing mechanisms on the arm and lock stretched the two devices towards each other. Stuart tapped her track screen, and the docking lock light flashed on—everyone felt a gentle jolt as the lock and arm made firm contact and joined together. A small motor whirred and the docking arm latched in position.

"Pressurizing," spoke Haddad. His voice echoed across the intercom. The craft shook a bit harder, then the green light flashed on the dash panel: LOCK COMPLETE.

"Okay guys," started Stuart, "remember we did train for this, right?" The team nodded, somewhat in unison, "Lets stick to the plan...get locked away and inventory your stations first off. It's still the same ship."

"Yes Boss," answered Haddad, and the crew nodded together like a group of school children.

TWO

WREN RELEASED the safety latch on her belt and tried holding back the vomit as her body floated up from her seat. She clung to the tiny rails running down the ceiling: the ladder they'd climbed earlier was recessed in the floor and now covered by a black lid, making it look like a smooth path of black tile. Wren tried holding her body in the upright position as her legs and torso flopped around in the zero gravity; her arms already ached from holding her swaying body at bay.

She clumsily wiggled her way towards the hatch, just enough that Galloway could release out of his harness. His blue eyes were bloodshot and his pale skin bloomed in roses of color on his stubbled cheeks, which he would later blame on smoke—not the stream of tears he cried for the planet. Wren smiled weakly at Galloway again, feeling somehow like an asshole for even surviving.

Wren tensed as she watched Williams wrestle with the door lock. He looked like something out of a Thor comic book as he strained against the stubborn latch; Williams somehow had the strength to wedge his nearly six-foot body against the frame without letting the lack of gravity get to him, even with a space suit on. The door latch finally let go with a rough screech and Wren jumped—she had quick nightmares of the cabin depressurizing and all the occupants imploding, leaving entrails and blood to coat the cabin. Her heartbeat calmed, though, as she remembered they were all wearing their safety suits and helmets for a reason. The door groaned and opened onto a narrow hallway that resembled an aircraft bridge at the jetport.

Williams gave himself one good push from the hull and floated up towards the second air lock. His trajectory was straight and smooth, like he'd been born in space. He reached the other end and started straining on the wheel that locked the second door, which came easier and turned with only a minor bit of effort. He pulled the second hatch door open and looked over the entire compartment within: there were seats on both sides of the aisle, just enough to fit 10 bodies for gravity adjustment. Sufficiently sure the area was safe, he waved the rest of the team forward. Wren and Galloway were first out the door.

Wren hated the topsy-turvy way her body floated—it made her feel humiliatingly out of control. Flying around and bumping her feet on the ceiling was not her way of impressing co-workers or having a good time; she found a hold on the tiny metal rail running down the side of the docking tube and pulled herself slowly along instead. Halfway down the docking tube, she looked out the window and over at the launch craft cockpit, locking eyes with Haddad who still sat in the co-pilot seat. She felt an electric jolt, then caught herself and blushed, hoping Galloway hadn't noticed.

She held her breath as Galloway decided to try the "Williams" route and pushed off from the launch pod door. He flew straight until about the middle of the tube, then lost his balance and caught Wren with one of his flailing arms. She lost her grip on the wall and suddenly they were both spinning helplessly; on one pass they bumped helmets and Wren yelped.

"Okay," spoke Williams in a tone usually reserved for

tussling fourth-graders, "enough of the shenanigans." He pushed off from the hatch and gently grabbed Wren's arm. "Let's go."

Wren went limp and let Williams do all the floating for her. Despite countless test flights, endless trips to the bottom of a pool, and her share of missions in space, she still didn't have the hang of weightlessness—her gratitude for Williams' natural aptitude in the matter was palpable. Williams floated her to the hatch door, then watched patiently as she gripped the door and pulled herself inside. Wren found the closest seat and pulled the shoulder straps hanging above the seat down over each shoulder. A small three-point buckle extended between her legs, and she snapped both straps into the buckle with a click. The harness held her comfortably in place with no more floating, and she breathed a long sigh of relief.

Galloway was bound and determined to make it to the hatch unaided, and he waved off Williams' first attempt to grab him. Williams' countenance darkened only slightly, and he grabbed Galloway's arm after the second pass.

"We need your head alive and not bruised, Bill." Williams added with what he felt was a caring tone. "No doctor equals bad news."

Wren held back a giggle as she watched the normally world-renowned doctor go limp like a three-year-old in the middle of a tantrum. Williams gamely held Galloway's hand and dragged him floating towards the chamber hatch, as Galloway finally obliged.

Once near the hatch, Williams gently swung Galloway towards the grab handle on the wall. Galloway caught it mid-flight, and his momentum shot him awkwardly into the edge of the hatch. Galloway grunted as the wind left his lungs.

"My bad, Bill." Williams called out from behind, pieces of his curly brown hair already sticking to his forehead with sweat.

"Yeah," answered Galloway with a strained tone in his voice, a mild frown accentuating the slight wrinkles on his forehead. "Thanks Pete." Williams looked mildly shamed.

Galloway pushed off from the docking hall bulkhead and floated into the chamber hatch. He swam his arms like a child doing the dog-paddle until he reached the seat opposite Wren.

"I give you a perfect 10," she gave Galloway a sly grin.

"Why thank you," he smiled.

"Better luck next time." Wren gave Galloway a thumbs-up.

"Yup," Galloway answered softly. His voice was muted from staring at the straps hanging over his shoulders and in between his legs; he grabbed the one over his left shoulder and fastened it to his crotch strap. Galloway's body hung awkwardly for a moment as the lack of gravity tried sucking him out of the harness, but he found the second shoulder strap and fastened it securely between his legs. Once finished, he locked eyes with Wren and matched her thumbs-up gesture.

STUART SAT FIXED in her seat, staring blankly at the controls; her head spun trying to reconcile what had just happened. There was no comforting voice over the headset to bounce ideas off of —Stuart had to suppress her tears because she realized there would never be voices on the other end again. A blank empty feeling overtook her whole body and her limbs felt numb.

She looked over at Haddad, trying hard to put on a brave face. All she could get out of her mouth was, "Hey."

Haddad looked over at Stuart, his brown eyes wide and blank like he'd been hypnotized. He stared out the window before twitching and looking over at Stuart, like he'd been woken from a trance. "Hey." His voice croaked and was barely audible over the shared intercom.

Both Stuart and Haddad stared out the cockpit window at the growing expanses of fire covering Earth, silent in their horror. Stuart couldn't take her eyes off the formerly blue planet, now aflame from the comet impact.

Haddad broke the silence. "Should we head to the Metis?"

Stuart spoke so softly her voice almost sounded like a sigh. "Yeah." She couldn't take her eyes from the charred husk of Earth, finding it perverse that even she couldn't resist staring at destruction.

Both captain and co-pilot unbuckled their safety restraints simultaneously and turned to face each other. Haddad was struck by how young Stuart suddenly seemed: her dark hair was cut close and hidden under her helmet cap, but her smooth taupe skin and youthful build made her look like a high schooler in the middle of a spaceship, as if she'd signed up for Space Camp but somehow got thrown in on a deep space exploratory mission instead.

Only he had seen how proficiently she handled a ship, had been in awe of her multiple missions to Mars, and her long journey to Pluto and back. Stuart's Pluto team was the first to visit the distant former planet, and they also held the distinction of being the first humans to travel to the edges of the solar system. When Haddad had gotten the news he'd made this mission as co-pilot to her captain, he was instantly excited to learn from the woman people at Space Command nicknamed "the queen": she did things with a spacecraft none of the other commanders could replicate.

The rest of the crew seemed to forget that the long periods in deep-space cryostasis had left Stuart looking years younger than her numerical age of forty; to the outsider, she still looked like a twenty-five-year-old punk Korean kid. Haddad prayed she had some good idea on how to get them out of this mess, given the years of experience she had handling unexpected situations on Mars and Pluto.

Stuart turned and watched the remainder of her crew fumble with their restraints, and one by one they each released themselves into weightlessness. It was easy to tell the people who had experience in space and who did not: all you had to do was watch how they tried moving in zero-g.

She made a mental inventory of the crew, and counted who was still left in her cabin; Stuart pressed the radio command module strapped to her throat and hailed Williams. "Pete, what's your count in the gravitation chamber?"

"Three strapped in, two on their way…that should leave you two left in the cabin, plus Louis and yourself."

"Good," Stuart answered. The count matched, and she could see Gutierrez and Simon through the cockpit window, working their way down the dock arm to the gravitation chamber. Patel and Forester were holding back in the cabin—Forester already looked green, and Patel tried her best to soothe him, taking Forester's arm and guiding him towards the dock corridor.

Patel surprised Stuart with her no-nonsense take on weight-lessness. She seemed to balance her petite body almost instinc-tually, and was able to hold onto the guide bars, move herself, and move Forester at the same time. Stuart felt bad for Forester: he was an expert on interstellar plant life, but a terrible astro-naut. Forester's six foot torso floated awkwardly behind Patel's five foot three frame, and he clung to her hand so hard it made Patel's brown skin turn white inside her suit. Stuart hoped Forester would make it to the gravitation chamber before he vomited—that was the last thing she needed today.

"You ready, Grace?" asked Haddad as Patel and Forester moved into the docking tube.

"Yup, guess so." She sighed as she scanned all the displays glowing dimly in standby mode.

"Well, onward." Haddad pushed himself off and glided down the aisle towards the hatch.

"Yeah." Stuart pushed off and followed him to the doorway. She looked ahead and saw seven pair of eyes looking back at her, all strapped in their gravity adjustment seats save for Williams who was floating next to the hatch door. Stuart felt their eyes boring into her flesh, and remembered the time she'd wet her pants while trying to do a book report in the second grade. Sometimes a room full of eyes still made her feel deeply inadequate—like a sham who only pretended to have the answers.

Stuart watched until Haddad made it to the gravity adjustment chamber hatch, then she turned, did a quick mental check down of all the systems in the launch pod, then closed the door and turned the lock handle until she heard the clunk. The green light next to the handle indicated the hatch was closed and sealed; Stuart pat the hatch door like a good dog, then pushed off towards the gravitation chamber. The entire crew watched as she gracefully flew head-first towards the chamber like an arrow, then quickly rose to the upright position as she approached the door. Stuart looked born to space life, and weightlessness brought out the years of experience she actually had. Under the old circumstances, this new ship would have been the flagship of Space Command—the first to have a full-time gravitational system. Now the novelty was lost in the charred wreckage of the planet below them.

She paused momentarily and looked out the docking tube window just in time to see what used to be the tip of Argentina —now it looked as if a giant had taken a bite out of the Earth's crust like an apple. The crater was unmistakable and the image etched itself into Stuart's brain.

The planet continued burning.

THREE

HADDAD FLOATED into the gravitation chamber and took a seat next to Galloway. They locked eyes for a moment and shared a weary look like two mountain climbers who were still a hundred feet from the summit. It worried Haddad to see the normally straightforward doctor shaking as he blinked furiously to suppress more tears springing from the corners of his eyes; Haddad felt just as broken by the day's events as his elders.

WEDNESDAY HAD DAWNED like any other training day: the crew arrived at zero five hundred to start the day's agenda briefing—on the menu had been a practice docking run, and a review of the cryosleep procedure. Normal, everyday types of training things one did in the month-long lead-up to departure.

Haddad had been working with Stuart in the simulator when they all heard the siren—an old-school wailing kind like they used in World War II. Commander Jensen came over the loud-speaker and demanded the entire team assemble in the confer-ence room. Haddad had looked at Stuart and raised his eyebrows—perhaps it was another of Jensen's drills to make sure the team was prepared for an invasion by some imaginary force, like kittens. Jensen seemed to like riling the team up at strange times to suit his own moods under the guise of "good preparation."

Stuart and Haddad joined the team in the conference room, and Haddad felt his heart sink and his bowels contract: Jensen's hands were shaking as he tried reading what was coming up on his tablet, then he finally put the computer down and stuffed his hands in his pockets with disgust. Jensen looked around the room with his hawkish eyes and tallied up the bodies present, then ran a hand absentmindedly over his bald head.

"There's been a change in plans, team." Jensen sniffed loudly. "Stuart, Haddad...I need to speak with you privately."

Both captain and first officer followed Jensen to his office. It was a white-walled room boasting only a chrome desk and three curved chairs, entirely dominated by a large window looking out on the Rocky Mountains; the only item on the immaculate glass desk was a picture of his daughter. Jensen's normally cool grey eyes were tear-stained and red.

"We need to prepare for immediate launch," Jensen said in the most controlled tone he could muster.

"Sir?" Stuart's eyes widened. "Now?" the tone in her voice covered the fact she thought this was another one of his crazy drills.

"You all know that comet PK662 was due to fly by Earth tomorrow." Jensen played absentmindedly with his wedding band.

Stuart nodded. "That's why we delayed the mission launch."

"Exactly," continued Jensen. "PK662's trajectory's changed. It's now on a direct collision course with Earth."

Haddad watched Stuart's beige skin go ashy.

"We're not going to survive this," Jensen muttered, almost to himself.

"Sir?" Stuart blinked and cocked her head.

"It'll be worse than the dinosaurs," Jensen sighed and stared out the window at some imaginary spot.

"Are they sure, sir?" Haddad piped up. "This isn't a drill?"

"They've calculated the path, and it will be a direct strike in about twenty-five hours. I need to call Caitlyn." Jensen looked out the window for a moment longer, then refocused and stared Stuart down. "Get to the Metis and get the ship out of the way of the immediate impact," he finished, looking at Haddad with his steely grey eyes.

Haddad turned to Stuart and saw the color hadn't returned to her face; in fact, she looked like she was about to pass out. Jensen turned to them and looked surprised they were still standing there.

"Get the Hell off this planet. Now!" He stared out the window at the mountains again, removing his wedding ring and playing with it like a coin. "Prepare the Metis."

"Yes sir," returned Stuart and Haddad simultaneously. They both saluted him and left the room; once outside, Haddad felt his knees getting loose and shaky.

"Jesus…is this for real?" he looked at Stuart with expectant eyes.

"It must be. I've never seen him like that." Stuart shook her head and ran a hand through her short ebony hair.

"What's the fastest you've gotten a launch ready?"

"Thirty hours," answered Stuart.

"Think we can do this one?"

"If we push it hard…I think so."

"Okay." Haddad nodded softly.

Stuart looked at him with gratitude in her dark eyes and a small smile. "Thanks."

Haddad felt the knot of fear in his belly twist and grab at his intestines. He'd seen Stuart go through drills of all sorts of crisis scenarios without breaking a sweat, but they'd never had one quite like this. If she said she could do the launch in under thirty hours, though, he believed her.

They walked briskly down the hallway back to the conference room where the team waited. Williams was watching the door intently like a Doberman and rose to greet the Captain and First Officer when they returned.

"What did he say?" Williams' eyes scanned the duo.

"We've got twenty-five hours to get launched," answered Stuart, nodding as she bit her lower lip.

"Twenty-five?" Williams' blue eyes widened.

"Barely...if that. We need to do it even faster if we can."

"Okey-dokey, Grace. You got this?" Williams searched Stuart's face.

"Yeah," Stuart said with a sigh, then added in a lower tone, "Remember we had to launch the *Beagle III* that fast, but that was twenty years ago with a totally different ship model." She quickly shook her head and her gaze hardened. "Doesn't matter. We have to make this. There's no other way."

"Okay," said Haddad in the bravest tone he could muster. "Tell us what we need to do."

"YOU ALL NEED TO know what's going on," started Stuart as she addressed the crew from a slender glass podium that Jensen usually used as his bully pulpit. Forester was scratching at his mop of unkempt brown hair, and alternating fiddling with his glasses and staring at his hands. Schwartz was messaging someone, but the rest of the team stared at her attentively.

Stuart cleared her throat. "Haddad and I just spoke with Commander Jensen, and he wants us to launch...immediately."

The entire room erupted in squawks of disapproval. A buzz of conversation followed as each member seemed to be asking the same question at the same time: "Why? Why now?"

Stuart held up her hand and the room quieted. "We all know we had to delay the launch because of PK662. New information has just come to light: the comet's trajectory's changed, and it's heading for a direct collision with Earth."

The room went eerily silent. Forester dropped his glasses on the floor and left them there; Schwartz clutched his message pad so tight his fingers turned white; Patel instinctively gripped Forester's hand. The entire team was so used to focusing on their mission, the news sent each one into their standard operating mode during a crisis: a level of shock that made you go numb and crave for any kind of work-related focus.

"I know we all need time to say goodbye to our loved ones. Use tonight to contact your families." Stuart's voice cracked, knowing the reason most of them had been chosen for the mission was their lack of husbands, wives and children—the only people the crew needed to notify were their parents.

Haddad's heart raced: he understood the time they needed to prepare for launch, and cutting an entire evening seemed terribly foolhardy. "Grace?" he asked softly with raised eyebrows. "You really think we can afford that?"

"We'll make it work," she added resolutely. "Everybody get moving, we meet back here at twenty-one hundred, and we'll work through the night. Take your checklists. If you finish early, go to your prep area and get everything on them ready to go. Patel? Forester? Can I talk with you privately?"

The two scientists looked at each other and rose to approach Stuart. They weren't used to her talking much to them, and Forester looked visibly uncomfortable like a dog that was in trouble, his broad shoulders hunching. Once they were close to her, Stuart spoke in a lower tone.

"You need to get anything in your experiments that you can use to reconstitute and breed from DNA."

Patel's mouth hung open in shock. "Some of our experiments aren't suited for that kind of research."

"Doesn't matter. Throw whatever you don't need out, bring whatever you need to re-start life. I hate to burden you both with this, but the Metis is no longer a research vessel—it's an ark."

Forester stayed silent and looked over at Patel. She locked eyes with him for a second, then refocused on Stuart. "We don't have enough time to do this."

"You gotta do it." Stuart's eyes pleaded with the scientists, as the shock of things slowly pushed the feeling out of her extremities. "Go through your lists and inventories. Bring whatever you might need. Forester, do you know anything about the seed bank on Mars?"

"Yes, from the reports I've read..." His voice barely broke the level between a whisper and a normal speaking voice.

"Good. Does your lab on the Metis have the appropriate measures to grow them?"

"Yeah," Forester nodded. "I was going to be running some soil-free growing experiments on Titan. We should be good on that front."

"Can you grow us food?" Stuart looked almost plaintive as she asked.

Forester blanched. "Food?"

"Yes, in case we run out."

"For all of us?"

"Yes."

Forester's eyes opened wide, but his glasses obscured most of the change, "Yeah, I can make it happen."

"Prepare for it."

Stuart turned and walked towards the door, "Say goodbye to your families as fast as you can. Get working on what you need for survival—meet back here at twenty-one hundred."

Both scientists turned and followed her out the door. Haddad watched them leave in stunned silence and felt instant pity for Forester and Patel: they were very capable scientists, but nothing in their studies had prepared them for this. The full force of the situation hit Haddad again like a punch to the gut; his stomach wiggled and a little vomit crawled up his esophagus. He restrained the urge and walked out of the conference room.

Once out the door, Haddad looked up and down the hallway. He saw Stuart and hailed her. "You need me?"

"You go talk to your family, Lou." She ordered him in a slightly scolding tone. "Say your goodbyes. I'll start the launch preparations and meet you back in a couple hours."

He could tell by the kind-but-firm tone of her voice she meant business, so he didn't question her. He knew her parents were dead anyway, and that was an uncomfortable subject. "Okay. I'll call you when I'm done."

Haddad turned and ran towards his office; inside was his trusty desk and call monitor. He tapped the lower corner of the screen and it lit up.

"Call Mom," he instructed the monitor. It displayed a little telephone icon and made the beep-beep tone that indicated it was trying to reach the intended party. The screen suddenly lit up with his mother's face, and Haddad immediately started crying.

"Mum? Have you heard?"

"Yes, darling."

"Is Dad with you?"

"He is."

"Go get him."

Haddad's mother called over her shoulder in a clean London accent tinged with the Egyptian she brought with her when she emigrated. "Hassim? Louis is on the monitor."

He recognized vague movement around the sides of the camera view, and soon his father's face filled the second half of the screen; he could tell his father had been crying too. It shocked Haddad to see the old man's red eyes— this was the Hassim Haddad who sat stoic at his own mother's funeral.

"Hi Son," Hassim choked.

"Hi Dad," answered Haddad—his face fell and his sobs ratcheted up a notch. "I love you so much!" he blurted out, and buried his face in his hands. Haddad cried for a minute while feeling the warmth of his face touching his fingers and the moist tears falling in his palm. After Haddad felt like he could control himself, he raised his head and wiped each eye with all his fingers.

"They're having us launch." Haddad's voice sounded low and gravelly.

"Yes?" Aisha Haddad's eyebrows raised expectantly and her eyes glimmered through the tears.

"Yeah." Haddad wished he could reach through the monitor and take his mother's hand. "We're supposed to take the Metis and get it out of the way."

"Do they think you'll make it?" Hassim stood straighter in his chair.

"I don't know." Haddad swallowed his tears and coughed. "We have to try."

"Good, son, good," his father nodded, "at least you've got a fighting chance. You've made us so proud." At this point all three cried even harder, but they didn't lose eye contact across the monitor.

"I love you, Dad!" sobbed Haddad. He looked over to his mother and blurted out, "Mum!" His face fell tragically and his lower lip quivered. "I don't know how to do this. I don't know how to do goodbye."

"You just do it," said his father. "You just do. Don't worry about your mum and I. We've had a good life, and we'll be thinking of you 'till it's done." Hassim paused for a second. "It will give me the greatest peace to spend my final moments knowing that you might escape this. I am proud my son will be one of the last."

To this, Haddad tried smiling through his quivering lips. "I'll make you proud, Dad," he whispered.

"Good boy." Hassim smiled painfully and nodded. "You go now and get that big ship ready."

"Yes, Louie," concurred his mother. "You go and beat this." She added with a naughty smile: "Tell that bloody comet 'Fuck You' for the both of us."

Haddad couldn't help but laugh, hearing his mother curse. She always spoke in such sweet tones that he couldn't fathom the 'F' word coming out of her mouth. Tears still fell but his face brightened, "I love you so much, Mum. I'll do that for you."

She smiled back at him across the screen and reached over to grab his father's hand. "We'll be thinking of you until the last minute."

"I will too," said Haddad with a pained smile.

"You go now, son," countered Haddad's father. "The telly's saying there's only the night until impact. You get off this planet."

"Yes, sir," answered Haddad with a resolute nod, then he reached out to the screen with his right hand. His fingers created a small distortion as they touched the screen, "I love you both beyond the Universe."

His parents both reached out towards their screen, and Haddad could practically feel them through the distance. "We love you too," they both said softly in unison.

FOUR

HADDAD TRIED HIDING the tear escaping the corner of his right eye—turning his head away from Stuart and hoping she hadn't seen it. His limbs grew heavier and heavier as the room acclimated to the simulated gravity inside the Metis, but his lungs were another story: they ached from the new gravitational system, and it temporarily hurt to talk.

He looked around the room at the rest of the team and noted all the crew sat close to their counterpart, almost out of rote memory: Simon and Gutierrez sat side-by-side in seats across from Stuart and Haddad, Schwartz sat next to Gutierrez, then Galloway and Wren finished out the row where it terminated in the docking arm bulkhead. Sitting on the same side of the compartment with Stuart and Haddad were Forester, Patel, and Williams.

No one made eye contact. Forester inspected his hands as if they were the most fascinating object he'd ever seen; Gutierrez stared in the direction of Stuart's navel; Patel looked at the ceiling, and Schwartz did too; the rest stared dully at the feet of the person across from them. The room was silent save for the whooshing noise while the gravitation system worked away.

Haddad didn't know if he was glad or sad that he'd left no one behind, save his parents. He knew all the crew were single; it had to be that way on a mission of this duration. The original plan had been to fly in cryostasis until they reached Titan, then they'd been scheduled to perform experiments for five years, send probes to the surface, and possibly a lander with a crew as well. All his training was for that purpose, and Haddad felt lost now there was no mission control to perform experiments for.

As his legs got heavier, Haddad's head ached. The gravitational generator on the Metis was something completely new to the space program, and Haddad had never tested it personally. The designers assured them it was safe: it hadn't killed any of the rats in testing, and he remembered the rats looking happy on the generator test video he'd watched. Haddad prayed the long-gone designers were right—there would be no one to fix the team if the gravitational field ripped them apart.

Haddad turned his head with effort and watched the control panel on the wall; it showed the balance of gravity in the acclimation pod slowly growing. He remembered the designers stressed a slow introduction to the artificial gravity, much like a scuba diver who needed to decompress when they came up from the depths of the sea. Scuba divers got "the Bends" and Haddad was terrified of what the equivalent of "the Bends" might look like in space. The control panel counted down the time to full gravity, and showed the gravitation percentage the generator had already achieved. They still needed to wait another thirty minutes.

Stuart looked over and her eyes made contact with Haddad's. He couldn't tell anything about what she was feeling—her eyes betrayed nothing but a clear, focused gaze. The corner of her mouth twitched in a tiny, forced smile, and he matched her smile with a tiny one of his own. Slowly Simon and Gutierrez raised their gazes and made contact with Stuart and Haddad as well. Neither smiled—their eyes still wide like deer caught in the headlights of a car.

Haddad looked down the line towards the bulkhead and saw Forester's hands fiddling with his gloves, apparently because he couldn't get to his cuticles. The sound of his gloves scratching against each other was the only noise in the chamber other than the whooshing gravitational system. Wren also watched Forester with an expression that was a combination of sadness and irritation, as Forester tapped his fingers in a way that reminded her of her five-year-old.

Further down the line, Williams stared across at Schwartz. The two men traded gazes that looked strong; they didn't exactly stare each other down, but neither seemed to be backing off the intensity. The two were like strange sphinxes, similar but also different: though they both stood just a hair shy of six feet, Williams' curly brown hair and gentle expression deviated severely from Schwartz's brown crew cut and hard blue eyes. Haddad knew both men well: they were seasoned astronauts with entirely different backgrounds—Williams had worked with Captain Stuart on all of her Mars and Pluto missions, and Schwartz had done his time managing the engines of the now-defunct Lunar fleet. He could tell Schwartz was still sore about Williams getting the lead engineer command, so the staring contest was understandable. Schwartz was still nursing that grudge like a bad puppy.

Next to Williams, Patel held her hands in her lap, gripping each other so fiercely it puckerered the material of her safety gloves. She breathed deeply in through her nose and out through her mouth, so hard that her faceplate was slightly fogged in front of her mouth. Galloway looked over and gave Haddad a strained smile; Haddad nodded his acknowledgement.

Haddad looked back at Stuart. She stared straight ahead at a point slightly over Gutierrez's shoulder, blinking slowly on occasion—the only movement betraying she was still alive. Her breath was slow and controlled and silent. Stuart, more than anyone else on the team, knew what space was like: she had seen the wonders of Mars and the lonely life in cryosleep. Haddad wondered if she was actually secretly happy to make space her permanent home.

They all sat like this as the seconds ticked down on the control panel, and Haddad felt his gaze returning to the pad's glow over and over. He remembered the old adage his father told him about waiting for water to boil, and he wondered if his father ever imagined it applied to waiting for gravity as well: it never went fast enough, especially when you watched it.

Finally the control pad turned green, beeped loudly, then a sterile female voice called out: "Gravitational systems ready." Williams unhooked his harness and walked over to the hatch door next to the panel. On the other side was the Metis, their new home. Williams pressed a few icons on the control pad, a chime that sounded like a bike bell rang, and the light above the hatch door turned green. "Systems normal," continued the robotic female voice. Williams looked to Stuart with expectant eyes and raised brows. She nodded, unhooked her harness, and turned to address the team.

"I honestly don't know what to say, guys." She paused and sighed. "Let's get in and get everything secured, maybe that will help us all a little." Stuart nodded at Williams, and he pressed the hatch release button.

The door swung open and the entire team got their first gaze at the insides of their new home.

———————

STUART BLINKED to clear the fogginess from her eyes and looked inside the Metis for the first time. It was sparklingly clean and white, a deep departure from the dark and cramped ship *Columbia* which had carried her Pluto mission. She couldn't believe how new everything looked: Space Command had spared no expense on this mission, and she felt a pang in her stomach realizing the designers probably had no idea what the craft would inadvertently become.

Williams held the door open and looked at her expectantly, "First in, Grace?" He held his hand out like the doorman of a New York skyscraper, and Stuart stepped over the edge of the bulkhead and placed her foot on the smooth tile floor. The tiles looked like marble, but she knew better—most likely some kind of synthetic composite. Everything glistened.

The storage bay was triangular, with the door to the hallway at the tip. The white tile floors extended to white metal walls, and the break between the two was so smooth it was almost invisible. The unintended effect was that one felt like they were in a white bubble, and it was sometimes hard to tell where the floor ended and the walls began. Stuart inadvertently thought about a white padded cell and shuddered, reminding herself to simulate some type of decorations to break up the monotony.

The Metis had been launched on an autopilot program over a year ago. Mission Command was hesitant to put astronauts on an untested craft: they'd wanted to test the ship's capabilities "dry."

Stuart participated in the early meetings and knew the original designers really hadn't wanted a human crew on board at all; they wanted the Metis to fly unaided to Titan, but early tests had proven the usefulness of the humans. Plus, the President had wanted to "send a crew to Titan" to make his final term look good—that way no one could disprove his dominance. Sadly, he would never see the fruits of his ego. As much as Stuart disliked the pompous little man, she realized he had unexpectedly saved her life.

She brought her other foot over the bulkhead and felt suddenly connected to the Metis. It hit Stuart that she was the commander of this beautiful ship, and it was like being given the greatest toy in all the world; the thrill temporarily replaced the pain of mourning in her gut. She smiled and walked further into the belly of the docking bay as Williams held the rest of the team back per the drill they'd rehearsed in the simulator. After five steps in, Stuart released the locking mechanisms on her helmet, hearing the hiss and click as she freed her head from its confinement. She breathed in deeply, relishing the fresh air that didn't smell like her sweat and tears.

Behind Stuart, the rest of the team began removing their safety helmets too, happy their captain had finally taken hers off. It was standard Space Command protocol to wait until the captain okayed helmet removal inside any spacecraft, and it had seemed like days since they put their protective gear on inside an empty command center.

Gutierrez smiled and pulled off her helmet and under-cap, revealing a frizzy shock of brown hair still tied in a rough pony-tail. She took a deep breath of the ship's air and brightened just slightly, her smooth brown skin glowing again. Simon followed her lead and removed his as well, revealing the face of a man who could have doubled as an ancient Nubian king in the movies. His hair was cut close to the scalp, but he kept a thin mustache along his upper lip that made him look like an African Errol Flynn. The two waited just inside the threshold, watching Stuart as she made her way across the storage bay floor. The rest of the crew behind them removed their own helmets and a chorus of sighs emanated from the gravitational adjustment room.

On either side of the docking bay were two small ships: the landers intended to go to Titan's surface. Both were engineered for flight either with a human crew or unaided on autopilot; Stuart smiled when she recognized the shape of both ships—

they were almost identical to the ones she'd taken to Mars. She chuckled softly, remembering the bumpy ride through Mars' atmosphere where she cussed profusely at the autopilot program, then switched to manual over the vocal opposition of her first officer. Kurowski had been terrified a "punk kid" was going to take the helm of his (at the time) state-of-the art landing craft—she remembered his face turning white, then red when she landed the machine perfectly on Mars' surface. Barely a bump, and when she'd banished the autopilot the ride down had been much better too—computers could only get you so far.

"Grace?" Williams' voice jolted Stuart awake and she realized, embarrassed, that she'd stopped and was stroking the side of one of the landers.

"Sorry—fond memories of these landers," she said absent-mindedly as she continued walking towards the com pad. Once at the pad, Stuart entered her command code and the pad sprung to life with a variety of bright colors. A tinny female voice spoke from the pad: "Welcome Commander Stuart."

"Authorization program twelve, sixteen, twenty-four begin." Stuart neared the pad and held her eye close while a tiny beam reached out and scanned her retina. Once it finished, all the lights suddenly leapt to life in the docking bay; a hum started up and the female voice now spoke over the ceiling speakers, "startup confirmed."

"Okay, we're in." Stuart turned to the team waiting in the gravitation bay. "It's safe now."

Haddad was the next in the bay and Stuart had to stifle a laugh; he looked like a kid in a candy store—and they were only in the storage bay. His soft brown eyes goggled at the beautiful surroundings and he swiveled his head to take it all in, because no simulator could do the actual ship justice. Haddad's eyes were focused on everything except where he was walking, and he bumped into the wing of one of the landers. "Shit!" he blurted out and blushed furiously.

As Haddad approached Stuart, the rest of the team followed him into the bay. Schwartz cut in front of the scientific staff and followed Haddad, behaving like the President's son he was; he waved Gutierrez forward and she and Simon followed single file. Patel nudged Forester to follow Simon, and he moved carefully forward watching his feet to make sure he didn't trip on the edge of the bulkhead. Patel followed Forester, her head craning to take everything in—she didn't seem to care about the landers, but the beautiful white interior made her feel like a strange kind of angel in heaven. The smell was even pleasant, like a new car.

Galloway and Wren followed Patel, and Galloway seemed neither excited nor disappointed: both doctors had been on plenty of space missions before, and they'd seen their fair share of ships. Wren smiled, though, as this was her first time on a brand-new craft. She usually got to go on missions that used the dingy, cramped *Explorer* ships that ferried people to and from the missions exploring the Moon. Galloway had recommended her for the promotion to the new *Antares* class, of which the Metis was supposed to be the first.

Williams followed last, being the good head of engineering and security he was—he'd also been on many missions, and he took his job seriously: with the exception of the Captain and First Officer he was always the last on and off. Stuart had worked with him on multiple missions to Mars and Pluto, and she personally made sure he was on the ship. Both officers looked deceptively young thanks to the preservation effects of long-term cryosleep: Williams was tall and muscular with light curly brown hair that bordered on blonde—a look that got him a fair share of ladies in his youth, but once he met Grace Stuart on the *Beagle III*, he'd only had eyes for her.

Williams closed the door to the gravitational chamber and pressed the red LOCK icon on the control pad. The bellows on the door hissed and pulled the door secure, and the locking bolts closed into place with a loud noise that bordered between a click and a clunk. A tiny bell rang from the control panel and the screen turned red: it displayed a flashing LOCKED icon.

Stuart surveyed the group of nine clustered around her at the entrance door. Each member of the team looked at her with tired eyes.

"Welcome home," she said as the bay doors opened.

FIVE

STUART STEPPED THROUGH THE THRESHOLD. Behind was a hall about two and a half meters wide, with walls the same shade of white as the docking bay and covered with the same marble-like tile. Everything was spotless like a brand-new diamond. Stuart could see doors to her left and right that led to the two engine rooms, and beyond them was the crossroads to the main hallway. The hallway branched off to the left and right and acted like the artery to the ship's "wings." Straight ahead from the bay were the doors leading to the bridge. Stuart looked back at her crew waiting in the storage bay, then turned to approach them; as she walked, she started unfastening the straps and zippers on her space suit, revealing a blue standard-issue Space Command jumpsuit underneath.

"Let's all get out of these suits and leave them here in the bay for now." Stuart wrestled with a particularly stubborn portion of her zipper that was stuck.

"Cool," agreed Williams as he started matching Stuart's progress and the other crew members followed his lead. They left the safety suits hanging on a row of hangers seemingly designed for the exact purpose.

Stuart looked at the group and made eye contact with Haddad. "Guys, we've all done this in the simulator—let's everybody head to their facilities and check them over. Post me your results as soon as you're done. Then we can get some rest." Stuart felt like an asshole demanding her team keep to the mission, despite everything they'd just gone through.

The crew nodded in semi-stunned unison and dispersed. Patel and Forester turned to the left and headed towards the bio labs; Galloway and Wren turned right to inspect the medical facilities; Schwartz and Williams each went to one of the engine rooms—Schwartz to the right and Williams to the left. Gutierrez and Simon followed Haddad and Stuart to the bridge. Each walked in silence.

Every step closer to the bridge made Stuart's heart race faster and she felt her belly breaking out in a nervous sweat. The nearer she got to the captain's chair, the less she felt like the Grace Stuart who was afraid to jump in the swimming pool when she was five years old; she wore an emotional mask that expertly covered little Gracie up. Stuart could never explain to her family the way piloting a craft made her feel—it was like you became bigger than you thought you were.

She reached the door and the two panes parted, sliding into recessed holes in the wall; beyond was a stunning view of the moon, brilliant behind the large window viewscreens that expanded in all directions. She'd seen this view a thousand times in the simulator, but seeing in person took her breath away. Stuart complemented the ship designers *in mortem*—they had created a craft of unusual beauty: it made the old *Explorer* crafts look downright barbaric and fit for the fictional Klingons of *Star Trek* fame.

The bridge had a bank of technical equipment, a large viewscreen system that covered all the exposed walls, a few seats for guests, and four com terminals. The four control desks sat in an egalitarian line in the center of the room; each small desk-like terminal stood in front of a chair that looked like the lower half of the letter 'S.' Stuart smiled—it all matched the training simulations perfectly, but somehow seemed magnificent in its simple practicality. The room tapered to a triangular point where the ship's wings became the apex of the Metis' nose, and when you turned all the viewscreens on and stood at that point, you felt like you were leaping naked into space.

Haddad, Gutierrez and Simon all dispersed to their stations: Haddad sat in the center just right of Stuart's seat, Gutierrez sat next to Haddad, and Simon took the seat to Stuart's left. Haddad touched the com screens and inspected the propulsion controls, Simon ran the start program on the navigational equipment, and Gutierrez started activating the planetary analysis controls. Stuart walked forward almost tentatively towards her captain's seat.

She knew she shouldn't be afraid, but a part of her felt a tiny uncertain twinge when she took the helm. Stuart knew how to command ships, but the long time in cryosleep to and from Pluto only made her mature on paper; in both looks and attitude she still felt thirty. Each step closer to the chair made her palms sweat, until she stood next to her command seat.

It was a beautiful curved piece of furniture, clearly designed for comfort and a commanding presence at the same time: the padding was a light mint color, adding to the strangely exposed and airy feel on the bridge. The décor was what surprised Stuart —it was like the designers had thought about futuristic comfort as well as the mission. Stuart wondered how many fights they'd had with Mission Command over the balance of beauty and function on the Metis.

She took another small breath and realized Haddad, Gutierrez and Simon were all looking at her with expectant gazes. Stuart blushed slightly and took her seat, feeling an immediate connection run from her tailbone up her spine as her heart pumped faster. The excitement of taking over a brand-new craft was a pleasure very rarely experienced, and only for the best pilots in Space Command. Stuart felt instantly like the Metis was her baby, friend and lover all at the same time—she couldn't help but break into a small grin.

"Seat fits, Captain?" Haddad gave Stuart an approving smile.

"Perfect. Just perfect." Stuart spoke softly, almost to herself in a trance. She snapped out of her pleasure and ran through the ignition drill in her head; her hands followed suit and worked the controls on the panel in front of her like a pianist. Though portions of her heart bleated in pain for the loss of her planet, another, colder, part of Stuart's psyche told her to numb the pain and get to work—she figured her crew-mates were feeling a similar call to duty.

Stuart first ran a diagnostic on the ship's integrity; the program checked the status of the engines, hull, life support systems, and each room on the ship. There were ten sleeping quarters, two labs, two engine rooms, a gym and a conference room that doubled as a mess hall. The computer program ran a body heat scan and Stuart was glad to see each member of the team at their stations, diligently getting started on their own status checks. The program went so far as to show her pictures of each room, as well as the heat signatures of the humans in the rooms. They all were running a bit warm, but that was to be expected given the day's stress levels.

Once the scan completed inspecting each room it continued checking all the hatches, doors, and the structural integrity of the ship's outer skin—all with excellent results. Next came the engine check; Stuart saw engine one was already online, and she silently thanked the Universe for Williams and his fanatic preparation. He had an almost obsessive love for different propulsion mechanisms, and she knew he'd been terribly excited to work with the new Ares 1 engines. He'd babbled on about them every night on Earth before they went to bed—it became the white noise that lulled Stuart to sleep.

Stuart turned her attention to engine two and her brow knit as a frown drew the corners of her mouth down. She saw Schwartz in the engine room, but his engine wasn't online yet.

She turned to Haddad. "Can you open a com line to engine room two?" Her hands were currently occupied with two different scanning programs.

"Yup." He tapped on his terminal and the window in front of Stuart suddenly turned opaque; a screen appeared with an icon flashing in the center. After about 30 seconds waiting, Schwartz's face appeared on the screen.

"How're things going, Jimmy?"

"Having a bit of trouble with this one, Captain." Stuart could hear the irritation in his voice, and he never called her by her first name. She was always, irritatingly, "captain" to him.

"What's the problem?"

"Can't seem to get it to initialize."

"I'll hail Pete and send him over. He's got Number One up and ready to go." She saw a flicker of frustration and anger cross Schwartz's face, but Stuart really didn't give a shit if he hated help—they needed to get the engines online ASAP to get the ship away from the damage zone.

"Yes, Captain." Schwartz sounded like a sullen twelve-year-old.

Stuart tamped down her frustration at Schwartz and closed the com screen. She returned to her diagnostics and noticed a few minutes later that engine two was finally online, and she smiled and praised Williams again. The rest of the systems checks were uneventful, and within five minutes they had the confirmation on the screen the craft was ready for ignition.

She turned to the bridge team. "You guys ready to fire her up?"

"All systems ready," they each responded.

Stuart touched the ignition program START icon and the craft came to life; each person on the ship heard a soft hum and felt a vibration like the buzzing of insect wings under their feet. Stuart felt it not just in her feet, but it traveled up her body and seemed to fill every pore: it made her feel alive.

"Let's bring her around to port," she called to Simon, never taking her eyes off the moon swelling in front of the viewscreen.

THE METIS TURNED and the entire crew felt the ground beneath them shift. In the medical room Galloway and Wren held on to the exam table to catch their balance, and in the engine rooms Schwartz and Williams each watched their respective engine like paranoid hover-parents. Their eyes were glued to the diagnostic screens, searching for any indicators of engine malfunction. Williams subconsciously held his breath, praying the engines continued working smoothly; Schwartz stared blank-eyed at his drive panel and picked at the dirt under his fingernails.

Forester and Patel left their lab and walked across the hall to one of the sleeping quarters. The room didn't have a resident yet, but the window viewscreen provided an outlet for Patel and Forester's curiosity to see where they were going. The lab had a window viewscreen too, but it faced towards the rear of the craft; it was human nature, they guessed, to want to see what was coming ahead.

The ship turned slowly and the view from the giant viewscreen in the bridge pulled away from the surface of the moon, gradually turning towards Earth. Simon watched his controls like a hawk, on guard for any more rogue satellites washed off course by the comet's impact; Stuart stared straight ahead, scanning the sky for visual clues of the same threat. She wasn't sure if the comet's blast had pulverized most of the debris from the force, or if there were further bits of rock and satellite loose in the planet's shadow.

The ship turned further and Earth slowly came into view. Stuart gasped and tried keeping her composure at the sight in front of her: the planet was no longer blue and green. What was left in the comet's wake was a planet of charred black and burning red; fires still burned on some of the continents, but the seas were all gone. They had been replaced with vast expanses of dull brown and black, and where the continents had already burned, the earth was a scorched black. The entire planet looked like the embodiment of Hell, and Stuart fought the urge to cry, but lost.

Beside her, Haddad, Simon and Gutierrez all shared the same shocked expressions. Haddad watched the blackened lump that used to be Great Britain, and started crying for the mother he missed and the hug from her he'd never receive again. Simon's dark eyes filled with tears and his lower lip quivered; Gutierrez sat with a pallid face and a blank expression, her legs shaking like an electric current ran through them.

In the sleeping quarters, Forester and Patel both got their first good look at the planet they once called home: Forester let out a primal cry of pain and collapsed on the floor, burying his head in his hands, and Patel kneeled to touch his shoulder, her tears flowing freely and dripping down both cheeks. They held each other and cried. Patel had known this was coming, but it still didn't prepare her for the sight of her blackened former home: to spend one's whole life studying the living things on a planet, and then to have them all suddenly disappear in one afternoon felt like the most crushing kind of defeat. It made all the DNA samples in their lab seem suddenly precious like the most rare element.

Williams was somehow glad he was in the engine room: his imagination already told him what to expect, and he didn't want to see what had become of Earth. To him, it was like going to a funeral with an open casket—something he'd much rather avoid. Williams consciously chose to remember the Earth that was blue and green, not the raging inferno he'd witnessed after liftoff. He sat and watched the engine screen like it was a candle in a dark room.

Schwartz couldn't help himself, he had to see what had become of Earth. He left his station and crossed the hallway to one of the other personal rooms, opening the sliding door to a full view of the charred and scarred planet. His face betrayed no emotion as Schwartz sat and stared at the view, and while he watched, the planet turned slowly—exposing the giant crater where Argentina used to be. It dwarfed anything he'd ever seen, and the only crater that came close in his mind was the SPA Basin on the Moon. Schwartz stared blankly at the window and blinked, his hand resting ponderously on his chin, while inside he thrilled carnally at the raw destruction.

Galloway and Wren also couldn't resist seeing Earth. They left the medical room and crossed the hallway just like Patel and Forester had done, and again like the others, they opened the door to a huge view of the destroyed planet. Wren clapped both hands to her mouth and cried in deep heaving sobs. Galloway hadn't made two steps in the door when his legs buckled and collapsed; he sat on his knees staring in shock at the crater. He was so stunned the tears didn't come—instead Galloway felt the crazy urge to laugh, then he threw up on the floor.

Stuart continued watching the planet turn, and she caught her breath as the crater came into view. It rivaled some of the ones she'd seen on Mars, and the similarity between the planets was eerie. She saw fires still burning towards the North Pole, but the whole of the Americas was now a blackened, charred mass. She felt a deep emptiness in her stomach and her innards seemed to drop to her knees—nothing in her travels had prepared her for this. She touched the control panel to open the ship-wide communication channels and her hand shook as she reached for the screen.

"I know we're all seeing this." She strained to talk through the knot in her throat. "We still have each other. Remember that."

Every crew member sat where they were, each staring shocked at the wreck of Earth. Galloway crawled forward on his knees to the window screen and placed his palm on the material, imagining he could feel the cold of space through his hand, like it could pierce his soul. Finally, the numbness broke and he started crying as hard as Wren. She moved to his side, dropped to her knees as well and held his hand; the warmth from her palm counteracted the coldness like a pin prick.

"Laurance, get us to the far side of the moon." Stuart's voice broke as she looked away from the screen.

SIX

THE ENGINES PUSHED into gear as Stuart increased the Metis' speed. The ship's power quietly surprised her—another improvement over the old *Explorer* and *Ranger* classes; it figured, after the feedback her crew had given Space Command on the one-and-only *Ranger*-class ever made. The *Columbia* was designed for deep-space travel to the outer reaches of the solar system, but the dark, cluttered interior of that ship inspired the crew to sleep long hours and fight with each other. The depression and claustrophobia suffered by the *Columbia's* crew was the warning signal the designers at Space Command needed to get the okay for a complete overhaul of the entire ship program. The Metis was the result of this progress, and Stuart had a quick flashback to how it felt the first time her mom gave her the keys to the car.

The Moon loomed huge in the bridge's window screen. Just as it looked like they might be on a collision course, Simon turned the Metis to port and guided the ship around the Moon's orbit. Stuart smiled; she had never flown with Simon outside a simulator, but already liked the navigator's crisp flight mechanics—the guys at Mission Command knew her style and played an expert job at matchmaker when picking her crew.

The Metis looped gently around the Moon and was soon on the other side. The machine made the journey effortlessly and Stuart already had good hope for wherever they were going; she watched the sky in front of them fade from the brightness of the moon's sunny side to the darkness beyond. Stuart felt her skin crawl and goose bumps rippled along her arms.

Once safely on the other side of the Moon, Stuart opened up the com lines. "We're on the far side of the Moon, and I think this holding pattern's pretty free from the debris. Let's all meet in the mess hall in 5 minutes."

GALLOWAY AND WREN looked at each other while still sitting on their knees; Wren shrugged and Galloway tried meeting her gaze with hollow eyes. She took his hand and stood up, pulling him with her, and Galloway looked at his vomit puddle on the floor with shame. "Guess this'll be my room..." He croaked sheepishly.

"Hey, it's as good a way as any to mark your territory." Wren tried coaxing a smile out of Galloway, but it didn't work—Wren immediately blushed so profusely it made her translucently pale skin glow like Rudolph's nose. She hunched her shoulders and headed towards the door trying to escape quickly and Galloway followed, stepping gingerly over the vomit; it smelled acidic and foul.

WILLIAMS STOOD up from his chair at the engine controls and checked his area diligently. The numbers on Engine 1 looked excellent, well within the appropriate operating range, and it hummed softly in front of him. Williams felt the desire to embrace the white box holding the engine: it was like a new kind of heartbeat that soothed the ache from his own chest in a primal way—reminding him of the time he heard the sound of a Tibetan Singing Bowl. He walked around the control panel and put his hands lovingly on the side of the engine. "Good girl," he spoke to the machine, feeling his heart somehow attached to the faithful power center. Sufficiently pleased, Williams turned and walked towards the entry door; a quick turn left led him towards the mess hall.

Once in the hallway, Williams checked both ways at the crossroads for the other crewmembers, but didn't see anyone. His neck tensed and he knit his brows in frustration, combatting the urge to go and round up all the other crew and give them an earful to get moving. Instead, he resisted and dutifully walked towards the mess hall.

Inside was a room the size of a corporate boardroom, dominated by a large meeting table and new-age chairs that seemed to be some Swedish designer's best approximation of something "comfortable." The décor was the same as the rest of the ship: a pearlescent white with the same marble-looking tiles. Viewscreens covered each wall, but they were all turned off, so the walls remained their usual white color. Williams took a seat at the back of the room facing the door—a strange, instinctual desire he'd carried with him since childhood.

FORESTER AND PATEL stood and hugged each other one more time, then turned and walked like zombies out of the sleeping quarters, remaining silent. Forester wiped tears from his eyes, then wrinkled his nose slightly at the smudges on his glasses from his fingers reaching repeatedly behind the lenses. He pulled them off and wiped them on his jumpsuit sleeve while

Patel bit her lip so hard her brown skin turned white. She didn't draw blood, but the sharp pain radiating from her lip somehow made her feel good.

SCHWARTZ LEFT his room and walked towards the mess hall. He saw Patel and Forester coming towards him and they all met in the apex, walking together the final distance then turning right into the mess hall. Williams was waiting for them, and each silently took a seat at the table.

STUART STOOD SLOWLY and felt her left knee pop when she rose, sending a small shock up her leg. She turned and walked towards Haddad, Simon and Gutierrez. "Ready?" She made eye contact with all three.

"Yup." Haddad nodded.

"Yes." Simon gravely whispered.

Gutierrez stared solemnly like she was in a trance.

All three turned and Stuart felt her arms spread out to herd them like a flock of geese. She wondered if her Aunt Nancy would be proud that she hadn't forgotten the skills honed on Nancy's farm; even when the geese bit her, Stuart never backed down.

Haddad pressed the pad next to the door and the panels opened softly. All four took the couple steps from the bridge, turned left, and immediately reached the mess hall. Stuart locked eyes with Williams at the back of the room and they nodded in silent agreement as Stuart and her team sat across the table. Stuart sat directly across from Williams, Haddad took the seat to Stuart's left, Simon sat next to Haddad, and Gutierrez next to him.

"Where's Galloway and Wren?" Stuart looked at Williams and he shrugged.

"Not sure, should I call them?"

"No, let's give them a couple more minutes, then I will."

The entire team waited in uncomfortable silence. Williams and Stuart looked at each other as if they were speaking telepathically, and Haddad watched them. Schwartz seemed obsessed with a small piece of string coming from the wrist of his jumpsuit; Forester returned to picking at his cuticles; Patel stared off in to the space over Simon's shoulder. Simon and Gutierrez followed Haddad's lead, watching Stuart and Williams intently.

Stuart heard the footfalls coming down the hallway and turned to see Galloway and Wren walk through the door; Wren looked fairly calm, but Galloway looked like shit—he was still pale and smelled like vomit. Wren shrugged sheepishly as she made eye contact with Stuart, while Galloway avoided all eye contact and slunk towards his seat. His eyes were hollow and had a grey ring around them as he stared at the table surface, his peppery beard stubble already springing from his cheeks.

Stuart looked down the line of people sitting on both sides of the table. "We need to talk about where we're gonna go now."

"ARE WE STILL GOING TO TITAN?" asked Patel, her voice cracking the silence like a whip.

"I don't think we should," responded Stuart sadly, "there's no one to do experiments for anymore, and there's no infrastructure from there on out of the solar system." Stuart now regretted the scrapped plan to put a small research base up on Pluto; thanks to the loss of the Moon colony during the SPRINGTIME riots, their options in the solar system were now supremely limited.

"How long can we live on the Metis?" piped up Forester, all the crew's eyes registered shock at even hearing his voice.

"The Metis was designed for us to live on it for up to ten years," Williams spoke up. "It was in the system design to keep us in cryosleep until we got to Titan, as well as back again. I think we could stretch the distance considerably if we stay in cryosleep longer, but we'd need to run some numbers on that."

"I'll start working on the calculations...can you get me a new list of what we have on board?" Simon looked at Williams pointedly.

"Yeah." Williams nodded. "I'll work on that as soon as I can."

"But what are we actually planning for?" Scwhartz puffed his lips and sighed. "Just to live a few more years before we die?" He slouched back in his chair.

"Yeah." Galloway spoke up. "Without the Moon, we're fucking stuck."

The crew sat silent for a minute, as each person pondered the cruel twist that happened only two years prior: riots between the workers and management had destroyed the Moon bases in their entirety. What could have been a safe haven for humanity had been destroyed by the management's greed and the responding worker's rage.

Wren looked around nervously. "If we're just postponing the inevitable, what point is there?"

"I don't want to die in a tin can in space," Schwartz blurted. "I didn't sign up for that kind of a mission." His eyes looked around the table like a dog ready to bite.

Williams sounded like an exasperated parent. "Neither did I, but that's where we are, Jimmy."

"This fucking sucks," Schwartz hissed as he sat back in his seat again.

The room suddenly devolved into a din of voices. Each person spoke over the others, and no actual conversation could be heard; the voices raised louder and louder and Stuart sat back and watched it all. The panicked faces, the irritation, Patel started crying and then Forester followed her lead. Schwartz looked at both of the scientists like they were filthy children and you could feel the disgust rolling off him in waves. Williams stared daggers at Schwartz, and Galloway and Wren kept trying to be heard with louder and louder voices. Suddenly Stuart couldn't take it. She stood up.

"Hey, hey, hey!" she shouted and slammed her fist on the table for effect. The room fell instantly silent and all eyes turned towards her. "I do have a plan. I've been to Mars, there are some bases still left there. I suggest we go there and see what shape they're in. At the very least we could clean them out for supplies."

"How will we land there?" shot back Schwartz.

"The landers in the bay will do just fine. They're very similar to what I piloted on my last mission there."

"You sure you can fly them, Captain?" Schwartz's voice dripped with a sarcasm that made Stuart want to strangle him right then and there on the table.

"Yes, I can, and I have made more missions in that craft before you were the age of ten than you ever will." Stuart snapped and glared down the table at Schwartz; she looked so young, but in that instant her eyes spoke her true age. Schwartz snapped his mouth shut and sank back into his chair, shoulders slumped.

Stuart continued. "I know the bases there, I know where they're located, I know where the DNA banks we planted below the surface are. The bases were designed for short-term scientific use, but I think we can make them self-sustaining."

"There's nothing left for us here, anyway." Haddad tried not sounding morose, but failed miserably.

"Any other suggestions?" Stuart tried softening her voice as she made eye contact with each of the people surrounding the table.

Gutierrez spoke first. "Sounds good to me. I think that's our best hope of gathering whatever resources we've got left in the solar system."

"There's the old Brinks supply buoy too," added Simon, "It still has some matter left from the last mission to Mars."

"He's right." Williams nodded his head vigorously and looked at Simon. "Thanks, Laurance, I hadn't even thought of that option." Simon tipped his head in acknowledgement.

"Any other bases or stations between us and Mars we can check?" Stuart felt so foolish: in her haste, she hadn't thought about the other human structures peppered across the solar system.

"Yup, beyond the Brinks we've got a few supply buoy stations that were put in place for the expeditions to Neptune," added Simon. "I helped design them."

Stuart was becoming more impressed by her Parisian crewmember by the minute. "Anything left on them?"

"Not sure, but we could check them too." Simon finished but didn't seem pleased.

"Good." Stuart couldn't hide the relief in her voice. "I think our short-term plan should be to prepare for Mars. We'll hit Brinks on the way, then go into cryosleep for the final approach to Mars orbit—that'll save us as much as we can."

The team all nodded in unison.

"In the meantime, let's all go pick out a room and get some rest. Reconvene in twelve hours?"

The crew nodded again and each person stood. Chairs squeaked and screeched across the tile floor, and still no one made eye contact with each other; they all walked out the door in single file, each person moving in a daze. Galloway turned towards the room he threw up in to clean up his mess and make it his own.

Patel and Forester turned right and walked down the hallway towards their lab. They chose rooms adjacent to each other and across the hall from their bio lab; Wren picked the room directly across from the medical lab. Schwartz turned left and followed the hallway all the way to the end, choosing the wedge-shaped room at the tip of the craft's right wing. Gutierrez picked the room next to Wren's, and Simon joined her on that side of the craft in the room between her and Schwartz.

Stuart turned right and walked in the opposite direction from Schwartz. She passed all the larger crew quarters on her right and walked directly to the smaller wedge-shaped room at the tip of the left wing. Haddad followed her lead and chose the room next to hers, and Williams followed Haddad with a somewhat suspicious look in his eyes, choosing the last room available—the one directly between Haddad and Patel. He smiled a little bit realizing he was nice and close to his dear Engine One, plus Grace was only a door away.

Haddad entered his quarters and looked out his window screen, revealing nothing but the unending expanse of space. He grimaced slightly, then turned the screen off.

SEVEN

STUART CLOSED the door to her quarters and shivered. She turned a full circle and surveyed the space: a small bed lined the wall to her right, next to it was her cryosleep pod imbedded in the wall. She turned and walked towards the pod; it had a small panel on the front displaying the interior status as OPEN. A flashing icon inquired if Stuart wanted to do a readiness check, and she pressed the YES command.

A soft hissing noise filled the room as the gaskets lining the pod tightened and sealed off the air inside, and a loud click jolted her awake as the outer lock closed secure. Stuart watched the lighting inside the pod change from pink to blue, then saw the steam from the cooling devices running their test cycle. While she waited, Stuart turned and looked at the rest of her quarters.

She faced the giant full-wall window screen and looked out into the dark space beyond; the pin-pricks of faraway stars shone like little specks of dust catching the light in a sunbeam. Stuart turned and looked at the sterile little table sitting next to the window screen and couldn't help thinking of a blanched kidney bean; there was a small, curved chair she could move around the table or stand independently anywhere in the room, and she sat down in the curved seat and leaned back. It was surprisingly comfortable, given the bizarre shape: like the conference room chairs, the room chair looked like it came from a Swedish design catalog of the most eclectic order.

Stuart spun the chair around like a little kid playing on a barstool. She watched the room spin around her, all the surfaces blending together in their uniform whiteness. It was like being in the middle of a milkshake, the dizziness wrapping her brain around itself. Stuart caught the floor with the toe of her right shoe and the friction made the sole squeak loudly on the floor; the spinning chair stopped immediately and Stuart shifted her body weight so the momentum change wouldn't throw her onto the floor.

The chair stopped facing the window screen and Stuart looked out into the unending darkness beyond the moon again. She felt all at once like her whole body was being drawn into the never-ending space, like a tractor beam had locked onto her body and had her in its grasp. She stood and walked towards the window screen until her body and face hit the material with an awkward thump. The tip of Stuart's nose made contact with the screen and she felt the cold pressure push her backwards—her eyes watered from the impact.

Stuart sat back down in the chair and cried; once the tears started, she couldn't get them in control. She buried her face in her hands, sat back down in the chair and laid her head face-down on the table; sobbing deeper and deeper, her whole back hitched up and down in jagged fits with each passing breath. Her body and face contorted in pain, but she made absolutely no noise as she cried—her tears ran down her cheeks and pooled on the table's immaculate surface.

Stuart's tears made the room all blurry and she blinked furiously to clear her view. More tears escaped the corners of her eyes and she wiped them hurriedly, hoping it might exorcise the memory of her momentary breakdown. She rubbed them, pulled the outer corners of each eye, then wiped the white goo out of her tear ducts. The cryo pod gave three loud tones in quick succession to notify her its test cycle was complete.

Stuart walked over to the cryo pod and tapped on the diagnostic icons prompting her to look at the readiness of the various functions. The chilling function was working properly, the life support tested perfect, and all readings looked within parameters. Satisfied, Stuart tapped the SHUT DOWN icon and the pod began its rest sequence. The seal bladders deflated, the hatch unlocked, and the light inside dimmed to darkness. Stuart felt relief these pods were the latest cryosleep model—earlier versions made you inhale a special goop, and she hated puking the goop up like an infant each time she woke.

She turned and walked over to the spartan bed next to the cryosleep pod. The thin white mattress lay over yet another harder white surface; Stuart cringed imagining what the bed must feel like, but she gamely lay down on it to test. The pad layer quickly adjusted to her body shape and started warming like a heated blanket; just like the funny chair, the bed was surprisingly comfortable even though it looked like a possible torture device.

Stuart lay quietly staring at the ceiling, remembering the days when she had little glow-in-the dark stars plastered over her childhood bed. She'd instructed her mother to put up tiny replicas of her favorite constellations and Stuart smiled remembering her mother tottering on the tall ladder as she tried sticking each little star perfectly. Madeline Stuart created beautiful replicas of the Big Dipper, Orion, Taurus, Canis Major and Minor, as well as a fantastic version of Pegasus she'd even illustrated by drawing a picture of a Pegasus around the constellation.

Stuart remembered her early obsession with Pegasus and unicorns fondly—she'd had posters of them all around her room; little Grace Yuna Stuart even asked Santa for a unicorn faithfully every Christmas from ages three to eight. At eight she'd asked for a spaceship, which Santa finally brought her when she was eighteen: the *Aurelia* from Space Command. Stuart suddenly wanted to go back to that bedroom very badly.

Her parents had spared no expense for their only, precious child; Madeline had tried for years to get pregnant, and when she and Larry finally threw in the towel they turned to a friend who worked at an agency specializing in placing Korean children for adoption. Grace came into their lives as Yuna, a tiny little girl already one year old and starting to speak short Korean phrases. The agency loved that Larry worked in aerospace engineering and Madeline was a biochemist; they figured the Stuarts would give the little girl who was already speaking eloquently and learning her numbers a good home. They were correct, and Stuart figured parental encouragement was equally to blame for her career in the stars.

Minutes slowly passed and Stuart felt her eyes drooping. The bed was more comfortable than she expected, and Stuart felt all the last week's stress wash over her like a wave. Her body ached, her head was getting fuzzy, and every inch of her screamed to go to sleep. Stuart fought the urge for a few minutes, then finally obliged.

HADDAD LOCKED eyes briefly with Williams and they dutifully followed Stuart down the hall towards engine room one and the Bio Lab, on the search for their new sleeping quarters. In the hurry to launch, Space Command hadn't gotten a chance to assign quarters to any member of the team, so now they had to decide for themselves in an all-out rush like a group of gold miners staking their claims. Haddad looked in the first two doors to his right, but Forester and Patel stared back out of the rooms at him with slightly animal-like possession. Their eyes painfully said: move on.

He kept going down the hallway and nodded to Williams when Stuart chose the room at the far end. Haddad took the room right next to her and Williams grabbed the last available room in between Haddad and Patel.

Williams locked eyes with Haddad one more time and raised his eyebrows in an expectant look. "You good with that one?"

Haddad grimaced slightly and nodded. "Yeah, I guess they're all kind of the same, anyway." He looked in the open doorway, then back at Williams.

"'Night." Williams waved at Haddad and headed into his own room.

"'Night." Answered Haddad, then he turned and entered his new quarters.

Haddad's room was undeniably cold and blindingly sterile white just like all the other rooms on the Metis. He was already tired of white everywhere, and his eyes were instinctually drawn to the darkness beckoning from his window screen—he stared at the stars, temporarily mesmerized. Haddad's eyes lost their focus and the number of stars he saw doubled, then he felt a strange lightness in the head and an almost overwhelming state of calm rolled over him from head to toe. He breathed deeply and stood in that position for a while.

As if on cue, Haddad broke from his trance and breathed in a snort of air. His eyes refocused and the stars now looked like brilliant pin pricks floating at unknown distances from him. Haddad still couldn't shake the feeling he was falling into the stars whenever he faced the window screen, and he suddenly wished Stuart had faced the craft towards the moon; at least the abandoned hunk of rock was more comforting than the unknown distances staring him down now.

Haddad found his chair with his right hand, then slid down to the sitting position with his back lightly pressed against the chair's surface. It felt like a strange caress: his skin tingled as the chair warmed to meet his body temperature. As he settled into the seat a small control panel lit up on the arm, and Haddad manually selected a higher temperature. He thanked the designers for their work on the intuitive furniture—it looked strange, but functioned beautifully.

He slid lower and lower in the seat until his back was curved like a grade-schooler's scraggly "S." Haddad's lower back protested slightly with a twinge, but he ignored the sensation, and his breathing slowed further as he observed his hands with a strange kind of misplaced intensity. His nails were clean, the skin on the tops of his hands was still firm and smooth, and his well-plumped veins tracked their patterns across the back of his hand. Haddad turned his hands over and admired the smooth, uncalloused palms; he couldn't smell the hand soap he used that morning anymore.

Haddad turned towards his bed and observed the sleeping space, as well as the cryo pod and tiny food simulator window. He was glad for this latest little bit of technology: each person had their own personal meal-making machine in their room. It sure beat having a communal kitchen where no one had to fight with Schwartz over the perfect kind of pasta—or who was doing dishes. Space Command had hoped individual sleeping quarters might take the edge off long-term space missions, and so far, Haddad believed their hypothesis.

The cryo pod let out a small beep and Haddad stood a little too quickly; his knees clipped the underside of the table and he barked a string of curses in Egyptian. Haddad felt the bruises forming under his jumper fabric already as he walked gingerly over to the pod and looked at the prompt on the control screen, beckoning him to run the auto test program. He hit the START icon with the tip of his middle finger, hoping it didn't look too much like he was giving the machine an obscene gesture; he certainly had no love for the cryosleep procedure.

While he waited, Haddad turned to the wall over his bed and felt around until a round blue icon the size of his thumb lit up on the wall panel. He pressed the icon, and the viewscreen built into his wall turned on to a blank blue screensaver, with a menu waiting in the corner. Haddad tapped the menu and chose the screensaver setting, looking through all the options until he found what he was looking for: a screensaver of the Scottish coastline, a vacation spot his family favored. He selected that screensaver, then went to the other two walls and chose different Scottish-themed screensavers for each of them as well. With most of the numbingly-white surfaces now broken up, Haddad felt like he could relax a little. His cryopod beeped in the corner, and he could tell from where he was standing that the test process was complete.

Confident the pod was functional, Haddad turned his attention wearily towards his bed. It seemed cold and hard like the rest of his room, but when he sat down the bed caressed his bottom just like the chair did. It looked so sterile but gave off the ultimate comfortable touch—Haddad didn't know how it could be done, but he was grateful for anything that took his mind off the course of the day's events; he crossed his hands above his heart and closed his eyes.

Haddad tried and tried, but no matter how tired he felt, he could not persuade his eyes to go to sleep; he kept thinking about the launch, and he worried if they'd gotten all the DNA and survival gear on the ship. A series of questions burned through his brain and made his stomach churn: had they gotten the proper supplies up to the Metis? How long would the food generator hold up? Would they find anything left in the buoys as they made their way towards Mars? Could they even land on Mars? Haddad's mind raced and he felt his heart beating faster as his chest tightened and his palms started sweating; a chill ran down his back at the same time.

As if on cue, Haddad started breathing deeply in through his nose and out his mouth—long and slow, and almost completely silent. Space Command had made sure to train all its astronauts in a variety of panic-calming techniques, and Haddad dutifully followed them now. His pupils dilated then snapped back into focus, then Haddad took one more full breath and his diaphragm strained upward at the extra push from his lungs.

A tiny tear trickled from the corner of Haddad's eye, and he made no effort to wipe it away.

EIGHT

GALLOWAY OPENED the door to his quarters and the sharp smell of vomit immediately hit his nose and made him cringe. His eyes focused on the puddle halfway between the door and the window screen and he shook his head, while an internal voice immediately berated him for being such a weak fool in front of Wren—she'd probably never respect him again. He prayed no one would learn about his "accident."

His eyes scanned the sterile room, desperate for any sign of cleaning supplies. The walls seemed completely smooth and he couldn't make out the slits for the doors or storage like they'd talked about in the preliminary ship meetings. They'd spent countless hours learning how to work the machinery in their respective work areas via the visual simulator programs, but no simulator had focused on the simple things like how to make your food or clean your laundry; that was the stuff that got lost during the aborted launch month. Galloway turned a full circle carefully in the center of the room, conscious to avoid the vomit puddle. He saw a small, kidney-shaped table, a funny curved chair, a small bed, and his cryosleep pod tucked away in the back corner: no closets, also no sign of the bathroom. Galloway tensed and a cranky expression came over his face, as he wrinkled his nose and spoke to himself, "Where's the fucking bathroom switch?!"

Galloway walked carefully around the perimeter of his room. He touched the wall gently at six-inch intervals, hoping some kind of door might open up. He chastised himself for not paying better attention during the training modules, but made it only a foot down the left wall when his fingers touched a small spot halfway between the floor and ceiling. A bright yellow light in the shape of a circle lit up and a piece of the wall about six feet long suddenly pulled forward about an inch, then slid sideways to the right.

The panel opened up and slid in front of the remaining wall. Behind it was a compartment containing a small sonic shower, a toilet, a vanity with a mirrored cabinet above it, and a small storage cabinet full of the tech towels that were easy to clean in the sonic shower. Galloway grabbed one of the towels and took it back into the main room. He sighed when he looked at the vomit puddle again, then lowered himself slowly to his knees and started wiping at the puddle's edges. The tech towel absorbed all the fluid until it was nearly double its size and Galloway didn't flinch when his hands touched the wetness inside it. Undaunted, he dutifully finished cleaning up his mess.

Galloway wiped in small scooping strokes towards the center of the vomit puddle; with each stroking motion the pile of food chunks in the puddle's center got taller and more compact. After he'd cleaned up all of the fluid, Galloway reached his hand over the little pile with the tech towel loosely held by all five fingers. He closed his hand around the pile and scooped it neatly into the folds. Galloway walked over to the toilet and turned the closed towel over as little bits of his last meal fell in the toilet—which flushed automatically. Galloway threw the towel in the sonic shower and pressed the LAUNDRY cycle and START button on the control pad embedded in the wall.

The shower started its INITIATION cycle with a strong humming noise. He saw the towel vibrating, then UV lights sprang to life in all the walls, ceiling and floor—they focused on the towel and bathed it in a blue light. The shower hummed louder and the towel vibrated so much it bounced around on the floor like an old-fashioned jumping bean. A loud click came from the right wall and all the lights shut off, the humming stopped, and a huge blast of steam shot out from the back wall in a forceful plume. Galloway jumped slightly and shook his head, laughing nervously. After another minute or two in the steam bath, another bell sounded and the icon on the control panel flashed a bright green COMPLETE icon.

Galloway opened the door and took the towel in his right hand: it was clean as new and smelled fresh with a tinge of lemon. He sniffed the towel again and smiled—it made him think about his mother, arms deep in a sink of dishes with an apron on. He always gave her a hard time about doing dishes the "old fashioned way" but she would laugh back and tell him she loved feeling the pride from her own handiwork. "The human body needs to see what it can do with its own hands every once in a while," Galloway's mother always tilted her head pointedly at him when she said that line.

He took the towel and folded it back to its original shape. Galloway's fingers worked expertly like an origami master and he didn't even have to watch what they were doing; he set the towel back on the top of the stack and nodded his head curtly like he was satisfied with a job well done. Galloway turned carefully so he wouldn't bump his elbows or rear on anything in the tiny bathroom, then stepped back into the main room.

There was still a tinge of vomit in the air: it made Galloway's stomach churn again in sympathy pangs. He felt bile rising in his throat but swallowed it back down with an uncomfortable gulp as he walked over to the room control panel next to the food simulator and punched the ROOM FRESHEN icon.

Five small vents opened in the ceiling and started sucking air inward; Galloway's salty brown hair stood slightly on end from the powerful intake, as a clicking noise came from the ceiling, then the vents reversed their flow and blew air back into the room. This air smelled as fresh and lemony as the towel, and Galloway closed his eyes while he breathed deeply—there was no lingering trace of the smell from his accident.

He turned and eyed the tiny table and uncomfortable-looking chair and thought about sitting for a moment—his legs were still shaky from getting sick and all the stress from the day. Galloway took a seat and stared out into the black space on his viewscreen, wishing he could see the sunset over Texas instead.

WREN TOUCHED the pad on the right side of her doorway and the two panels parted with a swooshing noise highly reminiscent of the old show "Star Trek." She touched her hair with a shaking hand and stepped through, her eyes scanning the cold white walls, ceiling and floor. Wren kept hoping the white color would calm the jittery feeling crawling under her skin because she wanted to hit something or break something, but nothing in the room seemed to fit the bill. Wren clenched and unclenched her hands, leaving small red marks where her fingernails bit her palms.

She walked over to the curved, modern chair next to the table that reminded her of the kidney beans her grandma always ate. Wren's stomach turned a somersault as she thought about the nasty, gritty taste of those beans—no amount of seasoning ever made them better. Wren ran her hands along the surface of the table: it was smooth, silky, and so tremendously cold. She sat down and lay her face on the hard plastic, feeling the cold radiate through her hot cheek.

The window screen beckoned and Wren took a look outside.

There were thousands of tiny pin-pricks glimmering out of the darkness at her, clustering and flowing, alone or nestled inside foggy nebulas. She had a hard time comprehending each of those tiny dots was actually a sun, quite likely one much larger than the one Earth orbited. Would they have planets and life going about their surfaces? Could some of those planets suffer a comet impact just like Earth? Were other species orphans in space like them? She sighed and kept staring.

The darkness felt like it surrounded her, and Wren prayed it would dissolve the burning itch under her skin. She relaxed her eyes and breathed like she'd been taught in the mission prep sessions, feeling her heart relax, but her hands still felt like they had bugs in them.

She jumped up and lay down on the hard floor on her back. Wren raised her legs so they looked like she was sitting in an invisible chair, then started furiously doing crunches. Her stomach heaved and her breath shortened, the muscles burning, but Wren continued her furious movement. She lay back for a second breathing heavily in jagged gasps, but the crawly feeling in her hands persisted. Wren raised her legs into the imaginary chair position and did crunches facing her right leg; after fifty of these crunches she turned and did the same movement towards her left leg. Her muscles screamed and Wren fought the urge to pee, laying back exhausted. Yet the crawling feeling persisted, compounded with a sensation that was like having invisible hands squeezing her shoulders.

Wren stood and left her quarters, suddenly desperate to go anywhere other than that cramped white room. She took a left from her door and jogged down the hallway, observing Galloway's room, Gutierrez's room, Simon's room and Schwartz's room to her left, and the three doors representing the engine room, med lab, and storage bay to her right. They passed by in a blur, and within seconds she was at the bulkhead where the ship ended. She turned and sprinted back down the hall, passing the crossroads within a few strides, and ending at the wing terminus next to Stuart's quarters. The total run took less than a minute, and Wren made the return trip nearly as fast; she ran this circuit for the next ten minutes, alternating jogging with blistering sprints that made her legs quiver. Finally, after many repetitions, Wren finally felt her hands and body relax: the crawling feeling was gone. She walked slowly back to her door, her chest heaving.

Back in her room, Wren walked to the food simulator in the corner, tapping the screen to the right until it lit up, emitting a cheery trill. The screen flashed WELCOME in bright yellow lettering; Wren looked at the screen dully as the yellow light illuminated her face. The screen offered her a multitude of different eating options: she could have beverages, meat, grains, desserts, and many other types of food. Wren tapped the BEVERAGES icon and a long list came up with handy pictures of the drink next to them. She tapped the EXERCISE DRINK icon and a list of drinks from protein shakes to calorie-free fizzies filled the screen. Wren selected the SPORTS REPLEN-ISHMENT DRINK picture and chose the flavor ORANGE, the option accompanied by a cheery image of a fresh Florida orange.

The machine hummed and Wren felt a small, warm exhaust coming from the closed window; when she lowered her head down closer she heard the humming get louder. She stood up and continued watching the window patiently until a beep came from the machine and the screen flashed a bright green COMPLETE icon across the pane. The green hue momentarily lit Wren's face again and made her look like The Hulk, then the door opened and a glass of bright orange drink lay waiting.

Wren grabbed the drink in her left hand and drank thirstily, stopping and coughing after a minute to curse herself about the perils of greedy thinking. After a bout of racking coughs, Wren took a tiny sip of the orange drink; satisfied, she finished the glass and set it back in the window.

She turned towards the screen and hit the RECYCLE icon on the pad. The window closed and Wren heard a crunching noise, then another loud hum. Wren stepped back and watched for a minute longer until the window opened empty. The screen flashed: RECYCLE COMPLETE - WOULD YOU LIKE ANOTHER ORDER? She turned her back on the screen wearily and walked away from the machine.

Wren moved towards her bed and lay down. She pulled a small portable screen from the side of the headboard and touched it to wake it from sleep function; it took a moment, but the screen came to life with a variety of bright pastel colors. Wren shielded her eyes slightly from the glare: there were option icons on the screen telling Wren she could control the softness and temperature of the bed, as well as its angle. The bed could also vibrate or massage and had an auto-clean feature.

Wren felt her body relax as it responded to the instant comfort the bed offered—a welcome finish to the second-worst day in her life.

NINE

SCHWARTZ SAT cross-legged on the floor of his white room; his shoes sat next to him on the floor, and his socks exhaled a particularly cheesy odor. He'd tried doing some of the meditating the Space Command shrinks told him would work for stress release, but nothing happened other than his own thoughts chasing one another like squirrels in a cage. It'd been such a bad day that he was desperate for any relief, so desperate he even tried the woo-woo meditation stuff. Now it was on to something he knew would work: masturbation.

Something about that act was always calming and soothing for Schwartz, and he made a point to usually take care of the need at least once a day. He likened it to good system maintenance of his entire body, and the relaxation afterward was good for the blood pressure. He thought about a particularly hot blonde he'd fucked only a week prior to their emergency launch, then began stroking himself. The thoughts progressed from her sucking him off to her being bent over a chair, to the look on her face when he fucked her really hard. The last thought rang the bell for Schwartz, and he climaxed.

Schwartz sat still as a statue while the semen dried on the

crotch of his jumpsuit and over his hand; he did not move a finger. At that moment he resembled a mannequin more than a man, his features more suited to the looks of a perfect china doll or a classic painting than a twenty-seven-year-old spacedrive engineer. His father had often berated him for his pretty face, but Schwartz knew the old bastard was only jealous. Jimmy Schwartz had always had his pick of the women, thanks to good genes.

A loud beep rang out from the main control panel and Schwartz jolted awake. He felt the tightness in his crotch and looked down to see the mess he'd made of himself; his brow knit tight and his face fell into a frown. He stood with his face still in the funny scowl and turned towards the sonic cleaner, then stripped naked and threw all the soiled garments in the machine. He pressed the START button and stood back from the cleaner's doors as the humming began; satisfied, he turned back to face the unending blackness of space.

Schwartz felt like a new baby in front of the darkness: it was like being born, again. He spread his arms wide as if crucified and turned his head—a fairly accurate depiction of the Man on the Cross, except he had no loincloth to cover his genitals. He smirked as he exposed himself. *Shit*, he thought, *it's not like God hasn't seen me naked before.* After a minute, he left the viewscreen and turned towards the small mirror above his bathroom sink.

His dark brows rose slowly and his face pointed straight ahead as he evaluated his body in the mirror's reflection; he was getting a bit older, granted—it took more effort to keep his physique now, but his abdomen and upper body still rippled with muscles. Schwartz missed the days of endless beers and pizza that never stuck to his gut; now he feasted on a Cobb salad and savored every bite of cheese. *Well, it's the price I pay for this beautiful piece of art,* he thought, rubbing his taut stomach that reminded him of a Roman gladiator's. It made him crave steak and blood.

Schwartz stared at himself and picked at the bumps on his face—he searched his skin for pimples, of which there were none—only smooth creamy flesh. His eyes were bloodshot, a bit veiny, but at least still in his head. He gave a somewhat bemused smile to the man in the high tower, and he imagined that man smiling back. Schwartz put his hands on his hips and started a series of deep knee bends, feeling his skin tingle and his legs get warm.

He cocked his head and beheld himself in the mirror. Schwartz smiled a little wider, then bared his teeth in a simian-type grimace while he squinted. This version of him looked a little scary, he thought: it was like looking at the madman part of oneself, which pleased Schwartz deep in the crevices of his heart.

A new beeping noise came from the cleaning chamber and Schwartz turned to face it: his clothes were ready. He pulled the clothing out and set them in a heap on the tile floor, then stepped into the cleaner and clicked the MAN-NORMAL WASH button right before he closed the door.

Schwartz felt the vibrations penetrating his skin—it was like getting a good, vigorous licking from a giant cat. He couldn't resist urinating as the waves hit him, and enjoyed every bit of dirt, grime and sweat lifting from his body. He also loved how the machine exfoliated his face. Schwartz's vanity drove him to love the machine that perfectly cleaned his masterpiece of a body, while the rest of the crew held the sonic shower with some distaste. Schwartz loved the brutality of it: he felt like getting clean was a rite of manhood, and it also made things perfectly clear he was in space.

A new beep sounded from the control panel and the sonic wave machine shut off. Schwartz stepped out of the enclosure and onto the tile floor—he was perfectly dry, so there was no need for a towel. He put on each clean jumpsuit layer and walked to the small toiletry cabinet above the sonic sink.

Schwartz used his fingers and a little bit of saliva to style the front tips of his bangs, then turned to face the door. Curiosity made him think about going out on the prowl to see who was awake, but tonight was probably better suited to rest.

Schwartz walked in an even step towards his desk, where he sat and turned on the the view monitor embedded in the table's surface; he scrolled through the selections until he found a movie he liked—*The Fast and The Furious*, one of his favorites.

PATEL WALKED into her new apartment and looked briefly around. She sighed at the bland white interior, but at least it wasn't a dark hole like the last ship she'd been on. *Better to be blinded than depressed*, she thought. Patel looked to her left, eyes scanning the wall for the break that the crew's manual said would mark the opening to her bathing quarters. She didn't see anything and had to walk a few steps closer before her eyes discerned the fine line in the smooth white wall panels.

She raised her thumb and waved it at the wall like a hitch-hiker; her tongue sticking out just slightly at the corner of her mouth, the example of concentration. Patel's brows furrowed over her dark eyes. About midway down the panel, Patel's thumb moved over an area that immediately shot out a tiny laser and scanned her thumbprint. A bell that sounded like it belonged to a tiny bicycle rang and the panel lit up. WELCOME DR PATEL it displayed in cheery yellow print.

The screen opened up to a wide array of option icons. One beckoned Patel to access the bath chamber, and she touched that icon with a glimmer of relaxation in her eyes. The panel slid forward and recessed to the right-hand side with a silky grace, revealing her small sink, wash cubicle, and toilet.

The tiny room looked like it was made for a gymnast. Even Patel, who was one of the shortest members of the crew, had a hard time moving around in it. She laughed at the idea of Williams trying to wash himself in the sonic shower—his elbows probably hit everything. Patel approached the mirror and looked at her reflection; she made a straight face that was neither a frown nor a smile, then she licked her lips and rubbed them together to moisten both lobes.

Patel stared deep into the brown eyes that looked back at her from the mirror: they were so dark they almost seemed black, a look Patel always secretly hated. She'd also hated her deep brown skin that would have marked her as a Dalit in the olden days; nevertheless, she'd always been proud of her thick ebony hair, and she started working at it with her fingers.

Her hair was tied up in a tight bun fastened at the crown of her head. Patel pulled out the bobby pins holding the center at neat forty-five-degree angles and her hair fell into a slightly-corkscrewed ponytail. Next, she dug her fingernails into the rubber band holding the ponytail centered to her head: it pulled out and took a few pieces of hair with it. Patel winced as the hairs ripped free from her scalp and she bit her lip in frustration.

Patel looked at herself in the mirror. She ran her fingers through her hair and untangled it, the pieces coming loose from the tight twist in loose waves. She looked for a brush, then remembered her training and headed to the simulator. "Hair Brush" she spoke to the window, then she selected her preferred hair brush from a massive array of options. The screen lit up and an engine whirred behind the wall, and in only a few seconds the panel beeped, the window rose, and Patel beheld a small new hairbrush with soft bristles. Patel smiled and grabbed it in her right hand, then brushed at her hair with strokes like a long-haired cat licking its coat.

She stared at her reflection, entranced; slowly, mindlessly, Patel unzipped the front of her jumpsuit and peeled it off both shoulders. The suit fell lifelessly around her waist, bagging around her hips as the torso fell backward. Patel wriggled the suit down her legs, then stepped carefully out of the entire piece —leaving the jumpsuit on the floor like a discarded husk. Patel approached the sonic shower and looked at the control panel flashing on its door: there were many bath cycle options to choose from. Patel selected the WOMAN - LONG HAIR - MOISTURIZE setting and stepped into the machine.

The vibrating made Patel's cellulite jiggle and her nipples harden. She simultaneously loved and hated the prickly feeling the cleaner made, but she did dearly enjoy the clean feeling afterward—Patel needed that after the day she'd had. She endured the vibrational assault from the shower and after a few minutes a pleasant peach smell puffed out of a small nozzle in the shower's ceiling, then it sprayed a fine mist of conditioner in her hair. Patel rubbed the conditioner into her locks and discarded any loose strands on the shower floor.

The machine beeped and Patel heard the latch on the door automatically open. The door slid outward and she stepped out of the doorway, one foot carefully following the other, pointing her toes like a princess in an old Disney movie. Patel grabbed one of the small towels and rubbed herself down out of habit, not need: her legs, arms and other body parts had been automatically shaved as part of the cleaning cycle, and she enjoyed that smooth, silky feeling. Patel stroked her calf and nodded, pleased.

She stood and looked at her naked body in the mirror. Patel used to chastise herself for being a little chubby, but now that she was one of the last women alive, who would care if she carried a few extra pounds? Patel shivered at the thought of having a baby; she thought that path for her ended years ago when Ravi cancelled their engagement, but now having a baby was a biological imperative for the future of the species. Patel started to look at herself in the same way she did any endangered species: young from her womb was now of the utmost importance.

Patel knew the rest of the crew hadn't thought of that, yet. It was her job to concern herself with these things: the contingency plans, the genetics. Patel knew how many different variations they could get from all the different breeding patterns, plus what they could create from the DNA they carried onboard. She'd done contingency survival studies as a young lab student, but she'd never thought hard about how those in the breeding program felt. Now wearing the shoes of a test subject, Patel thought it felt weird; she shuddered at the idea of having to have Schwartz's baby in the name of genetic diversity.

She looked back at the woman in the mirror, shrugged her shoulders, then turned and walked to the generator window next to her cryo pod. At that window she tapped the screen and spoke, "Pajamas," then selected her preferred option. The window whirred and quickly produced a pair of soft pink pajamas in a women's Petite Large. Patel pulled the pants up and fastened them at the waist, then she pulled the soft top down over her head. The smooth, warm feeling made her stomach settle and she just wanted to hug herself.

Patel walked over to her bed and lay down, imagining Ravi was cuddling her from behind. She smiled and closed her eyes.

TEN

"IT IS NOW zero seven hundred hours," called a strange female voice from the ceiling.

Gutierrez woke with a start. She sat straight up and looked out ahead, expecting to see the blue sky and her view of the launch pads, but the darkness of space greeted her instead. She sighed and turned, hanging her legs off the side of the bed, and a cold shock from the tile radiated up her legs to her groin when her feet touched the floor. It immediately woke up her up, and she desperately needed to pee.

Padding across the room in her bare feet to the area in the wall where their training said the bath compartment door was, Gutierrez waved her thumb over the spot mid-way down the panel and the scanner read her print. It beeped, then the panel slid against the right wall. She walked over to where the toilet seat stood flipped up against the wall for storage, pressed her thumb to the panel in between the toilet seat and the vanity mirror, and the toilet seat dropped slowly into place like a drawbridge lowering after a large ship. It locked into position with a loud snap that reverberated off the slick white walls.

Gutierrez lowered her pajama bottoms and sat on the toilet.

She stared straight ahead, a view that looked out on her bed and cryo pod. She traced the lines of the cryo pod with her eyes and mentally made the bed, wishing she'd remembered to grab her reading pad in the hurry to leave the planet—even a fashion magazine would have been welcome. She sat and tried finishing her morning constitutional; an old military habit so ingrained, Gutierrez still made sure to evacuate every morning.

The toilet automatically flushed when it sensed she was finished, while vents above the bath area opened to allow a tiny fan to clean the air. Gutierrez walked to the vanity and looked at herself: her hair was tousled and ratted from the restless night before. She ran her fingers through it and tried using a bit of simulated water from the sink to moisten it, getting the frizz and knots loose, then she simulated a brush and worked at it a little more.

Gutierrez sniffed her jumpsuit armpits and wrinkled her nose—the entire garment stunk of fear sweat and nightmares. She pulled off her clothes down to her underwear and threw them in the sonic shower; a few quick taps on the control screen and the machine was off and running—her clothing was clean within two minutes. Gutierrez removed each clean piece and put it back on her body, failing to get in the machine herself. She hated climbing in the sonic shower—there was no way to characterize the violated feeling she got each time she had to bathe. She simulated some deodorant and applied that liberally instead.

Clean and somewhat awake, Gutierrez turned to the simulator sandwiched in the corner of the room between the cryo pod and the wall. She touched the screen and chose the FOOD option, and under the FOOD section there were sub-sections for which meal of the day. Gutierrez selected the BREAKFAST icon, then chose a bowl of cereal and milk; for cereal she selected strawberry-flavored rice puffs, her favorite thing to eat in the morning. The simulator whirred for a minute then the window opened displaying a little red bowl filled with the pink balls and white milk. Gutierrez smiled and removed the bowl—the machine had even created a red spoon to match.

There had been many mornings when Luisa Gutierrez's mother had entreated her to eat something different, something healthier in her opinion; Guadalupe Gutierrez always tried to get her daughter to eat eggs or rice or chorizo, but Luisa always clung stubbornly to her cereal. The rice puffs were a perennial favorite, which Guadalupe clucked her tongue and decried as "fake food." As she grew older, Luisa noted her penchant for meal uniformity, but no amount of begging by her family or girl-friends could get her to give up the habit; she loved the comfort of a meal she knew she could trust.

She walked over to her table and sat, crunched her cereal and tapped the table's upper right-hand corner; the entire panel flashed to life and she saw it was, indeed, a large video screen. She pulled up the MOVIE function and typed the name, *The Hunger Games* into the title box. The screen identified the film and suddenly the credits filled the center portion of her table. Gutierrez watched Jennifer Lawrence for a few minutes, feeling her heart and nether regions warm for a woman who was already long-dead. Going back to her first crush was almost as calming as eating her favorite cereal.

Gutierrez ate at a pace that was not military-fast, but not leisurely either. She finished her meal quickly, with just enough time to watch the tragic selection of her hero for the movie's namesake event. She turned off the view screen in the table and took her dish back to the simulator's window, this time pressing the RECYCLE button as the simulator door closed. She imag-ined the simulator breaking down the used bowl into its atoms, then storing the energy to make something else later on; the little window stayed shut while she watched.

She turned and cracked her knuckles as she walked, rubbing the back of her neck with her fingertips, as she headed back to the vanity in the bath compartment. Gutierrez pressed the mirror at the lower right-hand corner and the entire panel released and opened: inside were a variety of simulated toiletries. She grabbed the toothbrush and toothpaste, then brushed her teeth using the simulated water that came out of the sink's faucet. It was all incredibly lifelike: the atom-manipulation technology had only been in its infancy when Earth met the comet, but it still opened up a world of useful possibilities.

Once finished with her morning routine, Gutierrez felt ready to face the day. She walked towards the door and stopped right at its threshold, took a deep breath in and exhaled, then stepped through the door and out into the hall. Gutierrez turned right and walked towards the bridge, where she met with Williams and Haddad at the intersection—Haddad beckoned her to walk first. She heard his footsteps clicking on the tile behind her as Williams turned and walked to his engine room. Gutierrez and Haddad stopped before the bridge entrance and looked at each other for a moment, meeting each other's gaze.

The doors opened up on a new morning in space.

STUART CLICKED the screen at her station. The little pad woke up and brightly displayed a variety of metrics on the ship's performance, orbit, and exterior space analysis. The Metis had spent the night observing the damage to Earth and wanted someone to see its findings.

Stuart sighed as she watched the debris churn around the destroyed planet. It looked like the debris field was predominantly between Earth and the Moon, so the Metis automatically positioned itself just outside the damage zone. The field contained large chunks of the planet's surface and sub layers and Stuart privately wondered if the field might create a ring someday like those of Saturn, or if it might coalesce into a tiny moon. The ship kept a distance great enough to exceed the Moon's gravitational pull as well as the Earth's, so it sat in a unique place to view the carnage.

The Moon pulled out of view and the crushed husk of a planet came into focus. It was remarkably brown and black now, with fires scarring the face where volcanoes spontaneously erupted; some of the lava fields were so large Stuart could still see their curves in space. They looked like giant bloody fingers tracing the planet's charred skin.

The massive crater obliterating the tip of South America was dark and desolate. The impact was so severe the spontaneous blast field had consumed everything in its path. *At least the people didn't suffer,* Stuart thought morbidly. She wondered where souls went when the planet was totally destroyed. Did they go to another planet somewhere far away? Would she be reunited with them someday? Or did they get scattered and recycled to the wind? Stuart shook her head and looked down at her control screen.

The screen gave Stuart an analysis of the greater space area, and confirmed the path between Earth and Mars looked relatively clean. Stuart breathed a sigh of relief—she wouldn't have to worry about some bit of space junk or an asteroid hitting the craft and killing them all while they were tucked away in their cryo tubes. She knew those pods could last and hold up in space for a long time, but a nagging voice in her head questioned *how long?*

She bit her lower lip and stared at the main window ahead. The scarred view of Earth was so incredibly sickening, yet Stuart controlled the urge to cry and vomit and felt a cold burn rise in her stomach. She vowed to make it through the morning, then burped quietly under her breath.

"How's it looking, Grace?" Gutierrez spoke softly from Stuart's left side.

"Not awesome." Stuart sighed. "The Metis took a whole

bunch of readings during the night, you'll probably want to take a peek at them before we head off."

"Yeah." Gutierrez nodded somberly. "I'll hop in right now."

"Thanks." Stuart gave Gutierrez a reticent smile, then tapped at her screen and wiped her nose briefly. "Let's get a com line open to everybody."

"One second." Haddad worked furiously to open all the com lines on the ship. "Ready Grace," he called back quietly as Stuart stood up.

"Hey guys," her voice reverberated over the entire craft. "We're sitting in a long orbit for a couple hours. I need each of you to go to your assigned workstations and get me an inventory of everything in your respective areas. Every nut, bolt and plant. Even the smallest things need to be inventoried." She paused to take in a breath, then continued. "Once you're done, get the supply level readings on your simulators too...all of them. Bring these numbers to the meeting room in two hours. Let me know if you need longer."

Each person in every room looked at the other occupants and shrugged or shook their heads. Galloway and Wren took turns divvying up the respective regions of the medical suite, while Patel and Forester separated out their DNA banks cleanly: Patel did the animal and insect life, Forester did all the types of plant life. The minerals were in their own separate bank, consisting of tiny samples down to the atomic size.

Schwartz and Williams each went to their engine rooms and the bridge team split up the storage bays; once everyone was in their assigned sections, the tallying began.

WREN GRABBED her scanner and waved it around her corner of the patient room. It scanned, identified and counted each of the items in that corner, then made a panoramic picture of everything it found in the specified area. The items were analyzed and tallied, then they were added to a growing spreadsheet. Galloway did the same thing on his side of the medical quarters and watched the item list grow on his screen. Occasionally he'd switch to VIEW mode and see the item images and watch the tally grow that way—something about seeing things as pictures brought out the child in him like Christmas Day.

WILLIAMS WALKED in his engine room and lay his hand gently on the storage housing and insulation holding the power core. He stroked the lid again with his fingers like he would a dog getting praise; "How's my girl this morning?" he smiled. Williams grabbed the portable screen sitting on the table and tapped the icons to wake his system up, then selected the visual inventory mode and scanned the open expanse of the engine room.

There was a lot of machinery for the craft power and control systems, but the engine itself was tiny: a miniaturized fusion reactor. The thing could last forever, as far as he knew. Williams felt it was the pinnacle of his career to get a chance to work with one of the engines in person; the last time he'd been to Pluto with Stuart the reactors had been in the theoretical stages. To get back and see the actual machine in action was truly a shock and a miracle to him, but he felt conflicted about how the post came his way. Williams bit his lip and continued smiling weakly at the corners—it gave him a strangely sad expression.

It struck Williams just then: they were the last ones left. Perhaps there were more people in cryo tubes adrift in space, but most of the human race was now fried to a fritter. Williams had the sick realization he needed to have kids, and the idea made his balls ache and itch. He'd never planned on signing up

for that rodeo, yet here he was contemplating fatherhood—
Williams somehow felt more paternal towards his engine.

STUART GRABBED a scanner and went to the main storage bay
housing the landing craft. She circled small groups of items and
inventoried them. This room was the biggest and should usually
have taken an average person the longest, but Stuart had a
method that made the room take hardly any time at all; and she
even got a perfect rating by the tallying software. She walked
over to the lander craft and stared at the ship's skin: it was cold,
but didn't feel like metal—more like very smooth polished
stone. Like something ancient and new all at the same time.

Stuart turned and left the storage bay. She carried her pad
with her to the meeting room and took her seat at the head of
the table, prepared to wait.

ELEVEN

HADDAD FOLLOWED Schwartz down the hallway, and felt a shiver of relief when Schwartz headed towards engine room two. Haddad continued further down the hall and turned in the doors just past the medical bay, into a storage room that curved to the Metis' wingtip. He stood in the center of the odd-shaped room and turned in a circle, scanning the room with his inventory screen as it made a panoramic view, tallying up all the items it sensed.

The room scan came back deficient and Haddad sighed as the screen turned from a sunny blue to bright red. It flashed the areas where the scan was incomplete, and he shrugged his shoulders with a resigned sigh then re-scanned those spots. In two places he was able to get a perfect scan on the second try, but in one spot the scan kept coming back wanting: the back corner that had the last part of the wing outside the bulkhead. Haddad walked closer to the corner and tried again, and again the screen blinked red.

"Fuck this." Haddad made a tiny pout. He tapped at the screen with a pointed index finger, not quite hard enough to damage the screen but enough to make the color turn at the edges of his finger. The re-scan started again. Haddad prayed to whatever God controlled computers and machines and hoped for a clean scan this time. "Please, please," he whispered under his breath. The screen blinked green and a happy tone sounded; SCAN COMPLETE flashed the icon in the center.

Haddad set down the pad and looked around the storage room: really just a room full of square, black, matter blocks to supply to the simulator machines. The blocks were about the size of a shoebox, but weighed close to ten kilos each. Once they ran out of atoms through enough recycling programs, the atoms had to be re-supplied, and the blocks upon blocks of atom matter in this bay were here to do exactly that. Haddad picked up the screen again and looked at the total tally: there were eight hundred blocks of matter packed tightly into the safe-load racks mounted to the room's ceiling and floors. Each block had enough matter to supply a single simulator for a year, so they had about forty years' worth of matter to resupply all the simulators on the Metis, or an eight-hundred-year supply if they just stuck to using one simulator only.

The machines could make anything 'material' a person wanted: from clothing, to food, to entertainment items, even live animals. When you wanted to get rid of an item, you just put it back in the simulator and the machine broke the items down to atoms, then stored them to use in the next sundry thing you might want. Someone could order up the entire collection from Versace every day for eight hundred years if they wanted to—not that Haddad would recommend that.

He stood back and admired the storeroom again: it was pretty much everything they needed to keep them going, but Haddad wondered if it would be enough to reach another habitable planet outside their solar system. They'd have to spend ages in cryosleep, and he shuddered at the thought. Haddad licked his lips, pursed them and scrunched his face like he was trying to massage all his face muscles; his whole expression rolled around in wacky ways for a minute, then Haddad yawned and covered his mouth with the back of his hand. He sighed, turned and walked back to the storeroom's entrance, where he tapped the screen on the right side of the door, affirming that his inventory had been completed one hundred percent. Then he turned to head back to the conference room.

Haddad paused as he passed close to Engine Room Two's doors: he wanted to touch that pad and open the doors so badly —his fingers even reached out and pointed at the pad, but he held back and refrained from fulfilling his doubting thoughts. He shook his head and hoped Schwartz was dutifully completing his inventory inside, and would rejoin them in the conference room quickly. Haddad resisted the urge to nag him.

He turned to head to the conference room and stopped, standing at the door's precipice for a moment; Haddad took a deep breath and stepped closer to the automatic reader, and the door panes slid open with nearly no noise. The sight of almost the entire crew greeted him, except Schwartz. Haddad frowned. "I'm the last?"

"Nope, not quite." Stuart nodded to the empty seat. "Jimmy's fallen in the engine, or something." She waved her hand dismissively.

"Hail him." Haddad kicked himself for not following his instincts the first time.

"Stuart to Schwartz." Stuart looked up at the ceiling.

"Hailing," answered the sterile female voice.

The screen at the end of the room flickered to life and the team saw Schwartz's back to them.

Stuart cleared her throat. "Jimmy," she spoke with an upturned chin and a small frown. He jumped and turned around quickly.

"Oh, am I the last one?"

Stuart wanted to slap the shit-eating faux-innocent grin off his face. "Yes."

"Damn! I'll be right there!" The com screen went blank. She couldn't hear the footsteps, but Stuart visualized Schwartz sprinting around the corner towards the conference room door. Right on time with her mental image, Schwartz came running in, slightly panting. "So sorry!" He shrugged apologetically.

"Well, now that we're all here, can I have your scan pads?"

Each team member passed their pad to their neighbor and the pile of pads grew until they reached Stuart. She took them, scanned the pads with her own, then laid them in a neat pile like a particularly perfectionistic child's building block toy. Her own pad took a moment to think, then came back with a score of one hundred percent. She nodded and smiled. "Looks like we're all good."

The entire crew sighed a breath of relief and the mood inside the conference room got noticeably warmer. "Well, you guys wanna talk about Mars?" Stuart tried making eye contact with each person in one quick pass, no matter how tight it made her gut feel.

THE TABLE FULL of curious eyes pierced Stuart and her back got sweaty, then suddenly cold—it was all she could do to suppress shivering. Everyone was uncomfortably silent and Stuart had to push herself to break it.

"We've got a pretty straight shot to Mars." Stuart cleared her throat. "I think we could do it in two different bouts of cryosleep, with a stop in between to check the supply buoy."

"Won't the quick cryo wake fuck us up?" Schwartz glared at Stuart and she fought the urge to punch him.

"Nope." Galloway answered before Stuart could even open her mouth, and for that she was grateful. "The sleep tube models we've got are the latest and best I've ever seen—

designed to have very few side effects, even on quick-turn-around wake and sleep cycles."

"No nausea?" Williams spoke up tentatively. He couldn't forget the massive vomiting attack he'd had on the last Mars trip. He'd thought his eyeballs might explode.

"No nausea." Galloway tried sounding reassuring to their lead engineer. "You'll feel surprisingly refreshed after this one."

"Really?" countered Schwartz sarcastically, chuckling for effect. "You've tried it?"

"As a matter of fact, I have." Galloway couldn't hide the irritation in his voice. "I was the guinea pig for the prototype. Wren and I both did a sleep-wake-sleep sequence on a two-week turn-around and felt just fine."

Wren nodded her head in agreement and added, "It almost felt like a spa—quite nice, actually." She tried sounding sincere.

"Only a crazy doctor would call cryosleep *nice*," muttered Schwartz under his breath. Wren shot him an icy gaze and he lowered his eyes and focused on his thumbs.

"The cryosleep will be just fine," interjected Stuart as she tried taking the reins back on the conversation. "We've got to prepare a plan to check and offload the supply buoy. That'll be the only time we'll need all hands available."

"Which buoy are we talking about?" asked Patel.

"The Brinks model 16 set up for the Neptune expeditions in 2064." Williams looked in Patel's direction.

"It's a good buoy." Stuart smiled remembering the last time she saw it. "We used it on my last mission to Pluto, and it still should have a good supply of matter on board. Simon, you have a route to it yet?"

"Oui." Simon smiled, happy he was already prepared. "I've got a clean shot to the area right next to it. Once in a comp orbit with the buoy, we'll probably have to use the remote docking mechanism to hook up."

"Shouldn't be a problem." Stuart was grateful for her capable navigator. "Our arm should match up just fine."

"I've piloted a similar plan," piped up Haddad. "We did some buoy retrieval and cleanup after the last Neptune mission on my most recent deployment."

"Sounds good." Stuart smiled. "Let's have another meeting and discuss the exact needs for the mission before we go in to cryosleep."

"Yes, Grace," answered Haddad with a smooth open tone. He sounded slightly like the old character James Bond.

"Laurance." Stuart looked at Simon and hadn't ever realized how dark his eyes were until she stared into them. "Can you work with Luisa to come up with the most fuel-efficient route to the buoys, and then from there to Mars?"

"Absolutely," he answered curtly, just a hint of his French accent tinging the words.

"How long will the sleep be, both to and beyond the buoys?" piped up a clear voice in the back: Forester. All the team stared in a semi-shocked silence since most, outside Patel, hardly ever heard his voice. They all knew he was trained at the top institutions, and that he was the planet's best at botanical reconstruction from DNA and also space botany but he always hid back during all the training drills and hardly ever spoke. They'd spent years together with him, yet most of the crew felt the most intimate detail they knew of Brian Forester was his penchant for drinking large cups of coffee at all times of day.

Forester was famous for his experiment with the growth of cannabis plants in weightlessness; the plants had been famously huge and all the stoners on Earth worshipped Forester like a god. A god who hardly spoke and hid behind his odd round glasses, a mop of brown hair obscuring his head.

Simon smiled and answered Forester in a kind and reassuring tone. "Given where we're at in Earth's orbit right now, it should be about a hundred days to the buoy and then another hundred and fifty-one to Mars."

"So that'll be a quick down and quick up freeze cycle," added Wren.

"You'll hardly feel it," reassured Galloway.

The entire team seemed to forget this was the science team's first mission with cryosleep—both Forester and Patel had done many individual missions safe in Earth's orbit, but neither had taken their experiments to this extreme yet. The original mission of the Metis had been the first planned, manned, expedition to observe life on Titan; Patel and Forester had been giddy at the prospect of being chosen, but that honor came with a price: cryosleep.

Forester made a strained grimace and took his glasses off. He cleaned them on the sleeve of his jumpsuit, then put them carefully back on, pushing the bridge of his glasses up his nose, securing them. "I just never got to test one before we had to leave," he added softly.

"Don't worry, Brian." Williams pat Forester on the shoulder. "It'll be great...forget those horror stories about the old fluid system."

"If you say so, Pete." Forester spoke even softer than before: the words came out under his breath as he stared down his ravaged cuticles.

"So, we're never going to Titan, then?" Patel spoke up as she played with a piece of her hair, twirling it. She often did that in the middle of tests in college, and now it was habit.

"Unfortunately so." Stuart looked over at her biologist. "I don't think Earth will need to know about the ice moss on Titan anymore."

"So what's our new mission?" countered Patel.

"Survive." Stuart's voice echoed around the conference room.

TWELVE

STUART EXCUSED the team meeting and Simon stood up from the table, nearly banging his knees on the underside of the table. He felt the tingling sensation as his legs woke up and struggled, suppressing his giggles as the tingle turned to a tickle. To save face he walked out quickly and proceeded to his workstation on the bridge.

Laurance Simon hailed from Paris but had a father who emigrated to the City of Light from Nigeria and a mother who hailed from Nice. The girls had always said he had pretty eyes, and they oohed and aahed about his smooth skin that was the color of fine dark chocolate. His face tapered in just the right way to give him the air of an Egyptian pharaoh, and his friends always joked he should become a model. Though he had the looks for it, Simon found the idea completely distasteful.

"You okay?" Stuart watched Simon hobble through the bridge door.

"Just some tickling in my legs...it will pass." Simon spoke softly, holding his mouth taut and trying to not burst out in perverse laughter.

"Okay..." Stuart turned and faced forward again.

Simon turned to his screen and couldn't help himself. If returning to Earth was out of the question, his brain screamed to know where they should go beyond Mars. The habit started in childhood: some youngsters doodled pictures they'd bring home, and Mommy and Daddy would put them on the fridge. Simon brought home spreadsheets calculating everything from the optimal amount of groceries a person could purchase with one hundred Euros, to the time it would take to drive around Europe if one maintained a constant eighty KMH speed. His parents supported everything, and got him different tablets or computing devices instead of paper and paint.

The old habit had resurfaced on the Metis, but the calculations coming out of his fingers didn't fuel some kind of fascination in his mind; instead, they calmed a gnawing sense of dread that made Simon's esophagus feel like it was on fire. His hands created the equations his brain directed, but something about the whole experience made him feel like he wasn't totally in control of his own body. Every equation had an answer, though, and it was the answers that quenched the sickness in his belly.

He had to figure out how much time they had—Simon's internal panic was getting the better of him, and he turned his screen to the CALCULATE function. A spreadsheet program came up and he calculated the amount of supplies they had for the simulators, the engine reactor life capacity, and how much energy supply they had for the life support and cryosleep pods. Next he played with the different sleep length options, and after that he calculated how far they could go in the maximum amount of time the sleep pods had in them. Thankfully, the sleep pods were powered by the engine reactors, so their lifespan was nearly limitless; it was just a question of how long the human body could go under such a deep program. He would have to get with Galloway or Wren about that.

Simon picked a general number, saying the pods could be set for a ten-year maximum for each program—he figured that might be an average time the human body could last under those conditions. Then he figured out how many of the ten-year cycles the machines could power—the answer was fairly good: almost a thousand years. He wondered what would happen to a human if they slept for that long, and he made a note to talk to Galloway about that too.

Back to his equations, Simon started a new set of numbers on how far they could go in a thousand human years at the ship's most fuel-efficient speed. It should get them at least to Alpha Centauri, and he was correct; they could get even further, if they wanted to, but the planets there hadn't been explored yet, nor had any of the further solar systems.

Next, Simon plotted distances to planets he knew of; they could hopscotch out of the solar system and on to the next, plotting sleep periods in between. He tried tallying up how many of these cycles their supplies would allow, then he looked out to where that distance might reach. It might get them into the next two solar systems before they would run out of supplies and die in space.

It was at least far enough to see if there were any habitable places along the way—something worth living for; a little piece of Simon just couldn't fathom staying trapped on Mars forever. Simon looked over to Gutierrez and smiled when he locked eyes with her; she smiled back and tried looking as comforting as possible. He felt her heartbeat even across the distance.

Simon looked over at Stuart. "Grace?"

"Yes, Laurance?"

"I've run some numbers and I think I have some ideas of where we could go to, beyond Mars, that is."

"That's great, Laurance." Stuart turned in her seat towards Simon. "Let's hear it."

"Well," he started, "I think we can get into the next solar system, and perhaps the one beyond it as well, if we run our supplies right."

"And if we get some more supplies from the buoy?"

"Hmmm…." Started Simon, "I hadn't thought of that. Damn!"

"Well, let's see where that might get us with the buoy's supplies added in."

"Will do," finished Simon, feeling stupid and smelling the sweat from his armpits.

Stuart nodded and turned back around as Simon returned to his calculations. He looked up information on the supply buoy's capacities and their estimated reserves remaining, then he added the weight of this estimate to the ship's information he'd already gathered. He recalculated the carrying balance of the spaceship—the amount of space it displaced during movement. With these new numbers he recalculated all of his original equations, and the new amounts were actually better with the extra supply: they would allow for a greater distance traveled.

"Good news, Grace." He turned back towards Stuart as she faced him.

"Yes?"

"It'll give us enough to get to the next three solar systems."

Stuart sat back in her chair, a strangely stunned look on her face. She nodded her acknowledgement. "Wow."

"Yeah."

They all stared in silence and let that information sink in.

———

SCHWARTZ SAT in his engine room with his feet up on the reactor, one of them tapping wildly. He stared at a spot on the wall, wondering what was on the other side: space, of course—but what about the planets and solar systems beyond?

He sucked at his lower lip; his upper and lower teeth pulled it into his mouth, bit it, then released it. Schwartz didn't even realize he was cutting bloody strips in the soft flesh with his front teeth—he looked like he was pouting intensely like an angry four-year-old close to a meltdown. A strange nervousness coursed through his veins that made him want to giggle: they were all far, far away from that planet. The thought made him feel naked, yet full at the same time.

He turned and let his feet drop off of the reactor's housing. They hit the floor left foot first, then the right tapped down—like a one-two punch. Schwartz spun the chair around and faced the door, cocking his head sideways like an owl and looking at the perpendicular line the door's edge made with the floor. He turned his head sideways in the opposite direction and felt his neck pop so loud it echoed across the room. Schwartz rolled his head back and forth and around in circles, gently massaging the nape of his neck.

He stood up and walked to the simulator in the corner and pressed through the options until he got to the FOOD icon; Schwartz pressed it with a sweaty finger, leaving a smudge on the screen. He tapped the icon for CUSTOM and pecked at the typing pad with one outstretched forefinger, spelling out the word GRAPE BUBBLE GUM on the screen, then sat back and watched as the door closed and the humming began. It only took a minute, then the screen chirped, flashed the DONE icon and the door opened.

A tiny square piece of purple bubble gum lay on a serving paper in the middle of the opening. Schwartz picked it up carefully between his index finger and thumb, examining it like a prospector eyeing a gem. He nodded his head and popped the square in his mouth; his jaw pumped up and down as he chewed the piece thoughtfully like a cow with her cud. After a minute of chewing, Schwartz blew outward and formed a large, soft bubble from his lips, which then popped—covering his face from chin to nose. Schwartz used his tongue to gather up the pieces of burst bubble, licking slowly on the skin to get every last shred of gum; it was smooth and left no sticky residue on his face.

Schwartz continued chewing the gum and walked over to the tiny reactor. He sat back down in his chair and turned it in circles with his feet, watching the world spin around him, all the while chewing the gum mindlessly. Every once in a while he'd blow another bubble and let it pop on his face. It was like being a little kid presented with the biggest, shiniest toy.

He stopped the chair's spin with one sneakered foot. It squeaked just a tiny bit on the smooth, white floor, but the shoe's tread did not leave a scuff mark. Schwartz looked over at the door and chewed some more, frowning slightly and cocking his head again, then his face opened into a shocking smile. It was not so much a friendly gesture as it was a terrifying grimace like a shark's open maw; Schwartz's eyes narrowed and he bared his teeth like dog. The chewing gum was clasped between his shining white teeth, looking like an extra line of purple flesh. Schwartz sucked at it from behind his teeth with his tongue—he loved the fake grape taste: it was nothing like the actual fruit, and something about that made him love it more.

Schwartz went back to the simulator window and pressed the pad to wake it up. He scanned through the option menus until he came on HOUSE GOODS, continuing further until he selected the PREMIUM DOWN PILLOW option. The simulator door closed dutifully and got to work. After a few minutes, the window opened and a beautiful white pillow sat gleaming in the opening. Schwartz grabbed it, turned back to the selection screen and chose AIR MATTRESS. He continued further until he had amassed a nice little bed on which to sleep; Schwartz lay down and snuggled into the black down sleeping bag he'd simulated. It contrast sharply with the white floor, and Schwartz's eyes struggled keeping focus between the two vastly different shades: it gave him a headache, so he decided to lie down—that was the best for headaches.

Schwartz crawled onto the soft air mattress, his knees bobbing on the undulating surface as he lay his body down. He wriggled himself into the sleeping bag and felt the interior warming in response to his own body heat; the sensation of warming up under a sleeping bag while camping had always been one of his favorites, and it comforted Schwartz now.

He thought about the different women in his life and each of the array of various, beautiful females passed through his memory. He remembered his ex, Nadine, who had exotic black hair that was long and straight and glossy. He'd loved wrapping his hands in that soft curtain and just feeling the strands passing through his fingers; the thought soothed him again and he rubbed at his own hair in a strange shadowing motion.

Schwartz lay exhausted under the soft sleeping bag. His brain buzzed with a fuzziness brought on by the day's stresses and he thought for a second he was falling through the floor and out into space. It startled him and he had to reach a hand out to touch the floor's surface: still cold and smooth, just like he'd left it.

Schwartz lay over on his left side and fell asleep.

"JIMMY, YOU THERE? SCHWARTZ!" he heard in the distance. The voice seemed to get louder and Schwartz raised his head groggily to reach the com screen. He swiveled the screen so no one could see his sleeping arrangement.

"Schwartz here, Captain," he spoke to the screen as it illuminated his face.

"There you are." Stuart sounded pissed off at him, like always.

"Sorry, was dazed a bit,"

"Well, don't let it happen again,"

"Yes Captain," he said as he was thinking, *you're such a*

whining cunt. His voice had a harsh little bit of insolence tainting it.

The com screen went dark and Schwartz turned. He wanted to contort his face in all sorts of shapes to mock her—a trick he'd maintained since kindergarten. He held off, though, and felt very proud of himself for keeping his good manners. Schwartz turned back to the bed, crawled into the sleeping bag, and fell back asleep.

THIRTEEN

FORESTER STARED down at his bloody cuticles, yet he couldn't stop himself from taking another pick at the scabs. His hands needed to do something, so they cannibalized themselves instead.

He looked over at the lab equipment laid out on the table. Most everything was specially prepared and synthesized for them already, but a few pieces had to be made on board, since they'd run out of preparation time before they left. Forester made a list of missing equipment in his mind, and walked over to the synthesizer machine at the end of the sterile white lab.

Behind an opalescent cover window was the largest synthesizer machine on board: big enough to make large instruments, big meals, even a small animal if they wanted. It could also make base matter they could add DNA to, then grow in test tubes. Forester started writing down each item he needed and in what quantities; his hands felt better—less itchy—when he was making a list.

The simulator machines could make nearly everything found on Earth, but the original creators had held back one option: simulating living creatures. The powers-that-be decided wantonly creating any kind of animal or plant was too dangerous for the average human to enjoy, so they limited the simulator's reach to inanimate objects. To create a living thing, you had to be a scientist with the appropriate credentials, approved by the United Nations, and actively working for a scientific employer—they had tried their best to deter any budding Dr. Frankensteins. Simulating living things entailed introducing live DNA to the simulator, a skill Brian Forester had been doing for years.

Forester stared ahead at the page and observed his chicken-scratch style handwriting; he so envied the pretty, curved script that differentiated Patel's writing from his. You could barely make out the vague meaning of what he might have scribbled down, but Patel you could read loud and clear. Forester wrote a list of the missing lab supplies with quantities in sharp script; *at least my numbers look okay,* he thought. He had always been especially addicted to the flow of numbers in the math classroom.

The door swished open and closed behind Forester and he cricked his head slightly to see who entered. Patel smiled up at him, made a funny face, and Forester's consternated expression melted to a smile as he gave a funny, guttural laugh that rattled like machine gun fire. Patel laughed back, then she took a seat beside him on the lab stool he'd just synthesized.

"How goes it?" she said as she pulled the list he'd made closer within her eyesight.

"Pretty good, you see anything I've missed?"

"I'd add a few of the warm pads to get the growth cycle started."

"Will do." Forester gave Patel a mock salute.

He turned to the synthesizer machine and started typing in the start of his list, beginning with the warm pads. A picture came up showing the pads, he tapped the image, and the machine went to work as they both heard the humming from behind the door. Within a minute the door opened and a new heating pad was waiting. Forester duplicated this sequence two more times, feeling Patel's eyes burning into his back, her head reaching to just below his shoulders.

PATEL ZONED out looking at Forester's back. She knew him from a distance anywhere, with his droopy shoulders that belied an athletic past; he'd always drooped, even when they were in college. Patel remembered being jealous of his brilliance in anything he touched: Brian Forester could get straight A-plusses in every class, but he couldn't talk to the girl across the hall. It had taken years before she knew what his voice even sounded like.

Forester looked around at just that moment and smiled at Patel. She never figured he'd be one of the last survivors of the human race, and he probably couldn't believe it either. She stared back at him and offered up another smile. "Looks good," she gave a thumbs-up sign, nodding towards his progress.

"Yup, it's going along," he answered in his soft Wisconsin accent. He'd never shed that, she thought to herself, even after years in London. Patel couldn't help but smile as he turned back towards the machine—he was a cute dork, she thought: the last dork.

FORESTER FOCUSED BACK on the machine and went to the next item on his list. He found a quantity of fifty test tubes, selected it, then set the machine to run. It closed the window, hummed again, and after a few minutes the window opened to fifty gleaming test tubes in already-synthesized holders. Forester pulled them out and set them on the counter to his right; Patel came from behind and removed them, taking them to an area next to her workbench.

They divided up the lab into two quadrants: one side was for Patel and her biology and animal experiments, the other was for Forester and his botany work. Each of them had a cabinet that pulled out from the wall, and inside the cabinets were many small shelves of tiny vials. Each vial contained the essential DNA of every major species alive on the planet at the time the comet hit.

Forester walked over to his cabinet and stroked the wall where he could see a tiny seam in the smooth hide; the wall reader scanned and recognized his fingerprint and opened the cabinet with a hiss. A little touchpad waited beside a door inside the cabinet, prompting him to enter the name of the item he wanted; Forester typed in: ALOE VERA, and listened to the vial filing system clack from behind the wall. After about a half a minute, a little door raised and the appropriate DNA vials for *Aloe barbadensis Mill.* sat waiting in a clear vial holder. Forester sniffed his nose and touched the RETURN icon, and the door closed while he listened to the Aloe vials being returned to their storage spot deep in the wall. Their entire DNA storage system was cleverly built into the lab walls, with a temperature control unit that kept all the samples stable. Within Forester's lab was enough DNA to re-make nearly every plant species from Earth on another planet—if they could find a planet to support them, that was.

He looked over at Patel admiring her own large collection of DNA samples from Orangutans to Caribou. Forester hoped the matter-machines had enough juice to revive every one of the species they had: if they could do that, they would be hailed as some kind of latter-day Noah and the Metis would be their Ark. *Hailed by whom?* Wondered Forester to himself. *Would there be anyone to care?*

Forester pushed at the outer edge of his cabinet and closed

it, marveling at the engineers who thought up that system; had they been challenged to create the wall storage over a beer? In any case, he was grateful.

"Wanna go chill for a bit?" Patel nodded towards the door.

"Yeah." Forester smiled. "That sounds nice."

They both walked together towards the door, but Forester didn't have the courage to take her hand.

GUTIERREZ SHOOK her head and sweat droplets fell from her brow to her chin. The music on her player blared an old punk-like song from a band called the Donnas. She bit her lower lip and pushed harder on the exercise cycle; Gutierrez wanted to feel the burn in her quads so badly it would take her mind off the situation—she wanted the hurt to help her forget about Earth.

Exercise had always been Gutierrez's way to iron out her emotions; growing up the middle of three children, she'd always had to find ways to channel the frustration when her mom would tend to her brothers over little Luisa. Boys had called her "stuck up" and "standoffish" growing up, despite the looks her mother had graced her with. In truth, Luisa Gutierrez didn't want any of the boys at all: she hid her girlfriend Pilar from her parents, and even from her own crew mates. Now she had to mourn in silence, finally understanding why the other members of the Metis' crew had chosen to remain single prior to their launch.

Outside the gym's window screen was the vastness of space; she couldn't help turning the thing on because it was better than staring at a blank white wall while she rode the bike—even though the only things Gutierrez saw were the never-ending stars. Gutierrez got a cold shiver thinking how the Metis was their new "home" planet now, and she felt claustrophobic for the first time in her life.

The tune changed to an upbeat hip-hop song and Gutierrez pumped harder, pushing in time to the music and watching the metrics on the monitor climb even higher. She smiled a fierce grin and winced as she looked towards the ceiling, then pulled her hands off the handlebars and sat upwards, legs still churning, her stomach muscles tightening to give the legs extra push. The metrics on the readout didn't dip.

Pushing the pedals harder, Gutierrez suddenly had the urge to soil herself and vomit all at the same time. It was her maximum, and Gutierrez slowed her pace to an RPM closer to that of a leisurely weekend-warrior. Her legs loosened, the cramping subsided, and she felt her blood surge upward and downward at the same time—almost like a high. Gutierrez stepped off the cycle and headed to the exercise mats where the wall window screen touched the floor, her thighs throbbing like they did after sex.

She sat down as close to the window screen as possible; the effect was like sitting at the edge of an infinity pool on the edge of the ocean, but the infinity she beheld was space. Gutierrez felt like she was going to fall outward into the stars, and the visual quality of the window screen amazed her—it felt as real as any regular window, but screens couldn't explode into space or be damaged like a real window could.

Gutierrez raised one arm and stretched it out towards her pointed foot. Her torso curved like a ballet dancer and both her hands reached out delicately and touched the tips of her toes. She repeated this move on her opposite leg, then slid her body towards the window making her legs do the splits against the massive screen—there was a tiny distortion where her toes touched the material. A muscle on the inside of her thigh cramped in protest, so Gutierrez pulled her knees back, wrapped her arms around her legs and sat staring out the window like a little child—her eyes fixed on the darkness.

On impulse, Gutierrez reached out her right hand and stretched it towards the window screen, and her index and middle fingers touched the pane. The screen distorted and little rings of light emanated from her fingers, but the material felt disturbingly cold. Gutierrez scooted away from the screen, stood, turned, then walked straight out the entry door, almost all the way down the hallway to her quarters while still shaking on rubbery legs.

She turned and tapped the entry pad to the right side of her door and the pad recognized her fingerprint with a green flash CONFIRMED; the door opened and she walked inside. The endless dark view greeted her again and she walked to her screen, turned it off, then immediately changed her mind when the all-white room made her feel like she was trapped in an insane asylum—at least the stars were moving enough to distract her.

Gutierrez walked to the bathroom entrance and stripped off her dirty gym clothes as she walked. Her muscled shoulders flexed while she pulled off each garment, and she threw everything in the sonic cleaner then pressed the LAUNDRY cycle.

While she waited, Gutierrez turned and observed her skin in the bath vanity; her pores were open and sweaty, but everything looked fairly clean. She grabbed one of the absorbent towels and wiped the sweat off her face, then proceeded to wash her entire face and moisturize it. The towel made long strokes down her cheek like a mother animal's tongue.

The cleaner beeped behind her and Gutierrez turned to see the pad flashing CYCLE FINISHED. She opened the door, picked up her bra and underwear and put those on first, then came the pants and top. Gutierrez grabbed her jumpsuit from its peg in the corner and pulled it on over top of the athletic wear—it felt cool and fresh against her sweaty skin. She shivered again so hard she fought the urge to pee.

Gutierrez turned to her simulator machine and tapped the screen until it read PROTEIN SHAKE. She selected one with Marionberries and blueberries with almond milk and extra plant protein, and the machine whirred into action; soon her frosty shake stood waiting behind the open door as Gutierrez pulled it out and drank greedily from the glass. A bit of the liquid rolled up on her lip giving her a protein-shake mustache.

She stopped and licked the shake from her upper lip, then proceeded to finish it in a series of greedy gulps, until a pain lanced over the crown of her head: too much cold liquid drunk too fast. Her brain cramped and she winced, setting the glass down on her table just as the tears started flowing. Gutierrez cried silently, hurriedly wiping her cheeks as quickly as they fell. After giving herself the usual minute to feel her sadness, Gutierrez tottered towards her bed where she lay a hand over her forehead and prayed for sleep.

FOURTEEN

SCHWARTZ TAPPED the com screen and selected the VIEW application. He looked through the different options available and started hitting icons. First, he touched the BRIDGE icon: the screen flickered and suddenly there was a clear view of the bridge from the ceiling's vantage point. He saw Stuart sitting like a queen in her captain's chair while Simon sat next to her doing something on a screen in front of him, Haddad sat at his station tapping a screen and talking to Stuart. Schwartz couldn't hear what they were saying, but the body language seemed cordial.

He scratched his back and the neck of his jumpsuit, then picked a small piece of skin at the corner of his mouth. Schwartz could only watch so much of Stuart and her party buddies before he was sick of the scene; he tapped the screen and picked the MEDICAL LAB view.

In this image Galloway and Wren were chatting with each other and walking around the lab: Galloway was holding a list and Wren was digging around in the cabinets for something. She pulled out a box and set it on the examining table that also doubled for surgery. Schwartz shuddered at the idea of Galloway performing surgery on anyone—he didn't trust any sawbones more than he could throw them. Wren, on the other hand; he'd let her cut on him just to feel her hands on his skin.

Schwartz watched Wren and Galloway as they opened up the box on the table and pulled out the contents. It looked like they were inventorying different medical devices, and this one had two paddles and a box attached to them; as old-fashioned as it seemed, the defibrillator was still a necessity. He watched the two doctors inspect the unit and then put it back in its storage cubby. Schwartz scratched where his hairline met his neck, pulled a scab from his scalp and inspected it as it balanced on his thumbnail; the blood was dried and almost black, and he crushed it between his fingernails.

Back to the screen, Schwartz tapped the CHANGE VIEW icon and flipped through all the different rooms on the ship. One image showed Williams sitting steadfastly next to his respective engine and looking at something on a screen in his lap. A litany of images showed the deserted private quarters of every other crew member.

Schwartz flipped to the view of Lab 1: Forester and Patel doing something with their tiny sample vials. Schwartz knew the samples were the DNA of every living species on Earth because he'd paid at least some attention during the briefings. He didn't really care for all the test-tube shit, but give him a new reactor to play with and a shiny new ship, and he was as happy as a clam.

He kept flipping channels—looking at the deserted conference room, the storage rooms all quiet and secure, and finally he flipped to the gym. Gutierrez's image filled the screen, and Schwartz watched her pumping away on the stationary cycle. All the exercise machinery was designed to harvest energy from the exerciser and feed it back into the ship, so Gutierrez's workout would not only burn her stress, but it would build a tiny power reservoir for the Metis.

Good little mousie, thought Schwartz.

He couldn't help but stare at Gutierrez as she sweated away. The image was great, and Schwartz could see the sweat glistening on her skin and could almost smell the acrid combination of flowery deodorant and sharp female essence. Schwartz brought his face so close to the screen his nose almost touched it, then he pulled back and let the entire image roll back into focus again.

Gutierrez kept exercising. Schwartz watched the way her thighs churned, and he watched her bite her lip. *It must be a hard workout*, he thought. He undressed her with his eyes, observing her shapely calves and legs, rolling up into a butt that begged to be shook with the impact of a man—or at least caressed and squeezed. Her waist was nothing special, but the breasts were another thing all together—they were large and round and somehow never seemed to sag. *Best tits on the crew*, voted Schwartz in his mind, *no question about it*. A tiny voice in his head wondered if she'd let him squeeze them like pillows.

Schwartz watched as Gutierrez suddenly stopped pedaling and sat up staring out the window, chest heaving from the last push on the bike. Schwartz touched the screen with his finger and traced the outline of her chest with the point of his index finger. He pulled the finger back and stuck it in his mouth like a coy teenager, sucking on the tip; on the screen, Gutierrez dismounted the bike, walked up to the window and started stretching. Schwartz wanted to moan, but he stayed quiet.

He watched as she went through all her stretches at the window screen like some kind of ballet dancer, then she touched the screen for some strange reason. It only took a second, but Schwartz couldn't help but be curious about what she was thinking: did the darkness fascinate her too? He bit his lip and kept watching.

Gutierrez left the gym and Schwartz lost her view from his screen, so he tapped on the view menu and selected MAIN

HALL. Gutierrez flashed into view again, this time walking towards her apartment. He watched the hall image go from her approaching the camera, to her walking past, then a beautiful view of her ass as she walked to her apartment.

Schwartz knew he shouldn't watch her in her quarters, but he just couldn't help himself—he stared at the screen greedily as Gutierrez disrobed and washed her clothing. He could see her staring at the mirror, and there was now a perfect view of her naked, shapely, perfect body. Schwartz wanted to touch himself, but instead held the feeling tight in his belly.

He watched.

STUART SAT DOWN and her mind hummed. Reaching three different solar systems was longer than any human had traveled in space, and without Space Command to create a game plan, she felt daunted. She turned her head to Haddad and Simon.

"What do you guys think our chances are in the next three solar systems?"

"Well," started Simon, "There are ten planets in Alpha Centauri around all the various stars, then a couple around Barnard's, and they still think a couple around Luhman 16."

"Ahhh." Stuart sat back in her chair. "Any of them remotely habitable?"

"Only the Alpha Centauri ones." Simon sighed. "When the Victoria probe blew up we lost the ability to test them—that was the first probe with an engine strong enough to even reach those systems."

Williams walked in the door quietly behind them and watched silently.

"You think we could make it?" Stuart looked at Simon.

"Yes." Simon scratched his head. "I've run the numbers multiple times, and I've come up with a range that should get us about seven light years' worth of travel distance—enough to get to the Alpha Centauri system at least."

"Wow," said Stuart as if she were talking to herself.

Simon continued. "There are at least three Earth-sized planets in the Alpha Centauri complex, way better potential than Barnards or Luhman."

"How much time will we need to evaluate each planet?"

"Normally I would say a year each," piped up Haddad, "about the same length as Command's Neptune mission."

"Is that do-able?"

"One second." Simon stroked his chin, tapped the screen in front of him, and paused a second to look at what came up. He frowned, then tapped furiously again. After a couple silent minutes he spoke, and the sharpness of the sound as it echoed through the silent air made Stuart, Haddad and Williams jump.

"If we try to stretch the cryosleep time to the max, then we'd have enough supplies to inspect each planet for seven days."

"Damn." Haddad exhaled.

"Mmmm." Stuart pursed her lips and betrayed no emotion. "What do you think, Louis?"

Haddad jumped at the question. It'd been so long since she'd asked him his opinion and he couldn't get used to the feeling. "I'd do what readings I can off probes, if they come back favorable, then a quick ground mission. Really, I'd do probes as much as I can. They're not sexy, but they'll get the job done quick. We could conceivably run them all off Mars."

"I like it." Stuart smiled. "How many probes will we need?"

"Eighty, maybe?" Haddad looked at Stuart and marveled at how beautifully smooth and soft her taupe skin looked that morning. "I'd give us ten probes per planet we know of, and then another twenty in case we run in to any more."

"We have enough material to fabricate that many?"

"Yes," interrupted Simon, "More than enough, especially if based from Mars."

"How long will it take to make them?"

"With one person manning one machine, we'll have them done in a day," interrupted Williams, the rest of the bridge crew jumped and looked at him as he came in the door.

"Can we store them?" Haddad couldn't get over the shaky feeling in his legs after being surprised by Williams.

"We could put them in the bay with the landers." Williams approached the command chairs. "I can fabricate a holding rack too—like that one I did for the Pluto mission."

"Good, make me a schedule...we'll make the probes when we get to Mars." Stuart locked eyes with Williams, smiling slightly.

"Alrighty." Williams grinned with a mock salute.

Stuart couldn't help it, her gentle smile cracked into a full-blown grin. "You ready for dinner, guys?"

"I could do some," said Haddad as his stomach growled loudly, "Simon, you in?

"Oui," Simon sounded surprisingly French for a man who tried hiding his accent.

"You in, Williams?"

"But of course." Williams agreed as he pulled closer to the group.

They walked together to the conference room and took the seats closest to the simulator. Stuart stood for a minute debating in front of the screen, then finally decided on a turkey sandwich on German-style rye bread. The machine hummed briefly and the doors opened to her little sandwich on a clean, white plate. She selected again and chose coconut water to drink. One minute longer and the door opened to a clear glass filled with a slightly pink liquid; Stuart pulled both aside and set them on the conference table, then sat down and started eating before Haddad even had time to press the START button.

Haddad scrolled through the options and debated back and forth between a Reuben or a green salad with chicken. The

Reuben made his stomach growl, but the salad made his waist-line happy. He thought about the last two days briefly, then chose the sandwich; when the machine spat it out it was exactly like the picture, dripping with sauerkraut, cheese and sauce. He selected a pint of India Pale ale and joined Stuart when everything was made; she chewed on her sandwich, less greedily and more thoughtfully now.

"How's it tasting?" Haddad asked as he sat down.

"Mmmmf...good!" Stuart mumbled out between bites. Haddad swore the longer you spent in cryosleep, the worse your manners got.

They both looked up when the smell of Williams' hamburger hit their noses. He sat down and started taking huge bites while Haddad noted a second example of his theory.

Simon selected a baguette with thin-sliced salami and butter, a childhood favorite. He remembered when his mother packed these sandwiches on hikes through the countryside on week-ends, and Simon could almost smell the warm grass and the pastures where she'd let him pet cows on the nose. Simon suddenly felt very sad, wishing he could see her; he hid his frown when he sat down next to Haddad.

Stuart looked up and swallowed her half-chewed bite. She surveyed the room with her eyes, found the com screen, and selected the PRIVATE icon. In theory, all com lines into the room were supposed to be blocked at this point, so Stuart turned to the group with a sigh.

"I'm still trying to wrap my head around my job switching from the captain of a glorified PR mission to a latter-day Noah," she said with a straight face, no hint of a smile.

"Yeah," agreed Haddad over a particularly stubborn bite. "May I speak freely?"

"Sure. Always." Stuart took another bite of sandwich.

"I know this sounds a little soft, but I miss my mother," he sighed. "I don't know how to mourn her."

Simon looked up abruptly and concurred. "Me too."

Stuart didn't know what to say, she didn't miss her mother, who was long dead before the comet struck.

"I've thought about re-creating a replica of her presumed ashes," continued Haddad, "you think that's a bit morbid?"

"Perhaps a bit." Williams set down his hamburger for a second.

"Do you think the simulators could do a good job of that? If I got her DNA code?" Haddad asked as his lower lip quivered for a blink of a second.

"Maybe." Stuart cleared her throat. "We'd have to ask Patel." She reached out her hand and took Haddad's as tears escaped the corner of his eyes. "I'm sorry, buddy. Maybe we could make a nice urn, at least?" She raised her eyebrows hopefully and felt her heart clench, seeing her First Officer in tears. He was always so typically British—unemotional to a fault. That he would open up in front of any of them meant his pain was important and real.

Haddad nodded through tears, and his voice was hoarse. "Yeah, that'd be nice."

Stuart hugged Haddad and let him cry out his worries, feeling his tears moisten the shoulder of her jumpsuit. She stroked his back like a child, and for the first time didn't feel uncomfortable with the physical peer contact.

FIFTEEN

GALLOWAY SMILED AT WREN. "You good if I call it a night?

"Yeah," she spoke with an exhausted voice, "thought you'd never ask."

"I'll set my alarm for zero seven hundred and see you at eight." He felt her weariness too—one could only count and reorganize the medical supplies so many times.

"Sounds like a plan, Sam." Wren sounded cheerful but didn't look it: Galloway could still hear the strain hiding behind her light tone. She turned toward the door, gave Galloway a little wave as she stepped through, and headed to her quarters. The door closed silently behind her.

He was all alone in the medical bay. Galloway looked around his new workspace and surveyed all the equipment they'd simulated that day: each piece was nicely done, every bit as authentic as the manufactured original. They'd gone past the point of human hands and even robot hands making things—the new simulator machines made everything small seem readily possible.

Galloway sat down at his new work desk and stared at the flat panel screen below his fingertips. It functioned like a desk and a computer, just like the other work stations in the ship. He could pull up any medical information he needed, as well as a giant history of different health conditions; the little desk took the place of an entire medical library on a server. Again, Galloway marveled at the advances on display in the Metis, he just wished the ship could go home to Earth after the mission.

Earth.

Even the word made his stomach churn and his eyes water. He'd done a pretty good job of avoiding the waterworks in front of the whole team, but he couldn't stop them now. The tears started softly at first: just a tiny one squeezing itself from the corner of his right eye, then the flood came and he broke down sobbing. Galloway laid his head on the table like a child playing a classroom game and cried, his tears pooling on the flat black surface as he wiped them up with his jumpsuit sleeve.

Galloway looked up and stared straight forward. His eyes and face were red and chapped from the tear moisture and he wiped up a tiny bit of snot with an errant tissue. *Gonna need to give this suit a good washing*, he thought, staring down at the splotches on the front of his jumpsuit, *especially after today*. He sat up and rubbed his thighs briefly, then the back of his neck— a headache was rising from his cervical spine like a cobra.

He stood up and walked around the med bay one more time, looking at the sleek walls with hidden panels that held all of their equipment. Mission control had given them a huge list of necessary materials, and they'd marked every item off the list; Galloway took turns with Wren at the simulator, but he'd spent a bit more time at the machine than she had. He'd wanted Wren to organize the cabinets, since she was always a wizard at that and rarely let him touch her handiwork.

As he walked past the cabinets he stopped suddenly: one particular door called him darkly. He looked at the flat panel, pinched himself, then walked back to his desk; Galloway sat down, but his legs started fidgeting and his fingers tapped the black panel. He knit his brows and bit his lip—the itch would not go away.

Galloway felt his scalp crawling. He scratched the nape of his neck again, then the crawling moved to his right temple, then up to the crown of his head. His fingers followed the itch as his foot tapped up and down like a drum player hitting the bass; he felt crawly and sick and a primal part of him screamed to go back to that cabinet. Galloway stared at the cabinet from across the room. He quit scratching, tapped his hand on the side of the desk, then stood and walked over to it.

With one touch Galloway had the cabinet open. The large panel clicked and recessed back into the wall, exposing an arsenal of medicines and supplements hidden within; each was housed in a tiny cylinder that kept the liquid medicine stable until it was time to administer it. Galloway scanned the vials looking at the labels, occasionally touching one. The vials were in alphabetical order and he made his way through all the letters of the alphabet until he hit "M." He kept scanning "M" until his eyes fell upon the prize.

Galloway picked up the bottle labeled MORPHINE and held it between his thumb and forefinger. He raised the bottle to eye level and turned it back and forth, observing the moving liquid inside: it looked smooth and beautiful in the little clear vial, like liquid life.

He turned and walked to the cabinet where he'd stored the prescription administration device. It was a small pen-like contraption that reminded him of the injectable devices of old, but this one was extra sweet: instead of piercing the skin it infused the medicine right through—a process so painless even the most needle-phobic person could administer themselves comfortably. Galloway grabbed the device and loaded the cartridge in.

He sat back down at his desk and stared at the vial. It was locked and loaded and he somehow felt like he was staring down the barrel of a gun; one part of his brain screamed to leave it be, to walk away, to throw the vial on the floor and shatter it, or perhaps call Wren to talk to her.

The other voice spoke soothingly and told him it would be okay. The world had just ended and he was alone. His family was dead. Even his dog was dead. He hurt and he was scared, and what would be wrong about having a little treat to take the edge off? He'd just survived a comet, a crazy launch, flying space debris, and now he was one of the last surviving humans in the universe. He deserved it.

Galloway touched the small tip of the infuser to his right thigh and pressed the administration button. He felt his whole body go warm, then seemingly melt away.

———

HADDAD WATCHED Stuart leave towards her room and felt a mixture of sadness for her, and gratitude for the hug she'd given him. He'd read Stuart's dossier when he'd been assigned to the mission: admitted to Space Command right out of high school, led her first mission by nineteen, was on the mission to Mars by twenty; she'd had the fast track to success all her life. Cryosleep had kept her body from aging, but her mind was as pitted and old like the rest of them.

One commander had called her "prickly." Haddad felt like that was an accurate description. They'd worked together for over a three years training and she'd never once taken him up on the offer for dinner, and it took the end of the world for her to give him a hug. He knew she thought he was trying to pick up on her, but in reality, he saw how lonely she was and only wanted to be nice.

He sighed and turned towards the exercise lounge. The room was full of a beautiful array of workout equipment: each machine hooked up to a tiny generator that then fed in to the ship's energy bank so they wouldn't waste even the tiniest amount of power. Haddad hated that hamster-on-a-wheel feeling of going nowhere, but sweating had always helped him relax. Plus, it would burn off dinner.

He chose a sleek elliptical machine and climbed aboard. It didn't match the long runs he used to do up in the mountains, but in space beggars could not be choosers; at least the artificial gravity kept them from having the same bone loss the earlier explorers faced. Nevertheless, Haddad still felt the primal urge to run—it itched under his skin.

He pressed a few buttons on the screen and selected a light grade with a medium resistance. Haddad grabbed the machine's handles and made the same motion he would while running as the machine kicked into gear and moved silently. He pressed on the screen and selected the MUSIC icon. The elliptical not only powered the ship slightly, but had access to all the entertainment files the builders had stored. Originally the idea had been to keep the astronauts entertained on their long mission; now they would also serve as the last reference to what life was like on Earth.

He tapped through the different genre selections, pausing on the BRITISH PUNK icon, then he decided against it and selected DEATH METAL. Loud screaming voices came out of the machine's speakers along with the thrumming sound of guitar. Haddad felt his pulse quicken and he upped the grade and tension on the elliptical, pushing hard to the music and slipping into an exercise trance.

Staring out the window, his thoughts suddenly turned to his mother; she'd looked so brave in that last call, so at peace. That had always been her style, he thought: Aisha Haddad had been the one to gather the whole family for dinners to break the fast during Ramadan, the one to babysit neighbor's children, and the one who'd held her grown son without judgment when he bawled on her shoulder following the loss of his wife.

Haddad knew it was the wrong reason to sign up for a mission, but that was the exact reason he'd wanted to go on the Metis: he'd hoped being planets away from his pain might make it go away, but now it was even worse. Not only had he lost Karen, but he'd lost his mother as well. In a way Haddad felt naked, yet he was fully clothed: it was strange to be standing completely on his own.

He increased the incline on the elliptical to its maximum and tried running even harder. His thighs screamed with lactic acid and felt like they could give out any second, but Haddad ignored them and continued. The music blared and sweat dripped from his forehead onto the control screen, the droplets running down the smooth screen plate and dripping to the floor. Haddad paid no attention to his bodily mess.

A sudden image crossed his brain: it was his mother smiling over a birthday cake—her sixtieth, and she'd worked all day on her own concoction. She'd always been so picky about what cakes she would eat…Haddad chocked it up to her early days as a baker in college, and she agreed when he'd asked her one time. "When you've had the best," Aisha intoned, "it's that or nothing!"

That night she'd made her favorite: key lime cake with coconut frosting. His taste buds had danced after every bite, and the entire room oohed and aaahed over Aisha's cooking. She just sat back and smiled, deflecting all the praise and thanking her visitors for coming—typical Aisha. Haddad thought about asking the simulator to make that cake flavor custom but quickly changed his mind—he wanted to remember her cake forever.

Haddad's quad cramped and he stopped the machine suddenly. He tried rubbing it out with the heel of his palm, but the cramp was not going away without a fight. Even Haddad's own legs didn't want the punishment he so badly tried to dole out. The mind made orders, but the body didn't necessarily always have to obey, so he stepped gingerly off the machine and limped to the recovery booth.

He walked to the corner of the room where a phone-booth-shaped machine was nestled flush to both walls. As a young man he'd called recovery machines "Superman Machines" thanks to their resemblance to the Man of Steel's preferred changing room, as well as for their physical effects. Once inside he pressed the WORKOUT RECOVERY command and the machine closed the door and purred into action.

Haddad stood with both arms slightly raised and felt the energy waves do their magic: they coursed from his feet to his head and worked out all the lactic acid and kinks along the way —it was like having a giant all-over body massage without anyone touching you. He sighed and felt the quad cramp loosen, then magically disappear. Since the invention of the recovery machine athletics had never been the same; after the first year they were available, almost all the Olympic records had been broken.

The machine beeped to mark the end of the cycle and Haddad stepped out into the gym. Still alone, he walked out the door without a glance behind him.

SHE DIDN'T KNOW why she did it, but Wren walked down the hall from her room and into the medical lab. It was almost like some kind of trance—the kind where you wake up and realize you're in a totally different place. The doors slid open and that's when she saw him:

Galloway was slumped over sitting against the wall, so pale his skin was almost gray, his eyes closed. She saw the administration device lying askew on the floor next to his foot. She didn't have to guess what was in it.

"Shit! Bill!" Wren shouted as she ran over to him. Her hand

slapped him across the face almost instinctually. "Come back to me, buddy..." she pleaded. There was no look of acknowledgement, no flutter of the eyelids, instead a tiny string of drool rolled from the corner of his mouth. "C'mon..." said Wren as she shook him by the shoulders, "You can't do this to me!" Panic made her voice get shrill.

Wren jumped to her feet and ran to the medical cabinet. She tried fumbling through all the vials, hoping to find the one that could revive him before it was too late. Her fingers shook as she touched each bottle and turned it to see the label.

HADDAD WAS at the apex of the two halls when he heard some shouting coming from the medical lab. Curiosity piqued, he turned towards the noise—there was nothing for him to go to in his room anyway. He walked in the lab to the scene of Galloway slumped over, his body almost totally touching the floor, and Wren frantically clawing through the medicine cabinet.

"Oh God, what's happened?" he asked, aghast.

"Fucking applicators," Wren hissed, almost not recognizing Haddad had spoken.

Haddad took four quick steps and was at Galloway's side. His skin was cold and his body ashy. Haddad shook Galloway and Galloway's eyes rolled back in his sockets.

"Is he sick?" Haddad's hands were shaking and Galloway felt cold and wrong all over.

"OD'ing." Wren wailed over her shoulder, her eyes still fixed on the bottles.

"On what?" asked Haddad.

"He had a thing for Morphine a few years ago. Cost him his marriage...I thought he was clean," Wren said as tears started squirting from her eyes. She wiped at them and continued searching for the right revival tube.

Haddad laid his ear against Galloway's chest and heard him breathing very slowly. Then that seemed to stop and he started panicking.

"He's not breathing!" Haddad yelped to Wren.

"Fuck!" shouted Wren as she started throwing bottles across the room behind her, "Where are you??!" she yelled at the cabinet.

"C'mon, buddy..." pleaded Haddad as he shook Galloway. Galloway's head lolled to the side like his neck was broken; Haddad felt his own breathing getting tight and his legs felt numb. He lay Galloway down on the ground and gave two short breaths into his mouth, praying to see Galloway's lungs respond in kind. Nothing moved, and Haddad began the breathing again.

"Ahhhh...yess!!!" yelled Wren in a shout that came close to a shriek. Her fingers found the bottle labeled NALOXONE and she ran towards Galloway, ripped the morphine bottle out of the infusion device and snapped the Naloxone bottle into place. She pressed the applicator against Galloway's leg and touched the administration button. The device made a tiny click as it infused the medicine in Galloway's thigh.

Wren and Haddad sat kneeling over Galloway's limp body, staring at him with intense desperation. Wren massaged his hand and put two fingers to his throat: there was a pulse beating very lightly. She pursed her lips and pulled back Galloway's eyelids—his eyes rolled around but at least they weren't totally gone.

"C'mon, buddy," she said as she rubbed his shoulder. "Help me get him up," Wren looked to Haddad as she grabbed Galloway by the back and rib cage.

"Yup." Haddad matched her position on the opposite side of Galloway's body, then they got him sitting in a more upright position against the wall.

Galloway suddenly took a deep breath in and his eyes fluttered open. Wren's eyes lit up and she smiled with full relief.

"Hey, buddy," she called to him softly, "come on back to us." She continued rubbing his left hand with her right one. Galloway looked at her and almost through her at the same time and Wren could see the Naloxone starting to clear his brain, but his pupils were dilated like a cat's during the hunt. He stared over her right shoulder.

"Is the stuff working?" Wren could hear the worry in Haddad's normally cool British voice.

"I think so…" Wren knit her brows and looked like a lost little girl.

"Hey doctor." Haddad poked Galloway in the chest with his finger, trying to get a reaction. When that didn't work, he changed his tack, "Hey you, sawbones!" he barked at Galloway. Normally this would get Galloway cussing, but Galloway just stared off over Wren's shoulder. "It's not working…" he sighed forlornly.

"He's alive." Wren spoke softly, almost trying to reassure herself. "At least he's alive." She sighed.

They both waited endless minutes watching Galloway for any sign of recognition. Wren kept rubbing his hand and Haddad took the other, but Galloway's skin was still cold. They both took turns staring at the patient, but neither Wren nor Haddad met each other's gaze. Haddad finally broke the silence.

"What're we going to do?" he whispered.

"I don't know." Wren shook her head and stared at the floor.

"We've got to call Grace." Haddad's voice cracked.

Wren nodded.

SIXTEEN

STUART WAS SITTING QUIETLY CONTEMPLATING her bowl of ice cream when the voice came over the intercom—she could hardly recognize Haddad because his British accent was suddenly very strong in his panic.

"Captain? I think you need to come to the medical bay." His voice sounded grizzled like he'd been through Hell.

"What's the matter?"

"It's Bill, Grace." Haddad choked on his words. "He's in some trouble."

Stuart jumped to her feet like she'd been shocked by a cattle prod. "I'll be right there." She made it to her door in three bounding steps, then practically sprinted down the hall towards the med lab. She'd known Galloway's problem even though she didn't talk about it, and her worst fears played out like a little horror movie in her mind.

When she got to the bay it was like the nightmare came alive: the door opened to Haddad and Wren kneeling next to Galloway's comatose body. He stared off into space over Haddad's shoulder, not quite in Stuart's direction.

"Fuck," was the only thing Stuart could say. Wren just looked at her with a painful gaze.

"Morphine again?" Stuart spoke somberly. Wren nodded and Stuart could see a couple tears escape the corners of her eyes. "Oh Bill," Stuart said softly as she knelt down next to Haddad and grabbed Galloway's hand. She rubbed his cold fingers and squeezed them.

"Shitty time for this beast to rear its ugly head." Wren kept staring at her hands.

"Yeah," agreed Stuart, "I thought he'd kicked it."

"I did too." Wren sobbed sadly, the corners of her mouth drooping in a macabre frown. She wiped at the corners of her eyes, then her hand migrated down and wiped her nose.

Haddad just sat and watched the two women dumbfounded. He'd known nothing of this. No one had told him that the head surgeon had a problem with morphine. No one had told him that his other crewmates knew about it—he felt so stupid and useless. All he could do was watch Galloway and count his breaths.

"You think he's going to wake up?" Stuart rubbed Galloway's hand and looked up at Wren.

"God I hope so," sighed Wren.

"Where do you think we should keep him?" As soon as the thought came out Haddad felt like an idiot—even though it was a valid question.

"Let's get him to the med pod. I can run a detox program."

"Good call," agreed Stuart, "Can you keep him here under observation?"

"Yeah. He won't leave my sight."

"Will the med tube be able to get him better?" Haddad again felt foolish.

"I think so," said Wren, making Haddad feel a flutter of joy that maybe he wasn't stupid after all, "it worked on him the last time he did this."

"It's happened before?" Haddad couldn't hide the shock in his whisper.

"Yes," Stuart sighed. "He went off the deep end after we lost a guy on the Pluto mission. I think he originally started the shit to help him sleep through the nightmares."

"But it became his nightmare," added Wren.

"How did Space Command clear him for this mission?" asked Haddad with a hint of disgust in his voice.

"Because I assured them he was clean and ready to go," Stuart's voice cracked and dropped to a whisper. "Fuck, it hurts to be wrong."

Haddad snapped his mouth shut and instantly felt embarrassed again. He doubled down and gripped Galloway's shoulder, then looked Stuart in the eye, "What can I do to help?"

Stuart looked at Wren. "Get him in the tube?"

"Yeah," said Wren. "Can you help me move him, Lou?"

Haddad nodded. "Absolutely."

"Okay." Wren stood up. "Grace, Lou, can you each take an arm and get him to his feet?"

"Yup," Stuart stood and moved to Galloway's left side. "You take that shoulder." She nodded at Haddad.

"Absolutely." Haddad went to where he was directed and stood by Galloway's right side, feeling maybe fewer words were better—that way he wouldn't shove his foot in his mouth again.

Wren left Galloway's side and went to the med tube in the middle of the lab, where she pressed a few buttons on its side and the lid hissed open. She stood back and watched Haddad and Stuart's progress.

Haddad crouched to his knees and Stuart mirrored his motions on Galloway's opposite side. They both rose to their feet at the same time, grunting under Galloway's supine weight. His legs flopped numbly below him like a rag doll, his feet dragging along the floor as the tip of one shoe squeaked on the tile.

It was about then that Wren chastised herself for not simulating some kind of a stretcher first, but they were already halfway to the tube, so too late to turn back.

Moving Galloway reminded Haddad of the time he had to babysit his cousin Mohammed and the little boy threw a temper tantrum so severe that he flopped down on the floor and refused to move. Haddad remembered grabbing little Mo by the armpits and trying to get him to stand, only to see Mo fall back down in a heap of angry frustration. Galloway was a bit like this, minus the demands to go to the movies.

They got Galloway over to the side of the pod and Wren picked up his feet, hanging Galloway suspended like a pig on a spit and lifting him into the pod. Haddad felt a twinge in his lower back as he heaved Galloway over the pod's rim.

Once they had Galloway inside, Wren jumped to work pressing little monitor probes and medication patches on his body; Galloway stared off into space over her shoulder and she prayed any brain damage could be corrected by the med pod's programs. The preparation only took a couple minutes and she closed the lid as soon as she was done. The pod's interior faded to a dark blue and Wren saw the medication indicators starting to move: the detox drugs began their work.

Wren turned to Stuart and said nothing. Then she let out an exhausted sigh.

"Well," said Stuart as she wearily clapped Wren on the shoulder, "looks like you're Chief of Medicine now."

WREN WALKED BACK to her quarters barely able to feel her legs. Her entire body felt numb and her chest ached; her foot caught the floor as she tried crossing the threshold so she had to grab the doorway for support. Inside her quarters she walked over to her table and sat down, staring out the screen into space.

After a few minutes Wren tried thinking about what she

needed to do next, but her mind came back with a blank—it just sat and spun like the old computer icons when a machine was frozen. Wren blinked a couple times and tried clearing her vision, rubbing at the corners of her eyes.

In one brief moment Wren's face went from stoic and blank to crumbling. Her mouth quivered until she could control it no longer and her whole face fell. The tears flowed fast and Wren's sobs echoed around the room; her shoulders shook with the effort. She tried controlling her crying but all that came out were a few barking sobs that bounced around the hard surfaces like a voice in a canyon.

She'd already lost so much. Now Bill.

She wiped her nose with her jumpsuit sleeve and cringed when it came away still wet. Wren tried sniffling some of the mucus back in her nose and jumped up to run to the toilet, where she grabbed some toilet paper and finished her cleaning. She looked again at her sleeve, wrinkled her nose, and unzipped her suit: in three quick moves she had the suit open and down off both shoulders, then it was off to the sonic cleaner.

Wren turned her back on the cleaner and walked towards her chair, sat down, and turned to look out into space again. Her hands lay palms-down on her thighs and she started taking gentle breaths in and out, just like the Space Command class said. She counted the length of the intake, held it for a few seconds, then exhaled to the same count. She repeated this breathing exercise over and over until her head felt clearer and her heartbeat slowed.

Wren took to any prescribed calming routine out of self-preservation; her psychologist suggested meditation long ago after the tenth antidepressant failed to make even a dent in her mood. She thought he was full of shit, but she didn't quite want to kill herself, and without any intervention that was certainly where she had been headed at that time. There was still a huge chunk of her that didn't want to walk the planet without Will or Joey by her side.

───────────

THEY'D GONE out for ice cream. She'd wanted chocolate peanut butter, Will wanted strawberry cheesecake and Joey wanted mint chocolate chip. At the last minute one of her clients had called in a panic over a supposed heart murmur and she'd let the boys head out to go and get the dessert while she tried calming Mrs. Whitaker down.

They made it to the grocery store in record time. Will called to confirm her choice right after Mrs. Whitaker hung up, and she reiterated that chocolate peanut butter was what her body demanded right now; it was her period, and she would eat chocolate all day if it came to that. Will laughed and agreed with her, "You're much nicer person when you eat chocolate," he laughed with a grin so large she could hear it over the phone.

"Yeah, yeah, just get me what Aunt Flo wants!" she laughed back. She could hear Joe saying something to Will about ice cream cones. "No, honey," Wren said through the phone, somehow hoping Joe would hear it, "we'll eat with spoons right out of the containers when you get home...won't that be fun?"

Will repeated what she said to Joe and she could hear his "Yay!" loud and clear through the tiny speaker.

"Sounds like the critter agrees?" Wren grinned into the phone.

"Yes, he agrees and is trying to open his container right now...hey, hey, hey, little fella!" Will trailed off as he tried keeping Joe from eating his ice cream on the store floor.

"Better let you go, then," Wren added as she heard his attention fading.

"Yeah, I'll see you when we get home," he agreed.

"Sure, will do...love you!"

"Love you too!"

It was the last time she heard his voice. On the way home an old lady ran the stop sign five blocks from their house. Wren was never sure if it was out of actual senility or just pure laziness, but the woman broadsided Will and Joey hard enough that it sent their vehicle spinning into the path of an oncoming transport truck. The old lady killed Will, but the transport vehicle killed Joe when it crushed the entire passenger side.

She'd waited for thirty minutes before calling Will's phone. Wren figured they must have taken a drive to the park to watch the ducks—one of Joe's favorites. When a strange voice greeted her on the other end of the phone her heart dropped to her toes.

Wren joined Space Command after that. As a child she'd always dreamed of being an astronaut, but she bailed on that plan when she'd met Will. They didn't take "attached" people for the long deep-space missions, and she couldn't fathom leaving the man who made her strange versions of French toast every Sunday morning. Joe had finalized that decision; she could never leave that funny little boy with the shock of bright red hair to go on a space mission. Ten years was too long to leave a child.

WREN SIGHED and looked straight ahead. Outside she saw the stars shining and wondered if one of them might be Joe and the other Will. A single tear dripped down her cheek and she wiped it away. Why did all her career moves seem to come from tragedy?

SEVENTEEN

FORESTER WALKED into his apartment and immediately found the main control pad; he reset the room temperature to 68 degrees and chose floor heating, then walked over to his bed and untied his shoes as he sat. In two quick movements both shoes were off and he pulled at his socks until they slid off and turned inside out in the process. He threw them in the corner and wiggled his toes on the tile floor, already feeling the tiles getting warmer. Forester stood up and padded around the apartment in bare feet.

He walked over to the simulator machine and started looking through the different food options: there were countless offerings, but something in him craved breakfast. It didn't matter that it was seven pm at night—it was nighttime all the time now, anyway.

He chose BELGIAN WAFFLES and watched patiently as the machine fired into action. It took a minute, but the window opened to a beautiful golden waffle, piping hot with a side dish of whipped butter. Forester looked at it greedily and took it to his table, slathering the entire ball of butter all over the warm waffle, leaving a shiny trail where it melted.

As his waffle cooled, Forester went back to the machine and ordered up a small bottle of fake maple syrup and a little cup of applesauce. He'd never liked real maple syrup for some reason, even though the rest of his family had craved it; instead, he preferred the version many old-timers called "Log Cabin." Forester took the applesauce and upended it on his waffle, then he smoothed it flat with his knife and drizzled the syrup on top —a method he'd learned from his mother. He closed his eyes in ecstasy as he took the first bite, chewing slowly and looking like a boy having his first orgasm.

Forester turned on his table screen. He surfed through the different options and chose a nature program focusing on the lemurs of Madagascar—the little creatures had been his favorite since grade school. He remembered doing a very thorough report on the Ring-Tailed Lemur for his second-grade presentation in a biologically-accurate lemur costume his mother had sewn, complete with a puffy tail on a bendable rod. The other second-graders had been duly impressed—it was one of the only times he spoke in public.

Forester's fork screeched across his plate and he realized he was out of waffle. He looked at the empty plate and thought about getting another one, but decided against it; his stomach was taut and full and he rubbed it like a pregnant woman fondling her unborn child. He figured it would be a miracle if any woman on the crew found him attractive, and he wasn't sure if he should maintain his figure or let himself go. For now, Forester decided to abstain from out-and-out gluttony.

He was full, but Forester still craved something. He looked at his simulator and thought about the screen he'd found the night before titled INTOXICANTS and laughed that Mission Control had even included this option. He chose CANNABIS and selected a small piece of taffy. Forester sucked on the strange-tasting "watermelon" flavored piece until it dissolved completely on his tongue, then he sat back in the strangely comfortable space chair turning it to look out the window screen.

Forester stared deep into space, feeling like the stars were pulling at him; it was exhilarating, and he thought he was melting into his seat. He smiled and leaned his head back, then clucked his tongue to the roof of his mouth: it felt like sandpaper, and he craved something moist to banish the desert-type feeling. He returned to the simulator.

Back facing the selection screen, Forester chose the BEVERAGE option and picked the picture displaying a tall cold glass of Pepsi. The machine whirred again and his drink appeared within a minute; Forester gulped it thirstily, belched, then sipped it more modestly. He went back to his chair, setting the drink on the table, all the while remembering his father's admonishments that little Brian should be 'a Coke man.'

Forester walked over to the synthesizer again and perused the plant options that didn't require a DNA infusion. His finger traced the screen lovingly as he selected the FABRIC ORCHIDS menu and settled on a spectacular cream Phalaenopsis orchid with pink stripes etched in its skin. The machine went to work and he waited patiently. After a minute that seemed endless, the panel beeped and the doors opened: inside was a medium-sized fabric orchid, looking just like a real orchid planted and mature with blooms. He smiled and pulled the imitation plant out, lovingly stroking its fake leaves like the real thing, then he set the orchid down on his table.

Forester sat and admired the orchid's petals; they were soft and sleek and beautifully colored and the stamen stuck out in a pseudo-sexual way—it was hard to tell that the plant wasn't real. He wrinkled his nose and took the plant by the pot, marched back to the synthesizer and placed the orchid back in the window. He hit RECYCLE on the screen menu and the doors closed as the machine broke the fake orchid down to its atoms again. The basic matter, less a little burnoff, was returned back to the matter storage.

After a second contemplation of the fabric orchid menu, Forester picked a bright blue plant. He admired the deep velvet-blue hue as the window opened, looked one more time, shook his head, and placed the plant back in the window to destruction. The synthesizer broke this decorative plant back to its atoms just as quickly as it had the first.

Forester went back to the menu a third time and selected a plant with a beautiful orangey-pink hue that looked like a sunset. He smiled as he beheld this final orchid—it was every bit as beautiful as the picture portrayed. He removed it from the simulator and placed it on his desk corner.

Curiosity piqued, Forester let his brain wander to all the animals on the planet he loved; as a child he'd wanted to bring home every creature he found, but none made it past the front door. Mother wouldn't have it, and little Brian had returned many a lizard, snake, mouse, dog, cat and chicken. It broke his heart every time, and that's why Forester started keeping plants as pets instead.

His mother loved his orchids but hated Forester's obsession with breeding cannabis plants. She'd chided him that he was "killing brain cells" every time. So much for her warnings, Forester thought, here he was an astronaut and one of the last surviving humans.

Forester suddenly wondered if he could simulate a kitten.

He stood up with a firm start—in one thought his aimless evening had a purpose, and he walked out his door and across the hall to the lab. Forester opened up Patel's case and took out one of the vials of housecat DNA. He only needed a drop of the stuff, and he used a syringe to draw out the tiniest amount. Once finished, he put the DNA sample back in the cabinet and went to the big lab simulator.

The screen flashed and Forester selected the CUSTOM

option; once on the screen, he typed in the words HOUSE CAT. The machine took a minute to think, then the prompt INSERT DNA appeared. He squeezed the tiny amount of serum on a little glass slide and the doors closed. The machine started working, but he could tell it was going much slower—the humming was lower and more intermittent. All in all, the cycle took nearly an hour, and at the end of the hour the signal beeped and Forester turned to look at the door like a little boy on Christmas morning.

As the door opened Forester got his first look: behind was a tiny ball of black fur. He approached closer and his stomach sank because he saw nothing moving, but as he got nearer the kitten popped its head up and stared at him with eerily blue eyes—the kitten was entirely black except for its electric blue eyes. Forester started crying as he looked at the tiny animal, and it looked back at him and mewed.

He reached forward and picked the kitten up, cradling it close to his heart.

STUART LEFT the sick bay and stopped right outside the door. She felt a huge weight settle on her shoulders and a blank empty feeling in her chest; her legs wouldn't support her weight and she leaned back against the wall, legs slowly collapsing until she sat on the ground. Stuart stared straight ahead.

How could she be so wrong about Bill? Galloway had promised his drug troubles were over. He'd even sworn he wanted to eat nails more than he wanted to shoot up again, and she'd believed him. Stuart felt so stupid...she'd believed him.

She wanted to cry right there in the hallway because she felt complicit in his downfall; perhaps the mission was too much for him to take and she should have never recommended Galloway. A voice in her head coldly reminded her that if she hadn't recommended him, Galloway would be a remnant of ash on Earth right now. Stuart brushed that thought aside and continued the blame game.

The voice in her head told Stuart over and over how much of a failure she was; how she didn't know people at all, and so, obviously, she'd picked the wrong chief surgeon. For that matter, she'd probably picked the whole crew wrong. They'd all fumble along in space until they died, and the loss of the human race would be on her hands—all because she didn't socialize more in school as a kid.

A different voice tried desperately to counteract each and every nasty word Stuart thought. It disproved the arguments and assured Stuart she was a very good captain: she'd had excellent missions before that had always gone as planned and on budget, and she knew how to fly the ship better than any human —Space Command knew that when they picked her to fly the Metis. She was their best, and the kind voice pleaded with her to come back to her center.

Stuart stood slowly and walked with a shuffling pace towards her room. She felt like someone had placed a fifty-pound sack on her shoulders, and she hunched ever so slightly as she continued into her quarters, alone.

INSIDE THE SAFETY of her sleeping area, Stuart made a beeline to the simulator and ordered up an ice cream sundae with a scoop of vanilla, a scoop of chocolate, and a scoop of coffee. The machine made it true to the image, with a perfect tuft of whipped cream and a little red cherry on top. Fine strands of chocolate syrup striped across the top; the bowl holding the sundae sat on a white dish with a doily underneath and a spoon neatly resting on the rim.

Stuart reached out and took the sundae greedily like a child.

She turned and walked to her desk, eating spoonfuls of the chocolate ice cream as she went. Once she reached the table she sat in the curved chair and set her ice cream on the smooth black screen.

Something about losing Galloway made her think of her parents; Stuart had been on her mission to Pluto when they both died. Madeline had gotten a pancreatic tumor that took her quickly, so fast that Larry hadn't even had time to prepare for life without her. One day, she was just gone.

He had spent two months living alone without his wife of forty years—trying to make food like she did, cleaning the house like she did, and keeping up with their group of friends, but every day the empty seat beside him wore on him more and more. When Madeline wasn't there to offer her usual critique of his barbecue recipes, that was the final straw.

Larry had taken the family shotgun out into the pasture, where he cradled his wife's ashes beside himself and took his own life.

Grace got the message about her parents when she woke from one of the sleep cycles on the Pluto trip. The cold white text on the screen simply said: YOUR PARENTS HAVE PASSED AWAY. DEEPEST CONDOLENCES. There was nothing about what had happened, and Grace had to come back to Earth to find out that her father had killed himself. Despair was a tricky thing, and it found even the strongest, most positive-thinking person like Larry Stuart a delicious treat. That it had settled on her father and taken him so quickly was a greater shock than learning about the cancer that claimed Madeline. It made Stuart feel helpless, sitting there in space and mourning parents who were dead a million miles away. That same helpless feeling crept into her heart when she was dealing with Galloway.

This thought hit Stuart deep in her gut and she started crying: so deep she made no sound at all and sucked air in heaving gasps.

She hugged her midsection with her arms and her eyes looked down the cold desk and the sharp edge it made with the black space outside. She focused on one particular star and kept crying.

After the last sobs faded, Stuart looked up and peered in her ice cream bowl. The three flavors were half-melted and pooling together in a wet puddle and she immediately had the urge to do something she'd learned as a child: she started chopping at the remaining ice cream and squishing it together with the flat side of her spoon, blending the flavors until they were a soft mass of light brown mash.

Stuart sucked down the first spoonful of homemade soft-serve, relishing the feeling of the cold mass sliding down her throat as it soothed the rawness. She'd tried eating ice cream this way when her wisdom teeth were pulled, and also learned a person could live off ice cream and Jell-O for over a week without getting tired of it. Stuart took her free hand, cold from holding the ice cream bowl, and pressed it against her puffy eyelids—relishing the cool spreading across her burning face. Ice cream had always been one of Stuart's favorite comfort foods, especially when stress torched her nerves.

Once finished with her sundae, Stuart returned the empty bowl to the simulator; the machine dutifully went through its recycling program and returned what was left of the item to base matter. She walked over to her bed and sat down on the mattress' edge, unzipping her jumpsuit and peeling the top off her shoulders. The entire suit slid down and Stuart wriggled it off until it was laying on the floor, then she sat on the edge of the bed in her prim-but-effective black sports bra and shorts.

The mattress adjusted to her body weight and set itself to a perfect medium-firm stiffness. Stuart tried sleeping but couldn't seem to get her father's face out of her mind: she could see his soft eyes and cheery smile, and the vision of him seemed to burn from behind closed eyelids. She opened her eyes half expecting him to be there, but an empty white room greeted her instead. Stuart shut her eyes again.

It was after she lost her parents that things got serious with Williams for the first time. He'd seen her alone in her room, and despite the years of casual sex between them, Pete had never given Grace a hug before. Pete had sat down next to Grace on the bed and let her lean into his shoulder, where she cried softly for many minutes, soaking his jumpsuit with her tears. Williams just let Stuart cry, rocking her gently and humming like her father used to do when Stuart was little.

Grace Stuart had never been like the girls who begged for a boyfriend every chance they got. Way too stubborn and aloof, always obsessed with winning, Stuart didn't attract the boys like the other girls did. It didn't matter if it was grades, a soccer match, or a so-called "friendly" game of pool, Stuart always wanted to be the best when she was young, and that focus blinded her to the interests of the opposite sex. She obliviously thought that no boys in her class liked her, so Stuart focused on her studies and work instead. It only occurred to her later that any interested boys had been probably scared away by Grace's preternaturally focused life plan.

Her parents had never known Pete Williams, and Williams had only seen the pictures Stuart kept of Larry and Madeline on her photo tablet. He'd heard the tales about Larry's obsession with raising the perfectly-spotted goat, and Madeline's love of everything Tolkien, but they were only mists on the wind compared to meeting the actual people. That didn't stop Williams from mourning them with Stuart, however, and from that point on they had quietly supported each other through any work arrangement.

It was challenging to keep a relationship quiet in any workplace, much less a spaceship, but Stuart and Williams were painfully aware of how things might look if the head engineer were screwing the captain. They had taken to meeting late at night, and cuddling for hurried moments, then Williams would scurry back to his quarters. That had been Pete's idea: making it look like they were having an official work-related meeting, just to throw people off the scent.

They had kept their relationship such a good secret that not even Space Command knew until they watched old video of the Pluto mission, and Jensen tacitly approved of their union as long as they didn't make it a distraction. That had been Jensen's gift to them both: he'd been the one to approve Williams for the Metis mission, and he carefully turned a blind eye to the fact that the ship's captain and head engineer went to bed in the same quarters from 01:00 hours to 04:00 hours every night.

Williams was in his quarters, waiting for their rendezvous time, but Stuart tossed and turned, laying back on her side facing the room with her back to the wall. She imagined Pete holding her, and the vision felt so real she actually thought she felt arms hugging her from behind; Stuart cuddled further back into that imaginary friend. The thought soothed her and she dropped into a deep sleep, waiting for the real man to arrive.

EIGHTEEN

SCHWARTZ FLIPPED THROUGH THE SCREENS, taking in the scene amongst all the crew members: he saw the commotion over Galloway and sat fascinated, but didn't get up to offer help —it was more interesting watching the man and wondering if Galloway would live or die. He saw Haddad and Stuart both tending to Galloway, and Wren looking for things on the other side of the lab. Schwartz watched as Haddad and Stuart awkwardly hefted Galloway into the med repair tube and Schwartz frowned—he kind of wanted to see what would happen if the doctor kicked the bucket.

Schwartz kept flipping back to Stuart. As much as he wanted to see the doctor in the final throes of a morphine-induced death, Schwartz couldn't break himself from watching the reactions of the captain as she tried saving her head surgeon.

That bitch, he thought as he watched her with an intense predatory gaze, *she has no idea how to handle this*—it would've been so much better if he'd gotten the command job over her. That was Father's final last kick in the balls for little Jimmy: to watch the command of the Metis go to a Korean woman who looked like she was twenty-five and always seemed to have a chip on her shoulder.

He wanted to fuck her and strangle her at the same time, and wondered if that would make her slanty eyes seem bigger— perhaps make her look like an actual white person for once. He touched himself while he watched her on the monitor, and when she went outside and started crying he grinned wide like a predator.

Why didn't Father love him enough to give him this last little present? All he'd wanted was to be the captain of a space-ship, and he'd joined Space Command to prove his Dad wrong: that he could stand up with the big boys and take a shot. When he'd made it to the commander ranking training he knew his father pulled a few strings to get him past the tests Jimmy didn't pass, but he didn't begrudge the old man that.

It was just this: the ship was supposed to be his...not hers. She was supposed to be the cute little first mate, or the engineer —she was supposed to look pretty and keep her mouth shut. She was supposed to do her duty. He'd liked Stuart originally because he saw a photo of her and thought she looked hot, but once he was actually working with her he realized what a mistake it had been.

The chick was a bitch...plain and simple. She wore the pants and then some, and seemed to have a thing out for him: he'd always done his best during the drills, it was only a few times he screwed up in the simulator. She treated him like he'd destroyed the whole planet, not just some bungled up simulator session. The comet had done plenty to wipe Earth off the map...much more than he had.

She didn't care, she never did. It was all her business or none and he silently hated her for that—especially when she bailed him out of the one simulator session where they were destined for certain doom. He'd looked like an idiot in that one: all thanks to that bitch.

It felt good to call her that; he'd only ever used the word in his head, but it had a certain spark—it made him feel his rage. She'd usurped his assumed next step and he'd fallen back to engine-keeper, and he was so much more than a lowly engineer —she knew it. That's why he treated his engine like shit: just to show her.

Schwartz watched as Stuart went into her room and indulged in a heap of ice cream. Schwartz wondered if she knew how detailed the intra-ship com screens could be as he watched her intently—she probably didn't know she could watch anything else besides her precious bridge. Perhaps that was his father's final gift: total access. Maybe she didn't have that, so he had the upper hand.

Schwartz sat and thought about what might happen if he used his access to his fullest: perhaps get everyone in one room and lock them up? That sounded good, and he could pull out the woman of his choice and impregnate her—and if she didn't like it he'd put her in cryosleep and do her then. He would be the father of a new race: the human race would be his.

Schwartz felt the seams in his pants tighten in his excitement. He held that feeling and reveled in the power and burn, dreaming black thoughts of how the ship would be his.

HADDAD STARED at the slice of berry pie. It sat on his plate, steaming, but Haddad just couldn't quite take a bite; he rubbed his chin and kept a cold gaze pointed at the buttery wedge on the tiny white plate. The meal was visually perfect—the simulator always knew how to make food to the atomic level, which put countless chefs out of business in the day. Not that it mattered anymore.

He picked at the pile of vanilla ice cream sitting next to the flaky piece of pastry and ate it in tiny pieces. Haddad savored the bits of crisp pastry and ripe berries like they were a fine wine, dipping each bite in a pile of melting ice cream, then chewing slowly. He licked his lips after each piece, then went back to staring at the plate; his gaze hungered for it, but somehow the stomach was fighting the urge to dive right in.

Haddad raised his thumbs to his lips and pursed them as his fingers pinched his upper lip. He frowned and cocked his head sideways at the pie piece and couldn't help thinking this was a dream—that he was staring at some photo of pie instead. The pie's realness soon took over and the smell of it overcame the sickness in the pit of his stomach—Haddad reached down and ate the pie piece in large chomping bites which belied no sense of pleasure: he ate like it was his job.

After the force-fed dessert, Haddad lay down on his bed, staring at the ceiling and willing his eyes to close. They wouldn't, so after sixty long-counted minutes he finally asked the computer: "run *Princess Bride*."

His first girlfriend got him turned on to the film. It was sophomore year and he would have done anything for Katherine, so a fluffy old fantasy movie didn't seem so bad. He didn't expect to actually like the film, but it became almost like comfort food for Haddad: he loved the giants and swordsmen and harbored a secret crush on Buttercup. Haddad never admitted about the teenaged night he masturbated to the entire film.

He watched the scene where the giant riddled about rocks ahead and cringed at the final rhyme, "If there are, we all be dead." His mind immediately flashed to the picture of a carved-out Earth, hemorrhaging where the comet hit. Haddad shook his head and cleared the tightness in his throat, but kept staring forward while the helpless feeling ate at him like a cancer.

His mind wandered back to Katherine—it honestly scared him at first how much Stuart looked like her; he'd had to refrain from trying to pat her bottom, remembering only Kate liked that. Kate had seen him as a handsome boy before any of the other girls realized it, and loved him when he'd gawkily sat next to her in biology—where they'd bonded over their mutual love of owls. She'd been one of the prettiest girls in school and had nothing but eyes for Louis Haddad. As he'd gotten older and taller and filled out, all the other girls were jealous of Kate— she'd gotten the jump on them.

They'd skipped school one day and taken the train to London; running around the city sans parents and teachers seemed so exhilarating. They'd been free and young and he'd brought just enough money to afford a small flat for the afternoon. The little condom had practically burned a hole through his pocket. He'd been terrible, but she was very kind and didn't say anything mean; Haddad worked hard over the next two years to repay her initial patience, and he'd figured out quite a lot with practice.

Leaving for university was the end of all that for both of them; he'd gone off to school in America and she'd stayed behind to go to Cambridge. They'd kept up the façade of a relationship for a couple months, doing video chats as often as possible, but the chats became fewer as the months rolled on. Finally, she'd missed one of his calls and then another after that. The first time he'd chocked it up to miscommunication, but the second time hurt—he'd gone and fucked a girl down the dorm hall after that. The girl hadn't been anything special, but she broke the spell.

The hard part was Kate nearly ruined him for other women; he couldn't ever seem to find another girl who was up to her level, so he danced through a series of long-term girlfriends everyone else thought were perfect for him—but he secretly felt empty with all of them. Until he met Karen, who'd blissfully chosen to marry him, despite his shoddy prior reputation. It was the cruelest slap of all to lose Karen and their baby while she was trying to give birth—that wasn't supposed to happen any more. Going to space was only an excuse for Louis Haddad to escape the memories of all the women he'd lost.

Haddad watched aptly as Westley was tortured for love and brought back again, staring at the screen and blinking ever so softly—the smile on his face evoked the small boy he hadn't been for a very long time. He rubbed his nose and sniffled as the movie finished and the screen went blank, then he rolled on his side and finally slept.

NINETEEN

STUART WOKE up and stared at the shiny panels covering her ceiling—they seemed to go on without beginning or end, and her eyes were already growing numb to all the white. They'd been on the Metis for over a week now, and she looked at the large tile above her head as it lit up abruptly and showed her a welcome screen: GOOD MORNING CAPTAIN STUART! it advertised in red text on a bright yellow background. *The computer must think yellow will wake us up,* she thought.

Stuart walked to the bathroom and stripped her undergarments off in front of the mirror; her sweat from the last night was particularly rancid, and it had soaked through her clothing. She sniffed her bra and winced, throwing all her garments in the sonic wash, then turning to the washbasin while she waited. She fired up her little toothbrush and methodically cleaned each tooth—the tiny humming machine vibrated in her head and made her inner ears mysteriously itch. Stuart put up with that feeling, because she loved the smooth texture of her clean teeth afterward.

She looked over at the sonic shower's door when it ceremoniously beeped at the end of the cycle, the control screen lit up and the door itself opened just a tiny crack: it tantalized coyly, promising something special inside. Stuart pulled the door open and grabbed the bra and underwear, throwing them over in the corner next to the toilet and begrudgingly entering the shower herself.

The machine sensed her climbing in. It scanned and read her DNA and automatically accessed the ship's crew manifest, where the data bank told the shower almost instantly Stuart preferred a warm temperature and a gentle cycle. The pod's interior warmed and she felt her muscles relaxing, then the hum started and Stuart braced for the cleaning.

Sound waves emanated from the back wall, buffeting her skin with tiny vibrations; Stuart always felt tingly and prickly when they hit her body and had always been jealous of other people who thought the sonic shower was ecstasy—to her it was borderline uncomfortable. It did get the skin clean, though. Stuart stood perfectly still and tried not peeing on her legs as the machine worked the skin directly over her bladder. After nearly four unbearable minutes, the machine made another celebratory beep and released her from its clutches; Stuart stepped out the door and shuddered as she crossed the threshold.

She walked to the corner simulator and fired up the same breakfast as the day before: the bowl of oatmeal with raisins always looked so wholesome and comforting. *It could be a cereal box cover model,* Stuart thought, *back when you used to get cereal in boxes.* She'd seen that in the movies.

She finished her breakfast quickly and watched a short part of *Some Like it Hot*. It seemed strange to her that people thought dressing in opposite-sex clothing was shocking and funny back in those days. The old-timers would've practically died if they'd seen the exhibitionist groups walking the New York streets in leather straps and practically nothing else, daring anyone to stare. Marilyn lived in an innocent age bathed in a golden glow and Stuart wanted to go there.

Stuart walked out her door and turned left; the long hallway stretched out in front of her and she was half surprised to see no one else there. She felt like the little boy in another one of her favorite films, *the Shining*, riding his big wheel tricycle round and round a deserted hotel. Stuart half expected to see two ghostly little girls waiting for her but none appeared, and she made her usual walk to the bridge.

Gutierrez was at the helm, running an autopilot test sequence on Stuart's monitor. When she saw the captain arrive on deck she jumped up out of the center seat, cheeks flushed. Stuart made a patting motion with her hand, the any-language sign to calm down.

"Hey, it's cool." Stuart grinned and saw Gutierrez relax. "How's the test sequence going?"

"Pretty good." Gutierrez took a large breath in. "All the metrics are coming out normal, and we've got excellent readings from all the energy sources. We're ready to test the cryosleep sequencing."

"Good, I'll let Wren know." Stuart looked at her command panel as she took her seat. "She can pick the first victim."

Gutierrez made a thin, knowing smile. She and Stuart had been around this block a time or two, and both instinctually hated cryosleep. Even though Galloway assured them the new pods were vastly more comfortable, Gutierrez couldn't get over the spins that made her want to crawl into bed and die. She wondered if Stuart got them too.

Stuart had learned to ride the beast that was cryosleep at a very early age, and figured that might be part of the reason she'd always been okay with the deep-space missions. Contrary to the sonic shower, the sleep pod functions never left her with a hang-over or an icky feeling; she didn't wake up necessarily refreshed, but she did feel okay most of the time. There had been one time of projectile vomiting right at the start, however, and Stuart's mind flashed back to the splash of partially-digested spaghetti sauce all over the hot male cryosleep instructor's shirt at the academy. The memory made her cheeks flush.

"HEY CINDY." The screen in the corner of the lab jumped to life. "Can you come to the bridge?"

Wren looked at Stuart's face on the monitor and it almost filled the screen—reminding her of the giant head in the "Wizard of Oz." To her knowledge, Stuart did not reside behind a magic curtain.

"Yup, be there in a sec." Wren set down the medicine applicator she was working on.

The screen flicked off and Wren took the quick jaunt down the hall to the bridge, the door swishing softly as she entered the command center. Stuart's back faced Wren, but she turned quickly.

"That was fast!" Stuart gave a small laugh.

"Yup, I got wings on my feet." Wren returned the smile, but it still felt forced after their ordeal with Galloway.

"The diagnostics are done." Stuart sighed. "I think we're ready to get going on the cryosleep rotation."

"Sounds good." Wren pointed at the door and Stuart followed her gaze. "You want to come and see the beasts?"

Stuart nodded. "You good with the bridge?" She looked over at Gutierrez.

"Yup. Go for it." Gutierrez answered.

Wren walked two steps behind Stuart as she followed her to the medical lab: the cryosleep pod used in the lab was specially designed for testing and other short-term cycles. Wren remembered on her last mission how the engineer hit his head and they put him in a sleep cycle until his brain healed; the man still needed some speech therapy afterward, but that was better than being a vegetable.

Stuart walked over to Wren's desk and sat down in the chair opposite hers. "We're gonna need some type of rotation order. I'm thinking a two week on, two week off type schedule." Wren nodded her head to agree and pressed the little speaker icon on her desk screen, which started recording and transcribing their conversation.

"Haddad and I will rotate constantly so one of us is always awake and in command."

"You want the rest of the crew to do the same?"

"No," Stuart continued, "engineers and bridge crew can rotate on the weekly schedule, but I was thinking a nine-month cycle for the scientists."

Wren's eyes widened a tiny bit and Stuart added nervously, "You can monitor that, can't you?"

"Yeah," Wren nodded. "But waking up from that long a sleep's gonna be a bitch!" Their eyes locked; Wren's were clear and true, full of her concern.

Stuart sighed. "I get that. We gotta save our matter stores, though, and they don't really need to be awake until Mars. You have any better ideas?"

"Not really, I guess," Wren answered with a sigh. "There's no prototype for an indefinite mission."

"Yeah." Stuart stared off at an imaginary object just over Wren's left shoulder. The weight of things suddenly came down on her and she had an ugly feeling they were wandering off to their doom; they didn't die on Earth, so now they could go and die slowly in space, and no one even knew if there were any habitable planets out there. Now she understood why Galloway wanted the comfort of his needle.

Stuart felt her stomach acid rising and resisted burping. Something about that last sentence rang so true: there honstly was no place to go to, no one to save them—they were all alone in a tin can in space. She knew it was some kind of honor to be one of the last, but it sure did suck. An itch started tugging beneath her skin and she scratched at it absently.

Stuart blinked her eyes and returned her focus to Wren's face. "You ready to give it a shot?"

"On you?" Wren's eyes widened.

"Hear me out," Stuart started, "I can go in and out smoothly. I don't want to torture any of the rest of the crew."

"I understand, but you're the captain. What happens if something goes wrong?"

"Then Haddad takes over."

"Okay." Wren tapped the start sequence initiation on her desk screen. "Head on over to the tube," she added with a flourish, beckoning Stuart to the corner of the room.

Stuart walked over to the cryosleep pod next to the med pod Galloway occupied and pressed the OPEN icon on the side. The lid hissed and cracked open, gradually exposing the sleep bed inside which was more like an upright restraining system— Stuart thought the whole thing looked like a coffin leaning against the wall, ready for its next victim. She climbed inside and strapped the retaining belts around her ankles, knees, hips, waist, and finally the chest. Wren finished up by securing Stuart's arms and shoulders, her face looming large in the window as she closed the lid.

Stuart smelled the gas first; it filled in through a small tube in the corner of the pod. Stuart felt like she was floating on a gauzy cloud and her ears rang, her vision blurred and she felt like she was melting into the floor.

———

SUDDENLY STUART AWOKE WITH A JOLT. She heard the whirring cycle while the cryosleep pod warmed her up, but her feet felt like blocks of ice and the burning sensation quickly became a gut-wrenching pain as her toes thawed. If she hadn't known better, Stuart might have thought someone was crushing her toes one-by-one in a nutcracker. She tried relaxing and breathing through the pain.

Outside the cryosleep tube, Wren looked at the test results on her screen: Stuart had been out for half a day and all her vitals checked out perfect—she didn't even throw up when Wren opened the pod.

Stuart nodded her head as she sucked her lips inward through partly-closed teeth. "Works!" Her voice cracked. "How long was I out?"

"Half a day." Wren looked at something on the screen in her hand. "You did well."

"Good." Stuart wiggled to get her circulation going while Wren unclipped all the restraining belts, then Stuart stepped cautiously free of the tangled mess. Her fist step was a little bit shaky, but anything was better than the whirling spinning room she experienced after her first go-around in cryosleep.

Stuart gingerly took her next step. "I think we're ready to go."

TWENTY

STUART WALKED BACK to the bridge and breathed deeply as she went; the cryosleep had left her legs a little bit rubbery and she had to focus intently every time her foot hit the ground. She used to take pride in the fact she could function so quickly after a cryosleep session, but now it just seemed like any other wakeup period.

She turned the corner and walked the short distance to the bridge and hesitated just slightly at the door when black spots started dancing in front of her eyes, then playfully globbed together in the center of her vision. She reached out and touched the wall until the spots returned to nothingness again, then stepped closer to the door, which sensed her and opened.

Inside, Gutierrez and Simon were chatting with Haddad, all clustered around his workstation. Their heads turned to Stuart as she walked through the door.

"How'd it go?" Haddad's eyes looked Stuart up and down like he was inspecting a loved one who had just been in a car accident.

"Pretty good." Stuart smiled but the corners of her mouth didn't want to budge without a fight. "I can't really tell if it's any better than the old machines, but maybe I'm not really the best judge of that."

"Yeah, lucky you…" Haddad imitated a jealous teenage girl. "I wish I could roll through it as well as you can."

"Seriously." agreed Gutierrez. Simon stayed quiet but watched Stuart's face intently and nodded.

Stuart walked closer to the group. "You guys got a minute?"

"Always." Haddad beckoned Stuart to her captain's chair. "What's up?"

"I've talked with Cindy and we're going to do a split cycle. The four of us plus the engineers will take turns being awake to man the bridge, and the rest of the team will sleep until we hit the supply buoy."

"Whoo…that's gonna be a good long sleep. You talked to Brian and Aditi about this yet?" Haddad whistled.

"I know, but Cindy says we've got to do longer cycles to conserve our matter supply."

"Makes sense." Haddad nodded.

Stuart sighed and sat back in her seat, feeling the warm material caress her. "I guess I've gotta break it to them."

Haddad looked grim. "Have either of them done a full long-sleep test yet?"

"I don't think so." Stuart's expression matched Haddad's as she thought about her first cryosleep trip again. "But they're gonna have to. Let's get them in the conference room." She looked over to Haddad and nodded as he opened up the com lines on his station.

"Guys, this is Grace." She kept her face steady, realizing she might also be on the video monitor. "I've got some news to share about our trip. Let's meet in the conference room in ten minutes." She tapped the com link on the screen before Haddad could even lift a finger.

"Now let's talk." Stuart said looking around the circle like a quarterback in the huddle.

"How long you do you want us to sleep?" Simon looked at Stuart with concern.

"I thought we'd do two weeks awake at a time."

"That's manageable." Gutierrez nodded.

"Yeah, that's what I thought too." Stuart looked at her crewmates. "I know you guys aren't the biggest fans of cryosleep, but I figured we'd keep it somewhat fair that way."

"I like it," Haddad smiled. "We going to do this after the supply buoy?"

"I'm debating that." Stuart scratched her chin. "It's about even between us and Mars. If it were up to me, I'd have us be awake the whole way, but Wren does have a point."

"Yeah, saving matter is important," agreed Gutierrez.

"It is," seconded Haddad. Simon nodded.

Haddad sat back in his chair. "So, who gets to go on watch first?"

"I'll go first," said Stuart, "that way I can show you what happened while you're out."

Haddad didn't look surprised. "Sounds good."

Stuart smiled, looking relieved. "Thanks."

"Definitely."

Stuart turned to Simon and Gutierrez. She made sure to look each of them in the eye, "You guys cool with that too?"

"Yeah," Gutierrez grinned and elbowed Simon in the ribs. "But I'll miss this guy!" She laughed.

"And I will go with you?" asked Simon, looking at Stuart while his French accent made a surprise return.

"Yup, if that's all right?"

Simon nodded. "Yeah, that's good."

Stuart clapped her hands together. "Now let's talk about the buoy..."

"I've been tracking its movement and it's staying pretty steady." Simon sent his map to each of their view screens. "Our flight plan should take us right by it on our way to Mars."

"Good," nodded Stuart. "We'll all stay awake for that one."

"You want the science team up?" Haddad looked confused.

"No, they can sleep through," Stuart's expression bore a mixture of thoughtfulness and resolution. "Lou, you'll lead when I'm under, and you can team with Luisa and Pete. I'll team with Laurance and Jimmy."

Gutierrez looked visibly relieved, and Stuart realized there might be other crew members who weren't keen on the President's son.

"You guys good with that?" Stuart looked around the room and the entire group nodded. "Great, let's head to the conference room, then." They all followed her out the door.

"Do you have a mock-up of the supply buoy?" Haddad asked Gutierrez as they walked through the doorway.

"Yes, I'll pull it up when we get back," Gutierrez left the buoy schematic open on her viewscreen to be ready.

They all walked silently down the hall as Gutierrez's words echoed off the walls, then turned in the conference room. Each took a seat facing a companion, with Stuart at the head of the table, and they waited until the other crew members arrived to join them.

Stuart looked around the table at the crew: Forester looked like he'd just gotten up, as well as Patel and Wren. Schwartz was still eating his breakfast bar and Williams picked at his teeth with his tongue, while Haddad looked at Stuart expectantly with his big eyes, and Galloway was conspicuously absent.

"Guys, we need to talk about doing a cryosleep schedule." Stuart noted the displeased look in most of her crew's eyes but continued. "I think we all know how important conserving our matter stores is now, given this situation. We've gotta save as much of it as possible, and the best way to do that is decrease our resource consumption...which means cryosleep."

"All of us?" asked Patel hesitantly.

"Yeah, but in rotation." Stuart tried sounding as kind as she could.

"How long?" Forester already looked green.

"You and Aditi will go under until we reach Mars."

Forester let out a puff of air as his jaw dropped and Patel's eyes widened. Neither had done much cryosleep training yet; this would be the marathon session they both feared.

"How long for the rest of us?" Schwartz whined.

"The rest of the piloting crew will take turns on a two-week rotation. You, Schwartz," started Stuart, "will be the engineer on my rotation team."

Schwartz actually looked pleasantly surprised for a second, then his trademark smirk returned. "I can handle that," he shrugged.

Stuart continued around the table. "Pete, you'll be with Louis and Luisa. Laurance and Cindy, you're with me." The crew sat for a second, processing the news.

"What about Bill?" asked Forester. "How long will he be out?"

"Because of Bill's health incident, he's gonna need to be in that medically-induced cryosleep cycle probably until Mars." Wren spoke sadly. "I'll take his place on both rotations."

"How is it going to feel?" Patel spoke softly and her eyes were wide.

Wren stepped in, "You should honestly feel pretty good," she started, "the actual takedown and sleep phases will be very smooth—like going to sleep before a surgery. The life support systems will keep your body working at a very low temperature and your cell aging will stop—essentially you'll go into torpor until the awakening phase."

"And how is the awakening?" Patel's voice was unusually quiet, and Wren had to crane her head to hear.

"That part will be a little rough. I know you've had a some

single-day training, so you know how that goes." Wren gave a barely-audible sigh.

"Yeah, I know." Patel's voice grew shrill with irritation. "I just about fucking died after that…how do you think six months will be?"

"Hopefully pretty good." Wren continued, "I personally interviewed the test subjects on these new models and they said it felt like they'd only been under a week. That said, you'll still experience the symptoms felt after one week."

"Fuck." Patel whispered under her breath.

Wren tried not letting it get to her and kept going. "That will include nausea, vomiting, occasional diarrhea, night sweats and a ringing in your ears."

"I just about barfed my guts up last time," Patel said softly to Forester.

Forester took Patel's hand and spoke up. "I have a confession to make."

"What?" Stuart looked at Forester, amazed again at hearing his voice.

"One second." Forester released Patel's hand, stood up and left the room. The entire crew stayed silent and all the heads focused on the door, until it opened and Forester walked in with a tiny black kitten; she was purring.

"I asked the simulator to make her," he said like a child caught with his hand in the cookie jar.

"Brian!" Stuart tried not sounding like her scolding grandma. "That's strictly forbidden by the State."

"I know." Forester blushed and his shoulders hung while the kitten tried climbing up his jumpsuit. "But the State doesn't exist anymore," he continued as he nuzzled the purring ball of fluff, "and I was lonely."

"Has she been functioning okay?" Patel looked at the kitten like it was a test tube.

"Seems totally normal." Forester forgot he was in the conference room for a second. "Normal bodily functions and read-outs." The kitten mewed and attempted to eat a piece of his hair.

"We'll take care of her," said Stuart.

"You will?" Forester looked at Stuart hopefully and Stuart realized the man was quite handsome, if he'd stare you in the eyes.

"I can do it, since I'll be up the whole time," volunteered Wren.

Forester beamed and stroked the cat's head. "You want to hold her?" he asked with bright eyes—the crew had never seen him so animated.

Stuart surprised the crew even more when she answered, "Sure," and proceeded to beam like a new mother as she pet the little fuzzy creature in her lap. The kitten tried chewing on her finger, then settled for licking it instead. Stuart smiled and cooed, "What a cute little thing. You got a name for her?"

Forester smiled like a new parent. "Roxanna." At the sound of her name the kitten turned her head towards Forester and mewed once.

Stuart stared for a second at the kitten's unearthly blue eyes; the rest of Roxanna looked like a normal cat, but the eyes seemed to be from another world—they scared Stuart for a moment. The moment passed as quickly as it had arrived, though, and then Stuart went back to kissing and snuggling the baby feline. After a second it mewed and tried crawling down her leg to get to Forester and he closed the distance to scoop the kitten up in his arms.

"Darling kitty," Stuart smiled. "She just broke all the conventions on Earth."

"A space kitten," said Patel with a girlish smile. Forester smiled back at her with sheepish pride in his creation. "We'll have to talk more about how you did that later." Patel raised her eyebrows like she was scolding him and Forester nodded at her and sat back down in his seat, while Roxanna attempted to climb on top of his head.

"Okay." Stuart placed her hands palm-down on the table in front of her. "Brian," she said with a look sharply back in his direction, "Let's have you and I and Cindy meet at 17:00 to discuss the ongoing care and maintenance of our new ship cat, Roxanna."

"Yes Grace," Wren and Forester answered in unison.

"Okay, dismissed." The entire crew stood and left the room in silence.

Wren smiled as the door closed and thought about cuddling little Roxanna in her bed at night: her purr would be a little magic fire in the cold darkness of space.

TWENTY-ONE

STUART WALKED down the hallway towards Engine Room One. She paused at the door while the panes slid open; on the other side Williams sat looking intently at his desk screen. His back was turned to her, but the tight hunch in his shoulders gave his concentration away.

"How's it goin'?" Stuart spoke up. Williams jumped as her voice echoed off the clean white walls.

"Good." He craned his neck to see her and his body followed suit; the chair obligingly swiveled to turn his body the rest of the way towards Stuart. "Engine's running perfect, and I'm just hangin'."

"What, you didn't want to play cards with Jimmy?" Stuart teased. Williams's face contorted into a look of mock surprise.

"Are you kidding me?" He laughed. "I still can't believe I have to spend the rest of my life sharing a ship with that guy."

"I know, I know," Stuart walked over to Williams and put her hands on his shoulders. "You would have preferred we clone you, and then our engineering functions would have gone perfect to your plan."

"Precisely."

"But there are other engineers out there who are just as good —you can't hog all the jobs. Plus, if we'd actually had a clone on board we'd be screwed from a genetic standpoint. And a clone of you would just weird me out." She giggled softly.

"Yeah, you're right." Williams sighed. "Even punk bitch engineers need to eat."

"Hey!" countered Stuart like she was scolding a child.

"What?" Williams tried grinning innocently, but it came off looking like a sarcastic smirk. "You know none of us had a say in him getting the detail. It must be good to be the President's son."

"Well he's not the President's son anymore," Stuart shook her head. "Now he's just Jimmy Schwartz, engineer."

Williams got quiet and a sober expression came over his face. "Yeah, guess you're right about that." He sat back in his chair. "So, did you want to torture me with thoughts of my co-worker, or do you have something I can help you with?" He grinned saucily and reached for Stuart's behind.

"I need you to help Louis while I'm out...teach him more about the engines, and work with him on the landers."

"Yeah?"

"Yeah." Stuart nodded and put a hand on Williams' shoulder. "Everything you know I can do...he needs to know too."

"You planning on retiring?"

"No." Stuart crossed her arms. "But we need more versatility. The whole thing with Galloway got me thinking—what if I died? Lou can handle it...he's better than he realizes."

"Okay," Williams grinned like the Cheshire Cat. "I'll be his Jedi master. You sure you want to go solo with Schwartz? I still can't stand the idea of that monkey watching the ship while I sleep."

"That's the deal."

"Why?"

"You know we have to conserve matter."

"Yeah." Williams nodded his head slowly. He had a sad tone to his voice and a misty vacant look in his eyes as he stared over her left shoulder. Then his eyes sharpened, "You remember his dossier, right? Where he said he wanted to be a 'Captain of The Ladies' someday?"

"Yeah, so?"

"He's not going to take that well. .having to deal with you and Wren…"

"Well fuck him."

"Whatever you say, Boss." Williams gave Stuart a faux-salute and she started giggling at the old nickname he'd given her on their first trip to Mars. Williams smiled back and laughed too—that was one of the reasons she loved him. She'd been grateful Jensen approved him for the mission, and didn't regret it one bit: there wasn't a better man to spend the rest of your days with.

"Thanks," she spoke when she'd caught her breath. "I needed that."

"So did I," chuckled Williams. "We don't have enough fun on this crew."

"I could synthesize us a slip-n-slide to run down the main aisle." Stuart winked flirtatiously.

"And mission control would be none the wiser," answered Williams back before he caught himself. His mood darkened slightly and he knit his brows.

"Guess we can do whatever we want." Stuart put her hands in her jumper pockets and raised up slightly on her toes, shrugging her shoulders.

"Shit, what do we do?" Williams sounded mock-scared as he opened his eyes a little wider; they had a bit of their old sparkle back.

"Wanna get sexy?" Stuart winked back at him.

"Ohhh m'lady," Williams moaned. "Ready about 22:00?" his voice teased the answer out of Stuart.

"Your room or mine?"

"Do you even need to ask?" Williams' eyes flashed mischievously. "I know our arrangement…"

"Definitely." Stuart smiled and felt her nether regions warming already. She dreaded the short, lonely walk back to her room at night anyway.

"It's a date, then." Williams grinned. "We'll call this being even for having to cryosleep rotate with the foolio." He waved his hand in the general direction of Schwartz's engine room.

"Okay." Stuart patted Williams' shoulder. "A date." Her eyes sparkled like a young girl—a look Williams loved teasing out of her.

Stuart's eyes softened for a minute and she felt herself get warm and fuzzy at Williams' touch, enjoying the energy bridge between them for a flicker of a second. He smiled back at her, and they held the moment—savoring it like sucking on a candy. Stuart reached down quickly and pecked Williams on the lips, then blushed furiously and scampered to the exit—getting back to the bridge doors so quickly she nearly hit them. The entire time it felt like she was being transported by a moving walkway in a cloud. Haddad, Simon and Gutierrez all looked up at her as she entered.

"Welcome back!" Haddad grinned.

STUART KEPT GLANCING at the time ticking down in the corner of her command screen. She didn't want to seem too eager, but her stomach growled and she felt that familiar warmth building in her groin again; it was all she could do to not think about Williams. The way he smelled, his skin, his hair, the way his eyes twinkled when he laughed—she wanted him now, but had to wait.

The minutes kept ticking by like peanut butter dripping

down a window, and each time Stuart looked at the screen expecting it would be ten minutes later, she was sorely disappointed to see that only a few minutes had passed. The growling in her stomach got worse, and suddenly Stuart felt the urge to go to the bathroom.

"Excuse me for a second, guys." Stuart stood up quickly from her command station.

"You good, Grace?" Simon raised his eyebrows and that made his already large brown eyes look huge.

"Yup." Stuart grabbed her portable screen. "Just gotta go to the toilet." Simon nodded like he understood.

Stuart ran to her room, finished her business and dressed quickly. A cold chill hit her midsection between her bra and underwear where a thin film of sweat coated her navel—she pulled up her jumpsuit's torso and felt instant relief. The material Space Command used for the "grownup onesies" was soft and warm, and always seemed to be the right temperature; even though Stuart thought they made everyone look like some kind of cult member.

She zipped up her jumpsuit and looked at herself in the mirror, adjusting the pieces of hair sticking out along the side of her head. She turned her head side-to-side to check for any rogue pimples, and satisfied, Stuart walked slowly back to the bridge. Simon gave her a curious look as she returned to her seat, but she brushed it off and tried looking normal; inside, the butterflies in her stomach got worse by the second.

At 20:00 hours Simon stood up from his station and cleared his throat. "Grace, may I excuse myself for the evening?"

"Absolutely." She looked back and smiled at Simon, which he returned. "Good job tonight. I'll set the autopilot after I leave—you'll need to disable it when you start in the morning."

"Not a problem," he finished with a hint of his soft French accent. "I will see you in the morning."

"Goodnight!" called Stuart as Simon left the bridge.

"Goodnight, Grace." He waved over his shoulder as he walked through the doors.

Stuart watched the clock count down until it was 21:00 hours. When the icon rolled from 20:59 to 21:00 she stood up abruptly, like a person who'd sat on a bee, then she set the autopilot to maintain their heading towards the supply buoy, turning the screen off as she stood. A small pulsating blue light lit up the screen corner, letting everyone know the autopilot was on.

She turned and left the bridge with a quick step. Stuart felt like running to her cabin, but didn't want anyone in the crew to think something was amiss. It'd been eons since she'd been with Williams, but he was a drug she just couldn't quit: having him on the crew was both a challenge and an excitement. She tried keeping her feelings for him numb while they worked, but after hours the firm grip she had on her self control waned.

Stuart walked to her cabin and turned immediately towards the simulator near her cryopod. Pete had always liked lasagna, and the simulators made one that put the old freeze-dried space food to shame. She ordered up two servings of lasagna, garlic bread, and an order of asparagus with parmesan cheese sprinkled on top. The simulator dutifully responded and hummed into action, and within five minutes the meal was complete.

The table in the middle of her room looked forlornly naked, so Stuart turned back to the simulator and went to the HOUSE-WARES menu. She selected a small rectangular tablecloth in the traditional red-checked pattern most Italian restaurants seemed to have in abundant supply, then grinned naughtily and had the simulator make a candle in a wicker Chianti bottle too. If she was going to be cheesy to romance her paramour, then she might as well go all the way.

She set the plates down on either side of her table and took a quick second to simulate a small self-assembling chair for Williams. Stuart placed his chair on the opposite side from hers so she could watch him face-to-face. The chair squeaked on the white tile floor and the echo made Stuart jump; she calmed her nerves just in time to hear Williams come through the door.

Stuart turned and looked at Williams' smiling face, matching his expression. His brown eyes had always been the thing that got her attention first: their warm gaze made her feel settled in her stomach and good all over. Even though Pete boasted a very fit physique from all his years of space training, his eyes were the thing that attracted Stuart to him most. She grinned deeper like they were sharing a private joke and beckoned him towards the table.

"Oh, dang…you didn't!" Williams chuckled as he took his seat, looking at the plates of lasagna.

"Yeah, I did." Stuart tilted her head and looked coyly at Williams.

"What did I ever do to deserve this?" Williams' grin broadened.

"Kept my engines from blowing up. For that I thank you." Stuart pretended to be extremely formal and bowed like a Japanese businessman.

Williams cackled wildly. "I'll take the bribe, lady."

Stuart remained smiling as she sat down opposite Williams: he was already intently smelling his plate and making manly "mmmm" noises that rumbled in his chest. Stuart watched Williams as he took his first bite and exploded into an array of more orgasmic-sounding noises.

"Good?" Stuart raised her eyebrows.

"Amazing," Williams gushed with a mouthful of lasagna. To Stuart it came out sounding like: "rrmmazing." He held up his hand and finished chewing his large bite then continued: "These machines really put Betty Crocker to shame."

"Damn straight," grinned Stuart as she tasted her first bite, "you know it wasn't me who made this." It was the type of dish her mother was never quite able to achieve, but the simulator knew the molecular makeup of the most perfect lasagna and could manifest it at will, any time. The family dinner had never been the same since the machine's invention.

They both ate in silence for a moment, each making happy "mmm" noises on a particularly good bite. Stuart looked up and Williams burped; Williams blushed as the noise echoed around the room.

"Pardon me."

"No excuse for you!" Stuart scolded back with a wink.

"Complements to the chef."

"Go pat the machine," she waved her hand at the machine in the corner.

"Maybe I'll do just that," Williams answered back with an equally saucy tone. He checked over his shoulder and around the room. "You turned off the view availability?"

"Yup, it's in Privacy Mode."

"Good." Williams leaned across the table, took Stuart's chin in the hook of his finger and kissed her softly on the lips. Williams sat back and they both smiled.

"Thanks." Stuart knew he could see her blushing. She always blushed when they kissed, even after all the years together.

"I needed that." Williams' eyes beamed so brightly he winked, then he sucked red sauce off his thumb which Stuart found oddly erotic.

"You wanna have dessert?" Stuart eyed the simulator and thought about ice cream again.

"Sure." Williams cleaned his teeth with his tongue. "What would you like?"

"Ice cream?"

Williams started making new happy "mmmm" noises. "My baby's favorite…That sounds perfect!"

"You still like that orange chocolate flavor?"

"Yup," he agreed. "Coffee for you tonight? Or will it be mint chip?"

Stuart grinned like she'd been caught red-handed and nodded quickly like an excited teenager. "Mint chip."

Williams stood up and went to the simulator door, taking both their entrée plates with him; Stuart turned and watched him go, so impressed at a gentleman doing the dishes. He looked back over his shoulder and smiled, and she sat back in her chair and returned the expression again.

Williams walked to the window and set both plates inside, then tapped the RECYCLE icon on the pad and the doors closed. A couple minutes passed and he observed his shoe in an uncomfortable manner while he waited. The thought of Grace naked in bed, the sounds of pleasure in her voice ran through his head; if she could have known how hard he was working to keep his erection down, she would have laughed.

After what seemed like endless hours to Williams, the machine chimed and the doors opened to an empty compartment. Williams hit the touchscreen and skipped through the simulator menu until he found the two ice cream flavors they wanted. The machine whirred into action and proudly displayed two beautiful scoops of ice cream in clear bowls with chocolate sauce, whipped cream and a cherry on top. Stuart flashed back to the ice cream parlor her mother used to take her to on Fridays in grade school; how the walls were painted in red, white and blue pinstripes, and they would bang a large parade drum when it was your birthday.

Williams sat down and placed the light green-colored ice cream in front of Stuart and set the lump of chocolate ice cream in front of his spot, sighing as he sat down. Stuart dug into her sundae and scooped a big piece of ice cream out with a smudge of chocolate syrup on top, drizzled the cherry in the whipped cream and chocolate sauce, and licked the sauce off the cherry's skin. Williams couldn't control himself any longer: he took her hand and licked her index finger longingly, then she dipped it in her ice cream and he did it again. Stuart couldn't restrain her chuckles.

Williams finished licking her finger and sat back. He focused on his sundae and proceeded to eat it in almost military-methodical fashion. Huge chunks of ice cream went in his mouth in a flash; so fast, he got a momentary brain freeze and a frozen tongue. Stuart ate her whipped cream first, finished off the cherry in a seductive way, then ate all the melted ice cream mixed with chocolate syrup floating at the edges of her cup. Once she'd cleaned the melted stuff up, she took long, swirling strokes off her ice cream with the tip of her spoon, licking it slowly in a way Williams recognized. He moaned and shook his head like he was scolding her.

Stuart finished the last of her ice cream and stood, taking Williams' left hand and pulling him upward; he stood and let her lead him backwards towards the bed. She walked him right to the edge, sat him down, then pushed him backwards on the mattress and Williams fell back with a grin. Stuart started unzipping his jumpsuit and when it was fully open he wriggled his torso out of the top. The bottom he let Stuart take off, and she noted the bulge in his underwear as he moaned softly.

Stuart stood over the prone Williams and unzipped her own jumpsuit, stripping it off her shoulders and arms, then pulling it all the way down to her ankles—which removed her shoes as well. Williams watched her, enthralled. Stuart stood in only her underwear, and he sat up and pulled her closer to him, sliding a finger up her underwear cuff and stroking her leg softly. She took her own turn moaning.

Williams kissed Stuart's stomach and slid his fingers under the top band of her underwear. From the corner of his eyes he looked over at the blackness of space watching them; it seemed strange to "do it" with the windows open, he thought, but there was no one out there anymore. Williams pulled Stuart down, lifted up her sports-bra and hurriedly freed her right nipple from its constriction, then he sucked on it softly as she moaned again. Stuart rubbed his head and ran her fingers through his hair, touching his ears softly as he removed her bra the rest of the way.

Stuart grabbed Williams' underwear and yanked the elastic band downward; the cloth slid down his smooth behind and she felt it catch on his crotch. She cleared the snag and stroked him in the same motion and he moaned louder while biting his lip. She pushed him down backwards and mounted him; Williams whimpered and moaned in the same breath and gave in to her warmth. She held him and gripped him just so and he came exploding into her with cries of his mother on his breath and Stuart's joyful screams in his ears. They stayed locked together, shaking in each other's arms. Williams' breathing slowed and he lay with his cheek on her breast, stroking the opposite nipple.

"I guess we're doing that for real." Stuart consciously noted the lack of a condom and spoke so softly she could barely hear her own voice.

"Yup," Williams answered softly back. He moved his hand from her nipple to her navel and stroked her belly. "A little critter wouldn't be so bad."

"Yeah," Stuart smiled and kissed Williams again. "Guess not."

TWENTY-TWO

SCHWARTZ PICKED at the side of his jaw, itching a bump that had popped up overnight. He hated the imperfection and it galled him to think one could still get bad skin in space. *There should be a machine for that,* he thought, but again he lamented no one had invented something to zap acne before the comet. Now it would be up to him and the other morons who populated the ship to think of new inventions. He hated them all.

The only consolation he took was in his nightly masturbating sessions; he'd think about all the women he'd ever wronged, all the women he'd ever hated, all the women he'd thought were cute. Even the older gals who looked suspiciously like his mom. *Mom did have great tits, after all,* he thought.

President Schwartz had left his son James to his own devices as a child, and it hadn't taken long for young Jimmy to figure out how to work the system around the house. Anything he wanted, he could get from one of the servants or their "acquaintances."

Schwartz stalked around his cold white room, pacing off the steps; he walked round and round the walls until he'd counted four hundred and fifty rotations, then he stopped and stared out the window into space.

He figured he had to kiss the Old Man's boots metaphorically for giving him this magic ticket off the death trap—with hot chicks on board to boot. His father really must have had the gold balls to get his sonny that final gift: that was the perk of being President so long.

Schwartz smiled: he missed his old pops. President Schwartz was the kind of man who had a swig of scotch in the morning then went on to power through his day, strutting like the man of infinite importance he knew himself to be. President Schwartz was tough and he knew it—balls tough.

It hadn't taken very long for the younger Schwartz to figure out he could get away with murder—literally. He'd seen to the killings of his father's opponents so his father never seemed to leave office, and it gave Jimmy a thrill just thinking of it. The only thing he didn't get was the blood on his hands: he usually didn't do that kind of killing personally. It disappointed him, but the practical side of Jimmy Schwartz knew he had to keep those tastes on the down-low.

Schwartz rubbed his eyes, chasing a phantom itch that wouldn't go away. The space beyond their ship seemed like fuzzy inky darkness and he had trouble focusing, so he lay back in bed.

Tonight he thought about the captain. He remembered her from the last time she'd come back from Mars—back when young Jimmy had just been a teenager. She didn't look much older than he at that point, but Schwartz knew better: Stuart was almost old enough to be his mother. A hot mother.

The next time he'd met her she was walking into a room where he was already facing his father. He'd turned to observe the petite woman entering confidently, and when his father announced this little woman would be the new captain of the Metis, he'd almost melted down. Why the fuck had he trained so long? Only to be usurped by that little bitch? The President looked smug.

Schwartz didn't even want to go on Stuart's bridge—it made him sick. He'd worked so many hours in those fucking simulators, and he'd done pretty well, by his count. Only crashed a few simulated missions; most had made it intact. Stuart just remembered the one he crashed spectacularly, and that was on his third try. He'd gotten much better after that, but Schwartz always felt Stuart's stink-eye on him—she wouldn't let him touch her controls again.

But he wanted that bridge so much...it was his! It was promised to him: Father had told him about the job over a meal of endangered swordfish. Schwartz wondered if this was some kind of cosmic mission: one last challenge from Father. He would take that bridge, and show the old man who's boss—that would make the old bastard proud.

Schwartz thought for a second; he needed to either get the crew's cooperation or subdue them all. Cryosleep would help— half of them would be out anyway, which left only Stuart, Simon, and Wren. Two chicks and a French man...who could almost count as a third woman anyway, in his opinion. That would be no problem: he'd take over the com system, isolate them from each other and begin the gradual takedown. The women he'd keep, even if he had to stick them in the sleep tube —the French one he'd do away with. Didn't need the extra competition.

It was perfect: he would be in command, and they'd all get to the future safely—whether they wanted it or not.

STUART WOKE up and stared at the ceiling. She heard Williams snoring lightly in little puffs through his parted lips and she stroked his hair with the tips of her fingers. Her touch was so soft he didn't wake, but moaned pleasantly in his sleep. Stuart watched him with a beatific smile on her face.

She looked up again at the ceiling, where the screen panel above her recognized her retina and displayed the time: 03:30 am. Stuart hadn't planned on falling asleep with Williams after their tryst, but he'd cuddled her and they'd both drifted off to sleep clasped tight like two spoons. She breathed in and got a whiff of his body sweat mixed with the last drops of his cologne.

Her body relaxed from head to toe and every inch screamed to go back to sleep in his arms, but the pragmatic side of her brain knew better: Williams needed to get back to his quarters before the rest of the crew realized where he was. They'd have to cross that bridge sometime, but for now she wanted to keep her relationship with Williams to herself.

Stuart stroked Williams' hair a bit more vigorously and he woke with a small moan, blinked his eyes, then stared into Stuart's.

"Mornin'" Williams mumbled between sticky lips, yawning.

"Mornin'" Stuart answered back with a smile as she pet his hair again.

"What time is it?" Williams' voice slowly began to gain traction.

"03:30."

"Fwhew!" He puffed a bit of air out of his lips. "Bit early?"

"Yeah." Stuart kissed Williams again. "Figured you'd probably want to get back before the natives got restless."

"Mmm, good call." Williams rolled over top of Stuart's nude torso and stepped out on the cold tile floor; the floor immediately greeted his touch with warmth. Stuart admired his naked backside, then Williams pulled on his underwear—the jumpsuit followed, then he slipped on his shoes. Within minutes Williams was fully clothed, looking down at Stuart still snuggled under the covers.

"Damn, wish I could stay."

"Yeah, me too." Stuart sighed. "We're gonna have to figure this out."

Williams smiled tightly and lay his hand on Stuart's head. "For another day."

Stuart smiled back and snuggled back in to her covers, "'Night."

"Night." Williams bent down and kissed her one more time, stroking her cheek longingly with his fingers and caressing her chin. Then he turned and stumbled sleepily back towards his quarters. The "Walk of Shame" still hurt in space, he decided.

Stuart rolled back in bed and snuggled in the soft spot Williams left, trying to get as tight with his warmth as she could. His body smell still permeated her pillow and she breathed in deeply and smiled, then her eyes fluttered and drooped. In another minute she was back asleep.

STUART WOKE AGAIN, this time with a start; she sat up in bed and tried staring out the window screen, but the same endless set of stars greeted her. Stuart's body shook and her heart raced —she'd somehow soaked through all her sheets while dreaming about an octopus she couldn't stop, that eventually ate Pete. The clock read 04:35 am.

She groaned and climbed up out of bed, stripping the sheets off in a tugging motion. They stunk of strange nightmare sweat —Stuart took a quick whiff and pulled her head away in disgust. She held the sheets at arm's length pinched between her index finger and thumb and walked slowly towards her cleaning stall, dragging them over to the sonic cleaner like the old-fashioned cartoon character Linus and his pet blanket. At the stall, Stuart dropped both pieces unceremoniously in the center and closed the door. The machine purred and bombarded her stinky sheets with sound rays that worked to strip the fibers miraculously clean.

Stuart stood in the middle of her room and shivered: the cold air made her sweaty skin feel even colder. She wished she'd hopped in the cleaning booth before she'd thrown her sheets in, because a quick sniff of her armpits confirmed they smelled just as funky as her bedclothes. Stuart resigned herself to the fact she'd have to take one of those scratchy baths and her mind irresponsibly wondered if the large simulator in the engineering bay could make a hot bubble bath in a claw foot tub.

The machine chimed and Stuart pulled open the door on her sonic cleaner; she removed her sheets and placed them on the closed toilet lid, sighed softly and climbed in the sonic booth like a reluctant child. The sensors confirmed her occupancy and immediately sprang to action, reading Stuart's body metrics, scanning her DNA to double-confirm she was Captain Stuart, then the machine remembered her favorite wash cycle and commenced.

Stuart tried relaxing as that cat-tongue feeling started up. She thought about getting dry and warm, about how good being clean would feel—anything to take her mind off the sensation. It only took a minute, but Stuart's time in the sonic shower felt like eons. As soon as the chime sounded, Stuart was out the door and pulling a clean sleep shirt on; she grabbed a fresh pair of underwear and tried fumbling her feet in the leg holes while she sat on the toilet and went to the bathroom. Once finished, Stuart padded back to her bed carrying her sheets.

She groaned.

Her eyes drooped and she wanted to go back to sleep, but Stuart forced herself to go through the motions of putting the sheets back on the bed. Once finished, Stuart stepped back and admired her tidy work, then she lay down in the bed and ruined it. Not five minutes after she'd laid down, Stuart was back asleep.

THE SOUND of a rooster crowing woke Stuart. She rubbed her eyes and stared up at the clock in the ceiling panel: it flashed *06:00 am* over and over. Her sheets were dry this time and Stuart was grateful for that, so she skipped the morning shower and went straight to the washbasin where she splashed some cold simulated water on her face, then dried herself with the yellow towel hanging next to her mirror. She rubbed a bit of moisturizer on her face and elbows, then turned and walked over to the simulator next to her cryo pod.

Stuart stared at the screen, trying to think of what to have for breakfast. She'd eaten the same cereal for what seemed like weeks, and today her stomach was curious for something different; she scrolled through the options and spied a tasty looking order of French Toast. Stuart clicked the ORDER icon and the machine whirred into action.

After minutes that stretched like taffy, the door opened and Stuart looked upon a plate of French toast that appeared identical to the picture she'd chosen. A whiff of cinnamon vanilla scent hit her nose and her stomach growled greedily. Stuart grabbed her plate, sat down, and ate her food promptly.

Almost as quickly as she sat down, Stuart was back up again cleaning up her breakfast mess. She checked the clock: *06:25.* Stuart returned her plate to the simulator, brushed back her hair, and headed out the door. She turned left and walked down the hallway to the bridge.

Williams' door opened and he came out almost on cue as Stuart passed.

"Mornin'." He said pantomiming the gesture of tipping his hat. Stuart laughed and thought he looked like some cowboy dressed up in a Space Command jumpsuit.

"And good mornin' to you, good sir," she added, dropping a faux curtsy and pretending to lift an imaginary dress. The move made them both devolve into giggles, then chuckles, then full-blown laughter. Williams jumped in with his own booming staccato "ha, ha, ha."

"See you at the team meeting?" asked Stuart.

"Yup." Williams scratched his head. "It still on for 09:00?"

"Yup."

"Good." Williams waved as he headed for his engine room. "See you then!"

He turned right at Engine Room One's doors and gave a slight wave again as he walked through the door. Stuart waved back, then she headed on her way to the bridge. She was fairly surprised to see it so quiet; there was no one out in the halls, no voices, nothing—the eerie silence made her feel like something was watching her. Stuart turned the corner and walked the final few steps to the bridge, the doors opened and she stepped inside; it felt like coming home somehow, even more so than her room. Stuart sat in her command chair and tapped the screen panel in front of her.

The pane lit to life and displayed the ship's progress over the course of the night. The autopilot had worked perfectly and they were on a clean course to the supply buoy, probably reaching it within three months. She ran a diagnostic check on the ship's systems and everything came out clean.

On a whim, Stuart ran a ship scan to sense for body heat. The results showed five crewmembers still in their rooms, a couple still in bed. One person was in the gym, and one was walking towards the bridge. The doors opened and Haddad stepped inside.

"Good morning, Grace," Haddad said as the panes swished shut behind him.

Stuart turned her chair to face him and smiled sunnily. "Morning, Lou." Then she remembered what they had to do that day. "You ready for the cryosleep rotation?"

"Oh joyous. Am I ever." Haddad's British accent made the sarcasm seem that much deeper.

"Yeah," concurred Stuart. "Joyous."

The minutes ticked down and Stuart alternated calculating travel distance to different planets and staring out at the blackness ahead of them. She actually liked cryosleep because it cut out the boring parts of a space trip: the space in between. There were only so many stars you could look at when you saw them non-stop every day.

"You doing good, Louis?" Stuart called over her shoulder.

"Yup," he answered.

Stuart turned her chair so she was facing him, but not straight on. "How's your room treating you?"

"Very nice."

"You liking things with the crew so far?"

"Yes Grace." Haddad didn't know if he should tell her what he really thought of Schwartz. Or what his solution would be.

"You feeling okay about things?" she asked, rephrasing her previous question. "Really?"

"Well, I worry about Schwartz," Haddad started, deciding to take advantage of the opportunity.

"Yeah, so do I."

"You really sure you want to go solo with him?"

"He needs to learn respect somehow."

"You sure he respects anything?"

Stuart paused for a moment and gave that question thought. Even though Space Command had picked Haddad to be her first mate, she honestly did like his astute judgment. This time was no exception: Schwartz gave her the heebie-jeebies. She wished she could've stood up to the president and rejected his nomination, but she didn't know she'd be leading the last of the human race.

"Well, we'll just have to see," answered Stuart.

TWENTY-THREE

WREN STOOD and looked at the clock embedded in the medical bay's corner wall: 20:00 hours. She scratched her scalp—her dark red hair was fading to grey at the temples, and she didn't care anymore. Wren sniffed and walked over to the medical supply cabinet and pulled out a scanner, adjusting the hand loop so the machine fit snugly in her palm, then she turned and headed out the door.

Her shoulders slouched inside her jumpsuit. The cocky strut of the young doctor had slowly eroded under years of duty in space, going from one ship to another, always tending to the aches and pains of people she didn't feel she truly knew. The loss of Galloway made it that much worse. She felt like she was married to Space Command, here in the last ark of Earth, one of the final humans in creation, yet all alone. It boggled the mind, but all she wanted was to sleep.

She scratched the back of her neck as she walked down the hallway towards Patel's suite and pressed the doorbell out of courtesy; the tiny light glowed brightly under the wall skin as she touched it. Patel came to the door wearing a comfortable pair of pajamas: they had pink elephants all over them and Wren couldn't help but smile.

"I figured I should be comfortable in my long sleep," Patel shrugged, half joking and half serious.

"Hey, whatever works." Wren gave a disarming shrug of her own.

Patel turned and led Wren inside, where Wren saw Patel had covered over as much of the white wall as she could: every non-functioning panel without a screen was covered with a cloth, painting or some knick-knack to dress it up. She'd even synthesized a soft pink blanket to go inside her pod.

"What, no teddy bear?" asked Wren in a teasing voice.

"You think I should make one?" Patel opened her eyes, breathlessly. Wren couldn't tell if she was joking or not so she just laughed. Patel seemed to think that was funny and laughed along.

As Patel approached the pod, Wren saw her tense and clench her palms. Patel turned to look at Wren. "You sure it's going to be safe for us to go in that long?"

"Yes, perfectly safe," Wren assured her, feeling like a bastard for feeding Patel a white lie. The vomiting wouldn't be pretty.

"Okay." Patel pursed her lips and turned towards the pod again. Wren followed her and held her hand as she stepped inside.

"Thanks." Patel smiled demurely. Wren could tell Patel was trying to psych herself up before the pod started its cooling cycle.

"You're welcome." Wren tried being comforting, but it just came off hollow inside her heart—she heard the voice she reserved for condolences and newborns coming out of her mouth, but the emotion behind it was missing.

Patel climbed in the pod and looked at Wren expectantly. Wren fastened the security harness and stuck the tiny monitor dot at the soft part of Patel's throat where the jugular pulsed.

Wren took an IV cuff and placed it around Patel's wrist and the needle pricked Patel lightly, inserting itself automatically in the exact right spot in her vein. Patel didn't even jump and her eyes stayed locked with Wren's as Wren connected the IV cuff to a plug in the pod's side.

"You ready?" Wren asked. Patel nodded with wide eyes as Wren placed the oxygen mask over Patel's face, then pressed the SLEEP CYCLE icon on the pad embedded in the side of the cryosleep unit. A soothing gas drifted into the mask and Patel's eyes fluttered. Soon she was asleep and the machine began the next stage of the cycle.

The cryosleep fluids flowed slowly through the IV, gradually making Patel's blood like a kind of antifreeze. Wren watched the temperature on the monitor screen drop until Patel's bodily functions were just above the level of someone who was dead; the heart monitor in the corner showed just the tiniest bit of a heartbeat. Wren watched Patel's vitals until she was certain Patel was completely under and in the safe maintenance zone.

"See you soon." Wren spoke quietly and patted Patel's hand, then closed the pod's lid, which hissed as the air lock equalized. The monitor pad went from red to green and displayed a SLEEP CYCLE INITIATED icon. Wren inspected Patel's room one more time to make sure everything was stowed, then she turned and left.

"One down, four to go," Wren muttered under her breath. She walked next door to Forester's room, and as her finger touched the doorbell a thought flickered through her head: "Rinse, Wash, Repeat." She chuckled softly. Forester opened the door to see Wren giggling to herself and a cloud darkened his expression.

"You okay?" Forester asked tentatively.

"Yup, sorry." Wren grabbed the bridge of her nose. "I just had a thought that tickled my funny bone."

"Ah." Forester nodded. His voice sounded like he empathized, but his eyes were confused and uncertain.

"Shall we?" asked Wren as she beckoned towards the cryosleep tube.

"Can I see Roxy one more time?" Forester sounded very much like a ten-year-old and his eyes even looked the part.

"Sure." Wren consciously used her "this-won't-hurt" voice.

Forester smiled and went to the small cat crate sitting on his bed; Roxanna sat inside, looking at him with intent eyes. When he neared, she came to the crate front and mewed. Forester opened up the crate and swept the kitten into his arms, tears streaming from the corners of his eyes as his lower lip quivered.

"Bye honey," he said softly as he kissed the kitten's furry head, "I'll see you in six months." At that note his lip quivered even more until he broke down in sobs; his tears soaked the kitten's fur, but she didn't seem to mind. She purred and licked his cheek, which made Forester cry even more. He looked up at Wren, "Will she even remember me when I wake up?"

"I'll take good care of her." Wren put her hand on Forester's arm and Roxanna reached out for her with a tiny paw—Forester couldn't go into cryosleep if he was hysterical, and Wren knew it. Forester cuddled the kitten for another minute, then kissed her on the top of the head and put her back in the crate. The kitten mewed repeatedly as Forester walked over towards the pod and Wren could tell he was trying hard to gain his composure.

"Sorry," he said as he neared Wren.

"It's okay." Wren pat Forester's shoulder gently.

Forester walked to the tube and got in. He wore his simple jumpsuit and smelled like he'd just taken a sonic clean. Wren buckled his harness, attached the monitor and IV, then ran through the sleep cycle, watching Forester's eyes close and his breathing slow. His heartbeat went down to the same almost undetectable levels as Patel. Wren double-checked her work and

Forester's life support status, then she turned to the cat in the crate.

"Let's get you to my place," she said as she picked up the crate.

The kitten mewed forlornly.

WREN WORE a patient expression as Gutierrez wriggled her way out of her jumpsuit. Gutierrez put on a modest pair of blue plaid pajamas and slid a pair of slippers on her feet. Her foot caught slightly on the edge of the cryosleep pod as she climbed in, but she managed to maintain her balance.

"You ready?" Wren gave Gutierrez faux-cheery smile. She hoped it looked confident and calming.

"Guess so." Gutierrez spoke softly. She couldn't help crying a little bit—she hated waking up from cryosleep and was dreading it already. The vomiting scarred her mind.

"Hey." Wren took a step forward with genuine concern, the emotion flooding out as she quickly remembered the time Gutierrez saved the whole crew calmly during a water practice. It was strange seeing that cooly confident woman close to tears. "It'll be okay," she continued patting Gutierrez's back, "supposed to be way better in these newer chambers."

"That's what they say." Gutierrez tried looking resolved but her chin quivered to hold her tears in. "It's hard believing it, though."

"You can do it." Wren swallowed her saliva. "I really believe this time it'll be better."

"Okay," said Gutierrez as she sat back in the machine. She looked like a small child trying to get comfortable on their grandmother's antique sofa; Wren gave her strained smile again and closed the pod uncomfortably. Gutierrez smiled back thinly and shut her eyes.

The machine went to work: it sedated her, then sent her body into the deep low temperature sleep. Her body systems all lowered to a whisper and the display panel on the side of the pod registered her bodily functions. Wren double-checked her numbers and nodded, satisfied. She turned and walked out of the room and the lights dimmed after her—the only glow came from the function light on Guttierez's cryosleep pod.

Wren walked out of Gutierrez's chambers and turned to head towards Haddad's room. The first mate was already in a modest long-sleeved pajama-pant set: no frilly patterns, the top was light blue and the bottoms a dark navy. He smiled as he welcomed her in, and Wren had to combat the desire to suddenly kiss his full lips. His teeth were a little snaggly, in true British fashion, but the face and body attached were something any woman wanted a piece of: tan skin, curly dark hair, and eyes like Bambi's. Wren had wrestled with a crush on him since the first moment she laid eyes on Louis Haddad in the training seminar, and she tried maintaining her composure.

"You ready?" Wren asked in her most nonchalant and hopefully confident voice. She prayed he wasn't put off by her messy hair and flushed red face.

"Guess so." Haddad shrugged. "You ready to knock me out?"

"Ready." Wren smiled widely as they walked towards the pod together. When they reached the side, Haddad turned to Wren and drew a step nearer. She felt the urge to grab him close.

"You need to keep an eye on Schwartz," Haddad said in a low tone.

"Pardon?" Wren raised her eyebrows.

"You know what I mean." Haddad's forehead wrinkled, his countenance darkening. "He's a tricky one."

"You think he's going to try something funny?"

"Maybe." Haddad sighed and his shoulders heaved. "He's got some issues about power, if you get my drift."

Wren pursed her lips together. "What do you think?"

"Look out for Stuart."

"Stuart?"

"I would." Haddad's brown eyes suddenly turned darker and Wren felt the steeliness in his gaze. "Just in case. You know the drill, call an emergency meeting if you need to."

Wren knit her lips together again and nodded. "I will."

"Thanks." Haddad looked visibly relieved.

"No problem."

Haddad turned and Wren admired his lovely backside underneath the pajama pants, feeling like some kind of old lecher—but his was something spectacular to enjoy. She could only imagine the lucky ladies who got to be with him in the days back on Earth, but Louis never looked at Wren with anything other than a brotherly kindness, so she didn't think he was even remotely interested in her. She walked over to the side of the pod and beckoned him in like a game show hostess.

"Hop on in."

Haddad looked at her and smiled, patting her on the shoulder before he climbed in the pod. Wren avoided flinching as she felt the rush of sexual electricity course through her body —she was sure he felt nothing at all, even though he looked her in the eyes.

"Thanks for looking out for Grace," he said earnestly.

"I'll try my best." Wren gave a resolute nod.

"Okay," Haddad settled in to the pod's harness, "time for nighty-night."

"See you in two weeks."

"Sounds like a plan."

Wren shut the lid on Haddad and watched him close his eyes and try maintaining composure; he fidgeted in the harness like a child in a car seat, and she couldn't help but chuckle softly—it reminded her of Joey when he wanted to go to the bathroom. Wren pressed the INITIATE button on the pod's screen and the container sprang into action, while Haddad closed his eyes as if he'd done the procedure a hundred times. On second thought, Wren realized that he probably had done the cryosleep sequence hundreds of times—he and Stuart both. She was impressed they faced the side effects so bravely.

Haddad looked at Wren as he went under and waved his hand slightly—she waved back at him as he drifted off in to cryosleep. Wren watched his lips turn blue from the freezing cycle, then she watched the tiny flicker of his heart on the pod monitor. Wren kissed the tips of the fingers on her right hand and pressed them to the glass on his pod, just above his face.

"Goodnight," she said softly, her voice echoing off the silent walls.

TWENTY-FOUR

SCHWARTZ WALKED AROUND WILLIAMS' engine room and stroked the surfaces. *Right about now Williams should be going in to cryosleep*, thought Schwartz, *good*. This engine room was physically identical to the one Schwartz inhabited, but it felt better somehow: like a toy that you've watched the neighbor kid play with until you steal it at night and break it in your bedroom.

He walked to Williams' chair and sat down, crossing his fingers in front of his face and knit them together in a tight clench; his fingers cracked and Schwartz smiled. Schwartz spun Williams' chair around and let his feet stop him on the floor with a loud squeak, then he stood up and walked to the simulator in the corner.

Schwartz typed in the command: NUDE PHOTOS into the pad and a variety of pornographic images flashed across the screen. He settled on a particularly risqué calendar featuring nude women in Hawaii and pressed GO. The machine worked for only a couple seconds, then produced a glossy calendar featuring many naked women who were most certainly dead now. Schwartz took the calendar and posted it on the wall right next to Williams' engine, then smiled thinking about how pissed Williams would be when he woke up from cryosleep.

Satisfied, Schwartz made a cursory inspection of the engine functions, saw they matched his own engine perfectly, and decided to call it a night. He left the engine bay and walked the few steps back to his quarters. He didn't stop to check on any of the others—it pleased him just fine to know they were all practically dead to the world. *Let them sleep,* he thought as he walked to his room and peeked nervously at his own cryosleep machine, dreading the moment Wren would ask him to get in.

There was something nagging at Schwartz inside; he paced his apartment over and over and still felt the strange itch beneath his skin, torn between the desire to do something or to fall asleep. Schwartz went to his bed, sat down, then immediately stood back up again like he'd been bitten by a bug. He looked around and checked the bed's surface: nothing there, just his own imagination tricking him. He itched his scalp furiously for a second like a dog.

After a few minutes pacing, Schwartz left his room and went to the gym—climbing on the treadmill and setting the machine to six miles per hour. He ran as hard as he could until he felt his legs getting quivery and he couldn't keep up with the pace. Schwartz hit the keyboard a couple times and slowed the treadmill to a brisk three and a half miles per hour and continued walking on the revolving band; he felt his mind settling and the itch slowly eased from his muscles. After a few more minutes walking, he stepped off the treadmill and let it run a minute longer, staring at the moving band—it hummed softly as it continued its laps of nothingness. Schwartz thought about leaving the machine running and then decided to turn it off; it was the right thing to do, he decided.

For a second, Schwartz's mind ran to Gutierrez and her bouncing breasts on the treadmill—he wondered if she was already in cryosleep. A quick trip to the screen in the corner could cure his curiosity, and Schwartz couldn't fight the urge. He turned on the screen and started the locator function; with the system unlocked he could see where everyone in the ship was by their heat signature. He turned the view to Gutierrez's room: she was in there, and her heat signature was low. *Asleep already,* thought Schwartz with a smile.

He walked out of the gym and towards Gutierrez's quarters with a predatory focus, down the hallway until he was standing right in front of her door. Schwartz thought for a second about aborting his curiosity trip, but an urge pushed him through the door.

Inside, Gutierrez's quarters were tidy: she'd simulated some pictures to hang on the white walls as well as a blue blanket to cover her bed, and there was a stuffed teddy bear in the corner next to her pillow. Schwartz went over to her pod and stared at her; her lips were an ashy blue but he could tell by the screen on the side of her pod that she was still breathing, be it ever so slightly. He touched the glass and rubbed the areas directly above her breasts. *If only I could get my hands on the real thing,* he thought with a smirk.

Schwartz walked around Gutierrez's room and stared at her desk; he sat in her chair, smelled her hairbrush, and stroked the corners of her pillow. He found her empty jumpsuit in the corner and held it by both shoulders so it hung in front of him, looking at her nametag conveniently located over her left breast. Over the heart. A new urge gripped Schwartz and he grabbed the crotch of her jumpsuit and smelled it like a dog would sniff for a female in heat. He took long, lingering breaths of her smell: slightly sweet and rich like candy. Schwartz wanted that.

He walked over to her bed and lay down underneath her blue blanket, cuddling her teddy bear and smelled the crown of its head like a baby's—the bear also smelled like her. Schwartz's unzipped his jumpsuit and his hand slid lower on his body, gradually making its way under the band of his underwear. He stroked himself and smelled her teddy bear some more.

Satisfied, he fell asleep in Gutierrez's bed.

WILLIAMS FIDGETED in the doorway to his chambers, looking nervously over at the waiting cryo pod. He knew the things were pretty advanced, but he still didn't like using them—he only put on a brave face for the rest of the crew because he had to. It was a hard sell for anybody; the vomiting on wakeup was practically unavoidable and he hated that—so much so he avoided throwing up at all costs, which led to many uncomfortable too-drunk nights where he refused to purge the poison, and lay moaning on the bathroom floor instead.

It also felt weird to go under without Grace. He usually did cryosleep rotations with her, so they were always awake at the same time; this would be the first time he'd slept without her, and it felt oddly wrong somehow. Knowing that she'd be alone with Jimmy Schwartz stalking around the ship also made his balls tighten. Williams remembered the time he'd taken Jimmy out to get a drink, an ill-fated plan to try and get to know the President's son. Jimmy had dragged Pete out to a strip club, where Jimmy proceeded to manhandle the dancers and threatened the bouncer with a Presidential execution if the bouncer didn't allow Jimmy to continue his antics. Jimmy had sworn Pete to secrecy about the event, saying it was "just fun between us guys."

Williams went to the bath mirror and fixed his hair again: a little short on the sides but tapering to a nice length up top, where a couple of his curls always decided to do whatever they wanted. Williams usually spiked his hair with a bit of gel when it was short, giving it a nice uplifted look, but that was a challenge with his longer curls that didn't want to behave. He poked at the top of his head with the tips of the fingers on both hands, then smoothed the sides backwards and used his thumb and index finger to curl his bangs: they fell onto his forehead like some 1950's heartthrob. He stopped, finally satisfied, then the doorbell rang and he jumped as the chime echoed off the walls.

Wren stood on the other side of the door, smiling a grin that was almost a grimace.

"Hey," she said with a knowing tone.

"Hey." Williams tensed, preparing for what he knew was coming.

"You ready?" Wren saw the uncomfortable look in Willliams' eyes and she raised her brows.

"Guess so."

Wren motioned Williams towards the cryo pod and he walked the walk of a cow to the slaughterhouse, his shoulders drooping. Williams' mind was already playing back the last time he woke from cryosleep and threw up a green goopy substance.

Williams turned to look at Wren. "Here goes." He sighed and his shoulders dropped even further, making him resemble a wet cat.

"Yeah." She concurred.

"You'd think after how many of these I've done I'd be used to this by now." He shook his head. "Nah."

"You're right...even with all these 'improvements,' it still sucks." Wren put her hand on the pod and felt like some kind of shitty used car salesman.

Williams hopped into his pod and started fastening the harness all around himself; Wren watched as he attached the shoulder, leg, and crotch belts to the center monitor piece, which connected all the belts securely and also read his heartbeat and bodily functions. Wren placed the other monitor pieces on his body, and the tiny white dots stuck to his skin while already reading all his metrics, sending the information remotely to the pad on the side of his pod. The screen lit up displaying Williams' heartbeat, among other things; if Wren had been paying closer attention she would have seen it climbing.

"Let's get this over with." Williams spoke in a resigned tone.

Wren nodded and started closing the tube door. When the lid was almost totally down Williams undid his wrist strap and reached out and put his hand in the crevice. "Stop! Wait!"

"What's wrong?" asked Wren from the other side of the door.

He reached out and took her hand. "I'll see you soon," he smiled earnestly.

Wren felt shocked by the physical contact at first, then her heart softened. "Yeah," she said softly, closing the hatch door with a light swoosh. It clicked closed and she watched as Williams tried appearing relaxed. The machine sedated him and she watched his eyes droop, then close as his chin rested on his chest. The pod cooled the entire inner chamber until Williams' body rhythms were at their lowest point of being alive. Wren stayed a bit longer until she was sure he was comfortably under, then she turned and left his quarters.

Wren walked down the hall and suddenly felt lonely. Stuart and Simon were on the bridge, and she certainly didn't want to go hang with Schwartz—he made her fingers cringe.

Wren turned the corner at the crossroads and headed towards the bridge. The doors opened to the giant window screen proudly displaying the deepness of space in front of them; Stuart sat in her chair and Simon sat at Gutierrez's station monitoring functions. Stuart turned when she heard the doors open.

"Everybody down for the night?"

"All tucked in." Wren sighed.

"Good." Stuart smiled and Wren realized she hardly ever saw their captain look relaxed.

"You guys mind if I hang out here with you?" Wren looked at Stuart and Simon bashfully.

"Of course." Stuart beckoned to one of the open chairs. "Have a seat wherever you like, Cindy."

Wren walked around the captain's chair to a bank of mint-green couches extending out from the wall. She took a seat on the one closest to the captain, feeling too weird to sit in Simon or Haddad's stations. It made Wren giggle to think about how the bridge was the only place one found any color on the ship— her eyes instinctively took all of it in, dancing in the soft green color. She stroked the surface and found it looked like leather but felt velvety. Her shoulders relaxed and she snuggled into the backrest.

"You like the digs?" Stuart looked at Wren expectantly.

Wren was altogether shocked at the informality. "Yeah," she replied. "It's nice to see some color."

"I agree." Stuart tapped something on her screen. "Are all the numbers good on our sleepers?"

"So far, so good."

Stuart nodded. "Good."

The group sat in silence. Simon pretended to look at his screen where nothing moved, Stuart stared straight forward, watching the nonexistent horizon Wren watched them both with interested eyes, like a wildlife biologist in the jungles of Africa. Her gaze flitted back and forth between the two, until Stuart spoke up.

"You guys like pizza?" Her voice echoed slightly.

"Yeah." Wren thought it was the weirdest question she'd ever been asked by the captain.

"Yes." Simon gave a short nod. His eyes twinkled a little bit and Wren felt a twinge inside.

"You guys want to have some? Say around 19:00?"

"Sounds great!" Wren smiled and Simon concurred with a nod.

"Good." Stuart looked at Simon. "Laurance, can you invite Schwartz too?"

"Yeah, okay Grace," he answered with another nod, then stood from his chair and headed out the door towards the engine bay. Wren watched him go and did not envy him.

TWENTY-FIVE

SCHWARTZ STARED at the wall in Gutierrez's apartment. The surface was smooth and white, with nary a crack nor mar to be seen. His eyes lost focus, refocused again, then he sat up and rubbed the shock of hair sticking up from his head: it was pointed upward, entombed in its own grease. His father would've been so disappointed in him since he hadn't bathed in two days, but his father wasn't here anymore. Schwartz's mouth parted in a crooked, strangely smug and satisfied smile—he crossed his arms behind his head and heard his neck pop, stretched both shoulders, then stood up.

He turned to look at Gutierrez asleep in her pod and immediately felt like Prince Charming and she was his Sleeping Beauty. Schwartz stroked the side of her pod above her lips with the hand he'd just had down his pants, gave Gutierrez one more good look, and left her room.

It barely took four steps to get to his door, then Schwartz stepped into his cozy lair. He felt the angled room suited him— it was unique and the corners were oddly sharp, just like how he felt. It wasn't a coincidence he and Stuart occupied opposite ends of the ship: he knew how she thought and his thoughts were quite different.

Schwartz looked around his quarters and his stomach growled; he wanted something, but he wasn't sure what. He turned towards his simulator.

As he walked over to the simulator, Schwartz thought about what food sounded good, and only the unhealthy options made his stomach growl. He perused his simulator options and selected a cup of black coffee and a jelly doughnut: raspberry filled—his favorite splurge. Schwartz instantly forgot his perennial diet, his mind clouded with thoughts of Stuart and Gutierrez.

Schwartz sat down at his table with the doughnut and coffee, eating dainty bites off the edges of the doughnut, careful to get a bit of jelly and doughnut in each bite. About half way through he gave up eating sensibly and wolfed down the rest in two big bites. His cheeks puffed like a chipmunk as he chewed on a bite that almost didn't fit his mouth capacity.

Once the doughnut was demolished, Schwartz drank greedily from his coffee cup: he finished it in three large gulps. The liquid burned the tip of his tongue and he felt the scratchy scorched flesh. Schwartz sighed and took his empty tableware over to the simulator, then pressed the RECYCLE button as the doors closed to let the machine do its dirty work in privacy.

Schwartz had always loved the simulator—his family had gotten one before anybody else. That was the fun of being the President's son. He'd only known the political life: watching his father campaign first for mayor, then governor, then finally President. Schwartz had been ten by that point, and he spent his formative teenage years roaming the halls of the New White House.

When the simulator had been invented, his father got one put in the kitchen immediately. Slowly the cooking team dwindled from the huge staff of chefs and helpers down to the lonely

Head Chef; the chef had finally quit the night The President made his signature pot roast in the simulator instead of having it fresh-cooked. The chef had been heartbroken that the intricacies of his most prized recipe had been corrupted by a machine, and he committed suicide a year later. The President hadn't even blinked—he still got the same vanilla pudding every night, man or machine.

Schwartz suddenly wanted that pudding. He scrolled through the menu until he found PRESIDENT'S PUDDING. He grinned at the double meaning of that name and ordered it. Every person had the option to eat exactly what the President ate; the pudding came out creamy white in the bowl with a dollop of strawberry jam in the middle. Schwartz mixed the pudding and the jam together in fierce little swipes, then spooned a large portion in his mouth. He sucked it down and felt it trickle coolly on his tongue, then he finished the bowl almost as quickly as the doughnut. Anyone who didn't know Schwartz would have thought he was a starved slave.

Once finished, Schwartz returned the bowl to the simulator and walked over to his window. He pressed his nose to the screen and peered out into space; the vast and endless stretch of stars expanding out before him. He felt very small, and his testicles shrank as Schwartz suddenly thought of the time his father had forgotten him at the baseball game and he'd stood crying in the rain; the pain stabbing and burning in his heart. He sat down cross-legged at the base of the screen, knit his fingers in his lap and hugged his arms tight below his rib cage.

He thought back to his father and how proud he'd looked behind the desk in the New Oval Office. The man had owned the room like he was born to sit there and little Jimmy Schwartz had enjoyed free run of the entire New White House. He'd looked like a grown version of the protagonist in the cartoon "Calvin and Hobbes" and acted like it too: he'd terrorized the maids and other household workers and they'd finally gotten robots because so many quit. Jimmy looked cute, but he was a terror behind closed doors.

Schwartz looked out into space, feeling like he was channeling the spirit of his father; he felt his spine straighten and his chest puff out. His chin jutted out slightly and the smirk on his face took on an interesting new curve. It felt like space was his domain—his birthright. He looked around the room surveying his premises: all white, all cold, all his. He felt the cold machine through his tailbone and it radiated up his spine; Schwartz was grounded in something that was not completely alive.

A vision flashed through Schwartz's head: Stuart sitting in her Captain's chair. She looked very small in the chair—like a child sitting in their parent's place. He felt immediate disgust and desire at the same time: if you were going to have a leader, shouldn't it be someone who'd watched great leaders all his life? He knew he could do all of the things she did and more; he'd run all the scenarios in his head over and over and they played like gruesome movies all the time. He only listened to some of them, but the ones related to leading the ship pulled his attention.

He focused straight ahead and thought about how it would feel to sit in the captain's chair.

STUART TAPPED her fingers on the side of her desk. She looked at the supply buoy diagrams on her screen and felt her eyes struggle to focus—you could only look at blueprints so long. She tried memorizing every cranny of the container so she could make the best path to it with the docking arm. It'd been a few years, but she still felt the docking control movements in her fingertips: some things the body never forgot.

The buoy was a long cylinder highly reminiscent of an old grain silo. Except the "grain" in this "silo" was matter instead.

Its docking receptacle stuck out of the side like a strange indented nipple, with a gasket made to adapt to any model docking arm. At least the pod's builders had the foresight to design something that wouldn't be immediately redundant, and Stuart felt grateful for the designer's ill-fated prescience.

Stuart tapped the question mark-shaped icon on her screen and the search window sprung up. She typed SUPPLY BUOY MODEL and the machine drew up a picture of the buoy they were hunting. Stuart zoomed in on the picture until she could read the serial number printed on the sleek skin of the pod: number 4488. She smiled—the same one she'd almost scraped with the Mars explorer all those years ago.

STUART COULD STILL REMEMBER the blaring impact sirens and the panic in her first mate's voice, then the blissful sigh of relief as she'd slid the ship into the dock like a lover's kiss.

The gasket had been a little funky. It'd taken an extra ten minutes of re-trying the docking sequence for the gasket to finally form and take hold on the ship's side. The ship had already been dangerously low on matter at the time, and she'd panicked when she thought she couldn't dock—if they couldn't dock, then they couldn't load matter and if they couldn't load matter, then the ship's engines would slowly fail and they'd all starve to death.

Just as she was thinking about how terrible it would be to starve, the docking mechanism took hold and sealed to the ship with a soft thunk. The arm released its air pressure until both sides were equalized, then the light turned green at the top of her screen. She remembered Wilson, her first mate at the time, hooting for joy. Stuart had smiled, hoping he didn't see the sweat creeping from her armpits.

IF THIS WAS the same buoy, then Stuart had some worrying to do. She pulled up the maintenance records on the buoy from Space Command and saw it had been serviced and filled only a year earlier—hopefully they'd serviced that gasket too. This time the survival of humanity depended on it.

Stuart sat back in her chair and rubbed her eyes; both hands came back slick with a thin sheen of sweat from her worry. She scratched the back of her neck and chewed on her lower lip, then rubbed her nose and looked over at Simon. He had his back to her looking over his own screen.

She didn't know what to make of him at first. When Space Command told Stuart they were taking a French member aboard the team to be the head navigator, she'd immediately expected a geeky, frail fellow—with perhaps glasses and a goatee. What she'd gotten was a tall French man of African descent who was broad like a mountain and watched the world with intense eyes. She'd immediately liked those eyes that seemed so wise.

He'd been in university by age 8, one of the brightest physics students France had ever seen. Both his mother and father had been visibly proud when he went to school and practically destroyed every course he took. He ended up with a PhD in Astrophysics and a master's in Literature, specializing in the American Science Fiction genre.

Space naturally called him. Laurance Simon had always stared at the sky, even when he'd trip in a cobblestone hole because his nose was pointed towards Ursa Major. The more Stuart read about him, the more she liked him: the man knew his way around space-time, and had also done some ground-breaking research into the nature of the distortion found in black holes. Her bosses at Space Command had practically creamed themselves when they'd found out they'd negotiated his services from the French government.

Simon had practically re-engineered France's space program from the ground up: he'd mapped all their missions, made sure their equipment was on par with other nations, and almost ran the place single-handedly. Despite knowing his way in and out of a space ship, he'd never actually been in one until he'd started training for their mission. Stuart laughed when she remembered his face going ashy pale as he felt zero-g for the first time; he'd vomited, but they'd been able to capture the mess before it hit anybody.

He took to his training like a demon, though; bound and determined to get over the gravity sickness. He asked Stuart to take him up repeatedly until he made the whole flight with no vomit. She'd complied and made five more laps until his food stayed put. Thankfully she'd never gotten hit by his leftover lunch—after the first trip Simon always brought a plastic sickness bag.

Simon turned around and caught Stuart watching him, smiled, and she smiled back. He approached her chair in his long, smooth gait, holding a portable screen loaded with supply buoy diagrams.

"You ready?"

"Yup-those the plans?" Stuart answered.

"Yes," he continued. "We have all the different views of the interior and exterior, as well as the angles and video from the last ship to dock with it."

"Good." Stuart nodded. "Let's see it."

Simon handed over the screen and she looked at all the different angles; the video showed the Neptune exploration ship *Icarus* docking at the end of their mission and offloading a number of matter blocks. She couldn't tell how many off the bat, but one quick turn to the inventory list showed they'd transferred two hundred eighty-six back on the buoy. There they sat waiting for the next exploration ship—the one that would be the buoy's last offload ever.

Stuart opened up the last picture and the inventory diagrams side-by-side. She saw how tightly packed the buoy was, and her mind raced to match up the number of blocks with a vague idea of how big their own storage holds were. Hopefully there would be enough room to get all the matter blocks on board—if not, they'd all have to store matter in their rooms. A thought suddenly took her.

"You have the Metis's carrying ratings?" She looked over at Simon and caught his gaze.

"Yes, one minute."

Stuart watched as Simon flipped through a couple views on his screen until he settled on one that piqued his interest. After another minute reading, he looked up at Stuart.

"Can you get me the total inventory weight in that buoy?"

"Ten thousand Kilos," Stuart answered back quickly.

Simon tapped away at his screen and frowned for a second. He continued working on converting ship volume to matter volume until he sat back with a somewhat satisfied look.

"It'll be close, but I think we can hold them all."

Stuart sat back with a smile of relief. "Thank goodness."

"It came close—we'll have to make sure we don't have any excess additions. Otherwise we won't have much room left."

"Can we store them all in the existing storage bays?" Stuart thought about the landers surrounded by matter blocks.

"I think we'll all have to have a few blocks in our rooms." Simon answered and Stuart frowned slightly, a look so subtle Simon missed it. She was thinking about loose matter blocks sliding around each crew member's room.

"The crew's not going to like that."

"It's what we'll have to do." Simon knit his eyebrows resolutely.

"Guess so." Stuart sighed.

Simon stood abruptly and looked towards the door. "You hungry?"

"Starving, actually," she answered with a knowing look. "You want to have dinner now?"

"Sure," Simon raised his eyebrows. "Shall we call Schwartz?"

"Definitely." Stuart nodded, then walked back to her chair and opened a com line. "Jimmy? You there?"

"Yes, Captain!" said Schwartz doing a mock salute in his room.

"You still want to do some dinner and a movie?" Stuart tried making it sound like an invitation, not an order.

"Now?" Schwartz's voice sounded slightly surprised, like he'd been interrupted doing something.

"Yeah, if you're okay with that?" Stuart hated masking her distaste for Schwartz with the need for his cooperation. "Pizza still good?"

"Sounds nice!" Schwartz answered with a cheery tone in his voice that made Stuart shudder. "I'll see you there!"

TWENTY-SIX

STUART TOOK a peek at everyone's plates while eating chunks of her own Hawaiian pizza and missing Williams already. Simon placed his neat dish of pesto chicken pizza in front of him, cradling a petite glass of red wine in his palm and sipping it with a blissful expression. Wren dove in to a small green salad covered in chicken, goat cheese, and some candied walnuts—an appetizer before the greasy piece of pepperoni pizza waiting for her. Wren opted to drink a glass of iced tea that sat dripping condensation in front of her. Schwartz folded his piece dripping with ham, sausage, salami and every other meat imaginable in half and took giant bites that he gleefully chewed with a smacking noise; he drank from a glass of very light-colored beer, having foregone his usual diet-friendly glass of water. Stuart sipped off her mango-flavored seltzer water and watched him.

The entire group ate in silence. Stuart tried hiding her disgust as Schwartz's smacking noises echoed off the walls; she had flashbacks to a classmate in kindergarten chewing a bite of macaroni and cheese in her ear with his mouth open. For some reason the sound still made her want to lash out and hit something, but she restrained herself and tried calming the itching rage boiling under her skin.

Schwartz pushed the pizza crust around his plate like a child playing with a toy car. Occasionally he'd take a large bite of soaked bread, then continue sopping up the grease and sauce splotches with a fresh chunk. He took fingerfuls of fallen meat and shoved them in his mouth, gamely chewing the bites of flesh with relish. Stuart wondered how long he could keep on that diet before he'd have to worry about a heart attack.

"What were you thinking for a movie?" asked Wren over a bite of her salad.

"Hmmm...good question." Stuart paused for a moment. "Any suggestions?"

"You need subtitles, 'Pierre'?" said Schwartz looking over at Simon.

Simon hid his absolute distaste and rage at the racist nickname Schwartz had called him since the beginning of training, and answered back in a quiet but firm voice: "No," looking Schwartz direct in the eyes when he said it. Schwartz looked away after a second of locked gazes—Simon's large white eyes gave him the willies.

"Comedy? Horror?" Stuart tried redirecting the conversation.

"Action!" piped up Schwartz through a mouthful of sausage and pizza dough. He raised his fist in a mock-salute and Simon gave Stuart a withering look. She shared it back and hoped Schwartz hadn't noticed.

"Okay." Stuart sighed. "Any suggestions?"

"Did anyone get to see 'Breakdown' before we left?" asked Wren, looking around the table.

"Yeah, I saw that with my dad weeks ago!" Schwartz obliviously sopped up more grease with a new pizza crust, forgetting his privileged background.

"Well, would you mind watching it again?" Wren couldn't

hide the irritation in her voice. It was like living with a large version of Joey who had a bad attitude.

Schwartz let a puff of air whistle through his lips like a disgusted teenager. "Sure, I guess."

"'Breakdown' it is!" said Stuart as she got confirming looks from Simon and Wren. Schwartz looked mildly disgusted but stayed in his seat. "Play 'Breakdown'—Filleree, 2080." She commanded the screen on the wall. Stuart sat down in her seat and snuggled into the memory material center as it conformed to her body and warmed to her optimal temperature. Her eyelids fluttered but she fought sleep.

The screen lit up and the opening credits of "Breakdown" flashed across it. The film had come out only weeks prior to the change in their mission, and with all the insanity Stuart had never seen it; she knew most of the rest of the team hadn't either. As the movie started, the screen widened to a view encompassing the entire wall—Wren and Simon moved their chairs to the opposite side of the table and settled back down. Sound came out of speakers lining the entire room's circumference: it felt like sitting right up against the movie screen, but somehow was quite comfortable.

Two men walked on the screen, each holding the keys to a pod racer; Stuart watched them climb in and take off across the long deserts of Arabia. One pod racer got shot down by militants and the driver fell out in a bloodied heap while the other pod kept going over the dangerous Dead Zone. He tried to make it, but his pod ran out of matter and he crash-landed in the nuclear desert. From there the driver had to walk, and his trek took him across the endless wastes left after the Third World War.

Stuart watched the screen and suddenly felt sick. Her heart kicked in a funny way during the scene where the pod driver befriended a cat with four eyes, two tails and three legs, and she suddenly realized the film they were watching wasn't a depiction of "home" anymore. Stuart stared at the poisoned sands and was suddenly glad they'd been obliterated by the comet's wake; the giant rock finally purged all the nuclear waste from the land.

The remaining material from the impact zone now floated about Earth like a loose cloud. Perhaps in a few million years the rock and debris would congeal together to form a new moon, but for now it was a treacherous blanket of chunks. Stuart wondered if the new moon would be radioactive.

Stuart sat back and watched the film out of one eye and Schwartz out of the other. She couldn't tell if he was awake or sleeping—an art he must have mastered during his many years listening to his father's speeches. He sniffed once or twice and rubbed at his nose, but stayed put.

Stuart turned her gaze to the giant screen and watched the man and the cat walk along a road that seemed to cut the desert in two. The man was showing the signs of radiation sickness and his illness progressed until he was near death at the end of the film. It finished with him dying next to the cat, the cat licking his oozing pink hand.

All the films that seemed to be out right before they left had deep pro-government, almost threatening overtones. If you were bad, they could send you to the place that was sickness to its core, and no good citizen wanted that. It was no surprise Schwartz got to see it with his dad, Stuart thought.

She looked forward at the screen and sipped her seltzer water as the man lay dying with the cat, and Stuart instantly decided to cuddle Roxanna after the film was done.

SCHWARTZ CHEWED his tongue like gum inside his mouth. It was almost raw and bloody, and he couldn't wait to get out of the conference room. "Breakdown," made him sick the first time around. The coppery flavor of his own blood mixed with the raw sweetness of meat bloomed on his tastebuds and he relished the two contrasting flavors—so different, yet full of the same life.

Wren pulled at her long red ponytail and Schwartz felt his gaze swing her way. She watched the screen intently, absorbed in the struggles of the pod pilot and the mutant cat. If it had been him, thought Schwartz, he would have put a knife through one of the cat's four eyes, then he would have eaten it.

He'd been out in the desert before as a young boy: Schwartz's father had sent him out with a military excursion to "toughen him up." The group had gone to the edges of the Dead Zone, and he'd seen the desolation and hardship. One day he'd watched an old man bury a baby born with two heads and no limbs. Their guides ate with the locals and enjoyed the fruits of deformed goats, but Schwartz had stuck to his safe meal bars.

Schwartz loved being out in the desert. It was so raw and barren and full of animal-like desires—you could be anyone you wanted to be on the edge of that wasteland. He'd gone out one night and slit the throat of a goat herder just for fun, then left the goats to lick the boy's gaping throat; the desert made even the most rational creatures desperate, he noted with a cold awe. Schwartz had watched the boy's body until sunrise, then he'd headed quietly back to camp. The camp master had found him tucked in his cot and feigning snoring at seven am—his father never knew about that gem.

He peeked out of the corner of his eye at Simon. The man was a giant in Schwartz's opinion, a giant who ate too much food and should never have been let on this mission. Forget that he was also French, and black—Schwartz detested the people who'd mocked his father to his face when they'd visited for a diplomacy meeting.

Schwartz looked over at Simon again and tried seeing if he was mouthing French or English words along with the movie: his lips failed to move at all. Schwartz wanted to puff and fuss like a sixteen-year-old who didn't get a new Mercedes, but he continued to project a calm exterior—underneath he felt like a taut piano wire ready to snap; only a few more twists and he'd be ready to blow. Simon's dark skin made him feel that way, he was sure of it: the man had to have some kind of voodoo. The kind that only came from Africa.

His father always told him Africa was a dirty place and nothing good came of its peoples—that was behind closed doors, mind you. Outside of his private rooms, President Shane Schwartz spoke only kind words about the planet's many different ethnicities. He never hired a cabinet member who was black, though.

Schwartz looked away from Simon and imagined different scenarios where he would stab him and then slice him into little pieces. Then he would feed Simon's body back to the simulator and they could all eat his matter over and over again. He wanted to fidget so badly, but he kept his body still and watched the screen with blank eyes.

He peeked over at Wren again and thought about running his fingers through her ponytail, then he'd grab it and see where it went from there. Using his hand only felt good some of the time, but other times you just needed the feel of a wet mouth. He cringed for a second imagining what would happen if she bit down; that snapped him out of his daydream and the tiny stiffening in his crotch settled.

He thought about how much force it would take to snap Stuart's pretty neck: not much he guessed, given her slender nature. He'd practiced a similar situation in Krav Maga as a twelve-year-old. *Wouldn't be too much trouble,* he thought; twist the head to the right and it would be done. Schwartz stopped for a second—killing Stuart might not be the best solution, his mind told him, as he might need her later on. Schwartz revised his Stuart scenario; this time around he would pop a little sedative in her food and see what happened, then she'd go in her pod for a long sleep all preggers with his baby. He liked the sound of that one better.

Schwartz started picking at his cuticles in the dark. He pulled at a small tag of skin poking out from the corner of one nail, but it was deceptively smooth and his fingernails couldn't get a purchase. He lifted the nail to his mouth and bit the tiny piece off, then he chewed it thoughtfully: the flavor was dull compared to the blood. He scratched his nose somewhat surreptitiously until he found a rogue nose hair and pulled it out by the root.

The screen showed the pod driver slowly dying of radiation poisoning on the sand next to the mutant cat. Schwartz watched coldly as the man died and the cat began feasting on him during the closing credits. *That was a dark one*, he thought, but the soft fools needed to know what was out there if they strayed. He'd always loved the films that kept the little folk coming back to the fold.

STUART WOKE up groggy and strangely sore. She'd done nothing since watching the movie and heading to her quarters other than sleep, but it felt like she'd been hit by a train. She woke up and tried moving her neck, but it wouldn't budge in either direction, then she took her hand and rubbed at the knots on either side of her neck until they softened slightly, but not much. Forester's kitten mewed from between her contorted legs: she'd borrowed Roxy for the night from Wren. Stuart unraveled her limbs from around the cat and sat up in bed—Roxanna watched her but stayed cuddled in Stuart's discarded blankets like a baby bird inside the nest.

Stuart stood and hobbled over to the sonic shower, gingerly removing her undershirt and sleep pants with stiff arms. This time she selected the MASSAGE function and let the machine go to work. It hummed in a new way and she felt pulses of warmth rolling through her muscles like waves—strangely relaxing compared to the scratchy wash function. After only a few minutes she felt the hard muscles in her neck softening; Stuart turned her head from side to side and smiled.

She stepped out of the shower and looked at the kitten on the bed. "You hungry?" she asked across the room. The kitten watched her with its eerie eyes and mewed once. Stuart put her clothes on and walked to the simulator, ordered up a bowl of wet cat food and matching bowl of water and put the fresh bowls down next to her table. The kitten jumped off the bed and started eating vigorously.

Breakfast began the same as every day, some more oatmeal in a crisp white bowl with whole milk. Today she watched a little bit of an old cartoon called "The Little Mermaid." She couldn't help but cry when the mermaid sang to her love on shore, and Stuart thought again about Williams entombed in his cryosleep pod. Stuart wiped quickly at the corners of her eyes and blew her nose with her napkin. After a quick cleaning session she headed to the bridge.

"Bye, bye Roxanna!" she called as she left her quarters—the kitten mewed in return and curled back into the blankets on the bed. Stuart walked to the bridge and wished she could hide the cat in her pocket, just to feel it purring. She turned to Simon as she took her seat.

"Morning."

"Good morning," Simon answered back. "Sleep well?"

"Kind of"

Simon nodded. "How is the cat?"

"Doing her best job to be a furry chiropractor." Stuart gave a lovingly bemused shake of the head. "I woke up this morning feeling like I'd been rolled into a pretzel. She likes sleeping between my legs." Stuart chuckled.

"Ah." Simon smiled knowingly. "Le chat...they are the best at hogging the bed."

"Don't I know it." Stuart rubbed her neck again to check for any spasmed muscles. "She's eating, but seems pretty bummed still."

"She misses her Papa." Simon gave a small shrug.

"Yup. Don't know how to deal with that." Stuart sighed. "I don't feel comfortable cloning her a friend."

"I can't believe he got her made anyway." Simon sounded amazed and frustrated at the same time. "How could he get the simulator past its block codes?"

"Dunno." Stuart shook her head. "I should have asked him that before he went under."

"Perhaps when he wakes?"

"Definitely."

"You like the movie last night?" Simon continued.

"Honestly?".

"Honestly."

"Well, I started out feeling fine about it, but after he met the cat I just felt sicker and sicker by the scene."

"Me too," concurred Simon.

"What a shitty last film to come from Earth." Stuart sighed and sat back in her chair.

"Yes, not the best."

"Well," she said with a slightly happier tone as if she was trying to change the subject, "guess we don't have to deal with President Schwartz's film choices any more. Do we?"

Simon smiled back and it lit up his eyes.

TWENTY-SEVEN

SCHWARTZ WALKED down the hallway towards the medical bay, and his footsteps echoed on the hard tile floor, making tinny noises as they bounced off the walls. He slowed his step and started thinking about what it would be like if he was a tiger, and his body immediately softened; the sound from his feet quieted to a nearly silent shuffle. Schwartz smiled and his canines looked like fangs in the bright light.

Two steps further and he was at the threshold of the medical bay. The doors opened onto Wren, her back turned to him while she examined something in a low cabinet. He caught a glimpse of her ass stretching the jumpsuit taut and felt the overwhelmingly powerful desire for her again.

"Uh, Cindy?" he asked in his most plaintive voice. She jumped and hit her head on the upper part of the cabinet.

"Shit!" Wren barked as she rubbed the new bump forming on the crown of her head.

"Sorry, didn't mean to surprise you." Schwartz reached out for Wren apologetically. Secretly he loved the drama and didn't feel sorry at all.

Wren adjusted her ponytail and appeared more confident.

She straightened up and tugged down at the waist of her jump-suit, smoothing the material over her upper body.

"What can I do for you, James?" she asked after a quick sigh.

Suck me off, he thought, but with his mouth he answered, "I'm having some stomach troubles, got anything to help with that?"

"What kind of troubles?"

"A lot of cramping and gas. I haven't taken a shit in three days."

"Hmmm..." Wren stroked her chin thoughtfully. "Sounds like constipation. Mind if I take a look?"

"Be my guest." He started walking towards the exam table. "You want me up there?"

"Yup."

Schwartz climbed up on the table and lay down prone in front of Wren; part of him felt slightly aroused with her standing over him, but he lay quietly and let her use the diagnostic scanner. The machine made no noise, but beeped when she ran it over his colon. Wren changed the mode on the device and with one click of a button she could see the image of his intestines on the screen.

"Yup." She nodded with a doctorly tone. "Looks like you're a bit stopped up there."

"Yeah, no shit," Schwartz answered back.

Wren tried hiding her smile but failed and started giggling. "Sorry," she said apologetically.

"No pun intended there," Schwartz gave Wren a faux smile back. "You got anything to do the trick?"

"One sec." Wren walked towards the medical simulator. Schwartz tried watching over her shoulder as she entered the special medical code into the login screen; only she and Galloway could access that machine. All the rest of the simulators had a lock code to prevent them from being used to make strange medicines or drugs—it was one of the ways Space

Command kept their astronauts from becoming drug addicts. It didn't work for the chief surgeon, though.

While Wren fiddled on the simulator, Schwartz looked around the medical suite; all the wall panels looked smooth, but there were small brightly lit orange buttons every foot or so. The buttons opened up the different supply bins that were similar to the one Wren hit her head on. Schwartz wanted to get in them so badly, but he knew the buttons were specially programmed to only open for Wren, Galloway or Stuart's fingerprint. He'd have to just watch Wren do it for now.

"Whatcha thinkin' doc?" he asked as he admired her behind again.

"I think we're going to try a combination of herbs to help clear that for you," she said while staring intently on the simulator screen.

"Herbs?" Schwartz scoffed.

"Yup, in your situation that will clear things up best."

"Couldn't you just use some special injection?" he asked, slightly irritated. "That's what Galloway would do."

Wren turned to him with a hard look in her eyes, "Galloway uses pharmaceuticals for everything. If I gave you what he'd use you'd be shitting your pants for days."

"Oooh." Schwartz sat up with a genuinely surprised look. "Don't want that."

"Nope. You don't." Wren growled firmly. "These herbs will help loosen things without getting out of control." She tapped the screen a couple times then the door closed and the device fired into action. She kept her back turned to him, and Schwartz thought again about how it would feel to grab her ponytail. Her hair was thick and slightly wavy: a shade of auburn that wasn't quite a flaming red. He bet it felt soft.

"Can I ask you something, Doc?"

"Sure." Wren turned to face him.

"What do you think about this mission?"

"What do I think?" she asked, almost rhetorically.

"Yeah, you stoked to be on this ship for the rest of your life?"

Wren looked at him with a blank stare. "I hadn't really thought of that yet."

"Well, what do you think about it?"

"There's not much to think…it just is." She answered back with the same blank look. Inside, her heart was tugging with thoughts of Joey, but she refused to let Schwartz see her cry.

"You think the captain has a good idea where she's taking us?"

"I think if there's anyone who can keep us alive, it's her."

Schwartz tried not looking annoyed and agreed with her. "Yeah, that's why she's the boss lady."

The simulator chimed and Wren turned back towards the delivery window; it opened and there was a tiny vial of green liquid standing on the platform. Wren took it and loaded it into a transdermal injector, then she walked over to Schwartz holding the device. "You ready?"

"Guess so." Schwartz remained still and prone on the table.

Wren took Schwartz's wrist and turned it towards her, and he flinched slightly at her touch—she ignored it and placed the injector against his skin. With one touch of a button the device infused the medicine directly into his skin and bloodstream. Schwartz tried breathing deeply through the whole procedure— he hated anything the doctors did to him, no matter how minor.

"Well, you're done." Wren stood back with a satisfied air— she wanted him out of her general proximity. Schwartz sat up on the table and turned his feet towards the floor, and as he stood he felt little gas bubbles already moving in his abdomen.

"Think I'll go hit the John." He grinned as he turned to leave.

"Sounds good. Enjoy that."

Wren watched Schwartz leave and breathed a sigh of relief as the doors closed.

SCHWARTZ WALKED BACK SLOWLY towards his room, his wrist still stinging from where Wren injected him. He wasn't being totally honest when he'd complained of constipation, but watching Wren took the edge off. That's how he knew he was serious—no one would face their phobia just to make cute with a female doctor.

He strode slowly towards his door at the end of the hall; the room had an odd, misshapen feel to it—both angular and cold in all the wrong ways, which Schwartz loved. It made him feel strong and clean and strangely powerful to sit with two corners bordering the vastness of space; plus, he could keep out of the way from his crew mates.

Crew. Mate. He thought about Gutierrez and her creamy tan skin and luscious curves—she was one crew member he wanted to really mate. He'd enjoy Wren too, but Gutierrez was truly spectacular. Too bad she was in Stuart's pocket, just like all the rest of them.

They all were. He hated that about the rest of the group: they were all hand-picked by General Thomas, Jensen and Stuart. He knew he was the only one recommended by the President, and they all knew why: he'd loved being Father's Little Astronaut. President Schwartz put him in all the TV programs and made him the poster child for Space Command, and it wouldn't do to have the poster child stay home from the Titan mission. Father got him into flight school to begin with, even when the basic training instructor said Jimmy Schwartz should never be let near a spaceship—Father made sure everything happened.

When it came to Stuart, though, Father hadn't had enough pull. The woman had the cock of Space Command wrapped so far up her tight pussy she was all theirs for whatever they wanted. She was the General's woman, and he found out later she'd actually been his girlfriend back when they were younger. *Figures*, thought Schwartz, *that's how girls always get ahead.*

He walked towards his bath area and stripped clothes as he went. The garments got squished in a little ball that he threw over the chamber wall like it was a net; basketball had always been his thing, and he made sure to be on all the winning teams. Once he got too old to play, he owned the teams that made men play—good 'ol Father and his buddies helped finance that too.

'Trillionaire Astronaut Playboy.' He liked the sound of that; it had a better ring than 'President's Son'—enough to get plenty of tail in college and later in life. He'd even gotten head from a young cadet only hours before they left on this mission; it was amazing the things people would do when they were about to die. He'd screwed chicks pretty much up until the last day of the mission training: that was the same girl who gave him the blowjob.

Just thinking about a blowjob from Gutierrez was enough to get him enormously aroused. He reached down and looked at his naked form: it wasn't too bad right now—not as ripped as he'd been in his younger days, but still very acceptable in an adult male. He ran his hand down the side of his waist until he reached his groin and slowly stroked himself. Schwartz leaned his head back and let out a small moan no one on the crew would have recognized, stroking faster and rougher until he practically cried as he climaxed. His member stung from a small cut created by the chafing, so he went to his cabinet and took out the burn-healing wand; after a few light passes you couldn't even tell he'd hurt himself in his pleasure.

Schwartz walked naked across his living room to the synthesizer machine in the corner and ordered up a pair of silk pajamas, size Large. The machine delivered them within a minute. He loved the feel of smooth silk on his bare body—the texture of that fabric alone was purely sensual and it calmed him at the same time.

Schwartz climbed in bed thinking a short nap might be nice, then rolled over on his side and watched the screen across from his nose light up. It sensed his fatigue levels and showed a panorama of softly falling waves that he imagined sounded like the waves in front of Father's Long Island compound. The panel was the latest version of sonic soothing technology—a boon for young mothers since its invention. It'd made the art of child rearing seem almost pedantic as kids obediently followed their parents everywhere. Every kid except James Schwartz.

The President had wanted his son to be "all boy": that meant military excursions as a toddler, a gun in his hand by five, and his first kill by nine; human, that was—he'd started on small animals long before that. Once you got hooked on the sight of death, it was an addiction pretty hard to break.

Schwartz watched the waves and imagined what he'd like to do to Stuart.

TWENTY-EIGHT

WREN WOKE up before her alarm could even go off. She scratched her head and picked at the tiny scab she pulled out of her hair, which made her remember the time Joey came home from school with lice—her head went from itching to immediately crawling, and Wren's fingers couldn't help themselves as they combed her scalp for more bumps, itching furiously at the phantom vermin. With a sigh she sat up in bed.

"Lights on," she commanded the room computer and the interior automatically brightened. The ceiling panels were made of bioluminescent film that the ship charged with a tiny amount of electricity; it was enough to create a bright light that was almost as strong as the fluorescent bulbs of old, yet it used only a tiny fraction of the energy. Space Command had jumped on the technology and put it in all their deep space ships, but the only downside was the cost; the earlier model ships only had small strips of the film running down the center of each room. The dark walls made the old ships almost cave-like, and there'd been a lot of problems with crew depression; hence the all-white interior in the Metis. She wished she could have told the engineers that the all-white had just the opposite effect: she felt like she was in some kind of space-borne insane asylum.

It'd been many weeks and cryosleep rotations, but they were now nearly halfway to Mars, and the Brinks buoy was next on their itinerary. Wren had made it through all the up-down cryosleep cycles, nursing the whole team back and forth from near-death to life every time. She missed Bill, though, and her body was starting to tire of being the only crew member constantly awake. That said, she didn't miss having to wake up from cryosleep like the rest of the crew did—she experienced enough watching them puke their guts out.

Wren stood up and walked over to her mirror. Her face was puffy and pale with pink blotches below her eyes where she'd rubbed them. She splashed some cold water on her face and dried herself with the tidy green towel hanging from the bar between the sink and the toilet. Wren grabbed her hairbrush and started untangling the mess on top of her head, wincing as the brush snagged in a tangle of hair above her ear. With firm strokes she patiently brushed all the knots out and gathered her temporarily smooth hair into a rubber band. The ponytail hung down almost to the center of her shoulder blades.

Quickly, Wren wolfed down some breakfast and looked at the daily schedule she'd made for herself the night before: today she had to wake the crew for the buoy offload—a task she was already dreading. She smoothed the front of her jumpsuit as she stood from her table, taking her half-eaten plate of eggs and toast back to the simulator and starting the recycle sequence. The machine went to work as Wren left her room and headed down the hallway towards the medical bay.

Inside the med bay, the lights sprang to life as soon as Wren entered; she looked to her left and saw Galloway's pod in the corner. Galloway looked very pale inside the tube—his mouth was drawn in a small frown that made him look intensely serious. The hair on the side of his face was tousled and stuck out at all angles. Wren giggled for a second wondering what he'd think of his normally oh-so-perfect hair—it looked like he'd been licked vigorously by a large dog.

Wren approached the pod and tapped the pad on the side. The screen lit up and displayed all of his vital signs: heartbeat and respiration all looked good, his blood numbers looked fine, and his overall function was running perfect. The pod screen showed his numbers in a cheery shade of green. Wren stared down at him and stroked the glass—he would stay a little longer in his involuntary rehab.

Wren walked down the hall and crossed through the main intersection, continuing on to the end of the hall that terminated in the wing. To her right was Haddad's door; she stepped to the threshold and walked inside. Haddad's tube was in the corner, quiet in the slightly luminescent room.

Wren tapped the WAKE CYCLE icon on the pod's screen. The machine started humming and Wren took a step back, grabbing Haddad's chair and pulling it over to the pod's side, so she could watch the screen and his face simultaneously. Her foot tapped the floor so hard her whole leg vibrated, yet she remained focused on the vitals gradually increasing on the screen. Wren's fingers searched her scalp again for invisible itching bugs they would never find.

Haddad's heartbeat slowly increased in tandem with his respiration. His body temperature rose by tenths of a degree, but it was getting closer and closer to the normal 98.6 by the minute; Wren watched intently as his hand twitched and his fingers curled, then his leg twitched so violently his foot almost hit the pod's lid. The numbers inched higher and Wren saw his chest visibly rising and falling—the pad beeped as his respiration and heartbeat all rose to the acceptable range. It flashed a WAKE SEQUENCE COMPLETE icon in green.

Wren watched patiently as Haddad's eyes fluttered under his lids like a person in deep REM sleep. The fluttering went for a second longer, then his eyelids slowly opened; he looked out at Wren and she smiled back at him and waved. Haddad smiled back and tried waving before he remembered his hand was strapped down in the pod. He looked out at Wren with eyes pleading to let him out: she grabbed the handle on the side of the pod and released the door.

HADDAD OPENED his eyes and looked out at Wren's pale face. Her hair looked like it was painted in Technicolor and her face looked like it was in black and white. She smiled at him and he tried smiling back, but his face felt numb and it took all his effort to get his lips to part in a smile. His tongue stung and stuck to the top of his mouth, reminding Haddad of the time his buddy Corey made him lick salt out of his hand on a dare.

He watched as Wren moved to the side of his pod and tapped something on the screen pad; the pod warmed up and he heard the hiss of the air gaskets giving way. Wren opened the door and Haddad felt a huge rush of fresh air hit his nostrils: it smelled clean and washed away the scent of the body odor that polluted the pod while he slept.

"How're you feeling?" Wren raised her eyebrows.

Haddad tried answering back but his sticky dry tongue got caught in his throat. He had to swallow a few times before he could answer back, "Mmmmokay...Good?"

"Yup, looks like your sequence went fine." Wren unfastened his restraining harness.

"Crew?" Haddad asked as Wren undid the shoulder straps first, then the leg straps.

"All good." Wren stood back as his body slipped down the backrest and his feet touched the pod floor. Haddad's legs felt rubbery like a new fawn and they buckled immediately; he grabbed the side of the pod and Wren caught him under the arms.

"Whoah there, buddy!" Wren spoke in a soothing tone that Haddad thought came naturally to her.

"Thanks." Haddad tried smiling at Wren but his lips spread in a strange, still groggy grimace.

"You think you can make it to your bed?"

"No," he whispered back.

"Here, use my shoulder." Wren offered her shoulder as she took his hand. He wrapped his arm around her slim shoulders and heard her grunt softly as she tried taking on the burden of his weight. They were only a step or two away from the bed when it hit.

Suddenly the room felt like it was spinning and Haddad groaned; his knees gave way again and he dropped to the floor with a thud. Pain lanced up from his patellas as they hit the floor—he knew there would be dark bruises there come evening, perhaps they would even turn green. Haddad moaned again and curled up in the fetal position. Wren tried comforting him, but she felt woefully inadequate—all she could do was hold his hand and pet his back as he whimpered on the floor.

"Bad?" she asked in a kind tone. Haddad nodded. "You gonna throw up?" Haddad nodded again and Wren let go of his hand to run and fetch the trash can. It was becoming old hat for her: they always responded like this—everyone started vomiting within minutes.

Haddad clutched his stomach and moaned again. He sounded like a woman in the late stages of giving birth—a moan so strong it would have turned to a scream if he hadn't been so terrified of projectile vomiting on Wren's clean jumpsuit. He lay in the fetal position and stared out the window, feeling the touch of the floor on his cheek.

Wren returned and placed the trashcan beside Haddad. He pulled himself to his knees and evacuated what little was in his stomach into the pail: no food came out, just a stream of orange goo that turned to bile after a few heaves. Haddad continued moaning and rocking back and forth as he threw up more in the bucket; the smell made it even worse and he couldn't stop his stomach from rolling around like he was on a rough sea. The bile gave way to dry heaves and tears streamed out of the corners of Haddad's eyes.

"Bullshit. This is not easier than the old models." Haddad managed to hiss out in between heaves.

"Yeah, I know," said Wren apologetically. "It's been brutal on everyone."

Haddad clung to the bucket like it was a teddy bear until his heaving subsided, and Wren went to the simulator to order him an orange flavored sports drink and some saltine crackers. She brought them over to him and he took a sip of the sports drink; his stomach thought about sending the drink back, but miraculously held it down. Wren took the trash can to the simulator and ordered a new one just in case. When the new one was made, she recycled the old trash can full of vomit.

Haddad crawled his way over to his bed and lay down on his side—his eyes were glassy and his hands shook from the low blood sugar. Wren grabbed her body monitor and read his conditions: his blood sugar was really ugly. Wren shook her head and looked up at Haddad.

"You think you can get a little more drink in you?" Wren stroked Haddad's shoulder to comfort him. Haddad curled into a tighter ball, but reached out with a shaking hand for the orange drink. He lifted his head off the bed to take a couple more sips, then handed the glass back to Wren. She ran a second scan and shook her head. "I'm gonna run and grab something a little more powerful. Back in a sec."

He watched Wren leave the room and felt a new wave of nausea hit him. The trash can was close and he pulled it over to the side of the bed with a weak finger and retched into the pail.

Only little bits of bile came out along with the tiny bit of sports drink he'd managed to get down; Haddad couldn't help himself and started crying. For some reason this wake-up period was worse than the ones he'd gone through earlier on their trip. *I must be getting older*, he thought.

Wren returned with a tiny vial loaded into a transdermal injector. She placed the device against his wrist and pressed the button; the medicine went straight to his bloodstream and immediately he felt the nausea subside. Within minutes he felt so much better he could sit up in bed—Haddad looked at Wren and smiled when his stomach made a loud growl.

"Food sounding good now?" she asked. Haddad nodded. Wren handed him the crackers and sports drink and he slowly nibbled his first cracker, then he washed it down with another tiny sip of drink. Wren watched him carefully, like a scientist observing a rat performing an experiment. After a few minutes she stood up from his chair and pat him on the shoulder.

"Sorry," she sighed. "I should have come prepared with that injector. You want some food now?"

"Yeah," answered Haddad with a nod. "Pasta?" he asked with a plaintive voice. Wren went over to the simulator and ordered him a bowl of buttered noodles. She brought the warm bowl over to him and his stomach growled again at the smell.

"Eat it slow," instructed Wren like she used to tell Joey.

Haddad nodded and took one piece of noodle and placed it in his mouth. He chewed slowly and felt the explosion of joy in his head from the savory taste of butter, salt and pasta. After a couple more bites his stomach shut down and gave him the signal that he was full; he pushed the bowl away and lay back down on his bed.

"Get some rest," said Wren softly, "We'll be at the buoy tomorrow. I'll brief Grace on your progress."

Haddad nodded softly and drifted off to sleep.

TWENTY-NINE

STUART STARED at the buoy as it inched closer to the craft; from further back it looked like a strange baton floating in space. As they got closer she could make out the Space Command markings on its flank: the model number, the year in service, and the total holding capacity. This buoy was fourteen years old—on her last trip to Pluto it'd been brand new.

She watched the readings on her panel as Simon ran a program to slow the ship down. It decelerated gradually, pulling smoothly alongside the buoy. Stuart tapped her screen and took the giant craft out of autopilot mode; her fingers deftly touched the command pad as she prepared to manually dock with the buoy.

The door opened and Stuart jumped—startled out of her focus on the buoy docking collar. Gutierrez entered with Haddad, both still looking a bit green around the gills.

"Welcome, strangers!" Stuart called over her shoulder as Simon nodded his acknowledgement.

"Glad to be back," Haddad croaked hoarsely.

"Glad to have you back." Stuart smiled. "Grab your seats and get your stations ready, we're going to dock in five minutes."

Haddad took his seat and started tapping his screen to bring it back to life. The panel automatically recognized his finger-prints and brought up the First Officer's menu; he logged into the docking program already in progress and observed Stuart's maneuvering on his own control station. He carefully kept his fingers away from her docking program, lest he accidentally interrupt her progress.

Stuart sat focused on her screen, swiping her fingers deli-cately over the control icons: she could control the speed and thrust of the entire ship with the touch of a fingertip. Many captains practiced years before they were allowed to helm a manual flight program, but Stuart had mastered it by the time she was nineteen. From afar, it looked like she was stroking the strings of an electric harp.

The ship slowed and turned ever so slightly to the right, bringing its left flank alongside the buoy; the tip of the left wing passed the buoy with a thousand meters to spare. Once the wing was past the buoy's front side, Stuart set in just the perfect amount of opposing thrusters so the craft slowed to a standstill. Then she activated the thrusters at the nose of the Metis—all it took was a miniscule blast and the ship compliantly inched backwards.

"Lou, can you extend the docking arm?" she asked with her eyes still glued to her screen.

"Affirmative." Haddad activated the pulleys that opened the docking arm like a large tentacle, and it slowly extended straight out from the indentation in the rear docking bay until it reached past the wings of the Metis. Stuart had dropped off the lander craft earlier in a nearby orbit to help free up the arm for docking.

"Fifty meters," said Simon as he charted the arm's progress towards the docking sleeve.

"Good," Stuart muttered, her eyes still glued to the screen.

She continued her slow advance on the door; Haddad could see the arm drawing nearer, but there was something off.

"Arm's not straight, Grace," Haddad said in a slightly alarmed tone.

"One sec." Stuart activated the port wing thrusters and the ship moved starboard until she did a quick counterbalance program that brought the ship to a perfect halt: the arm was now directly in line with the docking sleeve. Haddad sat in amazement—he'd never seen someone do a dock like this on manual settings, and he finally grasped why they'd chosen Stuart over him to command the ship. Watching her in person made the choice clear.

"On course now," Haddad said in a breathlessly amazed voice. Stuart just nodded and remained laser-focused on the screen below her nose.

The ship inched towards the sleeve. Stuart saw it in her monitor, waiting like some kind of mechanical vagina; if she weren't so focused she would have laughed at the similarity. Someone at Space Command had really missed their wife when they designed the mating system between incoming ships and the hatch on the buoy's side: the soft membrane on either side of the door looked like a pair of deep space labia.

Stuart inched the craft closer as Simon provided a distance countdown from his chair beside her. She squinted as the arm drew nearer, watching the target on the door like an archer aiming at the bullseye. With only inches to spare she fired the counter rockets one more time and the arm slid neatly into place. The Metis made the slightest jolt, then she saw the docking arm mating with the door gasket. Stuart imagined hearing a click and then the indicator lights on both the hatch and the arm turned green.

"Good to go for compression," Stuart called over to Gutierrez. Gutierrez tapped her screen and the air started equalizing inside the docking arm while tiny magnets in the ceiling and floor worked in opposition to create the gravity inside. After only a minute of waiting, the light on Stuart's screen indicated the arm was fully pressurized and gravity was consistent; Stuart looked up from her screen and blinked.

"All hands on deck," she called out over the intercom, "Meet us in the storage bay in five."

Gutierrez stood up from her chair and felt like she needed to collapse again—the cryosleep wobble was still assaulting her legs; she grabbed the side of her workstation to balance before stepping forward. A quick glance over to Haddad showed his own fawn-like progress and she smiled at him—he met her with a look of resigned understanding.

Stuart stood up and straightened the front of her jumpsuit. She turned and met the gaze of all three bridge officers; Gutierrez and Haddad still looked a bit green, but Simon had a pleased yet strong air about him. She walked towards the door and almost bumped into Haddad as he took a lurching step and stumbled on his own feet.

"Sorry." Haddad sounded deeply ashamed.

"No problem, Lou." Stuart spoke softly and steadied Haddad with her arm; Haddad felt a jolt of electricity from the kindness. Stuart took his hand to steady him and Haddad felt like he would melt, or at the very least she'd feel his palm sweat. She didn't seem to notice, though, and he balanced himself right away.

"Thanks." Haddad looked weary but grateful.

The four officers walked straight down the hallway towards the main docking bay. As they passed through the crossroads between the halls, Williams and Schwartz joined them and walked just a step behind their commanding officers. The bay's doors parted and they all walked towards the hatch where they'd entered the Metis only months earlier; the light above the hatch glowed a bright green.

Stuart grabbed the handle on the door and pulled it upward

with a harsh yank. It took all her body weight to move the lever, but it opened reluctantly; they all heard the hissing as the gasket released and the door opened. Beyond was the docking arm's extended runway—Haddad thought it looked like some kind of space pirate's gangplank.

Stuart walked to the end of the arm and touched the side of the buoy's skin: it crackled under her fingertips.

"OKAY GUYS, gameplan time: we're going to put the first matter blocks in the main storage bay. Once that's full, we'll pack blocks in the engine rooms, then the conference room, the gym and the labs. Last resort, we may have to each take some blocks in our rooms." Stuart managed to get that out in one long breath; she used her "boss voice," hoping it sounded confident but not bitchy.

The entire team groaned and Schwartz spoke up from the rear. "Can we hold all those blocks?" Stuart looked back over her shoulder at him and Schwartz saw the tiniest hint of exasperation in her gaze. *Good,* Schwartz thought to himself.

Stuart cleared her throat. "Simon made the calculations and we should be able to handle the entire capacity. We'll need all of it." Schwartz looked at her and said nothing.

The rest of the team waited patiently in a line behind Stuart. She opened the door leading into the delivery elevator and the smell of stale air greeted them; Stuart wrinkled her nose slightly but pressed on inside. The room was plain and cold, tapering to the apex that was the matter block elevator. The buoy had no gravitational system, so Stuart floated to the elevator and tapped the screen on its lower right side, waking it to life. The machine read her fingerprint and retina almost simultaneously, then flashed WELCOME CAPTAIN STUART on the panel.

Stuart scanned through the load menu, checking to see if the number of blocks on board the buoy matched the list on the Metis: it did, and she pressed the OFFLOAD INITIATE icon to start the elevator. It whirred to life with an old mechanical whine and she heard the buoy vibrating. Within a minute the first block was waiting behind the door, which opened like a vending machine and spat the block out.

The matter blocks were rectangular in shape, a dark grey-black color, and came in one size: roughly one foot long by a half foot wide. They were designed to fit neatly in the window of a simulator for easy breakdown and unit refueling, but weighed more than they looked.

Haddad floated up from behind Stuart and grabbed the first block. In zero gravity the blocks were effortlessly light, but as soon as Haddad crossed the threshold into the Metis' gravitation fields, the block tumbled out of Haddad's hands and fell to the floor with a thud. Haddad groaned and picked up the block, hugging it to his chest and trying to support the extra weight from his core. All the crew stepped back towards the bulkhead to give him enough room to pass, but the matter block threw Haddad's weight off and he almost clipped Schwartz's toes—even though Haddad had tried squishing as close to the wall as possible. Schwartz glared at Haddad as he passed.

Haddad took his first block to the storage bay where a rack already held an array of neatly-stacked matter blocks. He grunted as he lifted his block onto the rack and felt a twinge in his lower back. *Better hit the recovery booth after this,* Haddad thought to himself as he returned to get back in line for the next block. He watched Simon carefully carry his block down the hallway towards the storage bay and they both shared a look of resigned effort. Haddad wondered how engineers could design a ship that catered to its occupants' every whim, yet didn't have a way to easily convey the heavy matter blocks. He figured the engineers forgot that the Metis had gravity, while all the older supply stations did not, and tried thinking of solutions as he waited in line.

Each crewmember took turns grabbing a block and carrying it back to the Metis. Stuart manned the control panel since it would only accept a Captain's command signature for offload— if anyone else tried touching the panel they'd get a nasty security shock.

GUTIERREZ GRABBED her block and felt the fingers on her right hand slip as soon as she hit the Metis' gravity. The block tumbled out of her hands right towards Schwartz. "Dammit!" she cried. Schwartz bent his knees and picked up the block, handing it back to Gutierrez. For a split second his hand touched hers and she blushed, pulling away quickly like she'd been burned. Schwartz showed happiness on the outside but seethed inside.

"Sorry," Gutierrez turned quickly.

Schwartz nodded back. "No problem."

Gutierrez carried her block to the storage bay and tried forgetting the creepy feeling she'd gotten when Schwartz touched her. She shuddered when she was out of sight of the rest of the team and wiped the back of her hand on her jumpsuit; Gutierrez hadn't believed in cooties since she was a fourth grader, but the way Schwartz looked at her burned. The block was heavy and she cursed the shitty engineers who didn't think of handling matter blocks when they designed the Metis—what she wouldn't give for a conveyor system of some sort. Her knees and back agreed.

Once she had her block up close to the storage rack, Gutierrez heard a loud beeping noise. The sound made her jerk upright and she looked for the source: Williams came towards her leading a small lift with a red revolving light on top.

"Good call!" Gutierrez gave Williams a high-five.

"Someone had to save all our backs!" Williams answered Gutierrez with a wide grin. "I went and synthesized this real quick."

Gutierrez watched as he expertly used the tongs to lift her block, then placed it neatly on the one Haddad had just brought. He ran the little lift like it was a part of his own body, and the little machine cooperated fluidly; as each block came in, Williams stacked it neatly like canned goods in a pantry. Soon the stack extended so far deep into the rack Williams had to stop his progress and move to the other side of the bay—he didn't want to overweight one side of the rack and send it falling on one of their lander vehicles.

THE TEAM WORKED like a little colony of ants, carrying the blocks from the elevator down the docking arm and into the Metis; everyone dutifully followed Williams as he filled up the main docking bay first. In a fit of ingenuity Williams made the lift just small enough to get through all the doors in the Metis, yet large enough to handle the heavy matter blocks. Stuart peeked back down the docking arm and saw Williams drive the little lift out the bay door and turn down the hallway to Engine Room One—she was yet again grateful he'd been able to get on the mission.

Stuart turned back to the control panel and loaded another block in the elevator, holding herself steady in the zero-g.

THIRTY

SCHWARTZ SEETHED with both joy and pain as he watched the team loading blocks in front of him, and was grateful he'd decided to wait on his takeover plan until after the depot offload —the thought of having to move all those blocks alone made his shoulders sore. He would've needed Stuart's codes to access the buoy anyway; and her retina.

He stared at Haddad's back as the line inched forward. Gutierrez came down the aisle carrying her block with considerable effort and almost dropped it on him. Schwartz admired her breasts as he bent down to pick the block up, his fingers brushing hers just slightly as he held himself in control. That warmth she had.

Finally, he was at the front of the line and Schwartz could get a good look inside the supply buoy: there was a tiny access room with an elevator and a control screen—just barely enough room to fit Stuart, a matter block, and the person moving said block through zero-g. Schwartz held back from the threshold and watched Haddad grab his block, then thought briefly about how good it would feel to stuff Haddad into one of the simulators and close the door.

Haddad moved his block down the gangway towards the open door and passed Schwartz. Stuart already had a block waiting and Schwartz grabbed it with both hands. The block was cold but not freezing, and Schwartz pulled the block to his chest carefully—grateful for the muscles he'd spent so long strengthening, and his skill in zero-g. Schwartz looked at everyone's feet as he walked by, trying to guess the owner by the foot stance; in most cases he was correct.

Schwartz cursed his fucking father for not getting an engineer to do something about a matter conveyor system on the Metis: this block carrying was bullshit. He wanted to cuss out the idiot who didn't think of these things, though he knew they'd gotten their just desserts in a fiery death by now. That fact made Schwartz smile.

As Schwartz moved down the line he managed a look at Gutierrez again and she returned his gaze with an expression that let him know she thought he was a snake. Good. She'd be rough to tame. He liked that almost better: the ones who were vicious. Those kind of thrills gave Schwartz life.

He got his block to the hallway and saw Williams directing him with a hand towards the other engine room.

"Gotta move to the other one, this guy's full." Williams waved his hand as he tried catching his breath.

"Alright." Schwartz nodded and felt his neck strain with the block's weight. *It would be so nice to crush his skull with one of these blocks*, Schwartz thought as he looked at Williams' back.

Schwartz followed Williams and lugged his block into the other storage bay: this one had ample room on the racks and Schwartz realized he'd be loading blocks all day to fill those shelves—a task that might break all of them.

"Hold on a second." Schwartz grunted as he set his matter block on the shelf.

"What up?" Williams looked at Schwartz with wide eyes.

"Got an idea." Schwartz raised his finger in the air. "Let me try this." He went to the large simulator in the corner and pressed on the control panel, found an option for HOVER STRETCHER, then specified the size as: FIFTEEN INCHES BY THREE FEET, THREE HUNDRED SIXTY POUNDS CAPACITY. Schwartz synthesized the first one and showed it to Williams with the pride of a child bringing home an "A" on his report card.

"What d'ya think?"

"Shit," said Williams with genuine awe. "Fucking great idea! Let's test it."

They loaded the stretcher full of eighteen matter blocks, then Schwartz led the stretcher around the storage bay, and out to the hallway. He turned the stretcher around in place, maneuvered it past the corner of the main hall, then returned to the storage bay. "It works," he nodded to Williams, and inside he felt something akin to joy and dominance combined.

"Williams to Stuart." Williams tapped the room's com system.

"Stuart here."

"Jimmy's got an idea," Williams called to the ceiling, "you might want to come and check it out. Would save our backs a ton."

STUART PERKED UP, hit the SUSPEND button and the buoy elevator stopped. "Hold here for a second," Stuart told Simon as he approached the door. Simon stood aside obediently and watched as Stuart walked down the hallway, then turned the corner into Engine Room 2. Stuart beheld Williams and Schwartz standing over a long, thin hover stretcher.

"What's that?"

"A conveyor stretcher," said Williams. Schwartz stood to Williams' side, trying to look innocently proud.

"Does it work?" Stuart poked the contraption, wondering how it could possibly carry a matter block.

"Watch," said Schwartz as he grabbed a couple matter blocks and set them on the stretcher, then he paraded the contraption around the storage bay, avoiding the landers and the sharp edges of the storage racks. The stretcher followed Schwartz like a humble puppy, easily guided with the touch of a finger. "It can hold up to eighteen matter blocks at a time." Schwartz looked at Stuart earnestly. "One of these for each of us, and we can get this done, double-time."

Stuart was genuinely amazed. She'd never thought the President's son actually possessed some intellect, yet here he was; coming up with a true engineer's solution. She wondered if all her judgements about Schwartz had been wrong.

"I like it," she said with a nod, "do it."

"Yes Captain."

WILLIAMS STARED at the two and couldn't believe the moment of civility he'd just witnessed: Stuart and Schwartz both treated each other like an actual valued crew member, not the intestinal parasite they both thought the other was. Williams was impressed by them—it was a nice change, and he wondered if space was finally softening Schwartz up a bit.

Schwartz walked to the simulator and ordered three more stretchers, and the simulator responded there would be a short wait time for the quantity to be completed. He pressed the PROCEED icon, and the simulator started to work. Stuart headed back to the hallway, the first stretcher in tow.

"Okay folks, listen up!" Stuart spoke over the din in the hallway. "Jimmy engineered us a conveyor solution for these blocks." The entire crew breathed a sigh of relief. "Change of plans for a little bit. Let's all load up this stretcher—Louis, you stay here with me in the buoy."

Haddad stayed at the head of the line while the rest watched, curiously.

"I'm going to have you stay here and help me load the blocks on each stretcher, you okay with that?" Stuart looked at Haddad. "You're good in this zero-g."

"Yes, Grace," said Haddad with a nod. Stuart fired the elevator back up and they both stared at the mechanism until a new block appeared in the window, then Haddad grabbed it and placed it on the stretcher, which Simon held in the doorway right where the gravity transitioned. Haddad was able to gently set the block on the stretcher, then slide it to the end as the gravity transitioned and sucked the block down under its own weight. In zero-g, moving matter blocks was easy, and Haddad's back relaxed as he loaded another block.

"Looks good." Stuart smiled at the dry run and wiped her hands like they had dust on them. "Let's fill this one up."

The stretchers arrived soon enough, and four hours later they had the entire buoy offloaded. Thanks to Schwartz's invention, no one's back got broken in the process.

Through the course of the offload, Stuart realized supply buoys were never meant to be entirely empty, nor used with a gravitational field: that's why Space Command had never thought of a conveyor system. No one ever needed more than a few blocks loaded from the buoy at a time, and when they did, they just floated the blocks onto their ship. Her heart sank a bit as she realized what the matter blocks from the buoy would do: extend their lonely little survival mission a few years more, but would they ever re-start humanity? She prayed to the All they would.

AFTER THE ENTIRE offload was done, Schwartz went back to his quarters. He sat down in his chair and wiped at his nose; his arms were a bit tired, but between his conveyor setup and Williams' forklift they'd gotten all the matter blocks offloaded in record time with minimal injury to body or mind. A part of him was happy with the teamwork, but a part of him hated melting in: he wanted to be at the head, not a component of the body. The thought started a little fire in his chest.

Schwartz went to the synthesizer and ordered up a bloody steak and sat down with a piece of bread. He sopped up the blood and ate the meat with relish, thinking about tearing off a piece of Stuart's thigh and chewing it like the steak.

As he swallowed, Schwartz wondered what human flesh tasted like.

STUART WALKED to her chambers and rubbed her lower back; it ached from floating so long at an odd angle while accessing the control panel, but she'd avoided the brunt of the block moving. She felt sorry for Haddad, having to handle all the blocks that came off the conveyor—he looked tired at the end of the night and waved goodbye with a limp arm as they retreated to their quarters. Stuart waved goodnight to him as well.

The doors opened to her room and she looked at a smiling Pete Williams, naked in her living area. Stuart cracked up and laughed behind a waving hand.

"What?" he asked with a hint of real uncertainty.

"Oh man," Stuart choked through laughter. "You are quite the stud."

"Really?"

"That you can even think about sex so soon after cryosleep..."

"Yeah!" Williams chuckled matter-of-factly as he approached her.

"Yeah." Stuart beamed and spoke softly as they leaned in close to each other, then kissed as they inched towards the bed. Stuart could tell Williams was cold, but the floor warmed to their feet as they walked on tiptoes and fell in a heap on the bed. The mattress adjusted to the combined weight and felt effortlessly perfect as Williams kissed her.

Stuart blushed and felt the hairs on her arms stand on end—the little ache that had longed for Williams during those lonely nights roared alive: she missed this. Fuck cryosleep...she wasn't going to let Williams go under again. She primally needed him, in order to make it through the cold darkness of space: he was her heat and fire and he gave her hope.

"Honey, I missed you." Stuart snuggled closer as Williams nuzzled her neck.

WILLIAMS BREATHED in Stuart's body and felt her heat seep through the skin on his torso. He'd missed her too—there was no way he'd go back into cryosleep and lose out on being with her again. He'd run every shift just so he could see her: Grace Stuart was the best thing out in space, and they were each other's. It was something neither had really thought about, but somehow instinctually knew. Williams smiled as he watched Stuart doze off on his shoulder; she snored little puffs of air against his neck while her cheekbone dug into his skin.

They dozed together sharing each other's heat, warm from the bed underneath them and warm from their love. Stuart moaned in her sleep and Williams looked down at her to make sure she didn't bite his shoulder—her mouth stayed shut and she rolled over onto his sternum. Williams stroked her shoulder and stared lovingly as Stuart twitched in her sleep.

It was after three-thirty am when the buzzer rang; Williams woke and touched the screen next to Stuart's bed, halting the alarm. Stuart moaned as she rolled over.

"Just five more minutes," Stuart pleaded with the alarm clock—she didn't want to be out of Williams' arms. Williams pulled her close and Stuart made a happy mumble, snuggling against his chest; it felt smooth and warm and smelled clean. Stuart smiled.

"Gotta go Babe." Williams peeled his arms off Stuart and rolled over.

"Really?"

"Gotta keep up appearances." Williams winked at Stuart.

"Fuck appearances!" She hissed with a smile.

"What do you think they'd do if they found out we were sleeping together?"

"No one can fire you now," Stuart smiled rakishly.

"Yeah, but really!"

Stuart sighed dejectedly. "They'd probably be pissed and think you were fucking your way up the chain of command."

Williams nodded and kissed Stuart in the center of her forehead. "That's why I should go tonight." He sighed back with a shrug. "That's the price you pay to be the boss man."

"Boss Lady!" Stuart corrected with a grin.

"Yah, Boss Lady," Williams finished, smiling too.

Williams stood up and went for his jumpsuit, grabbed his underwear off the floor and slid them on. Stuart put her underwear on as well: a trim sports bra went up top, the boyshort panties had a little bit of lace on the cuffs, yet were a dull heather grey. Williams loved them and playfully swatted at her bottom.

"Hey," Stuart giggled coyly. "You stop that naughty man!"

Williams looked at her saucily and raised his eyebrow at the mock-scolding. "Really?"

"Well," said Stuart as she pulled her bra back off again.

Williams unzipped his jumpsuit and started walking back towards the bed, shedding a layer with every step.

WREN WALKED up to Galloway's pod and stared at him; he sat quietly under the glass, sleeping away in his forced state of rehab. She checked his blood levels and verified the last of the heroin sequence had run its course: his body was fully detoxed, but his mind would be another matter. She'd never done the pod's mental reprogramming function before, but she and Galloway and Stuart were the only ones with access to the special software. Wren pressed ADDICTION PROGRAM INITIATE on the panel and watched Galloway's brain rhythms fluctuate on the screen.

The science said manipulating brainwaves would be the way to unlocking memories, perhaps erasing some. The mental reprogrammers all knew it was easy to erase the bad stuff, not so easy to erase the good; they had worked harder to perfect their theories, but now it was up to their science to save an integral part of humanity. Wren wondered if Galloway would pass his addiction on to his children—a thought to keep her up at night.

Galloway's brain rhythms bent and wove across the screen; she saw the first tics of reprogramming nano-beacons floating around and activating the trouble spots. They picked out an area of vulnerability and went to work cleaning it up. The results were amazing: on Earth they'd achieved a ninety-five-percent cure rate amongst all addicts and those who suffered mental afflictions. Society had blossomed for a short time, then it was wiped out.

She hoped this program would cure him of the heroin. Wren knew Galloway's disdain for the machine and its methods, but he was in bad need of some curing; the twelve-step program had only taken him so far. He'd sneaked the opiates all along, but paid off technicians to show he was clean—good enough to pass right under Space Command's nose. They didn't know their head surgeon was a junkie because he was so good at acting sober.

Wren knew because she'd been there all along. She'd been the one to bring him home from god-knows-where when he'd lost his house keys and somehow crashed his car into a tree. She'd known what they were up against when they'd hired Galloway to be part of the crew—another reason why she'd volunteered for the job. She knew someone needed to keep an eye on Bill, but she'd secretly hoped there'd be no need; Wren was sad she'd been wrong.

She walked over to Galloway's table and sat in his chair. *He's probably farted in this chair*, Wren thought. The Galloway of another world would've laughed and cackled at the idea... Galloway had a pretty sophomoric sense of humor and loved surprising people with that side of his nature: the dorky doctor with the teenager's taste in laughs. Wren initially thought Galloway was so serious, but then she'd gotten to know him.

Wren smiled and went back to the pod. The neural impulses were lulling Galloway to sleep, even within his sleep. He smiled a little. *Must be enjoying something*, thought Wren as she turned back to her desk.

HADDAD WALKED towards his quarters and rubbed his middle back. It ached from carrying all the blocks to the conveyor belt, but he knew it'd be screaming in the morning if he didn't get on the recovery machine, and fast. He walked into his room and turned towards the bathroom.

Inside was a small device about the length of an old-school chalkboard eraser. It had little bars protruding that emitted a beam of energy, which penetrated a person's muscles and made them right again. He turned it on and the device hummed, then Haddad held the wand behind his back so it hovered above the skin. The energy moved inside and cleared all the toxins out of his blood and he smiled as his back relaxed: it was blissfully good.

Haddad sat down in his chair and contemplated the stars: they moved slowly, though Haddad knew the ship was going at tremendous speed. He stared straight out, his pupils dilating, wondering if this was what every night would be like: sitting in his room, alone, watching the stars his every waking minute. No earth anymore. No trees. Suddenly Haddad wanted to hear the croak of a frog again—he missed the delicate creatures he'd once caught by the dozens as a child and kept in the bathroom sink at home, until his mother stepped on one and made him set them all free.

"Play frog song," Haddad commanded the ceiling com panel. The panel obeyed and the quiet melody of frogs calling in the night carried over the air; he felt his whole body relax and he breathed a deep sigh, his eyelids drooping and he walked to his bed. Haddad lay down and felt the bed growing warmer to the touch until sleep overcame him.

HADDAD WAS WALKING in a mossy forest, surrounded by trees of the darkest green. He smelled the mist on the air and breathed in deeply—feeling the touch of dew on his skin and the cool in the early evening. It was a luxurious feeling. He touched the moss on a tree and felt the bark like fur. Haddad smiled a little in his dream and that smile translated over to his sleeping body tucked in bed.

HE HADN'T BEEN DREAMING LONG when Haddad started awake and stared out into the black abyss again. The thought burned in his mind as he woke: He needed to get with Forester and Patel to see how to simulate a live tree. He needed that.

THIRTY-ONE

SCHWARTZ WOKE and checked his alarm panel: it read 03:30 hours, only a half hour shy of his original waking time. He got up and checked the survey program he'd set the night before, which read all the crew's body signatures. Stuart didn't know he could do such things, but there was a lot she didn't know about him. Schwartz looked in each room and saw all the crew sound asleep, tucked in their beds like little children. Good. Now it was time to get his plan going.

He walked to his shower and climbed in for a good quick clean. The machine performed its duty and Schwartz masturbated even though he was being scrubbed vigorously by the sonic waves. He didn't mind: it almost made him more aroused. Schwartz ejaculated right before the machine shut off and it cleaned the last bit of spilled semen in the cycle's finale; he stepped out of the box clean and smelling like nothing at all.

Schwartz walked over to the panel again and watched Gutierrez in her room. She slept on her side and a tiny soft bit in his heart wanted to spoon with her—she looked warm and he suddenly missed snuggling someone. Judging from her reaction when he'd touched her during the buoy offload, though,

Schwartz knew those dreams were only fantasy; if he tried climbing in bed with her for real, she might kick him in the balls.

He put on his soft "house" shoes and walked out of his room, turning right and heading towards the main intersection; instead of heading towards his engine room, Schwartz made a right turn and walked to the bridge. He stepped through the doors into an empty room, the autopilot sequence operating the ship from Stuart's command panel. Schwartz walked over to look at it.

He could see the course and trajectory that pointed them towards Mars; it was still probably the best first stop on their journey, so Schwartz didn't alter the flight plan. He tapped Stuart's screen and when the UNAUTHORIZED warning popped up, he entered a code his father had taught him in the corner: it was the President's master code, and it unlocked the full control functions for any Space Command ship. The Metis' mainframe obeyed and dutifully opened access to the entire control panel.

Schwartz felt a rush that made his skin feel hot. His hands shook a bit—he really hadn't expected the master code to work. Schwartz thought his dad had been full of bullshit, telling him the President could control any ship he liked; now Schwartz knew his pop was right—he had full control of the Metis. Schwartz walked around the bridge, smiling and snapping his fingers softly.

There were so many choices. What would be his first act as captain? Schwartz went to the control pad and started searching through the ship's security functions. Once he found the icon for LOCKDOWN he pressed it with a quiet smile; all the doors to each room locked immediately. Schwartz went through a manual picture of the ship and unlocked the doors he needed to the engine rooms, storage bays and workout room— he left the doors to every private quarter locked except the one to his own. On second thought, he unlocked Gutierrez's door too.

Next up, Schwartz disconnected the com lines to each room. One by one each activity light turned from green to red until he could see every private quarter was now its own quiet little kingdom. He wanted the ability to hail the rooms over the inter-com, but didn't want to be bothered by the little people calling out—Schwartz knew what his jailed crew mates would say to him and he didn't want to hear their shit right now. After a couple minutes each room was completely disconnected from the others, but Schwartz still had master control to talk to anyone he wanted.

Schwartz looked at the monitor one more time and read the vital functions on each person: they all were sleeping soundly. He watched the two bodies in Stuart's room with piqued interest and let Williams head back to his quarters before he locked the doors. Schwartz had never known Stuart and Williams were fucking—Schwartz totally understood now why he didn't get the master engineer job. Williams knew how to get his way...an age-old method once employed by women only, but Schwartz didn't put it past Williams to whore himself out. *Guess you gotta do what you gotta do to keep your job*, he thought.

He looked through the rooms and noticed the three cryosleep pods still on: Galloway's, Patel's and Forester's. He would probably keep Galloway and Forester in a permanent sleep state for now; a part of him wanted to just pull the plug on both machines and watch the two die quietly in their little cages. The other part of him remembered he might need the doctor at some point, and the botanist would come in handy if they ever did find a planet where they could make a home. His finger paused over the DISCONNECT button for a second, then he held his movement and turned away from the switch. *Best let sleeping dogs lie*, his father had always said.

Schwartz sat down in Stuart's chair, still feeling a little sleepy from his early wake time. Her chair warmed to his body and Schwartz felt it already conforming to his shape; he smiled and gripped both armrests, squeezing them a little with his fingers. The seat felt good, definitely better than he'd ever dreamed, and he'd expected a bigger fight for it. Now he was at the head of the ship: the place he'd always wanted and knew would be his. *Father would be so fucking proud,* he thought.

Schwartz watched as the bodies on the screen slept; one by one he flicked from room to room, observing all his captives like a warden. He wanted them contained but happy, so he left them all their living functions—everything except the door to get out and the com line to call and bitch at him. That was a fair trade-off, Schwartz figured.

He kept eyeing the com panel, waiting for the first person to wake up.

———

STUART'S EYES fluttered and she immediately missed Williams' warmth next to her. She stared at the ceiling and cursed herself for letting him leave—she wanted everyone to know he was hers, and having him spend the night would be the best way to show that. Instead, she took the cowards way out and let him walk out the door.

She rolled out of bed and walked to the bathroom, sitting on the toilet and putting her elbows on her knees, cupping her chin in her hands. Stuart blinked repeatedly as she remembered a dream she'd had where Williams rode a white horse—which was funny to Stuart, because she knew Williams hated horses. He'd never forgiven his sister's pony for biting him.

Stuart wiped at her nose as she stood up off the toilet; the machine flushed automatically when it felt her weight disappear. She turned to the vanity mirror and looked at her face in the reflection: there were little lines finally starting to crease the corners of her eyes, and a small fold forming at the corners of her mouth. *A frown line,* she thought, *how great.*

She went to the corner simulator and ordered up a vial of the best anti-wrinkle serum the doctors had concocted for wealthy women before the simulator became the great equalizer—her mother had sworn it did the trick and took years off a woman's face. Stuart had laughed at her mother then, but a nagging desire to look sexy for Williams drove her to try it now: she poured a small amount in her hands and spread the cream all over her face and neck. Satisfied, Stuart stored the vial in her medicine cabinet, where it looked out of place next to the deodorant and floss.

Stuart walked back to the simulator and thought about what she wanted for breakfast. The sensible woman in her wanted something simple like her usual oatmeal, but the hungry lover in her needed more sustenance: she ordered up two eggs, over-easy with wheat toast and strawberry jam. *That should be plenty to recover from my 'exercise',* she thought with a crooked grin.

Stuart broke the egg yolks with her fork and dipped the end of her toast piece in—that had always been her father's favorite way to eat his eggs. Tasting it brought him back so viscerally Stuart fought the urge to cry; Larry Stuart had been a strong and stern man, but deep down he had nothing but endless love for his daughter. He was the one who encouraged her to start flight training so young, taking her out in his own glider and teaching her beginning at age five. The pilot in him knew he had a prodigy on his hands, and he made sure his daughter developed her gift.

Stuart wiped at the corners of her eyes just a little as she finished her eggs. She spread jam on the last wedge of toast and stood to take her tray back to the simulator, which it gladly recycled, as always.

Breakfast finished, Stuart grabbed her jumpsuit and pulled it on; the zipper ran up the front and made a soft ripping noise as she fastened it. Dressed and satisfied, she turned and walked towards the door.

It didn't open.

Stuart had to stop herself mid-gait and pull back so she wouldn't break her nose on the pane. She looked up at the sensor and waved her hand back and forth.

Nothing.

Stuart walked backwards a few steps and tried going towards the door again. She got two steps away and realized it still wasn't opening. Irritated, Stuart walked over to the command panel by the door and opened up the programming: the panel advertised the LOCK PROGRAM was on. Stuart didn't remember locking the door that night and immediately wondered if Williams had set it for her when he left.

She tapped on the panel, trying to open a com line to Williams—if he'd set the door, maybe he'd know how to open it. Stuart felt like an idiot needing her man's help just to open a door, but he knew some special programs so perhaps he'd done something to play a practical joke on her. Stuart's mind flashed back to the time he'd reprogrammed her simulator on the Pluto trip to only make her fried SPAM—she'd had to beg and plead him to turn it back again. She wouldn't put it past Williams to try a naughty lover's trick again; he had that imp in him.

Stuart tapped the com line: nothing. She tapped it again. Nothing. She knit her brows and tried a third time. Same result. Flashes of *2001: A Space Odyssey* ran through her mind and she immediately worried about the computer mainframe going haywire. She ran a couple diagnostics from her panel and all came back normal, then she tried running through the settings again.

Stuart tested the door's override function. ACCESS DENIED flashed the panel. She tried again, going slower with her key strokes—ACCESS DENIED blinked the big red letters in response. She scrolled through the settings and saw the next red icon: COMMUNICATION LINES DISCONNECTED. Stuart bit her lip in frustration and tried the override key sequence again, using her Captain's Override code one more time. ACCESS DENIED the panel responded back.

"Fuck!" she yelled to no one and hit her fist against the wall. "Goddamn!" Stuart went back to the com screen and delved deeper into the functions, searching the authorization settings and pulling up the computer's command hierarchy. It showed a diagram much like a family tree, with her above Haddad, Haddad above Williams and Schwartz, Williams and Schwartz above Wren and Galloway, then the rest of the crew below Wren and Galloway. At the top of the diagram was a name that wasn't present on the ship: The President.

"Hello Ms. Stuart," said the com line as it suddenly opened up. Stuart heard the glee in Schwartz's voice, "guess I don't have to call you 'captain' anymore."

THIRTY-TWO

SCHWARTZ WATCHED, his smile growing ever larger. He watched Stuart wander around her apartment, oblivious during her morning routine; he watched as she cleaned up, ate breakfast, and dressed herself. It was almost too much...his mouth grinned so large he felt the edges cracking. It stretched larger like a maw as Stuart moved towards her door and he let out a triumphant crow as she nearly hit the door with her nose—it was too perfect.

Stuart walked to her panel and kept trying to get the door to open. He could see her trying all the command codes, all the things her training had taught her—it was all wrong. There was one thing she didn't know: the President had put his failsafe over all. *And the only one who has that code is yours truly,* thought Schwartz as he licked his lips with a predatory glee.

She kept monkeying with the door and Schwartz sat back in her command chair and put his feet up on the control panel. It was just the right height for a nice footstool, thought Schwartz as he crossed his arms behind his neck. After a few more minutes he couldn't take it any longer.

"Hello Ms. Stuart," said Schwartz with a grin and a slightly haughty air, "guess I don't have to call you 'captain' anymore."

Her head snapped up and she looked at the ceiling with a visage of fury that Schwartz had never seen before—he didn't think she was capable of it. The curiosity was uncontrollable and Schwartz opened the com line.

"What the fuck are you doing?" She asked in a voice so low the computer had to boost the volume. It sounded like the angry growl of a mother wolf defending her pups.

"Taking what should have been mine," answered Schwartz in a matter-of-fact tone. "You know he wanted me to do this mission, I think he caved to pick you because he was up for re-election."

"Open the fucking door," said Stuart as she looked right into the camera. Schwartz felt her eyes boring in to him even across the com link.

"No can do," he said as he shook his head, "I think you need a little time to cool down."

"Fucking open this door!" she snapped back.

"Now that's not a very nice tone," Schwartz scolded. "Did your mama teach you to talk like that?" he cooed.

"I don't give a shit," hissed Stuart, maintaining that steely gaze on Schwartz through the screen. "Open the door."

"That's nicer, but I still can't," answered Schwartz.

"You know where you're gonna take us?" said Stuart, changing the tack.

"Nope, not yet." Schwartz scratched his head and stifled a burp. "I do like your idea of Mars, but we'll see," he trailed off and rubbed his chin. There was a tiny bit of stubble sticking out like peach fuzz. He stroked his chin for a second, then refocused his gaze on Stuart.

"You plan to take us there yourself?" Stuart crossed her arms.

"The autopilot can get us there just fine."

"What if we encounter asteroids?" shot Stuart back.

"You know that I know that the autopilot is programmed to avoid any collision risks...I'm not that stupid, Grace."

"You plan on keeping us in our rooms the whole time?"

"If you're not nice, then yes."

"And if we're 'nice?'"

"Then you can come out to play."

Schwartz decided to leave it at that and shut off the com line. His direct screen went blank, but he could still see Stuart pacing in her room through his monitor. He watched as she walked back to her desk and started tapping away furiously at her panel. He knew she was probably trying to work some kind of hack in to his code, but if his father was right, she wouldn't get very far: the President's override code trumped all.

He could see Stuart as she pounded her fist against the panel in frustration; Schwartz knew she'd probably tried every override she could think of, and got nothing in return. He smiled and watched the panel like a cat eyeing a mouse. Stuart got up from her panel and went to the restroom; Schwartz watched gleefully as she dropped her pants and he got a quick glimpse of her underwear and privates. He was surprised to feel himself just the slightest bit aroused; he usually didn't get in to asian girls, but the challenge of conquering Stuart stirred something inside him. He'd probably have to drug her to get her compliant, but they'd make a really smart kid—not the best skin tone, but he had to father humanity, didn't he?

Schwartz continued watching as Stuart paced the inside of her room. She walked back and forth in front of the window, then started pacing circles around the perimeter. He could tell she was muttering something, but he didn't have the desire to open the voice line and hear what she was saying—probably only cussing at him anyway.

He walked over to Simon's station and looked at the course they were on: it took them straight to Mars and put them in an orbit around the planet. Schwartz smiled and went back to Stuart's chair—Mars would be a good stopping point, after all. He'd heard about the colony buildings being tested there, and his father had told him about the secret installation underground. Stuart's team had delivered parts to build the installation, but Schwartz didn't know if she knew what the parts were really for. The President had been a cagey man, and he knew how to diversify: the colonies on Mars had been his private project, and only little Jimmy knew about them.

Schwartz turned on the screen again and watched Stuart pace her room like a caged lion. He smiled as she beat on the door, then turned back to her bed and lay down with her hands covering her eyes. She looked like she was crying.

Schwartz grinned and turned off the monitor.

HADDAD WOKE up and stared at the clock in his ceiling—it was 06:00, his wake-up call. He sat up and rubbed his eyes, and they opened to the same darkness as every morning. Haddad wished they'd had time to install the video screens with screensavers across all the walls—at least then he wouldn't have had to stare at the endlessness of space for the rest of his years. He sighed and fought his despair back down into his heart.

Haddad stood up and walked over to the bathroom, groaning as he approached the toilet, his body suddenly screaming—it was all he could do to get over the rim before his bladder let loose. As he relieved himself, Haddad smiled ever so slightly and made a little satisfied "Hmph" noise, then he walked to the sink and washed his hands using the sonic cleanser mode. He wanted to use the water from the faucet, but sonic cleaners were the most efficient in space. Haddad wondered if Stuart might let them build a water-based recycling shower once they got to Mars.

Walking over to the simulator, Haddad knew already what he'd have for breakfast: two eggs, scrambled, with a scone. He ordered the scone WITH JAM, BUTTER AND CREAM, and the machine jumped in to action—soon he had his meal ready and waiting behind the door. Haddad ordered a cup of coffee, black, and chewed on the scone while he waited. Once the coffee was ready he grabbed the cup and took a long, lingering sip; Haddad felt the caffeine rushing to his brain and suddenly his eyelids didn't feel so heavy any more. He blinked a few times and continued working on his eggs.

Breakfast finished, Haddad took his recycling to the simulator and headed towards the door. He smashed into the panel and felt a sickening crunch as his nose broke, stars swimming in front of his eyes as they watered so heavily he felt blind. He felt the dripping wetness from the nosebleed already in progress; Haddad cursed and stepped away from the door, stumbling back over to his bathroom. He grabbed the tech towel hanging by the toilet and slapped it over his nose, the bleeding continuing until Haddad felt like he might pass out.

Minutes went by and Haddad stood by his vanity, holding his nose inside the towel at a slightly upturned angle; after a little bit, Haddad finally pulled the towel away from his face and gingerly touched his nose. He winced when his fingers brushed the side where he could see a slight bend in the bridge. "Shit," he whispered as he observed his profile in the mirror. Haddad grabbed the repair wand from his bathroom wall and turned it to the BONE: BROKEN setting. The machine took a minute to warm up, then rattled off three high-pitched beeps to alert Haddad it was ready.

He grabbed the wand and ran it over his nose area, feeling the tingling sensation that the wand always made as it did its work. At home on Earth it had become the mom's best friend: no more scrapes and bruises, no more trips to the doctor to set a broken bone—the average parent now had the power of an entire hospital at their fingertips. He thanked the machine's inventors as he felt his nose set back into place.

Broken nose better, Haddad walked back to the door that had caused the damage: he approached it slowly and got within inches before aborting, not wanting another broken nose. The door's automatic sensors seemed to be failing; that was the only explanation Haddad could think of to describe why the door wouldn't open. He walked to the panel next to the door and started running through all the diagnostic programs, and each test said the door was fine. Haddad scratched his head and returned to the main panel screen.

That's when he saw the tiny text at the bottom of the screen: SHIP LOCKDOWN INITIATED it flashed in red.

"What the fuck?" Haddad spoke to the empty room and his voice echoed off the walls. He immediately navigated to the ship control panel menu and started trying to go through the overnight alert codes: perhaps they'd hit something in the night and the hull was compromised. The diagnostics confirmed the ship was intact, though, so that was ruled out.

Haddad returned to the main screen and brought up the access codes panel. When he tried entering his first-officer's code the screen flashed: ACCESS DENIED. He re-entered his code, thinking perhaps his fingers had botched the first code: ACCESS DENIED flashed the screen again. He worked his way through every diagnostic he could think of, and each one confirmed the ship was okay, but wouldn't explain why his door wouldn't open. Haddad slapped his forehead and suddenly went to the door diagnostic screen—he was sure that would solve his problems. The door diagnostic took a minute to run and Haddad groaned when he saw the results: the door was completely structurally sound.

"Why the fuck won't you open?" he asked the door. The door didn't answer, just stood silent and white.

Haddad walked back to the control panel screen next to the

door and started racking his brain for any clue as to why his door wouldn't open; he'd run through every scenario and none seemed to be the culprit. Haddad was almost ready to give up and chock the experience up to a ship manufacturing robot who had a bad day, but that still left him trapped in his room.

That's when a thought crossed Haddad's mind; his fingers tapped furiously at the wall panel as he entered a string of data into it. Haddad waited a minute while the panel thought on the questions he'd just asked: WHO IS IN CONTROL OF THE SHIP?

The computer answered: CAPTAIN SCHWARTZ.

THIRTY-THREE

STUART WIPED her eyes as she sank down on the smooth tile floor, feeling the heat from the surface as she brushed more tears off her cheeks and chin. She sat on her knees for a second, hands cupping her kneecaps, looking like a yoga practitioner or a person about to start their prayers. Stuart stared straight out the window and wiped her eyes again, sniffling softly. After a minute or two kneeling, Stuart stood up and went to her desk, but instead of running code to decipher Schwartz's whereabouts, she turned on a movie. She considered her choices for a second, and selected THE TERMINATOR.

She watched as Sarah Connor and Reece escaped the deadly machine only to lose each other, feeling haunted a little by the ending: the woman driving off into an ominous sunset. Stuart missed sunsets—the feeling of warmth on her skin, and the way the clouds danced through a rainbow of color before going dark. The viewscreen panels could replicate the look of a sunset, but they couldn't copy the warmth.

Stuart stared down at her hands and looked at her finger nails; they were short and smooth, but one pinkie finger was misshapen where she'd crushed it in a door as a child. She tried looking as nonchalant as possible to Schwartz on the overhead view monitor—she couldn't see him, but she was positive he could see her. It already galled Stuart he'd seen her crying; *the fucking little daddy's boy,* she thought, *he probably jizzed himself watching me cry.*

She sat and stared out the window, hoping from the camera angle Schwartz could only see her profile. He probably loved seeing her so small and him so strong and in control; Stuart had known it the instant she'd met him. Didn't even need to know James Schwartz was the President's son...he had that attitude about him: that he got everything he wanted—whether you wanted to give it to him or not. It was the glint in his eyes that gave away the deepest desires of his ego.

It galled Stuart he'd figured out how to take over her ship. He wasn't even that bright...the flight simulator stymied him. How did he think he could command a fully-powered ship when he couldn't even master a manual ship landing? That was why they'd focused Schwartz on the propulsion systems he was already an expert at.

She shuddered thinking about Schwartz putting the ship in manual to evade an asteroid belt. Even a couple small asteroids might be beyond him.

And their lives were now all in his hands.

This thought woke Stuart out of her futility-induced stupor. She jumped over to her pad and started trying all the com lines —anything to get something open to Schwartz. She tried the house communication line. Nothing. She tried her personal communication line. Nothing. She tried to hail Williams. Still nothing. Each time the computer screen flashed back ACCESS DENIED.

Stuart sat back and crossed her fingers under her chin, knitting them together like a basket. She rested her chin on her knuckles and stroked the cuticle on her thumb, then she suddenly sat upright and slapped her hand against the table in a kind of "a-ha" gesture. Stuart's fingers typed furiously on the screen, pressing so hard you could almost see the tips of her fingers turn white. After a minute of typing, Stuart sat back and pressed the SEND icon with finality.

"What do you plan to do about the Miller Belt?" she messaged Schwartz and waited for a response. Nothing came back.

Stuart paced around her suite, walking the circumference until the walls blended together. She tried getting the thought of Schwartz in control out of her head: it drove her crazy and sickened her all at the same time. She feared what he'd do to the crew and the ship—there wasn't a thing she wouldn't put past him, and he now had them all at his whim. Stuart wanted to scream and beat the walls and tear out her hair, but she knew watching that would give Schwartz too much pleasure.

In a fit of contrary, Stuart walked over to her bed and lay down. The mattress warmed to the perfect temperature and she felt herself drifting off to sleep again—crying sapped more energy than she thought, and her eyelids couldn't seem to stay open. Stuart figured it would be a fitting sign to Schwartz if she showed him just how much she didn't care about him from here on out. She fell asleep imagining Williams was holding her; she could almost smell him, and now she wished they'd had the balls enough to share the same bedroom.

STUART DREAMED she was running across a large field towards a house at the end. The grass cut her feet but she kept running. As she got to the house she tried opening the handle but it broke off in her hand, then she ran around to the back side and tried to get in the back door. That handle broke off in her hand too. She went to all the windows and looked in each one, trying each frame to see if it would open; each stuck hard and she realized the windows were painted shut. Stuart sat down on the porch and cried.

SHE WOKE up with a start and smelled the acrid scent of her own fear sweat. Stuart wiped her nose and rolled over, looking over at her wall screen just in time to see it flicker on unattended. It was a picture of Williams' quarters: he was asleep in his bed...same as her. She wished she were in that bed with him, snuggled up against his chest, hearing his breathing and the mumbles he made when he dreamed. Stuart missed him so badly all of a sudden her chest actually hurt. *Well at least he's letting me see Williams, even if he won't let us be together,* she thought.

Stuart watched Williams as he rolled over and faced the wall; it would've been so easy to spoon him if she'd been in his bed. Her eyes turned to the corner of his room where something moved: Williams' door opened and a figure walked in his quarters. It was Schwartz. Schwartz took a moment to look up at the central camera and smiled, and Stuart saw something shiny in his hands. He walked towards Williams' back and brought the shiny thing out in his right hand: a butcher's knife.

Stuart started screaming and beating the screen with both hands.

SCHWARTZ FINISHED UNLOCKING Gutierrez's door and turned his attention to Williams' room camera. The guy was passed out asleep and lay askew on his bed like he'd been shaken and laid down by a bear. Schwartz wondered how a guy like Williams could sleep so soundly in the aching endlessness of space—it made Schwartz want to tear his eyeballs out sometimes.

He walked over to Stuart's main panel and checked the heat

signatures in each room: every red blot of human body heat was located in his/her bed except for Stuart who was pacing back and forth in her room, and Haddad who was sitting at his desk. Schwartz touched the screen where Gutierrez slept in the fetal position; he ached to be beside her, dreaming about any physical contact. Schwartz guessed her skin was soft and smelled like honey.

It wasn't fair she didn't like him—he was built, a prime physical specimen in his own right. There were many women who'd loved him at home...he didn't care if they wanted him for his money, his father, or his looks–the fucking he gave them was all the same. Heck, there'd even been times when he'd had two bitches at once; granted, they were both drunk and high on a concoction his father's doctor had given him, but they'd both sucked him off, and the male enhancement he'd taken helped him perform on both girls equally. One had been blonde, the other a brunette...a delicious combination.

Schwartz turned his attention back to Gutierrez again. She'd rolled over in her bed and lay prone on her stomach, a good position to be bedded in; he watched her heat signature cool a little, then heat back up to blazingly hot. *Must be having quite a dream,* he thought. He couldn't stand it any longer and switched the view to her room camera—she slept soundly and he could see her hair wrapped around her head like she'd just walked through a windstorm. Gutierrez scratched her side and rolled again, this time facing the wall in the fetal position. Schwartz wondered if she dreamt of other men.

He turned the view back to Williams; he was the one Gutierrez probably got wet to. Schwartz imagined her fondling herself in the mirror, thinking about Pete Williams, not Jimmy Schwartz. It drove him mad. He reached for himself and didn't so much as fondle his penis, but manhandle it, and within a minute he had ejaculated and stripped out of his jumpsuit right in the middle of the bridge. He recycled it in the corner simulator and made himself a new uniform in under two minutes, while his penis still ached.

Schwartz had a new focus: Williams. Williams needed to go if Schwartz was going to have any chance at Gutierrez. It was the only way. He walked towards the door and stopped at the threshold.

How? It was a simple question but Schwartz suddenly had no answer. He looked down at his hands and remembered the time he'd strangled the little boy in India; it had felt so good, and no one even missed the little bugger. A life lost that didn't mean a thing, except to James Schwartz: he got hard every time he thought about it.

Death by gun he'd also done. He'd paid to hunt an African girl across the desert, where she'd tripped on a sand dune and he'd blown her head off. It went too quick and he always felt a little let down and lost when he thought about it.

Knife was new. Schwartz instantly thought of it and immediately approved the choice—that would be a much safer way to get the job done, and make sure the hull didn't get compromised. *One must always think about the ship's safety*, he thought to himself as he simulated a nice, sharp butcher's knife. The machine dutifully went to work and didn't ask questions, it just did his bidding and had the knife made in under a minute flat. Schwartz picked up the blade and looked it up and down, testing the edge—it took a small sliver of fingernail when he ran his thumbnail across it. Ready.

Taking a minute to turn Stuart's room camera on so she could watch the action, Schwartz walked out the door sufficiently armed, and padded towards Williams' suite. He'd seen the other engineer lying cuddled on his bed like he was sleeping with a sweet honey, perhaps even dreaming of Gutierrez. Oh how they'd both love that...rubbing it in Schwartz's face on a tiny ship for the rest of fucking eternity. His animosity fueled his rage: *better now before he fucks her and gets her pregnant*, Schwartz thought.

He walked down the hallway with a steady and confident gait, and moved with the knife in his right hand like some sort of special ops soldier. He walked into Williams' suite, looked up at the camera just to show Stuart who was boss, then walked over to Williams' bed where he lay with his back facing Schwartz. Schwartz stabbed him four times: once in each lung, his heart and his neck–severing the spine. His fighting and weaponry coach couldn't have done it better.

Schwartz wiped his blade on Williams' sheets, bowed to the camera like a samurai and walked from the room.

STUART BEAT her hands against the screen and screamed as she watched Schwartz plunge the knife into Williams' back over and over. Her wails of agony sounded like pain incarnate, and she rolled off the bed, sobbing uncontrollably. It was one thing to lose Earth: it was another thing completely to lose Pete. She sprinted to the door and threw herself at it, howling Pete's name over and over, but the door still didn't budge. Her legs gave out and she collapsed.

Nothing in her body wanted to work. Stuart lay on the floor wishing she was dead like Williams too, seeing Schwartz plunge the knife into his spine and watching him die right there on the bed over and over. Every inch of Stuart wanted to be in that room, defending her man and dying with him if necessary. To be held back and helpless in her own room didn't just scream frustration, it made her vibrate from every pore; she wanted to hold Williams, even if it was his lifeless body for the last time.

Stuart rolled over on her side and curled up in the fetal position on the floor. She cried so powerfully the blood vessels at the corners of her eyes burst, leaving sprays of tiny blood specks decorating her eyelids like some kind of avant-garde eyeshadow. Stuart cried with heavy wracking sobs and didn't care about the snot streaming from her nose or the saliva dripping from her mouth. She wailed to the darkness in space and wondered if anything out there heard her, if anything out in that blackness knew her pain.

Her shoulders hurt lying on the floor, but Stuart stayed still on the white surface; she felt it warming and her hand reached out and stroked the smooth tiles. She couldn't believe she was here alone now—who would hold her and make her laugh like Pete? Who would make her banana pancakes, even though the simulator could do them perfectly? Who would read her old stories at night until she fell asleep?

A sudden burst of rage came over Stuart. She stood up, went to her bed, and started beating at the mattress, pummeling it over and over, screaming her anger with every punch. Her right hand began to hurt, so she switched to her left and continued beating the mattress, wishing her hands were contacting Schwartz's groin instead of the fabric. She didn't give a shit if he was watching–it felt good to beat on something, anything.

Stuart beat on the mattress until her arms and legs gave out simultaneously and she sat crumpled on the floor again. Her tears flowed and she keened while rocking back and forth. She wrapped her arms around her torso and held her ribcage like a teddy bear, all the while emitting the tortured sound of a broken heart.

After endless minutes crying, Stuart crawled up on her mattress and lay down. The surface warmed like usual and she felt the empty blankness surround her. Stuart wanted to stay awake and feel her pain for Williams with every fiber of her being, but her body revolted and drifted off to sleep from exhaustion. She tried to fight the drowsiness, but her body gave in.

HE STROKED HER SHOULDER GENTLY, so soft in fact that Stuart thought it was the cat nuzzling her.

"Sorry, Bae," Williams said softly as he nuzzled her neck. Stuart shivered all over and rolled around to touch Williams' cheek, his stubble scratched her palm just a little, but she stroked his face and loved the prickly feel. "You alright?" he asked, looking Stuart straight in the eyes.

"Yeah," she said sheepishly. "I had a bad dream."

"What about?"

"You died," she said flatly, looking away towards the wall.

"Well that doesn't sound nice," he said with a chuckle, "any good story behind it?"

"Schwartz murdered you in your sleep and made me watch," she said with a sob.

"The fucker!" Williams flashed his sunny smile. "How dare he?!" Stuart could tell he was joking, but she didn't really appreciate the humor. Her skin still crawled.

"God, I'm so glad it was just a dream."

"Yeah," said Williams, his voice sounding sadder all of a sudden, then he brightened and changed the subject. "Did you hear about the President's master code?"

"What?" Stuart looked at Williams incredulously.

"You didn't know about it?"

"No."

"Seriously?"

"Nope...what is it?"

"I heard from one of the ship programmers the President had a master code that could override everyone else's clearances."

"You're shitting me!" Stuart scoffed.

"No joke." Williams looked suddenly serious. "He did it to have all the control...I don't think he realized he'd get that control after he was already dead."

"Grim," Stuart shook her head. "Do you know what it is?" she added with a feisty wink.

"You mean the number?"

"Yup." She grinned, rolling back on top of Williams.

"92565!" Williams blurted out like he was being tortured. Then he laughed.

"Are you serious?" asked Stuart. Williams nodded. She nuzzled deeper into his arms and smelled his cologne—it was the best way to fall asleep, in her opinion.

———

STUART WOKE SLICKED with sweat again. The cold air chilled her body and her nipples hardened like bullets. She felt instant sadness—she was alone. Stuart wanted to cry again but her tear ducts were dry, so she scratched her head and sat up instead. As if she were still dreaming, Stuart stood and padded to the door panel, her fingers entered "92565" as if in a trance.

The door opened.

THIRTY-FOUR

GUTIERREZ SAT up in bed and stared at the flawless beach sunrise—she'd finally decided to reprogram her window to another view other than the endless blackness of space. She rolled over, walked to her bathroom, skirted the shower while eyeing it warily, brushed her teeth in the vanity, then sat down for breakfast. Bread and butter, jam and tea, with a hardboiled egg—a meal her mother would have been proud of. Her morning routine took all of fifteen minutes, leaving Gutierrez plenty of time for a good workout before heading to the bridge.

She walked out her door and headed towards the gym. Gutierrez could see someone coming down the corridor towards her, but his head was obscured thanks to the slight curve in the hallway; by the walk she realized it was Schwartz, and felt her whole body stiffen.

"Hi, Luisa," called Schwartz as he approached her. "Top 'o the mornin'!" he continued, imitating an Irish brogue.

"Good morning." Gutierrez gave Schwartz a curt nod, which she hoped would be enough. Just as she turned her gaze to avoid making direct eye contact with him, she spotted something red on Schwartz's pant leg; looking up along his torso she saw more spots—most definitely blood. Her gaze carried her eyes higher, somehow thinking Schwartz might have a bloody nose and need help. Gutierrez locked eyes with him and saw the full extent of what he'd done in his expression.

"Yeah," said Schwartz, cocking his head ever so slightly, "about that…"

He tried to lunge out and grab Gutierrez's hand. She kicked his hand away and he barked a strained yelp, shaking his now-bruised wrist. Schwartz dropped his knife and tried grabbing Gutierrez around her torso, but she deflected both his arms and redirected his energy so he tripped and fell on his face. Gutierrez ran the five strides it took to pass him and turn the corner towards the gym. She sprinted through the door, then whipped around and hit the LOCK button as soon as the panes sealed. Gutierrez slid down the closed gym door and started crying.

She sat back against the doors and held her head in her hands. Gutierrez saw murder in Schwartz's eyes, but she didn't know whose blood was on his jumpsuit. She heard a beeping on the other side of the door panel. Gutierrez had only seconds to roll forward before the door behind her parted and Schwartz fell on top of her. Gutierrez cursed her rookie mistake: thinking she was safe.

"Yeah, I want this," he said with a smile as he pinned her arms underneath her body and tried reaching inside her pants. Gutierrez whipped her head backwards and felt the crown of her head connect with Schwartz's nose; stars blazed in front of her eyes as she felt a crunch and knew she'd gotten him where it counted. Schwartz shrieked and clapped both hands to his face. Gutierrez wriggled forward and rolled over so she was facing Schwartz, her back on the ground. She did this so quickly Schwartz had no time to move his hands from his nose to protect his crotch—Gutierrez kicked out with both feet and connected each with his testicles. She felt another crunch and heard all the air suck out of Schwartz's lungs, then Gutierrez whipped over to all fours and scampered back from Schwartz. He fell in the open doorway and Gutierrez sprinted around him out the gym door.

She ran down the hallway and headed towards her suite. In a fit of paranoid brilliance, she turned and slid into Engine Room Two. *He'd never suspect I'd go to his lair,* she thought with a smug smile.

Gutierrez had felt Schwartz's skeazy eyes all over her since the moment he'd been named to the mission; Schwartz had never disguised his lust for her, and she'd answered it with cold disregard. Each rebuff made Schwartz rage further for her, though, and Gutierrez feared he'd respond like this someday. A small dark corner of her mind asked if she should have just told him she was into women, but another part of her mind wondered if he would have believed that answer.

Gutierrez hid around the back side of the engine cover so the engine was between her and the door. She tried hunkering down below the top shape, but the tiniest bit of her hair stood out above the white surface. She prayed Schwartz wouldn't come in the engine room quite yet. Minutes ticked by and her knees ached; she needed to move, but was still terrified Schwartz might come busting through the door any minute. Gutierrez waited despite her agony.

More minutes passed and she couldn't take it any longer. Gutierrez's knees popped as she stood up, just in time to see Schwartz coming through the door. He locked eyes with her and Gutierrez's bladder almost gave out when she saw what was in his gaze: the blackness of the untold darkness, evil and sticky at its core. He looked at her coldly and smiled the forced, crazy-man smile.

"You know it's only a matter of time," he said almost sooth-ingly, shrugging his shoulders. "Why fight it?"

Gutierrez dodged to her left and Schwartz mimicked her move; she lunged right and he matched her yet again. He kept moving closer to the engine, and she realized she was stuck behind it. In a moment of desperate energy, Gutierrez scrambled up on top of the engine and tried leaping over Schwartz's head —he caught her legs and she fell on top of him in a kicking heap. She struck his face again with her shoe and he screamed. His grip loosened for a second, then tightened again.

Gutierrez screamed as she felt him tearing at her jumpsuit with something. A knife, she realized as he cut her skin in his haste to remove her undergarments. She screamed again and kicked at him, the knife sliced her thigh and blood spurted down her leg.

"Shit," said Schwartz as he tried to get her to stop kicking. She was getting blood all over his engine room.

Gutierrez kicked at him again and writhed across the floor, pushing herself out the engine room door.

"Help!" she screamed, "Someone help!!" she screamed so loudly her voice cracked.

"Sorry babe," said Schwartz as he walked out the door towards her. "They're all in beddy-bye."

Gutierrez shrieked again and tried standing. She stumbled towards her suite, hoping to make it before she got too dizzy from the blood loss. From behind her she heard a kissing noise, like a child getting a noisy peck from a grandmother. She turned out of instinctual curiosity.

Gutierrez's eyes locked with Schwartz's as he drew the knife blade across her throat. Her eyes widened with surprise just as he cut her open, almost in disbelief.

"Now look what you've made me do," said Schwartz with a shaming tone, reminiscent of his mother.

STUART HEARD the screams and ran to where the halls met. She stopped just in time to see Schwartz turn towards her, knife in hand, splattered with Gutierrez's blood. The pool spreading from Gutierrez's body was dark crimson against the white tile floor.

They locked eyes.

Stuart sprinted for the bridge.

STUART FOUGHT the urge to piss herself as she ran from Schwartz. Her inner radar told her he was only a few steps behind, and she ignored the desire to look back. Her eyes were focused on the door only steps away.

She bolted in the door and hit the emergency icon as soon as it closed. That bought her a couple seconds while the door thought about the particular emergency and prompted her for her code. Stuart entered 92565.

COMMAND ACCESS GRANTED flashed the screen and the door showed LOCKED in big red letters.

ON THE OTHER side of the door Schwartz dropped the knife and tried entering his dad's special code: 92565 on the pad. ACCESS DENIED, the screen flashed back in red letters.

WHY? Typed Schwartz into the pad.

PRESIDENTS CODE ALREADY IN USE - EMERGENCY PROTOCOL ENACTED.

"Fuck!" screamed Schwartz as he slammed the palm of his hand into the door.

STUART SAT in her chair and breathed deep for the first time in what seemed like ages. She sat back and rubbed the armrests on both sides with her palms. The smooth material calmed her down.

"Open view to outside bridge door," Stuart commanded the main computer. It obediently flashed to a view from just behind Schwartz's left shoulder. She could see him beating at the door with his fist; it looked broken at one point, but he kept hitting the pane. There was a smear of blood from his split knuckles.

Stuart smiled sickly, the rest of her face contorted in a scowl.

Schwartz paced back and forth for a while holding his mangled hand, then he slipped from the screen. Stuart switched to another view and watched him head towards the medical suite. She switched views again and saw him heading to the large regeneration machine at the corner of the sick bay, where he put his injured hand inside. Stuart hated to do it, but she pulled her attention away from Schwartz and back to the bridge.

She got up and checked Gutierrez's station. Everyone accounted for, except the now-dead planetary analysis officer and Pete; Stuart didn't know Gutierrez as well as she would have liked to, but she felt like crying. Losing Luisa was like losing something precious, and Stuart felt instant rage and sadness welling up inside her. She wanted to do to Schwartz what he did to Luisa. She wanted to do to him what he did to Pete. Tenfold. She wanted him to bleed so badly, to mewl and cry and beg for forgiveness as she stood over him with the knife as she sliced away little parts of him.

Something in her stomach twinged, and Stuart rubbed her solar plexus, then burped—the sadness felt dissipated somehow, the anger cooler. She started bringing up different views of each crew member: Haddad was pacing back and forth in his quarters, he was obviously up and he knew he was locked in; Forester, Patel and Galloway were all still asleep in their cryotubes, all vital functions normal. Stuart used the special code and locked all three of their tubes from tampering, hoping the tubes would remember her code first and deny Schwartz, just like the door.

Next Stuart turned her attention to Wren, who was asleep in her quarters, still presumably unaware of their capture. Simon was just getting up. Stuart watched him go through the same motions she'd gone through: the breakfast, the cleaning, up until he bonked his nose against the door. He tested the door and tried the keypad, just like Stuart and Haddad had done. Stuart felt kind of sick watching Simon figure out he was trapped—she didn't like being even remotely in the same shoes as Schwartz.

"Schwartz's gone rogue," she typed into her computer pad and touched SEND to both the message pads in Haddad and Simon's quarters. "Meet me on the bridge. Go now...he's in the medical bay." She finished the message and manually opened both the men's doors. Haddad was out the door like a bolt, running towards the bridge. Simon took a minute longer, still a little groggy and not quite sure what was going on—the sleep still had his brain.

Simon walked towards the bridge. Stuart and Haddad both held their breath as they watched Simon coming down the hallway on their monitors; he walked past the sick bay doors and Stuart breathed a sigh of relief. She switched her monitor view to inside the sick bay just in time to see Schwartz's body leaping like a lion out the door onto Simon with his knife outstretched. Schwartz stabbed Simon in the back and Haddad gasped as he watched Simon try to pull the bloody knife out from between his shoulder blades. Schwartz did it for him and stabbed the knife again towards the base of Simon's neck, and Simon dropped like a limp sack of grain as Schwartz severed his spinal cord. Stuart screamed, seeing visions of Williams as Simon fell.

Haddad screamed with her.

THIRTY-FIVE

WREN OPENED her door and beheld Simon's body collapsed and bleeding on the floor, with Schwartz standing crouched over Simon—a knife clasped between his teeth like some kind of space pirate. He was fiddling with something on Simon's jump-suit, but looked up at Wren like a predator disturbed mid-meal. His eyes glared blackly at Wren. She stepped back and closed the door quickly, pressing the LOCK icon on her way in.

Wren breathed a sigh of relief and started moving away from the door to her com pad. That was when her door opened. Wren made a tiny scream that was a half-squeak of terror as she turned to see Schwartz striding in her room towards her, knife in hand. He tapped a code into her panel as the doors closed.

"Here's how this is gonna go," he stated as he walked toward her. "You're going to be a good girl and stay quiet."

Wren walked backwards towards her bed, then turned slightly to lead Schwartz past the corner of her desk. She traced a circular pattern around her room. Roxanna cowered in the corner, instinctually terrified of Schwartz.

"What the fuck are you doing, Jimmy?" Wren asked as she walked backwards and kept her eyes on the man.

Schwartz shifted his knife from his right hand to his left hand and back again, all the while still speaking, while little droplets of blood ran down his hand and spattered on the white tile floor. "You're going to go lie down on that bed, or I'm going to do to you what I did to Simon and Williams." He grinned like a gargoyle.

Wren started when she heard the two names and she almost tripped over her feet. "What?" she asked in confusion.

"Gave 'em both a little poke," he said, miming the action with the knife hand. "You want a little poke?" he asked, poking the knife at Wren for effect.

She shook her head no.

"Good," said Schwartz in a satisfied tone, "go to your bed." He pointed with the non-knife hand towards Wren's bed. Her heart sank immediately and Wren felt a fear heat building in her loins: she knew what he wanted. She walked towards the bed, heart palpitating and quavering on legs that had suddenly gone numb.

"Go on," Schwartz nodded towards Wren, "take off your jumpsuit."

She did as she was told.

"All of it."

She removed her bra and underwear.

"Now take off mine."

She knelt forward feeling the cold floor on her naked knees; the air made her breasts contract and she felt a breeze between her legs. It was so deeply shaming. He held the knife to her throat and she could feel the blade pierce the tiniest bit of skin —it felt like when she cut herself shaving her legs. Wren unzipped his jumpsuit, then pulled it off his body like a banana peel.

"All of it," Schwartz said, like he was reminding a child.

Wren removed his underwear and he stepped out, all the while holding the knife like a razor against Wren's throat. His eyes never left her. They were cold and burned at the same time.

"On the bed."

Wren did as she was told, and lay on her back facing the ceiling. Schwartz held the knife to her throat and pressed in a little, delighting in the tiny trickle of blood that fell down Wren's neck. He entered her and she whimpered softly.

"Quiet," Schwartz growled.

She stayed silent as he took her. It was the same act performed by so many good men who she'd loved, but this time it was different: she could see the blackness in his eyes, and feel the pain of him inside of her. She cried out as he thrust particularly hard.

"Shut up!" he hissed at her as he dug the knife a little deeper in to her skin.

Tears squirted from the corner of Wren's eyes as she tried to stay quiet when all of her wanted to scream; she looked up into his eyes and saw the blackness that was the pure Devil in his gaze—there was no man there, only evil. It was like looking in to a pool where there was no reflection. The closest Wren could come to describing it, was thinking about the old horror movies where they put black contacts in someone's eyes to black them out, except this time there were no special effects.

Schwartz thrust deep into her one last time and she felt him orgasm. She wanted to cry and sob and scream and run from this beast in human skin, but some part of her deep inside told her to stay quiet and still: to survive at all costs. She listened.

"Well how does it feel to be saving humanity?" he asked her in a sickly chipper tone.

Wren stared back at him blankly.

"Don't you fucking kill that baby," he said as he brandished the knife back towards her neck. "We need that baby to survive."

Wren felt her whole body shaking and her hands felt so cold;

her body felt distant, like it wasn't hers. She watched him leave and immediately started sobbing and hugged her torso as the doors closed, rolling on her side and crying in deep wracking moans, curled up tight in the fetal position. She didn't feel like she owned herself any more.

Wren reached a hand down and felt her genitals. It stung and burned where he'd broke her skin, and her gut ached deep in throbbing contractions, the bruise against her cervix felt like it was going to tear her apart from the inside out. Her hips and pelvis hurt from where he'd used his free hand to pull her in to him, and one side of her pelvis felt dislocated—there was a bruise matching his handprint on her pelvic bone. Her hands shook as she explored further, coming back spotty with blood where he'd torn her perineum. She cried in deep wracking sobs.

She sat up and looked over at the sonic shower; it was then she so badly wanted an old-fashioned shower to wash it all away. Wren walked shakily over to the machine, feeling her whole body quiver from the fear and cold. She opened the shower door and shuffled in, careful not to move too much for fear of the gut pains.

The shower went to work and started scrubbing all the orifices on her body. Wren shook ever so slightly as the sonic waves scraped every last bit of Schwartz off the outside of her body—it just couldn't get rid of what was inside. Wren could still feel him inside of her, even though she also felt numb: it was like disgusting slime she couldn't escape.

Wren jumped when the shower beeped to signal the end of the wash cycle. She turned and felt her abdomen give a shock of protest when she moved too quickly, so she put a hand to her belly and rubbed it in a circular motion, which helped a little. Wren walked to the simulator in the corner and ordered up a recovery wand, a warm set of fleece pajamas and a blanket, then she used the little machine to treat the damaged areas around her vagina. When the machine beeped to signal it was done,

Wren set the device down on her table, then dressed herself like she was in a trance. Finally clothed but still feeling naked, Wren walked over to her chair by the desk, then sat down in the chair and pressed the control panel to HEAT. The chair warmed and Wren felt the heat penetrate and soothe her violated parts.

She stared out the window into the darkness, shaking, terrified to leave her room lest she encounter Schwartz again.

STUART AND HADDAD lost Schwartz from view.

"Shit!" spat Stuart as she tried getting the body scanning system to pull Schwartz's location up.

"I'll check the log…" said Haddad as he watched Stuart's frustration.

Haddad quickly went through all the camera views and watched an endless stream of Schwartz stabbing Simon, over and over. His eyes grew numb to the act after the first few times.

"I can't find him anywhere…" said Stuart mournfully.

"Got him!" Haddad yelped right as she finished. "Oh God," he continued, "he's in Wren's suite."

Stuart felt herself go cold. "Bring up her room!" she said with urgency.

All they could get was the heat signatures, but it was enough to see what he was doing to her.

"We gotta go, now!" shouted Stuart at Haddad who nodded with a vicious hunter's glare and turned towards the door. They both sprinted headlong into the pane that refused to open. Both hit the panel with a thud and bounced backwards.

"Dammit, no!!!" screamed Stuart as she jumped up and hit the door like a crazy animal trying to get out. Her shrieks rose higher and higher and Haddad tapped away furiously at the pad to get the doors to release.

"Grace, the code!!" he barked at Stuart, breaking her from her panic.

"92565!" she said, putting her face so close to the door she could feel its essence.

Haddad entered the code and the door opened again. They both sprinted out the bridge, down the hallway and around the corner towards Wren's quarters, each hoping to fall upon Schwartz leaving the scene of the crime, and beat him to death.

They rounded the corner to an empty hallway, devoid of any movement. Simon and Gutierrez's bodies lay askew in pools of their own blood. Stuart instinctively stepped around Simon's body as she moved to Wren's door. Haddad acted as if to barge in and Stuart stopped him with a stern glare—he halted in his tracks and followed Stuart's lead.

She entered the code in Wren's pad and held her breath as the door opened. A quick glance left and right showed nothing...In their panic neither heard the hum of the sonic shower while Wren tried to scrub the act away.

"He took her!" Stuart uttered breathlessly as she turned and headed towards the door. "Keep going!"

Haddad followed Stuart obediently; secretly not wanting to stumble on to the aftermath of what he knew had happened. He felt sick in a horrible way.

The two watched the door close then turned to each other.

"Where do you think he went?" asked Haddad.

"Storage bay?" she answered, hating how unsure she felt.

"Okay," Haddad nodded as he headed that direction. Stuart followed one step behind.

They both got to the storage bay doors and stopped. "Better be safe." Stuart gave Haddad a knowing gaze. Haddad nodded and they each took a side of the door, both hugging close to either edge with their backs to the wall. Haddad entered the President's Code into the panel and the door slid open. Stuart and Haddad both jumped out like police in an old-time cop drama, but they stayed silent. Each moved soundlessly into the storage bay.

The racks of matter blocks lined all the walls; there were so many in the bay you could only move about two yards into the room before hitting the first rack. Stuart looked upward to see the matter blocks extending all the way up to the ceiling. There was effectively no room to hide.

"Not here," Stuart said as she lowered her gaze.

"Nope," agreed Haddad.

They stepped back into the hallway and crossed over to the door that marked Schwartz's suite. He had a tip-of-the-wing room like Stuart, just on the opposite side of the craft. Haddad's chest got tight and his hands slicked with sweat. They both took similar positions on either side of the door, just like with the storage bay.

Haddad hit the President's Code into the pad one more time as they waited for the door to open. He heard the doors slide and prepared himself for the onslaught of man with a knife; better yet, a cornered man with a knife. Haddad regretted not simulating a knife for himself as well, just to even out the fight, but he trusted the self-defense and hand-to-hand combat skills he'd honed his entire life. Haddad protected his torso instinctually with his upraised arms as the door moved.

The pane opened and Stuart and Haddad both jumped out again, then walked simultaneously through the door. Stuart turned left to face the bathroom area and Haddad turned right to face the sleeping area: both were empty. Haddad felt his pulse drop suddenly and the urge to fight was replaced with the maddening urge to sleep. He felt his eyelids drooping and rubbed them to fight the post-adrenaline reflex.

"Now what?" Haddad looked around the room.

"He's here somewhere," said Stuart in a predatory tone. "This ship is only so big." She turned and walked out of the room, and Haddad followed again.

They moved to the next door: Gutierrez's room. Stuart and Haddad followed the same routine, entered the room together, and found nothing again. Stuart spotted the stuffed teddy bear Gutierrez had synthesized to use as a pillow and her stomach dropped to her feet. The loss of life was unbearable, even in a normal-sized population, but in a crew that represented the last of humanity it was absolutely an affront towards God. A deep underlying steely feeling took hold in Stuart's stomach—she had to stop that creature from inflicting any more damage.

They continued back to Wren's door and Haddad nodded. "Should we check back in there again?"

"Yeah." Nodded Stuart. "He could've snuck back in."

Stuart and Haddad walked up to the door side-by side. The pane opened to a view of the back of Wren's chair, and they saw her arm extending out, hanging limply, Roxanna desperately rubbing against her calves. Both Stuart and Haddad ran to her side, shocked to see their physician sitting in her chair almost comatose. No blood on her body, but wounded nonetheless.

"Cindy? Can you hear me?" Stuart asked softly. Haddad averted his eyes out of habit. He felt like a criminal just for being his gender at that moment.

Wren didn't move for a minute, then blinked. She looked up in to Stuart's eyes.

"Get him," Wren said to Stuart with a look of pure hate in her eyes.

THIRTY-SIX

SCHWARTZ COULDN'T UNDERSTAND how that bitch had gotten his code: that was his, given to him by his Father, and no one else was supposed to use it. He was the only agent of the President still left standing, so in a sense he was the only one authorized to have it. Stuart was hacking the system, and would need to be punished—Schwartz figured a good 'ol bun in the oven would do the trick, then into cryosleep before she went to term. That would keep Stuart in line and keep the species afloat. As the new Father of the Human Race, Schwartz felt that was an appropriate solution.

Without the primacy of the code, though, he would have to change his strategy. The plan was so much easier when he could just lock everyone up and play jailer, but now that some of his captives were on the loose and hunting him he had to do something different. *Stay one step ahead,* he thought to himself and smiled in pleased satisfaction.

Schwartz started by leaving the medical suite where he'd hid after impregnating Wren and moved to the science lab, where he used the code to log into the main monitoring system to see where Stuart was. She and Haddad were currently inspecting his room, and they looked like they were making their way suite-by-suite towards his location. He watched as they went from his room to Gutierrez's, and as soon as they entered Gutierrez's suite he ran back down the hallway all the way to the storage bay across the hall from his room.

Schwartz got a quick thrill as he ran by Gutierrez's doors, knowing Stuart and Haddad were inside but had no idea where he was. He slid inside the storage room and stood still for a second. It was one thing to play Hide and Seek, but Stuart and Haddad could still track him in this grownup version. Schwartz slid past a couple racks of matter blocks to the storage bay simulator on the left side of the door.

He squeezed his hand through the side of a rack and typed: HEAT BLOCKING SUIT. The simulator pulled up a couple different options of cloaking clothing he could use, and he picked a full-body jumpsuit that covered everything except his eyes in a size Large. The machine went to work and soon he had a full cloaking suit ready. Schwartz wriggled into the suit, pulled the mask over his head, and zipped the zipper at the front. He had the pad test his heat signature and smiled wickedly when the machine said it couldn't find him.

Schwartz slipped out the door and into his own quarters. With Stuart and Haddad moving on to Wren's room, he took a gamble they wouldn't retrace their steps. Inside his quarters, Schwartz leaned his back against the wall and sighed—he hadn't even noticed the huge erection he'd gotten just from running across the hall. The thrill of escaping capture made him want to fuck something so bad.

Schwartz looked at himself in the mirror; he was covered in a shiny silver material that made him look somewhat like the "spacemen" of old, or like some kind of metallic ninja. His eyes glared out from the holes and Schwartz almost imagined he could see himself in the court of a Japanese nobleman, there to defend the honor of the master. He smiled under the mask—the idea made him feel good.

Turning on the screen in his table, Schwartz sat down. There were camera views of every angle on the ship, and he wondered why Stuart hadn't bothered to consult any of them. Schwartz switched to the view of his room and saw himself as he looked in the silver jumpsuit: he blended a little, but still stood out from the white walls and floor surrounding him. Schwartz frowned for a second and walked over to his simulator, and in only a few minutes he'd swapped his silver cloaking suit for a newly-custom white cloaking suit. When he turned the camera on again Schwartz saw an empty room, and his smile widened to a predatory grimace under his mask.

In two steps Schwartz bounded over to his bed and lay down. He threw a white sleeping mask over his left eye; a quick check of his camera view confirmed he was pretty invisible, so Schwartz put the other half of the fabric over his right eye. He crossed his hands over his chest like a vampire and went down for a quick nap—being the new Father of The Human Race was tiring.

JIMMY SAT NEXT TO A BED. He saw his mother's frail little hand hanging over the edge, her skin so pale it was transparent —it somehow made Jimmy want to grab that hand, crush it, and see how purple it turned. He wanted to curse and scream at her for being such a selfish little bitch; for not getting him his dinner just right. He wanted to yell at her in all the ways he'd learned from his father. She looked like a beautiful First Lady on the outside of the Presidential Palace, but inside those walls she was abused and derided by her husband and son—it was no wonder she'd gotten cancer and it claimed her so fast. She had no will to live in that hellhole with the beasts she married and bore any more.

Jimmy watched as she rose from the bed like she was being pulled from above by a string. He tried to scream in horror and run but his legs were fused in place. He couldn't run, and his voice cracked into nothingness when he tried screaming.

She turned to face him. Her hair was stringy and her skin was pale and sweaty and her eyes had somehow turned black. She pointed at him slowly, fingers hanging in an accusatory claw.

Schwartz finally screamed.

———

HE WOKE up still screaming and clapped his hands over his mouth almost immediately. The white eye cover fell to the floor and Schwartz rolled to his belly so his eyes wouldn't show to the room camera. He looked at the floor and walked shakily to his chair.

Schwartz turned and stared out his window screen into the darkness.

THIRTY-SEVEN

AS SOON AS the doors to Wren's room closed, Haddad looked over to Stuart, his voice cracking. "What the fuck are we going to do?" he asked mournfully.

"We have to find him," Stuart's eyes flashed fiercely, her voice echoing Wren's words with a steely resolve. "We'll find him and make him pay for this."

"How?"

"We gotta plan this better," Stuart tried catching her breath. "Let's head to the bridge, enough of this running for a second. He could just be going room to room evading us." Her head felt hot and she wanted to scream and lash out at anything. She stopped her hand, though; because Haddad didn't deserve the beating she so wanted to give.

The two sprinted to the bridge, where Stuart entered the special code and the doors opened to an empty room. Stuart and Haddad both breathed a sigh of relief as Stuart closed the door and locked it with the code again. She stepped over to her control screen and frowned at the footprint marring one corner —she knew she hadn't left that; the only culprit was Schwartz. That made Stuart rage inside, knowing he'd invaded her space like that—it made her want to flay him alive, starting with the penis first.

Stuart ran a scan of all the lifeforms on the ship; the computer scanned the body heat signatures of all the occupants and came back with a total: six.

"Fuck." Stuart stared at the screen.

"What's wrong?" Haddad looked at her with concerned eyes.

"The ship's only counting six people, three in cryosleep." Stuart felt a knot in her belly twist hard, remembering they were already down three crew members.

"Where the fuck did he go?" Haddad sat down at his own desk and started up the scanning software for his own check.

Stuart rubbed her forehead, feeling a headache brewing. "I think he's synthesized a heat-blocking suit."

"Really? That fast?"

"Yeah. He knows we can track him with his body heat, so I'm sure that's one of the first things he thought of." Stuart ground her teeth, thinking about Schwartz hiding out on her ship somewhere.

"Fuck." Haddad seconded Stuart's frustrated response.

Stuart looked over at Haddad. "I think we need more hands on deck for this."

"Agreed." Haddad nodded. "Who?"

"Bill," Stuart spoke almost immediately. "We need him... sober or not."

"You think the rehab program worked?" Haddad raised his eyebrows.

"I'm praying so."

"Then let's do it."

Stuart nodded at Haddad and waved him to follow her. "Let's stick together."

"You got it." Haddad stood and followed Stuart to the door. They waited for a second while Stuart typed in the code, then he watched the hallway while Stuart locked the bridge door again behind her. She hoped the code would at least slow Schwartz down if he tried getting into the bridge while they weren't there. Once the bridge door was secure, the two sprinted towards the med bay, checking the corners and covering each other like police officers, only without guns. Stuart typed the special code into the med bay doors and then locked them with the code as soon as she and Haddad were inside.

They looked to the back corner, where Bill Galloway lay asleep in the med pod; the head surgeon looked peaceful, like a happy corpse. He had a little smile curling the corner of his mouth, and his hair was rumpled in a way Stuart found perversely funny.

"I hate to have to wake him," she said as she stared down at Galloway's face.

"Yeah," agreed Haddad. "Ignorance is bliss."

Stuart hit the WAKE sequence start button and the pod sprung to life: it hissed and they both watched as Galloway's skin got rosier, like he was transitioning back from the grave. Galloway moved around in the tube a little, Stuart watched as his hands twitched and jerked a few times, then started curling in and out of fists. He moaned and it was loud enough that both Stuart and Haddad heard it outside the pod.

"Almost done buddy!" Stuart called in a kindly voice, hoping Galloway could hear her. After a few more minutes the pod gave a beep and flashed WAKE COMPLETE on the screen. The door opened and Galloway blinked his eyes.

"Welcome to the land of the living," said Haddad, trying to sound jovial.

"What the fuck happened to me?" asked Galloway. He shuddered and immediately started vomiting. Stuart cursed herself for being unprepared and ran to the simulator to simulate a bowl. Once it was made, she ran back to Galloway and held it under his retching mouth. He took hold of the bowl with an exhausted yet grateful look and continued purging his system.

Stuart and Haddad both watched Galloway as he came back from cryosleep. A little clock ticked in the back of Stuart's mind, and she wondered where Schwartz was and who he was hurting right now. Her heart raced with the panic that they weren't moving fast enough.

Galloway finished vomiting and looked back and forth between Stuart and Haddad, "Why the honored wake-up call?"

"Long story," started Stuart. "Schwartz's gone rogue."

"More so than usual?" Galloway raised an eyebrow.

"He's killed Williams, Simon and Gutierrez, and raped Wren."

Galloway just stood like he'd been slapped, then promptly collapsed to his knees. "Oh Cindy," he said softly under his breath.

"She needs you and we need you," said Stuart, trying to refocus Galloway in a way that made her feel so mean. "Schwartz's loose in the ship and we have to hunt him down."

Galloway looked at Stuart with resolve. "What do you need me to do?"

"You sober?" asked Stuart, looking Galloway straight in the eyes.

He nodded.

"Can you stay that way?"

He nodded again.

"Good," said Stuart, relieved. "I couldn't risk losing you again. You scared the shit out of us with that...don't fucking do that to us again!"

"Yes Grace," said Galloway in a tone that firmly acknowledged his agreement. "I won't."

Stuart reached out and hugged Galloway tightly, almost out of instinct, and patted his back. "We missed you, Bill."

Galloway whispered back. "I'm sorry, Grace."

"I know." Stuart nodded as she released him from her embrace, understanding that he was apologizing for her losing

Pete as well. Galloway had been with them on the Pluto mission, and she figured he'd suspected something.

Haddad grabbed Galloway's jumpsuit and handed it to the head surgeon. Galloway put both his feet in, pulled the body up, zipped the front and looked at both Stuart and Haddad. "Ready."

"Good deal." Stuart forgot how quick Galloway was at cryosleep recovery. She went to the viewscreen in the med bay, turned it on, and set it to the view where every body heat signature glowed red on the screen. "We've been working our way down the hall trying to flush each room, but haven't found him yet."

"No sign?" asked Galloway.

"Not yet." Stuart grumbled, the frustration evident in her voice. She thought for a moment, then looked over at Galloway. "I think we need to wake up Forester and Patel."

Galloway looked surprised. "You really think they can fight this guy?"

"No." Stuart shook her head. "But it sure beats being killed in your sleep. At least this way they stand a fighting chance, and we can all stay together."

"Oh god." Galloway's voice broke as he imagined Schwartz cutting the plug to all the cryosleep tubes, killing the inhabitants. "He wouldn't really do that, would he?"

"I'm praying he hasn't made it that far yet," finished Stuart. "Given what Schwartz's already done, I'm sure he's going to try."

"I'll get down there and get on it," said Galloway as he started moving towards the door, then he stopped suddenly. "Weapons?"

"Fuck, that's right," said Stuart, suddenly realizing what she'd forgotten all along. "Let's do a few stun guns."

"Only stun?" asked Haddad.

"We cannot afford any more loss of life," said Stuart resolutely, "even his."

"If you say so..." Haddad's voice sounded eerily like Stuart's mother when she wasn't sure of a decision.

The three walked to the simulator and Stuart entered her captain's code. It still was the only code that could make weapons of importance: even the President's code couldn't. After a few minutes the machine spat out three stun devices and Stuart, Haddad and Galloway each took one.

Galloway suddenly stopped. "Can I see Cindy first?"

"Yeah," said Stuart, again feeling suddenly so shallow. "Absolutely, but keep your eyes peeled for Schwartz."

"Will do," Galloway mused. "You guys comfortable waking up Aditi and Brian?" asked Galloway to both Haddad and Stuart. Haddad and Stuart nodded. "I'll be there shortly," Galloway finished.

"Okay," agreed Stuart. She felt a pang of worry in her stomach about being temporarily split up, as Galloway turned away towards Wren's apartment.

GALLOWAY WALKED across the hall to Wren's room and took a deep breath before he entered. He tapped in the President's code he'd learned from Stuart and Haddad and watched the panes part like the Red Sea in the old Hebrew stories.

He beheld the room, sterile and cold. His heart panicked for a minute when he couldn't find Wren anywhere, then he spotted the two ankles visible from the lower part of Wren's chair. The kitten sat beside them, looking up at the chair's occupant. He approached closer on tiptoe, somehow feeling like a criminal himself. He settled himself and cleared his throat.

"Cindy?" he asked softly.

"Don't look at me!" she hissed from behind the chair.

Roxanna skittered back to the corner. He could hear Wren sobbing.

"Oh honey," he said, on the verge of tears.

"Don't call me that!" she hissed again, her voice cracking.

"I'm sorry and I love you," he whispered. Even then, the sound seemed to ring off the walls.

Wren turned her chair and he beheld her small frame, hunched and curled around her midsection. She looked even smaller than normal and her eyes were sunken. Galloway walked up to her and dropped to one knee, then took her left hand. Wren flinched like she'd been burned, but Galloway held her hand lightly.

"You're cold," he said softly, "let me get you another blanket."

Wren didn't respond but Galloway stroked her hand and went to the simulator. He ordered up the warmest, thickest, fuzziest blanket he could find and selected the color purple–her favorite. She started crying as soon as he draped the blanket around her and he held her immersed in warmth.

They both cried. Galloway stroked Wren's hair and tried wiping her tears, but his own tears got in the way. He didn't care, just held her as best as he could.

"I was too scared to stop him," whispered Wren through her sobs in to Galloway's chest.

Galloway rocked Wren back and forth. "It's okay."

"He wanted me pregnant," she said a little louder, with a note of anger in her voice. "He was acting like he wanted to be the father of the human race. It was so surgical."

Galloway held Wren closer. He didn't know how else to respond.

"Is it fucked up to say I don't know if I can abort it?" she asked Galloway. "Not after Joey...not with us being the last..." She sobbed into Galloway's chest and he could feel his jumper getting wet. "God, I miss Joey so much..." Her voice pinched and trailed off.

Galloway looked down at the crown of Wren's head, but spoke in a whisper. "I think that zygote is <u>yours</u>. You can do whatever you want with it." His eyes hardened. "I think that monster has no rights, with the act he committed."

Wren's eyes showed surprise, but she nodded.

Galloway continued, his face getting red with the power of his conviction. "I think he's permanently damaged his own soul. I think he's vacated any right to be called a man. What he did is what an animal would do, so he's no better than any lowly animal that can't control its urges. We geld bad animals so they can't breed or abuse any more—I think he deserves that. He's no longer a human in my eyes. He's spat in God's face with the one pure act that's supposed to be loving."

Wren exhaled a little puff of air. She sat back and pressed her hands to her uterus, still feeling conflicted whether she wanted to keep any possible pregnancy or abort it. In a normal situation, she would have taken a Levonorgestrel dose and terminated the prospective pregnancy immediately, but even Wren understood that their situation had changed dramatically: even the product of a rape was valuable genetic diversity for future generations, as hard as it was to process. Then she thought about holding baby Joey in her arms, and saw the little boy's impish smile.

"I claim this baby as mine," she said firmly. "I alone am its parent and teacher. May the sperm donor be cursed for his actions." She breathed deeply and exhaled slowly. When she was done she looked up at Galloway. Her eyes didn't seem as sunken any more: she wasn't smiling, but something in her seemed a bit better.

"I'll help you with the baby," said Galloway earnestly. "It'll be a joy...the first baby in space! Especially good that it'll have two doctors for parents," he finished with a smile.

"Yeah," Wren sighed, earnest in her own right. "Can I ask

you something personal, Bill?" She looked Galloway in the eyes, and he suddenly realized how blue Wren's eyes were.

"Fire away."

"You still craving the heroin?"

Galloway sat and thought for a minute. When she said the word it was the first time in all his recent memory that he hadn't gotten a chill from the name of the drug. "You know, I don't think so," he said with astonishment. "Damn!"

"The programming cycle worked!" A small smile brightened up Wren's face.

"Yeah," agreed Galloway. "I think it did."

"I wonder if it could take the sociopath out of him," Wren asked out loud.

"Schwartz?" Galloway paused. "It might." He scratched his chin. "If you'd asked me a year ago if I believed in the reprogramming software, I would've given you a tirade on how it was the end of mankind. Now, I think I'm actually grateful to that damn program."

"You really don't feel any urges?" asked Wren.

"Nope," said Galloway, sounding palpably relieved. "I didn't even get the shivers or a hard-on to the name."

"Good," Wren nodded. "I can't go through what you put me through again."

"Thank you, Cindy," said Galloway hoarsely. "I owe you for everything."

Wren was happy to finally hear those words coming out of Bill Galloway's mouth. "You're welcome," she said and squeezed his hand.

They both sat and stared at each other for a little while, then Galloway wrapped Wren back up in a hug. He knelt on his knees and embraced Wren's lower legs, laying his head in her lap. She stroked Galloway's hair, staring at the darkness beyond her viewscreen.

"I gotta call her," said Wren suddenly with a jerk.

"Who?" Galloway's eyes perked up.

"Grace," Wren answered. "I have to tell them not to kill Schwartz."

"What?" asked Galloway, surprised.

"I'm gonna reprogram him. I want that bastard alive."

THIRTY-EIGHT

STUART WALKED down the hallway and felt a strange urge to hold Louis' hand. She'd never noticed the electric charge crackling between him and her before, but it was there now, just dancing under the surface of their interactions.

They got down to Patel and Forester's doorways and Stuart nodded for Haddad to take Forester. She entered the President's Code into Patel's door panel and went inside.

Patel's window screen was dark, showing an evening view of a rainforest. Stuart walked over to Patel's pod and marveled at how the scientist could be so exacting yet also decorate her suite perfectly: the room didn't quite feel like it was on a spaceship, and Stuart told herself to ask Patel to decorate the whole ship if they made it through their encounter with Schwartz alive.

She approached Patel's pod and looked in on the scientist, so serene in her pink pajamas.

"Sorry Aditi," said Stuart as she pushed the wake sequence button, knowing the hateful nausea Patel had to look forward to.

The machine went to work and started the awakening process, activating Patel's tissues slowly to clear the cryosleep material from her system. The inhaled gases passed the old toxins and drugs into her bloodstream, then cleared everything out through another set of fluids delivered by IV upon awakening. They did the job remarkably well compared to some of the old water-immersion methods, but the side effect was still nausea.

Patel's eyes fluttered and Stuart held a bucket at the ready— she opened the cryosleep tube and as soon as Patel sat up Stuart handed her the bucket. Patel looked at Stuart with grateful eyes and began throwing up immediately. After minutes of retching she looked up at Stuart with sadly exhausted eyes and handed her the bucket.

"Here you go," answered Stuart and she handed Patel a glass of room-temperature water and some saltine crackers. Patel sipped the water and munched the crackers.

"How'd you know this would work?" Patel mumbled as she finished a cracker. "Thanks, by the way," she added quickly.

"It's my secret trick." Stuart smiled, momentarily forgetting the situation she was in. "I've had to do this sleep program so many times, you develop ways to make it more palatable. Water and crackers help, when you're ready I'll get you some sports drink."

Patel nodded and Stuart went to the simulator to get her a glass. She ordered the most basic flavor: orange. The glass came out frosty and cold and Stuart cursed in her head as she re-made the glass of drink to be room temperature. Anything cold would send Patel back to vomiting again—Stuart knew from experience.

"I'm really sorry we had to wake you early," Stuart walked back to Patel with the glass of sports drink in hand. "We've got a problem."

"What?" asked Patel, her eyebrows raising. "What's happened?"

"Schwartz's gone rogue."

"Shit."

"Yeah," answered Stuart, her voice hitching. "He's killed Williams, Gutierrez and Simon and raped Wren." Patel flinched at the last part.

"Why do you need us, then?" Patel waved her hands for effect. "What am I going to be able to do against a crazed engineer?"

"We wanted you awake so at least you stood a fighting chance," Stuart clasped her hands together as Patel's eyes widened with recognition. "We were worried he'd pull the plug while you were in cryosleep."

"Shit," sighed Patel. "I always wondered about that fucker. What can I do?"

"We need to form a plan to find him and kill him." Stuart's eyes looked particularly intense, focusing on Patel like a laser.

"Where is he?" Patel looked at her door on instinct, terrified Schwartz might come walking in.

"Don't know," said Stuart with a vexed tone to her voice, "he's been jumping from room to room. Not showing up on the infrared now."

"He got a heat-blocking suit." Patel nodded knowingly.

"Yup...my thoughts exactly."

"So how are we going to track him down?"

"Are there any ways to spot the heat signature in one of those suits?" Stuart looked Patel up and down.

"Yeah, you can just barely see the outline if you set the heat settings way below the normal reading threshold," said Patel. "I used that method to track some really interesting shrimp once."

"Could you do it from the bridge?" asked Stuart.

"Yeah," Patel scrunched her nose slightly before she continued. "I can download my software codes from Luisa's desk, I think." Patel inhaled sharply after mentioning Gutierrez and looked at her hands, suddenly remembering that the planetary scientist was dead.

"Good, let's go," Stuart's eyes trembled with urgency, "I'm praying we'll see Louis and Brian when we get there."

"Brian's okay?" Patel asked as her eyes lit up.

"I hope so," Stuart nodded. "Louis went next door to wake him and we've been running silent. I'm hoping to see them just as much as you are."

"Why do you think he did it?" asked Patel.

"Schwartz?"

"Yeah," said Patel.

"He has some special code that the President gave him. It was a master code that controlled almost everything on the ship—got him access to doors that should have stayed locked, and also let him simulate things he shouldn't have gotten," said Stuart as she watched Patel change from her pajamas into her jumpsuit. "My guess is the President tasked him with command takeover, and he's just doing what he's programmed to do."

"Fuck, really?" asked Patel.

"I wouldn't put it past our 'ol Presidente," said Stuart. "I had a bad vibe in the pit of my stomach ever since I found out he wanted little Jimmy on our flight."

"But why a science mission?" asked Patel, "we weren't doing anything that exciting, I thought…"

"Yeah, me too," agreed Stuart. "I don't understand either but there's just no other explanation I can come up with for him having that code. I've seen a couple Presidents in my time, and this one sure liked his control—I wouldn't have put it past him to send his son to do his dirty work."

"He makes even the skin on my toes crawl," said Patel as she followed Stuart out the door towards the bridge. "I think anything female felt his eyes."

"Yeah," Stuart pursed her lips like she tasted something bitter. She walked quickly around the corner just in front of Patel to check the hallway for Schwartz. With the coast cleared, she waved Patel on and the two trotted to the bridge doors. Stuart entered the now-infamous code and the doors parted.

Inside, Haddad waved to Stuart and Patel as he held a bucket for Forester who was dry-heaving over the top.

"I got him here as fast as I could."

"Thanks," Stuart sighed in relief and wiped the sweaty sheen from her nose.

"No problem," he answered. "You ok?" Haddad looked over at Forester, who gave the thumbs-up sign but continued retching in the bucket.

Stuart was about to talk when the intercom crackled to life.

"Grace...are you there?" asked Wren softly into the speaker.

"We're on the bridge, Cindy. You okay?"

"You have Schwartz?"

"No, not yet."

"Good."

"Wha?" Stuart looked confused at the ceiling, not sure how to respond.

"I want you to bring him to me alive," said Wren, sounding frightening on the other end of the intercom, then firm. "I want that fucker alive."

The connection clicked silent.

———

SCHWARTZ SAT up from his bed and walked over to his desk, careful to keep his eyes pointed downward so they wouldn't show up on the ceiling monitor. He sat down and immediately pulled up the views of every room in the ship, where he saw six red blobs communing on the bridge. *Shit,* he thought to himself while he watched the heat blobs move around on his viewscreen.

The bridge was not good. Six bodies moving around...that

meant they'd woken up the two scientists, and Galloway. Schwartz paced back and forth in front of his window. He stopped still in his tracks after a moment and realized he was probably visible against the black backdrop. He sat back in his chair and tried surreptitiously tapping the code to change his window covering from the black space outside to a white hologram that mimicked the room's three other walls. Once that was completed, he stood back up and started pacing again.

Schwartz walked round and round in his room; staring at his feet had the strange combination of making him feel dizzy but also more focused. He thought about how to get at those people on the bridge: they obviously had his code now, as evidenced by how that Korean bitch was able to get out of her room in the first place.

He seethed at how she'd been able to get that code. His father told him it was a secret between the two of them...why had his father betrayed him and given it to that whore of a captain? Why did she rate? He immediately conjured an image of Captain Stuart kneeling at his father's crotch and smirked. *Oh that's how...*he thought. *Wouldn't put anything past that cunt.*

Schwartz wanted to chew his fingernails but the cloaking suit's gloves got in the way. He sucked at the cloth and nibbled it; not quite the same, but still satisfying in some way. Exhausted, he lay down on his bed and rolled so his back faced the room camera, but he fought sleep—instantly terrified of his mother's pointing hand. Instead, Schwartz stared at the wall and started counting down from two million: he'd done that since he was a boy when he needed to calm down. It'd been the child psychologist who recommended it–*one of the only good things that asshole headshrinker ever did for me,* thought Schwartz.

His eyes started drifting and Schwartz settled down to sleep. After only a few minutes he started awake, again seeing his mother's pointing hand. Schwartz clapped a hand over his mouth when he tried screaming—he knew they could hear audio of his room too, so he wanted to be as silent as possible.

It was terrible. He couldn't stop that dream from running on a loop in his head. She was staring at him like she knew all the evil of his heart, and he instantly knew she was right: he was just as evil as her stare accused. He'd spent his life of privilege enjoying all the hedonism and ego fulfillment his heart desired, and had neglected any generosity. That he somehow made it on this ship as one of humanity's last creatures was somewhat of a miracle to him. It proved, in his mind, that God did not exist—if anything, it proved he <u>was</u> God.

Hunger growled in Schwartz's stomach and he wanted to go over to the simulator so badly he could taste it. He didn't think he could eat a meal quick enough to avoid detection, so he walked slowly to the simulator with his head down. He quickly ordered a nutrition juice pack, pierced the top of the packet with a straw, and sucked his dinner down while keeping his eyes to the floor. He hoped it was fast enough that no one saw.

This went on for three days; Schwartz checked his room clock occasionally and saw how time passed, always slowly and never-ending, surrounded by all that white. He paced the room until he was hungry, would drink a nutrition pack as quickly as he could, then return to pacing again. Occasionally he'd lie down, but now Schwartz had gotten smart: he put tape over his mouth so if he woke screaming nothing came out but a few muffled grunts. It was the only way he knew to avoid detection.

THEY'D BEEN WATCHING monitors for days.

"How the fuck did he disappear?" asked Galloway, pacing in the background while Wren sat quietly behind him.

"He's really good in that cloaking suit," Stuart growled, running a hand through her hair.

"Shit." Galloway rubbed his chin and paced some more.

Stuart scratched her temple. Her eyes were blurry and she felt like she'd been watching all the screens for an eternity. "Guys." She rubbed her eyes. "This isn't working. He's here somewhere, but I just can't tell where."

Patel's eyes brightened and she stood up, talking and walking in Stuart's direction at the same time. "Grace, I have an idea!" She looked like she'd just figured out a cure for some dangerous disease.

"What's up?" Stuart looked up, grateful for the break from staring at the screen.

"Hear me out guys." Patel breathed harder and Stuart saw a little sheen of sweat coating her upper lip. "What do prey animals do when there's a predator on the loose?"

Haddad looked confused. "Hide?"

Patel nodded. "Yeah, hiding for sure, but what else?"

"Camouflage?" Piped up Forester.

"Exactly!" Patel grinned and pointed at Forester like he'd just won a gameshow. "Schwartz is basically our predator right now, and we're his prey. But what if we turn the tables?" Patel's grin spread wickedly. "What if we play his game too, and we all wear those suits? We've got the numbers, and I think if we all stick together we can flush him out. Or at least wait him out, and we can fuck with him at the same time." Her eyes flashed fiercely, her smile wide.

"That's awesome, Aditi." Stuart stared at her biologist, watching as the petite woman seemed to grow larger in spirit, if not in size. They had all stayed put on the bridge and simulated some cots, where each person took turns on 'watch duty' looking for Jimmy. One person watched the door at all times, serving as the lookout, and they all slept on rotation.

Haddad nodded vigorously. "I like it, Grace. And I think I have just the thing to help us."

"What's that?" Stuart looked at Haddad and smiled, and the way her eyes glinted caught Haddad directly in the heart.

Haddad shivered, trying to tame his heart palpitations. "I think I can tweak the simulator code to make us a heat-blocking suit that can also be nearly invisible."

"How?" Galloway raised his eyebrows and focused on Haddad, interest streaming from his gaze.

"If I ask the simulator to cover the suit with an exo-layer of thin viewscreen material, then put little dot cameras on the suits, I think I can program them to read the area you're in, and make you invisible against it."

"Shit! Really, Louis?" Galloway looked impressed.

Haddad nodded. "Yeah. Let me try one first."

Haddad got to work running he custom program, designing the suit from his desk and sending the data to the simulator. The machine made a series of humming and buzzing noises, and at one point it made a groan that made the whole room jump. After nearly ten minutes of work, the doors opened and Haddad removed the garment.

It looked like any normal white hooded jumpsuit, but there were small dots at key points all over the garment. Haddad stepped his feet into the legs, then drew the cloaking suit up and put his arms in, as well as his head in the hood. He zipped the entire garment up, and when he was done he resembled a ninja or hazardous materials handler, clothed in white.

"Nice one, Lou." Stuart looked Haddad up and down.

"Alright," Haddad checked over his body, inspecting the suit's arms, legs and torso. "Let's try this." He pressed a button on the suit's arm, and suddenly only Haddad's face was visible, floating against the viewscreen background like some disembodied ghost.

"Whoa!" Patel chortled. "It's perfect, Lou!"

Haddad grinned. "Thanks, Aditi."

"Let's check it." Forester turned to Simon's desk, taking the seat and turning on the heat signature view of the bridge: it showed the hot red body heat images of Stuart, Patel, Galloway, Wren and Forester, as well as the bright red image of Haddad's face, floating like a balloon in space. "Works!" Forester chortled. "Great one, Lou."

"Thanks Brian." Haddad walked over to Forester's screen and looked at the image, and the rest of the crew gathered around like a group of surgical interns following their resident. Haddad frowned for a second, then looked up at the group. "I think I need to simulate a mask for this too." He turned to the simulator, where he ran his material hybridization code and fed it into the simulator program for a face mask. Within five minutes, he had a mask simulated, which he then put on.

The effect was eerie; Haddad had completely disappeared, except for his eyes, which floated in the vicinity where his face used to be visible. When he moved, there was a slight shimmer at the edges of the suit.

Patel shivered. "That's kinda creepy, Louis. But...wow!"

"I'll make one for each of us." Haddad spoke from the area of his floating eyes. "I think if we keep our eyes down on the screens, we'll be able to hide pretty well from him. Anyone sleeping can use an eye mask to cover up completely. I'll simulate those too."

Within the hour, they were all clothed in Haddad's new cloaking suits. The only way the crew could recognize each other was by their floating eyes, which made Stuart feel a little like she was in one of the old *Scooby Doo* cartoons where everyone was hiding in a dark, haunted castle. Haddad and Galloway had worked together at the beginning to simulate a couple futon-style mat beds, as well as a composting toilet and supplies for Roxanna. The ship's cat was the only creature not cloaked, and she looked oddly forlorn if you viewed her from any one of the viewscreen modes. She still smelled her humans, though, so they were occasionally given away when Roxy rubbed against someone's leg, which looked in the viewscreen like she was vigorously rubbing herself against some imaginary surface.

Gathered and prepared, the bridge crew waited for their quarry to reveal himself.

THIRTY-NINE

PATEL SAT STARING at Schwartz's room. She'd gotten the unlucky draw but felt obligated since she knew watching that room would freak Brian out: he was a sweet man, but not suited to a manhunt.

Aditi, on the other hand, loved a good chase: she figured that was why she was a biologist, and Forester a botanist—the action. She loved hunting down a zebra, tranquilizing it, then setting it free; he loved staring at an orchid for hours, but their friendship had honestly surprised them both.

They'd worked together on the ill-fated SPRINGTIME mission to colonize the moon; riots had taken place and destroyed the complexes only a year before the comet hit Earth. It was a shame, because there'd been enough humans and DNA in that colony to at least give the human race a fighting chance. Now there were only the few people left on the Metis.

Patel and Forester ran the botany and animal labs on that colony so well they'd had a full garden with animals on the moon within two years. The President had awarded them the Science Merit Medal for their feat, and they'd watched all their hard work burn when the angry colonists decided to riot against the management. The management had mis-handled the situation and used too much force, then someone ruptured an airlock and severed the electricity at the same time. The whole place decompressed and the fight was over. Both sides lost.

That mission had gotten them both on this ship, eager to recreate their miracle on a different moon: Titan. Patel figured if they ever got out of this shitshow with Schwartz they'd get their chance on Mars instead, and she'd already mapped out the setup in her head and knew how she'd like to get started. Forester would probably start with his base set of plants as well. She hoped they had enough room to get a few biomes going—that would help with diversity.

Suddenly she saw a flicker: something moved over by Schwartz's corner simulator. Patel rewound the video feed and watched it again on slow-motion, as a juice pack magically floated out of the simulator. She watched a tiny slot appear in thin air, then saw the juice pack's straw enter the slot. It was over in less than a minute, but Patel had her proof.

"The motherfucker's still in there!" Patel hissed to herself.

"What?" asked Forester, looking up from his screen.

"Schwartz's still in his room!"

"Really?" Forester moved to take a look at Patel's monitor.

"Look, see!" Patel rewound the video one more time and showed him the magical juice pack on slow-mo.

"I'll be damned!" Forester slapped his thigh. "What do we do?"

"Grace! Wake up!" Patel shouted into the quiet bridge air, unafraid if Schwartz heard her.

"Yuh?" Stuart mumbled, abruptly woken from her nap on the cots.

"I found him!" Patel's eyes glinted with sick glee.

"Schwartz?" Stuart's eyes widened and immediately focused.

"Yup," Patel breathed deeply. "The fucker's been hiding in his room the whole time!"

"Oh my God." Stuart sighed, both happy they'd found his hiding spot but frustrated at how they'd missed it too. "Is he still in there?"

"Yup," Patel grinned under her face mask, her voice slightly muffled. "I've got cameras on his door and the simulator now, looking for any more floating things."

"Floating?"

"It looks like a ghost is doing something funny when he's in the suit," Patel started, "stuff he's carrying looks like it's floating."

"He carries things?" said Stuart.

"Food, really," said Patel, "that's all I've seen."

"Is his door locked?" asked Stuart.

"Yes," answered Patel, "as good as it can be. But he'll just use that damned code to get out."

"Yeah, the thing's pretty well useless now," said Stuart.

"Yeah," agreed Patel, "just another code. What do we do next?"

"Let's see what he does."

STUART PULLED AT HER JUMPSUIT, smoothing it out and getting the bunched fabric out of her crotch. Even the couple minutes of sleep were worth it, and she felt revived like she'd been dipped in cool water. She looked down to the floor where Haddad was lying on an air mattresses he'd synthesized. She could only see the mat, but heard soft snores coming from the general vicinity of Haddad's head.

He was sleeping, half on and half off the edge so his hand almost touched the floor. Stuart could just make out his outline, which looked like a distorted shimmer laying on the mattress. A fine string of saliva dripped from the corner of his mouth through a small hole in the cloaking suit, which ended up looking like a drip coming from thin air. Stuart thought it was so cute; watching the beautiful first mate in a position he'd admittedly be embarrassed by, but it somehow made him even more adorable in her mind. Stuart shook her head, feeling bad she had to wake him.

"Louis," Stuart reached out to Haddad, trying to sound soft and kind. "Time to wake up!" She shook his shoulder gently.

Haddad sprung to life and almost hit Stuart in the face with his thrashing limbs, mildly confused since she was still in a cloaking suit. "Muh? Huh?" he grunted as he shook his head awake. "Oh my God, I'm so sorry Grace!" he said in a panic, realizing he'd just about hit her. "What's up?"

"Patel found him."

Haddad's eyes immediately focused, "Where?"

"In his room."

"His room?"

"Yup, the whole time."

"Fuck, don't I feel like an idiot." Haddad shook his head and wiped at his hair with his left hand.

"Me too," agreed Stuart.

The two got up off the sleep pads and went over to the stations where Patel and Forester were sitting, watching their screens intently.

"So how're we going to catch this guy?" Stuart put her hands on the back of Patel's chair, looking at the screen.

"He thinks we don't know where he is," Patel looked up as Stuart arrived behind her.

"How do you know?" Stuart raised her eyebrows under her cloaking mask.

"He's doing the same thing every day...pretty much on a routine," answered Patel. "I watch him eat his lunch, take a nap, and every once in a while I can see him pass by something. He paces the room."

"And this shows he thinks he's safe?" asked Stuart.

"Yeah," started Patel. "If he thought we were out to get him he'd be hiding somewhere else, on the offensive. By hiding in plain sight he's telling us all he thinks we're stupid, and weak."

"He thinks we're stupid?" asked Galloway, his distaste evident.

"And that might not be a bad thing," Stuart touched Galloway's arm, trying to gently redirect his anger. "It might be better for him to keep thinking that."

"Yeah," chimed in Patel. "The fact that he doesn't know, that we know, can be a good thing."

"It's our only advantage right now," added Haddad.

"Then what do we do with it?" Galloway looked around the room.

"Hold on a sec." Stuart walked to the synthesizer and made a piece of paper and a pen. She felt so strange using something so old-fashioned, but she suddenly didn't want any record of what would come next. "Huddle around, guys." They all huddled close over the paper so it was blocked from view. Stuart started writing first.

"We need to play to his weakness," she wrote on the sheet. "His pride."

Haddad gently plucked the pen from Stuart's fingers and wrote a response: "We need to get him out of his room. He knows we'll see him if he opens the door, so we need a reason for him to come out."

Stuart nodded, though the action was hidden by her cloaking suit. Patel took the pen with a glint in her eyes, "We need to make a trap." She looked at each of the crew members as she finished and nodded firmly like she meant business. Stuart suddenly loved this new side to her biologist; there was a hunter vibe going on and Patel seemed viciously excited. "I've done this before," Patel continued. "Just like hunting a tiger...we need to lure him in with some bait and then strike for the capture," she finished writing.

"How do we trap him?" wrote Forester, looking concerned at Patel.

"With a stun gun," wrote Patel.

"What bait do we use?" wrote Forester again.

"Me," wrote Patel.

Forester immediately broke from the circle and started pacing and waving his arms in the "no" gesture, his cloaking suit wasn't able to keep up with the sudden movement, and it smeared and streamed at the edges, making his movements temporarily visible. He shook his head and looked directly at Patel, then came back to the circle and wrote on the pad, "NO!" He underlined it for emphasis.

Patel looked at Forester with a firmness in her eyes, the walked over and hugged him. She pointed at him and then took the pen to start writing again.

"He wants women," she wrote. "He doesn't think I'm a problem. He'll think I'm weak."

"But what if he hurts you?" wrote Forester.

Patel turned the page over and continued writing. "He's going to hurt me anyway unless we stop him."

Stuart took the pen and started writing on the pad. "I'll do it. He hates me with a passion, and I know he wants to hurt me. If I show myself, he'll come."

"How?" wrote Patel. Stuart broke from the circle to go synthesize a couple more sheets of paper and they tightened the circle while she was gone.

"I'll take off my suit, and go to my room," wrote Stuart as she came back to the group with a pen for everyone and some extra paper.

"Good," wrote Patel. "We can hide in the room with you. Circle around the predator and surround him. We can wait against the walls."

"Let's do it pack-style." Haddad took his own pen and wrote on the corner of the sheet, then tapped it with the pen's tip.

"We can all walk together with Grace to her room, make it look like the rest of us are still on the bridge."

"But we won't be." Galloway's grin spread to his eyes, and they glinted behind his face mask.

Patel kept writing. "We'll have to wait until he falls for the bait. Could take a while."

"How long with tigers?" wrote Stuart.

"Sometimes weeks," wrote Patel.

Forester suddenly realized that he might be in for a long period in a cloaking suit and his eyes registered his shock behind the mask. Patel and Stuart both looked at him and Patel wrote, "You still good with this?"

Forester settled himself and wrote on the paper, "Yes." He had a new look of focused determination in his eyes, as he tried psyching himself up for the challenge.

"Ok," wrote Patel. "Thanks, Briar." She looked Forester in the eyes and smiled. He smiled back at her, knowing her smile anywhere—even if he could only see through the slits in her cloaking mask.

Stuart looked at the group and started writing again. "Let's all stay on the bridge here for a day to make it look like we're still afraid of him." The group nodded and she continued. "I'll wait until the evening, and make it look like I'm tired...like I just couldn't stand being on the bridge, so I left to go be in private."

"But why would you want to leave us?" Patel wrote, then looked up at Stuart.

Stuart's eyes started tearing, and her body shook as she cried silently. All of her crew mates stared in shock as they witnessed their captain cry for the first time. Her fingers trembled as she took the pen, the finality of what she was about to write hitting her suddenly. "Pete and I were a couple." She stopped writing for a minute while her crew mates took in the news in silent shock. "We'd been together since the Pluto mission. Jensen asked us to keep it from interfering with our jobs, so that's why we kept it from you guys."

Patel reached across the pad and embraced Stuart, and Stuart gave in and relaxed in the biologist's arms as she cried. It felt good to finally mourn in the open. Within a minute, all the members of the team had followed Patel's lead, and they all embraced their captain in a group-hug. Something in that gesture spread an energy among all of them, linking them and strengthening their will. After a long time hugging silently, each member peeled off the pile and returned to the paper and pen.

"What do we do in the meantime?" wrote Galloway.

"We'll each take turns watching him on the cameras and keep sleeping in rotation here. Anyone sees him move they holler," wrote Stuart.

The group nodded in agreement and Haddad started writing. "Let's watch him today, and lay the trap tonight."

"And after that?" wrote Galloway again.

"Go time." Haddad nodded and his eyes gleamed.

Stuart took the pieces of paper from their conversation and recycled them in the simulator.

FORTY

SCHWARTZ SAT and stared down at the floor. He hung his legs over the edge of the bed, careful to do it in such a way he didn't break his disguise in the cloaking suit. To the outside eye it looked like the wall moved for a second, then stilled.

Schwartz could just barely make out the edges of his hands against the backdrop of the floor; it was strange losing track of one's own body and the visual effect was a bit unnerving. He felt like he was floating somehow and he had to curl his toes repeatedly to try and bring some kind of grounding to his body.

It didn't work. His head started spinning and Schwartz sprinted to the toilet—he didn't care that his white body showed up against the grey bathroom background. Schwartz threw up in the toilet and watched the proceeds from his last two nutrient packs go down the drain. He'd have to drink another. Great.

Schwartz was sick of the chalky taste from those packets. The first couple days had been okay; the packs almost tasted like a marshmallow candy. After a few days of the same regimen, though, they brought instant nausea to Schwartz's gut. He dreaded the taste, but those packets were the easiest way to eat in his disguised state. He knew if he had more time to program the machine he could probably make a more delicious nutrient mixture, but in his hurry he only ever made the pre-mixed ones. The slog went ever onward...

He stared down at the remains in the toilet. They splattered the sides in the disgusting way everything did in a non-water world. He pressed the button on the side and the sonic cleaner inside the toilet went to work. It broke the refuse down to its base atoms and stored the matter away for later—everything could be broken down to its atoms.

That gave Schwartz a thought: if he only needed atoms to make anything he needed, he only needed a little bit of seed from his male crew members to create future generations—the males themselves were unnecessary. He smiled and thought of all the female crew members docile and pregnant as he stood watch over them all and their precious cargo. The rest of the males could be broken down to their matter once their seed was harvested. His plan was getting so much better.

Schwartz suddenly didn't care if anyone saw him anymore. He was sick of the fucking juice packs and sick of just hanging on for mere scraps—he wanted to live, not fester in a jail of his own making. Schwartz pulled the mask off his face and walked to his simulator. He ordered up a burger with fries and a beer, then sat down at his desk, turning on the view monitor.

Stuart was alone on the bridge. He watched as she milled around and did her work. Schwartz watched as her heat signature moved towards the door, and he sat up a little as the small signature approached the door, then walked through.

Schwartz set down his food and drank from the beer as he watched the little red blob on the screen walk down the hallway and turn into Stuart's room. The size matched her.

It was time.

———

HADDAD LOOKED over at Stuart and suddenly felt an overwhelming urge to touch her cheek, even though it was obscured by the cloaking mask. The sudden intimate thought disrupted Haddad, and he had to break from what he was watching on his screen; he walked over to the simulator to make a drink pack of coffee—a design he'd come up with to serve the crew all of their meals. He'd custom designed the packs with the same cloaking skin as their suits, so they could at least enjoy a little food surreptitiously while they waited for Schwartz.

"You want a coffee?" he asked softly as he neared the simulator.

"Oh yeah," she answered in a whisper. "Can you get me a pack of Ethiopian with vanilla creamer?"

"Coming right up."

"Vanilla creamer, again?" Galloway whispered in a slightly louder voice as he looked at Stuart with a raised eyebrow.

"Hey man, you know I've always liked it," defended Stuart with sheepish smile as she turned to look at Galloway. "I don't care how much crap you guys all give me. It's delicious and I will drink it until the simulators can make no more."

"Hey, someone's gotta keep you real," said Galloway with a wink. Next to Williams, Galloway had been on the next-most missions with Stuart. He missed getting Grace laughing like the old days.

"Yeah," answered Stuart, giving Galloway a hard time back. "Some of us just don't have the cast-iron gut from drinking quadruple Americano's like some people."

"Touché," Galloway laughed and he mocked a fanciful bow to Stuart, even though she couldn't see it.

"God what I wouldn't give for a piece of my mom's pie." Stuart sat back in her chair with a sigh. "She made the best blackberry one."

"Simulator?" asked Galloway.

"I tried it once." Stuart shook her head dejectedly. "Still wasn't the same."

"Even with the recipe?" asked Patel.

"Yup. Just wasn't right."

"I tried having it make my grandmother's ice cream once," said Haddad. "Same result."

"She made ice cream?" Stuart heard her stomach rumble at the mention of her dessert of choice.

"Yup," answered Haddad, "from scratch every time. She cooked until the end...called the simulator the 'spawn of the Devil'."

Stuart laughed, "What was her best flavor?"

"Vanilla actually." Haddad smiled and didn't realize he'd licked his lips. "She did one that was so smooth and rich. I've tried replicating it with the simulator and even cooking it myself...can't do it."

"That's a shame." Stuart looked back at Haddad.

"What's your favorite flavor?" Haddad looked Stuart in the eyes and she realized his were the color of brown sugar.

"Mint chocolate chip." Stuart answered, smiling slightly under her mask. "Yours?"

Haddad laughed for a second. "Same," he countered. "I swear I'm not copying you!" He brought Stuart her invisible pack of coffee and set it on the edge of her view panel.

Stuart took a sip, sneaking it under her cloaking mask. "Perfect, thanks!" She grinned, stealing a glance at Haddad.

Haddad felt a little shock of electricity grab him in the heart when they locked eyes. "You're welcome."

———

PATEL LOOKED at the clock on her display: it read 21:00. "I think it's time."

Stuart glanced at her screen, "Okay...here goes." She

stripped the cloaking suit from her body, leaving her feeling strangely naked as she stood in the middle of the bridge floor, still fully clothed in her Space Command jumpsuit.

"Yeah, looks good." Patel nodded, her eyes piercing and hard, then she turned back to the viewscreen. Stuart looked like she was alone on the bridge. "We're ready."

The entire team gathered together just behind Stuart, close enough to follow her through all the doors without the timing mechanisms giving them away. They looked like an invisible entourage following a movie star, as Stuart walked slowly to the bridge doors and entered the special code; the doors opened and she started her walk down the hallway.

The pack stayed close in Stuart's wake, following her quickly to her room. Stuart felt their energy behind her, but everyone took great care to move silently, and then into their positions in her room. Galloway hugged close to the walls in between Stuart's simulator and the cryosleep tube, Patel stayed close to the wall next to Stuart's bathroom, and Forester took the viewscreen wall, camouflaging deftly against the blackness of space. Haddad stood right next to the entry door, ready to pounce at the first sign of violence. Wren had remained on the bridge, partly to keep control of that location, and partly because she wasn't ready to see Schwartz's face yet.

Stuart sat down at her desk, as her team beheld a person slowly letting her 'captain' title go; She looked somehow more relaxed and it spread to the crew as a result. She nodded at the group, pursed her lips, and waited.

SCHWARTZ WATCHED Stuart as she walked down the hallway, went to her room and went inside. He saw her lock her door and he giggled a little bit. "That won't help," he whispered.

Stuart was fussing around in her quarters; it looked like she was making herself a little something in the simulator, then she ingested whatever it was and went to the washbasin in her bathroom. Schwartz assumed she was brushing her teeth because he could see her arm moving in a slightly zigzag motion. After a few more minutes grooming, Stuart turned and went over to her bed. Schwartz smiled as she lay down.

A sour smell suddenly caught Schwartz off guard. It came from his armpits and he sniffed them a little closer to make sure he was the culprit; confirmed, he walked to his simulator, stripped, and ordered a new jumpsuit. While he waited, Schwartz went to his bathroom and hopped in the sonic shower.

He suddenly felt so free being naked and visible at the same time. Schwartz didn't want to admit the extended period in the cloaking suit had actually gotten a bit difficult—it was nothing compared to some of the military undercover training he'd done as a boy, but it did wear on you after a time. So did the nutrition packs.

The sonic shower scrubbed away at Schwartz's body until it was clean to a microscopic level. He climbed out of the shower and went to his simulator where a new jumpsuit and cloaking suit were waiting, then he put them all back on, but stopped right before he zipped up the cloaking suit. In a fit of inspiration, Schwartz synthesized up a little bit of his favorite cologne and dabbed a some on his neck and chest. After a second thought, he put a little on his groin as well. *Doesn't hurt to make a good impression,* he thought as he zipped both suits up.

Sufficiently clean, Schwartz went back to his monitor to check on Stuart. She was asleep on her bed, and she rolled over to face the wall as he watched. *Perfect,* he thought, as he grabbed his knife and went out the door.

––––

"HE'S MOVING!" whispered Haddad with a hint of alarm.

Stuart watched her wall screen as a faint shape walked down the hallway, obscuring things like doors and panels as it passed. If a person wasn't looking closely, it would have been easy to mistake Schwartz in his cloaking suit for a viewscreen anomaly.

"Everyone ready?" Stuart looked to her crew mates hidden against the walls. They all whispered "yes" in unison, then went back to holding still like statues. Stuart watched as Schwartz walked past the bridge hallway on his way to her room. A few ghostly fingers tapped the President's Code on her door panel, then the panes opened.

SCHWARTZ WALKED down the hallway feeling slightly invincible. He couldn't believe they'd been so stupid to not find him in the first place, and he felt even better about the mission he was on. To be the Father of The New Human Race was an honor, and he wished his Mothers felt the same way. Patel would grow to love him, he figured; after all, weren't her people used to arranged marriages anyway? Stuart would be the hardest, and he was glad to take care of her now.

He walked to Stuart's door and stopped for a moment. Schwartz couldn't believe how fast his heart was beating, and he tried slowing it just for a minute. His cock was already hard and burning with excitement, and it surprised Schwartz that a little Korean would get him so aroused; maybe it wasn't her, per se, but what he wanted to do to her. He wondered if he could drug her enough to enjoy getting fucked from behind, but that was for a later date.

Schwartz tapped his father's code into the panel and went inside.

HADDAD'S EYES were starting to get fuzzy from trying to be alert for so long. He didn't know how Patel could do this: staying alert and awake to catch something. The constant adrenaline was fatiguing his body, and Haddad's fingers flexed on the cloaked stun gun in his hand. It'd been a long time since he'd shot one, but the man in him wanted to stand up and defend Stuart as she faced this dangerous mission. The realist was suddenly very afraid of what he had to do: capturing a dangerously experienced murderer was not a guaranteed situation. He prayed to the All for courage.

Stuart's door opened and Haddad tensed. He watched Schwartz come in the door and was suddenly so overcome with rage he jumped on Schwartz's back like a tiger instead of using the stun gun in his hand.

FORTY-ONE

SCHWARTZ PITCHED FORWARD as someone hit him from behind. He lost his knife in the process and it went skittering across the floor towards Stuart's cryotube. He snarled, buckled to his knees and threw the attacker over his head and onto the floor. The man grunted and Schwartz could just make him out: the guy was wearing his own cloaking suit, the fucker. Schwartz kicked him in the groin, then jumped on the torso he could make out. He felt for the assailant's head, grabbed it, and smashed it back into the floor. The attacker fell silent.

Schwartz ran over to Stuart's cryotube and grabbed his knife. Stuart sat up in bed and shrieked, playing the frightened prey. "You hold still, missy!" Schwartz snarled as he pointed the knife at Stuart. She jumped to her feet and tried running around her table to the door; Schwartz followed her, and on the view monitor all you could see was a floating knife following Stuart.

Stuart screamed again and tried making it around her table but she caught her hip on the corner and went sprawling. Schwartz was on top of her in an instant and he held the knife to her throat. "Just be good like Wren and stay quiet," hissed Schwartz through his mask.

"Fuck you!" snarled Stuart as she brought her knee firmly up into Schwartz's groin. He snarled and sliced her throat in an automatic reaction, one he quickly regretted.

Schwartz turned to the viewscreen, but two eyes peered out of the darkness at him. He nearly wet himself, remembering his mother's cold gaze from his nightmares.

"Hi," said Forester as he punched Schwartz in the face.

<hr>

HADDAD WOKE to see Schwartz collapsed by the viewscreen, his facemask askew, and Stuart laying in a pool of her own blood and holding her throat.

"Grace!" he screamed as he rose to his feet and stumbled towards Schwartz and Stuart, trying to ignore the flashing lights dancing in front of his eyes. All he saw on the floor was the red stain.

Schwartz looked up and Haddad felt a rage so powerful his muscles hummed. He charged across the room and fell upon Schwartz again, this time bowling Schwartz over towards the window and onto his back. Forester and Haddad pinned Schwartz, and Forester felt his knuckles split when he made the next punch into Schwartz's nose.

Haddad beat his fist into Schwartz's face and each impact felt better than the last: he used both arms to pummel the engineer all over his body. Haddad felt like he was in a trance—the hitting felt so good and his bloody knuckles were numb to the pain. He watched as Schwartz's pretty face became increasingly featureless, and smiled a snarl of a grin as he felt Schwartz's cheek bone break.

Forester moved a little lower and beat Schwartz's ribs until he felt bones snap inside as well. He screamed as he punched Schwartz's penis and testicles, wanting so badly to cut all of it off and shove it in Schwartz's shitty little mouth. That was what

Forester wanted to do, but then he remembered Wren's request: *bring him back alive.*

Forester held his next punch and looked at the broken unconscious man below him.

WREN SPRINTED down the hallway from her hiding spot on the bridge. She caught a glimpse of what was happening on the monitor as she left the bridge, and it didn't look good. She saw Haddad jump on Schwartz instead of stun him, and she knew Forester didn't have the training to keep up with a Delta Fighting-trained man. In her heart she prayed Forester could stay alive long enough for them to stop Schwartz.

She ran down the hallway and tripped as she turned the corner. Wren hit the door at a dead run and smashed her nose; Schwartz had auto-locked it when he'd entered Stuart's quarters.

Wren cursed and entered the special code in the door. The code didn't take and she realized she'd mis-entered a number. She tried a second time while working to still her shaking fingers.

The door opened and Wren could see a head barely visible above the top of Stuart's desk. As Wren walked in the room, she moved to the side to get a better view: Haddad and Forester kneeling bloodied over Schwartz's prone body. Stuart lay bleeding on the floor, but she'd clamped a hand to her throat and Galloway was already tending to her with a recovery wand.

"Lou?" Stuart croaked softly as soon as Galloway was finished.

Haddad looked up from staring down at Schwartz's mashed face as if woken from a trance. His eyes cleared and he locked them with Stuart's.

"Grace?" he asked, his face full of joyful surprise as he got up from Schwartz's body and embraced Stuart. Haddad still didn't feel his hands; the blood from his knuckles soaked through the cloaking suit and got on Stuart's sleep shirt.

"We did it!" Stuart said softly as she held Haddad close.

WREN STARED down at Schwartz's pulverized unconscious face and looked up disbelievingly at Forester. The botanist cradled his injured hands while Patel clucked and cooed over him.

"Can we get it to the sick bay?" she asked, pointing to Schwartz. "We'll be able to handle everyone from there."

"Everybody grab a limb," said Haddad as he picked up Schwartz's right arm, "don't feel bad if you bump him."

"I think he's been bumped enough," said Stuart, patting Forester and Haddad on their backs. "Lou and Brian beat him for all of us." Forester beamed sheepishly, but his eyes retained their focused look; he sidled over to Patel but couldn't wrap his injured arms around her yet. They stood next to each other, basking in the victory.

Stuart walked over to Schwartz and grabbed his left arm. Galloway took his left leg and Haddad took his right. Forester cupped his arms underneath Schwartz's midsection; his hands were starting to throb and he couldn't close his fingers any more. Patel grabbed Schwartz's right arm by the wrist with a look of disgust. The five followed Wren as she led them out of Stuart's room and down the hallway to the medical bay.

Inside, Wren directed the group to set Schwartz down on the medical table closest to the door. She motioned Forester and Haddad to sit on the table next to Schwartz, and then made a warding-off motion towards Schwartz's body.

"You take that thing, Bill," said Wren with audible disgust. "I like the way it looks now...I don't want to see it get its face back yet."

"No problem," said Galloway, "you want me to do a little plastic surgery?"

"Yeah," said Wren. "That might actually be a good thing."

"Facial transplant?"

"You've done one before?" asked Wren back. She never knew he'd done a surgery so complicated.

"Yup," said Galloway.

"Successful?"

"Yup." Galloway said again with a nod.

They both looked at Stuart. "You okay with this?"

Stuart looked at them both. "I'm fine with it, as long as you tone down his looks a bit—it gave him a big ego before. Don't want that coming back after the procedure."

"Okay then," said Galloway. "I'll do my best...You take Brian, Lou and Grace."

Wren turned to Haddad and he nodded her off and pointed to Stuart. "Do her first," he asked.

Wren obeyed and headed to Stuart's table. She ran the healing wand over Stuart and quickly finished the job Galloway had started on her neck. Once the gash was sealed she ran a SCAR function and removed the white line from Stuart's throat. Within five minutes Stuart looked like she'd never had her throat slit.

Next, Wren turned to Haddad. "She's fine," Wren began. "Can I do you now?"

"Okay," said Haddad softly. Stuart came over and hugged him from behind.

Wren went to work on Haddad's fingers, setting the bones in each first, then addressing the cuts and bruises that had flayed them open. The healing wand hummed softly and Haddad felt the warmth working: it was like having all the pain magically slip away. He wished he could hug the wand's inventors. When Wren finished, he flexed each finger and clenched both fists, looking at both hands in amazement.

"Good as new?" asked Wren.

"Yeah." Haddad nodded, his voice soft with awe.

"How's the thing?" asked Wren over her shoulder towards Galloway.

"Getting ready for his new life," said Galloway, never raising his head and concentrating at the task at hand.

Stuart and Haddad sat to the side and watched Galloway work on Schwartz; Galloway re-shaped Schwartz's cheekbones and nose, re-did his lips and chin and altered the forehead a bit too. When he was finished, Schwartz looked like no one they'd ever seen before: he was not quite handsome, but not quite ugly.

"Just right," said Galloway, admiring his masterpiece. "You ready for the next step, Cindy?"

"Yeah," said Wren, looking coolly at Galloway's creation. "Keep him sedated until we get to the pod."

"Already one step ahead of you," Galloway said with a sly grin. "Sleeping Beauty here won't wake until he's a new person."

They put Schwartz in the med tube, fastening all the straps as his head lolled to the side.

"What were you thinking for a program?" Galloway asked Wren.

"I've created a custom one...you'll see." Wren stared at the remains of Schwartz with a cold gaze. "While you guys caught him I made his jail."

Galloway closed the tube and turned to Wren. "All yours."

Wren looked down at Schwartz like he was some kind of specimen in a bottle. She scrunched her nose and knit her brow as she frowned and bit her lip, then her features all relaxed and she nodded.

"Looks good, Bill." She nodded to Galloway.

"You like?"

"Looks nothing like the creature," answered Wren. She

started tapping the screen on the side of the pod, initiating the reprogramming sequence. The pod beeped and a title for Schwartz's verdict came up: MALE – AGGRESSIVE SEX CRIME, MURDER. NAME – JAMES SCHWARTZ. The pod beeped again and showed the title of Wren's new program: MALE – SENSITIVE, COMPASSIONATE. NAME – BOB NEWMAN.

"Here's hoping he can finally become a man," said Wren as she touched the INITIATE button.

EPILOGUE

STUART WALKED into Schwartz's room and checked his pod; they'd removed it from the Metis on the last unload down to Mars. The ship sat docked in a permanent orbit but powered down, with a monitoring program running silently on Stuart's control pad. All the systems checked out normal.

———

THEY'D TAKEN everything off the Metis and broken it down to base matter, even the fixtures and chairs—the only things still intact on the ship were the actual rooms, doors, and functioning systems. Anything superfluous was now base matter stored on Mars, and the landers waited patiently outside their habitats on the Martian surface. Thanks to the discovery of the underground warren the President had built on Mars, there was enough matter to last the crew and their families for at least three hundred years if they lived lavishly, and up to nine hundred if they lived frugally.

The systems on Mars had been dormant since the last expedition. Back in Space Command's final days Mars had been next on the list for a colony, but after the Moon riots Space Command shuttered the program and focused on trying to examine Titan. They'd hoped a longer distance to Earth might make the colonists a little more amenable to Presidential control —that had been the hope, at least.

Mars had enough labs and dormant facilities that every crew member could have their own wing, if they wanted it. Each person had chosen the opposite, however, and they all lived communally in the main wing together. There were individual rooms, but a shared kitchen and main living space.

Everyone worked on a first name basis now. There was no "leader" any more and Stuart loved it that way: she'd never felt right in the "Captain's" skin. The pilot in her loved flying those big ships, but she never felt comfortable lording power over another person.

Now they all pitched in together and focused on what individual skills they could each bring to the pie: Galloway and Wren made sure everyone stayed healthy, Forester created a beautiful forest and garden in one of the science modules, and Patel created small animals to farm in the other one. A third and fourth science module sat dormant, awaiting more use. Stuart and Haddad both endeavored to learn Williams' job to maintain the fusion reactors so they could help power this new community, and they all worked to call Mars home.

THE WHOLE GROUP gathered for dinner in the main kitchen. Forester stood at the counter chopping vegetables from his garden, while Patel dressed a chicken she'd butchered from the inaugural hatching. The simulator sat in the corner, unused, that evening.

Wren wrestled with her daughter, Olivia, while the one-and-a-half-year-old tried wriggling away to grab Forester's spade so she could chew on it. Wren tried balancing her massive overprotective urges by remembering her mother's story about a baby Cindy Wren eating dirt before her birthday cupcake. Little Olivia Wren was following closely in her mother's footsteps.

Sara Williams-Stuart sat on the floor, trying to make new combinations with a pile of brightly-colored toy blocks. Roxanna walked by and Sara reached her hand out, stroking the cat's tail gently; Roxy turned and meowed at the child, tapping Sara gently with her paw.

Stuart laughed and looked down at Sara, who was now trying to grab Roxanna by the tail. "No, honey. Roxy doesn't like that."

Sara looked up into her mother's eyes, grinned, and let go. The cat turned and walked away, twitching her tail as if to taunt the toddler.

When the meal was ready, all six grownups, the two children, and the cat sat down at the table to eat.

———

STUART AND WREN approached Schwartz's pod like it was a dangerous casket filled with a vampire.

"You sure you want me to do this?" asked Stuart.

"Yeah, I have to see if it worked. I have to see his eyes," answered Wren. She stared at the cryopod like it was a bomb.

"Okay," said Stuart, a tad disapprovingly. "If he's still bad, you want me to put him back under or kill him?"

Wren's eyes hardened for a second. "If he even shows the remotest possibility of going to the dark places again, kill him."

"Alright," said Stuart as she pressed the INITIATE button.

The pod gradually woke 'Bob Newman' and he went through the customary vomiting period. Stuart gave him a bucket while Wren sat across the room, watching Mr. Newman with uneasy eyes. When the vomiting was done, Wren walked closer to Newman and looked him in the eyes.

"How're you feeling, Bob?"

"Good!" he said with a clear and easy smile.

Wren looked deep into Bob's eyes, searching. His eyes were the same color as Schwartz's, but the look from within was soft and kind.

Wren smiled.

"WE ALL GOOD?" asked Louis when Grace came back in the main quarters.

"Yup," Grace grinned, taking Sara from Louis' arms. "How was our little munchkin?"

"She threw a fit when I had to take her out of Brian's garden," Louis gave Grace a weary smile as he ruffled the tuft of brown hair on Sara's head. "She was sitting and staring at his orchids."

"Were you a naughty girl?" said Grace to the squirming infant. Sara grinned and babbled like she knew she'd been a little feisty. "You gotta be nice to Papa," said Grace as she bounced the girl on her hip and gave Louis a kiss on the cheek.

The two parents smiled and held hands, then walked off to watch the Martian sunset.

THE ADVENTURE of the Metis isn't over! Stay tuned for more Mars exploration in: *Refuge.*

ABOUT THE AUTHOR

Stephany Brandt is a speculative science fiction author based in Oregon. Her novels are set in the Pacific Northwest both in present and future times, and her tales focus predominantly on the battles between good and evil, and the nature of love during trying times. Her works bear the influence of writers like Robert A. Heinlein, Arthur C. Clark, Stephen Baxter, Stephen King and Ursula K. LeGuin.

Ms. Brandt is the author of the upcoming novels *Perfect*, *Here* and *Feeding*. She received her creative writing training at the University of Oregon, graduating in 2001.

Stephany lives in Bend, Oregon with her husband Tobin, their loving 19 year-old cat, a pug from outer space, and a passel of pet chickens.

Visit Ms. Brandt at: https://www.stephanybrandt.com

COMING SOON

Perfect

He was supposed to be her helper: a typical robot just like any other used to do human's bidding. But he came with a flaw that would change the world he lived in forever...what happens when a girl falls in love with her robot?

Here

Earthlings knew first contact would come some day, but when an alien race begs for asylum, will Humanity accept them?

Feeding

What would you do if you had to kill your pet? If today was your last day, but you didn't know it? If you can't flee the one who wants revenge? Nine tales of intrigue and horror from the days of our future.

SNEAK PEEK - PERFECT

Beth stared at the brightly-lit store in front of her. "Robots to fit your life!" the flashing sign advertised. She pursed her lips and crossed the parking lot, carefully avoiding the two distracted drivers who almost hit her. She automatically hunched her shoulders and avoided eye contact with the passing crowds, slipping quietly in the shop's front door.

"Welcome, can I help you?" A shiny sales robot rolled to the door as she entered the clean white room.

"Yes, can I have a human salesperson?"

The metal face turned to her and nodded, "Of course," its voice annoyingly agreeable like eating an over-sweetened candy.

She watched the robot head to the back room and hail someone from behind a door. A short chubby man with a flustered look on his face emerged from the room, looking like he'd been interrupted from something.

"Can I help you?" He scratched his head and the annoyance in his voice wasn't lost on Beth.

"Yes," Beth spoke softly. "I'm here to buy a robot?" She couldn't help sounding insecure—James always said she was too passive. That was one of the many issues he seemed to have with her before he left.

"Of course." The man looked her over. "You have something in mind?"

"No, that's why I need the human help. I've never bought a robot before."

The man's eyes lit up. He didn't see too many virgin customers any more. Most people wanted an upgrade on their unit and the robot salespeople were plenty good for that. This girl stared at the robots lining the room like they were from some other planet. He saw her eyes widen as she turned around the room.

"So, you're new to robots?" He tried sounding innocent. "What made you want to get one?" What he meant to ask was: *"How come it's taken you so long to join the real world? Are you some kind of freak?"* but he knew that would lose him the sale.

"I need a companion." Beth spoke so softly the salesman could barely hear her.

"Oooh," he gave her a saucy wink, "need a little lovin' in your life?"

"No." Beth blushed furiously. "I need one for protection—to watch the house."

The salesman's face fell and he decided to play it straight. He sensed the girl's frustration. She seemed like she was one foot out the door already, and he couldn't afford to lose a commission. His tone changed to the kindly one he used with his wife when she was really upset.

"Okay…a protection model?" He walked back towards a line of shiny titanium bodies.

"Well." Beth played with the ring on her index finger. "Kind of. Is there one that can protect and do house work too?"

"Oooh, have I got the one for you!" The salesman changed his trajectory and walked towards the back of the room. Along the back wall stood a huge line of what appeared to be mannequins. When you got closer, they started looking more life-like. "These are our 4400 models," he said with a sweeping gesture towards the waiting machines, "Top of the line—both pleasure and service functions."

Beth followed the salesman towards the wall and looked at the line of blank faces. They all were spotlessly beautiful, male and female, all clothed in a simple grey jumper; their eyes faced forward, glassy and clear. She held her breath as she approached them. "They're very nice." Beth shivered as she touched one of their cold hands.

"Yeah, they sure are." The salesman ran a hand over his non-existent hair. "We just got them in from the 'Haus." He pointed at the sign showing the logo of CyberHaus—the international robot corporation. "These are the newest top-of-the-line. Looks real, feels real, can do it all...if you get my gist..." He winked at Beth.

Beth walked the line, looking at all the different models in stock. Some were built to look female, with large breasts and pretty faces, and they made her think of the Barbie-dolls her mother forbade her from having as a child. The male ones were just like Ken, but "Ken" with different faces and all the appropriate organs below the belt. Some had blonde hair, some had dark hair, but all stood about six feet four and had the build of a football player.

"You got something in mind?" The salesman spoke behind Beth's right shoulder.

Beth jumped and prayed the salesman hadn't seen it. "Not sure." She crossed her arms and cupped her elbows with her palms. "What do most people get?"

"Well, the ladies are all pretty stoked on this fella," he said, pointing out a handsome robot with white-blonde hair and the tan of a surfer. He unzipped the jumpsuit and displayed the anatomically correct nether regions equipped with a particularly large member.

Beth pursed her lips and looked at the other robots. The blonde one looked too much like her cousin—she just couldn't fathom making love to something that made her think of being hunted by blow darts in the basement.

She walked down the line, observing each of the male-fashioned machines. One had a thick mane of dark hair that cascaded down his shoulders and a dark goatee to match. Another had curly brown hair and a sweet clean-cut expression. Two had matching crew-cuts in blonde and brown, clean-shaven in the military style. Beth walked by all of them, not feeling anything but a small tickle in her belly.

"Do you have any more?"

"Yeah, I got a few new ones in the back...none of these to your liking?"

"Not really."

"What's your type?"

"Not sure."

The salesman turned in a huff and disappeared into the back room again. While she waited, Beth turned and looked at the robot salesperson. "What do you think?" she asked the machine.

"If you want a unique model," the silver machine spoke with a gentle tone, "may I suggest the 4500?" It led her away from the line of 4400's towards a robot in the corner. He stood on a clear pedestal, seemingly bereft of company. NEW! the flashing screen above the model advertised.

Beth walked over to the robot and stared at his face. He was shorter than the rest of the 4400's, probably six feet to the 4400's six feet four. His hair was cut short and clean, and his eyes looked softer and friendly. His lips were full and his build was muscular without being too over-the-top: he looked like a fit lifeguard.

"Would you like me to turn him on?" The robot salesperson looked at Beth expectantly.

"Yes."

The salesrobot touched the back of the machine's skull where it met the neck. The head lifted at once and the eyes focused. The robot turned his head from side to side, then looked at Beth and smiled.

"Hello," he spoke softly, "My name is Michael."

www.ingramcontent.com/pod-product-compliance
Lightning Source LLC
Chambersburg PA
CBHW070200260626
47160CB00002B/402